KAREN ROBARDS

Morning Song

AVON
An Imprint of HarperCollinsPublishers

This is a work of fiction. Names, characters, places, and incidents are products of the author's imagination or are used fictitiously and are not to be construed as real. Any resemblance to actual events, locales, organizations, or persons, living or dead, is entirely coincidental.

AVON BOOKS
An Imprint of HarperCollins*Publishers*
10 East 53rd Street
New York, New York 10022-5299

First Avon Books paperback printing: January 1990

Avon Trademark Reg. U.S. Pat. Off. and in Other Countries, Marca Registrada, Hecho en U.S.A.
HarperCollins® is a registered trademark of HarperCollins Publishers.

Printed in the U.S.A.

20 19 18 17 16 15 14

To Doug and Peter,
as always, with much love;
And to Peggy, my dearest friend,
for twenty (can you believe it?) years:
This book's for you!

PROLOGUE

Clive McClintock was playing stud poker. He sat sprawled in his favored, back-to-the-wall chair at a round table in the smaller of the three public salons of the riverboat *Mississippi Belle*. A thin cheroot dangled from the side of his mouth, his neckcloth was loosened, and his long, booted legs stretched negligently out before him. The woman behind him, full-figured, scantily dressed, and beautiful, ran her fingers through the crisp black waves of his hair.

"Stop it, Luce, you're ruining my concentration," he drawled, flicking her a glance over his shoulder. She grinned down at him, a sly meaningful grin that drew envious looks from the other three men around the table. Luce ignored them. Her attention was all for Clive.

"Nothin' ruins your concentration, sugar." She ran her fingers caressingly down a dark-stubbled cheek, but then, as a concession to his protest, withdrew her hands while still retaining her position behind him. Her robin's-egg-blue eyes narrowed as she studied the hand he held. His eyes, an even paler, more arresting shade of blue, flicked back to the cards, expressionless.

"Damn it, McClintock, what are you gonna do?" The man to his left, whom Clive knew only as Hulton, was on edge, as well he might be. Most of his

1

greenbacks lay in the center of the table. The few left in front of him would not, in all likelihood, be enough to allow him to stay in the game. He had already tried to add his pocket watch to the pot in lieu of cash and had been declined. This was professional poker, played for high stakes, and it was a cash-only game. Hulton had been allowed in because he had the necessary ten thousand dollars to ante up. When he ran out of money, as he seemed certain to do within the next minute or so, he would be out of the game. It was as simple as that, and Hulton, like the rest of them, had known the rules before he ever sat down.

But the man's nervous desperation stirred an odd, faintly contemptuous pity in Clive. It had been clear from the man's wild bidding that he had, or thought he had, the hand of a lifetime, and he wasn't going to be able to make it pay off for him because he wasn't going to be able to stay in the game. It was a situation in which Clive had found himself a few times, and he could sympathize with Hulton's frustration. Still, the man shouldn't gamble. If he couldn't lose with a shrug and a smile, he had no business at a card table. Clive only hoped there weren't a wife and a passel of kiddies somewhere counting on the money that Hulton had just gambled away. Though why it should bother him one way or another Clive couldn't figure.

He'd been a professional gambler for twelve years now, since he'd boarded his first paddle wheeler as a downy-cheeked youngster of sixteen. Such distracting emotions as pity for an opponent—especially such a one as Hulton—should have been far behind him. At that moment his attention should have been focused on one thing, and one thing only—the game. But lately his vaunted concentration had had a tendency to wander, which was not a good sign. Maybe, after this game, he'd take some time off, maybe even go on a trip. And not by riverboat, either. He was getting as tired of riverboats

as he was of poker. The realization, coming as it did
when he was on the verge of winning, and winning
big, worried him. Clive frowned almost imperceptibly, then mentally took himself in hand. He could
not afford to think about that now. He had to focus
on the game.

As near as Clive could figure it—and his head for
figures was nearly as good as his head for cards—
forty-one thousand two hundred and six dollars now
lay in the center of the table. It was a fortune, and
if luck went his way just a little longer—and he could
keep from dissolving into tears over Hulton's
plight—it would be his.

"I'll call your hundred and raise you two hundred." Without responding directly to Hulton, Clive
addressed his remark to LeBoeuf, who sat on his
right, suiting the action to the words as he did so.

It was Hulton's turn. He glared at his cards for a
minute, then threw his hand on the table with a
curse.

"I'm out," he said bitterly, scooping up the few
greenbacks that remained to him while eyeing the
mound in the center of the table as if he would like
to grab that, too. He stood up, moving clumsily. His
chair toppled with a crash. He started to turn away,
then turned back, bending forward, his hands
braced flat on the tabletop, his eyes blazing hatred
as they moved from one to the other of the three
remaining players. A murmur went through the
gathered crowd of onlookers, and a few stepped out
of Hulton's way.

Clive's eyes were deceptively lazy as they lifted
from his cards to focus on Hulton. Killings over a
gambling loss much smaller than the one Hulton had
just suffered were not uncommon, and over the
years Clive had seen his full share. Despite the pro-
hibition against wearing arms onboard, which the
captain of the *Mississippi Belle* zealously enforced,
Clive was, in fact, prepared. A tiny custom-made
pistol was tucked snugly into a holster in his boot.

If Hulton made the wrong move, he would be history in a matter of seconds.

But unlike Clive, Hulton was apparently unarmed. He merely glared around the table, mouth working, then cursed viciously and turned away again. The onlookers parted for him. Clive watched him intently. Hulton had looked desperate, and desperate men could be dangerous. But if Hulton had intended violence, he had apparently thought better of it. Snatching his hat from a nearby hat rack, Hulton slammed it on his head and stormed out of the salon without looking back. As the doors swung shut behind him, Clive's eyes slid back to his hand. The play continued without further ado.

When it was over, Clive was, as he had expected to be, some forty-five thousand dollars richer.

"On a pair of treys!" Luce crowed in his ear as she bestowed a smacking victory kiss on him. With the game over, Clive allowed himself to relax.

"It's not so much what you've got, but how you use it that counts," Clive responded with a suggestive grin, his hands finding and squeezing two well-rounded buttocks as a means of illustration. As she giggled and nuzzled his neck, he tucked a wad of bills into the tempting cleavage that pressed against his chest.

"Oh, Clive," she breathed, feeling the cool prickle of the bills. Instantly she let go of his neck to fish out the money.

"For being my good-luck charm," he said, and pinched her satin-clad fanny. She squealed automatically, kissed him again, and turned away to count her money. Clive grinned, watching her. Luce had a head on her shoulders that was at least as hard as his. She liked men, himself in particular, but she liked money better. Just touching it gave her a thrill.

Clive accepted congratulations with a nod and a jest, conscious of being watched by nearly everyone in the salon as he scooped his winnings into his hat.

It was a good win, and a clean one. He'd learned to expertly palm aces and deal off the bottom and employ all the other tricks of the trade years ago. An ability to fuzz the cards was necessary to a gambler's survival. He did it when he had to, but he didn't like doing it. He hadn't needed to tonight, and as a result he felt exceptionally good about the win. A few more like this one and he could buy some land and get off the damned river and away from the smell of Mississippi mud forever.

He was not fool enough to keep such a large sum by him for any longer than he had to. Leaving the salon, he looked carefully both ways along the deck. It was late at night, or rather, early in the morning, and most of the passengers had long since retired to their staterooms. There was a lone man, unknown to Clive, standing a little way farther along, his hands gripping the rail as he looked toward the river's east bank. It was December 1840, and the river was rain-swollen and smelled peculiarly of worms. The night was clear, with a full moon casting enough light to reveal the muddy brown water, the pristine decks. The rhythmic sloshing of the paddle wheel churning and voices from the salon he'd just left were the only sounds. Everything looked just as it should, but Clive had not lived as long as he had by taking chances. Reaching down, he pulled the pistol from his boot and placed it atop the money in his hat. Then he proceeded to his cabin. In the morning he would take his winnings to the purser's office, where the money would travel the rest of the way to New Orleans in the *Mississippi Belle*'s safe. Once in New Orleans, it would go directly into his bank, where it would more than double the tidy little nest egg he'd been accumulating. Someday, not so far distant now, his gambling days would be behind him, except for the occasional gentlemanly wager. He'd earn his living by a means that would allow him to stay on dry land.

A few hours later, Clive was sleeping soundly in

his stateroom when a sense of something being dangerously wrong woke him. He came instantly awake, his senses honed by years of precarious living, to the knowledge that someone else was in the room. Not Luce, who was curled up in luxurious naked sleep beside him, but another someone else. Someone who, if his senses did not mislead him, was even now creeping toward the bed.

The cabin was dark as pitch. He couldn't see a thing.

Clive's hand snaked beneath the pillow, closed over his pistol, pulled it forth, and leveled it at the presence that was still more sensed than seen.

"Whoever you are, stop right there or I'll—"

He never got the rest out. Even as his eyes at last picked out the darker shadow creeping through the gloom, even as he released the safety on the pistol and spoke, all hell broke loose. Another shadow leaped to life from the floor beside the bed where he'd thought there was nothing, looming up out of the darkness with no more warning than a hoarse curse. Startled, Clive reacted reflexively. He jackknifed into a sitting position, jerking the mouth of the pistol toward the new danger. But before he could orient himself, before he could recover from the shock of this second threat enough to find the target and pull the trigger, a glancing sliver of light caught on the glinting blade of a knife as it plunged down, down . . .

"Ahhhh!"

Clive cried out as the knife sank through the flesh of the hand that held the pistol, feeling the blade first cold as ice, then hot as fire as it drove his hand down to pin it, palm down, fingers quivering, to the mattress. . . .

"Clive!" Beside him, Luce awoke with a start.

"Come on!" With silence no longer a necessity, the man closest to the door jerked it open and sprinted through it, calling to his partner, who abandoned the fight to run after him. By the lighter gray of the near dawn as it spilled in through the opened door, Clive glimpsed the second man, and recognized him as Hulton. Then he saw the silhouette of his own tall boot held tightly in Hulton's hand—his boot, where he'd hidden his winnings.

"Damn it to hell and back!" he swore, not hearing Luce's frightened cries as she scrambled off the bed, not aware of any sensation of pain as he grabbed the still vibrating hilt and yanked the knife out of his hand. The money; he had to get his money back. . . .

As soon as his hand was free, Clive hit the floor running, snatching up the pistol from where it had fallen on the mattress with his good hand, his left hand, and running after the would-be murdering thieves who'd robbed him. Blood poured from his wounded palm, splashed warm against his legs and feet. He was oblivious to it, just as he was oblivious to pain and his own nakedness. Pounding after the absconding pair, he leaped down stairs two at a time as they fled to the lower deck, toward where the paddle wheel roiled the water. He was shouting, but he wasn't aware of what he said. Behind him, Luce was screaming something as she ran after him. The officer of the watch popped out of the bridge to discover the cause of the commotion, but he was too far away to be of any help to Clive. The bastards had a punt tied to the rail.

"Edwards!" Hulton shouted to his accomplice, who was some two yards ahead of him. The first man turned to look without ever slackening his headlong flight. Even as Clive's hand came up, even as he paused to steady his aim because he'd never been as good a shot with his left hand as he was with his right, Hulton tossed the boot. The man in the lead caught it.

The first man was at the rail, about to leap into the punt.

Clive jerked the mouth of the pistol from its in-

tended target, Hulton, to aim it at the man who now
held the boot. The man with his money. . . .

The pistol barked. The man with the boot cried
out, staggered, and turned, falling heavily to the
deck. Despite the less-than-optimum conditions,
Clive's aim had been good: he'd shot the thieving
bastard clean through the back of the head.

Even as the man writhed in his death throes, Hulton leaped over him, snatched the rope from the rail,
and leaped over it, too, into the punt. The *Mississippi Belle* steamed forward. Hulton, rowing furiously in the opposite direction, disappeared into the
misty gray darkness of the river at dawn.

Clive sprinted to the downed man. Footsteps
thundered along the deck behind him, but he paid
no attention, just as he paid no attention to Hulton's
escape.

The boot. Where was the boot?

It was not on the deck, but the man had been
carrying it when Clive had shot him. Could it have
fallen overboard? Swearing, Clive shoved at the
body, turning the man over so that he lay faceup.
Blood streaked the corpse's face from the exit wound
above his right eye, matting hair nearly as dark as
Clive's own. Blue eyes stared sightlessly upward.
Clive spared the dead man barely a glance. He
wanted his boot—and there it lay. The body had
fallen on it. Discovering it, Clive felt a rush of relief.
Hunkering down to retrieve his money, he became
aware of the pain in his hand for the first time. Holy
Christ, the thing hurt!

But that was nothing compared with the pain he
felt when he looked into the boot, thrust his left
hand inside for good measure, and found it empty.

"Bloody goddamn bastards!" he yelled, throwing
the empty boot aside and leaping to his feet. He ran
to the rail, to lean glaring out into the swirling darkness into which the punt had disappeared. It was
maddeningly obvious that Hulton had only thrown

the boot as a decoy, while keeping the cash himself. . . .

"You shot him dead, Mr. McClintock," came the voice of the young ship's officer, sounding both awed and a little worried.

"Bastard!" Clive snarled, referring to the dead man. Unless he chose to swim in pursuit of his money, there would be no pursuit, he knew. Turning a paddle wheeler around was not the work of a few minutes. It required an hour or more, and could be tricky under the best of conditions. The *Mississippi Belle* would not be steaming in pursuit of the thief. The best Clive could hope for was that she would stop at the next town so that he could report the theft to the authorities. Much good might it do him.

Turning away from the rail, Clive stalked over to the dead man, barely resisting an urge to kick the corpse with his bare foot.

"Here, sugar." Luce had come panting up behind the ship's officer, who was kneeling over the body. She held out a sheet to him. Clive saw that she had the quilt that had covered them both earlier wrapped around herself, and realized that he was standing buck naked in the cool of predawn, on an open deck, with curious heads starting to crane in his direction from the open doors of nearby staterooms. He took the sheet and wrapped it around his middle while his blood ran onto the white linen, striping it with scarlet.

"Oh, Clive, your hand. . . ."

"To bloody hell with my hand! The bastards stole my money. Hulton, and this one. Who the hell is he? I've never seen him before in my life."

"I believe his name is Edwards. Stuart Edwards. He came aboard in St. Louis." The ship's officer stood up. "Mr. McClintock, I hate to bring it up at a time like this, but there's the matter of your pistol. . . ."

The man, either foolishly brave or stupid, held out

his hand, palm up. Clive looked at him for a disbelieving moment, then with a shake of his head handed the pistol over without uttering a word.

"Thank you. I'm sure there won't be any legal repercussions for you over this. . . ."

"Legal repercussions?" Clive laughed, the sound unpleasant. His right hand, still dripping blood, dangled at his side, throbbing and aching like the devil himself had pierced it with his pitchfork, but that was the least of Clive's concerns. He wanted his money! "Legal repercussions? I just had forty-five thousand dollars stolen from me, and you think I'm worried about legal repercussions for shooting the son of a bitch who did it? I'm worried about recovering my money!"

"Yes, well . . ."

Someone had evidently summoned the captain from his cabin, because he strode toward them along the deck, buttoning his shirt as he approached.

"Mr. Smithers! Mr. Smithers, what in the name of heaven is going on?"

Mr. Smithers, clearly the ship's officer, looked relieved to see his superior. He broke off whatever he'd been about to say and hurried over to confer with the captain in whispers. Luce moved to stand beside Clive, patting his bare arm comfortingly as he scowled down at the body of the man he had killed.

"You owe me, Stuart Edwards," he muttered at the corpse. "You owe me, you thieving bastard, and I bloody well mean to collect."

I

He was going to be trouble. Jessie knew it from the instant she laid eyes on him.

Disheveled and more than a little sweaty from her morning ride, she had just come up through the house from the stables and collapsed in a rocking chair on the second-story gallery, which, thankfully, was shady and situated to catch the faintest breeze. Her thick, curly auburn hair, having escaped from its careless bun long since, tumbled anyhow around her face and down her back. One particularly irritating strand had found its way inside her collar and tickled her neck. Grimacing, she scratched at the irritation, neither noticing nor caring about the smear of mud on her knuckles that her action dully transferred to her right cheek. Indeed, the dirty streak was not the abomination it might have been, so well did it blend with the general unkemptness of her appearance.

The riding dress she wore had been made for her when she was thirteen, five years before. It had once been deep bottle green, but it was so faded by years of hard use that in some spots it was the color of dust-dulled spring grass. To make matters worse, she had been considerably less well developed five years ago. The buttons up the front of the bodice strained to hold it together, mashing her generous

11

bosom nearly flat in the process, and this despite the fact that only the previous year Tudi had added wide insets of fabric to the garment's side seams. The skirt was much darned and some three inches too short, allowing far more of her worn black boots to show than propriety permitted. Not that propriety even entered Jessie's head as she lifted her feet, crossed them at the ankles, and rested her lower heel on the railing that ran around the gallery, putting a scandalous amount of white cotton stocking and thrice-turned petticoat on view.

"Here, now, you cain't do that! You put your laigs down and sit like a lady!" Tudi protested, scandalized. She was seated in another of the half-dozen rockers that lined the wide porch, her gnarled black hands buried deep in a bowl of string beans she was snapping for supper. Jessie gave an ill-used sigh but obeyed, letting her feet drop loudly. With a satisfied grunt Tudi returned her attention to the beans.

Beside the porch, a ruby-throated hummingbird flitted in and out of the pink-veined blossoms of the mimosa from which the vast cotton plantation took its name. The tiny bird's characteristic sound and bright plumage drew Jessie's eyes. Watching it, she bit with relish into the cherry tartlet she had purloined from Rosa, the cook, on her way through the house to tide her over until luncheon.

From the road that wound past the house came a series of rattles and clops as a buggy rolled smartly into view. Its appearance distracted Jessie from the feeding hummingbird, and she observed its approach with interest. When she saw that it would turn up the long drive that led to the house, instead of continuing on toward the nearby river, she frowned. It could only be a neighbor, none of whom she particularly cared to see, probably because they all disapproved of her and made few bones about it. "That wild Lindsay child," the planters' womenfolk called her. Their delicate daughters scorned her as a playmate, and their eligible sons seemed unaware that she was even alive. Which state of affairs, Jessie continually assured herself, suited her just fine!

Then, with even less enthusiasm than she would have awaited the arrival of one of the neighbors, Jessie recognized the petite, exquisitely turned-out woman perched beside the driver as her stepmother, Celia. Her eyes moved on to the dark-haired driver, where they fixed, narrowing. Him she did not recognize at all, and in a community where one knew all one's neighbors, from the wealthiest planters to the poorest of the dirt farmers, that was cause for surprise.

"Who's that?" Tudi looked up, too, as the carriage bowled toward them along the oak-lined drive. Her hands, busy with the beans, never faltered, but her eyes were wide and curious as they fastened on the stranger.

"I don't know," Jessie replied, which was the truth as far as it went. She shunned the neighborhood social doings as assiduously as she would a nest of vipers, so it was always possible that someone had a visitor whom she hadn't met. But it was quite clear that the man, whoever he was, was no stranger to Celia. Celia sat snuggled too closely against his side, so closely that their bodies touched. She wouldn't sit like that with any just-met beau. In addition, Celia smiled and chatted in blatant provocation, and her hand moved every few minutes to stroke the stranger's sleeve, or give his arm a pat. Such behavior was nothing short of *fast*. Coupled with Jessie's knowledge of her stepmother, it gave her a dreadful, disbelieving inkling of who the stranger must be: Celia's new lover.

She'd known for several weeks now that Celia had a new man. After ten years of living with her pretty blond stepmother, Jessie could tell. Jessie's father had been dead for nine years, and in that length of time Celia had had easily double that number of men. Celia was careful, but not careful enough to hide her indiscretions from the keen eyes of her less-

than-adoring stepdaughter. Jessie's first realization
of the true purpose behind Celia's frequent pro-
longed absences had come when she'd happened
upon a letter Celia had been penning to her latest
paramour and had accidentally left in the back parlor. Knowing that it was rude to read others' corre-
spondence, Jessie nevertheless did. The missive's
blue language and impassioned tone had made an
indelible impression on the innocent youngster she
had been then. Once her eyes had been opened, Jessie had learned to read her stepmother like a book:
the restlessness and petty meannesses when she was
between men, the secretiveness and lack of concern
over Jessie's most heinous transgressions when Celia
was involved with someone.

Over the past few weeks, Celia had moved about
the house with a sly little I-have-a-secret smile that
told Jessie a new lover was in the offing. From experience, Jessie had guessed that soon Celia would
be making another shopping trip to Jackson, or
would find herself invited to a house party in New
Orleans, or would manage to come up with some
other excuse to be gone for several weeks without
giving rise to scandal, while she pursued her new
interest away from watching eyes and the con-
straints of propriety. Such deviousness might fool
the neighbors, who would be shocked and loudly
condemning if they knew that the charming widow
Lindsay had had as many lovers as a cat in heat, but
it didn't deceive Jessie. After half a lifetime spent
observing her, Jessie was thoroughly familiar with
the real Celia, who bore only a surface resemblance
to the sweet, slightly silly female she pretended to
be. The real Celia was as hard and ruthless in pursuit of her desires as a tigress, and about as kind-
natured as one, too.

"First time she's brought one of 'em home," Tudi
muttered, scowling, her hands stilling in the bowl
of beans at last as the buggy rocked to a stop before
the front steps. It was true, Celia never brought her

men home, and that, of course, was one reason Jessie felt so uneasy at this one's advent. But to hear her disquiet echoed so succinctly by Tudi, before she'd even managed to pin the cause of it down herself . . .

Jessie glanced in sidelong surprise at her onetime nursemaid, who had taken over the reins of the housekeeping long since, when as a bride Celia had shown no disposition to do so. Though why Jessie should be surprised to discover that Tudi thoroughly understood the situation, Jessie couldn't fathom. Tudi, for all her comfortable girth and placid disposition, had the eyes of a hawk and the brain of a fox. Celia's subterfuges wouldn't have fooled her any more than had Jessie's inventive excuses for misdeeds when she was small.

The stranger stepped down from the buggy, and Jessie's eyes swung back to him. One of the yard boys ran up to take charge of the equipage, but Jessie's eyes never left the man. So intent were he and Celia on each other that neither noticed that they were under intense and hostile observation from the upper gallery. Tudi's hands were still plunged deep into the bowl of beans, unmoving, while Jessie had stopped both rocking and eating to watch.

Even from the back the stranger was worthy of feminine attention. He was tall, with broad shoulders, long muscular legs, and an abundance of wavy black hair. As far as Jessie could tell, his black coat and tan breeches bore not so much as a speck of dust or a wrinkle, which by itself was enough to distinguish him from the planters and their sons who were Celia's official callers. It was mid-May of 1841, not as hot and sultry as it would be later in the summer in the steamy Delta region, but still quite warm, and already the menfolk thereabouts were rumpled and smelled of sweat by midday. But this man—why, his boots even gleamed! Something about the very pristineness of that glossy brown leather set

Jessie's teeth on edge. Already she knew that this was not a man she was going to like.

She frowned as the stranger reached up to catch Celia around the waist and swing her from the buggy. Though the gesture was no more than any gentleman might offer to a lady, those long-fingered hands in the black leather driving gloves curled around Celia's tiny waist with far too much intimacy, and he held her for too long to be quite proper. Watching, Jessie felt a stirring of embarrassment, as if she were witnessing something that should have been private. Celia, of course, was beaming at him—which was nothing to be surprised at. If he was her lover, and Jessie was becoming more convinced with every passing moment that he was, then she would certainly smile at him. And he would look down at her with sickening ardency, and be reluctant to take his hands from her person. In other words, he would behave just as he was doing.

Celia was giggling appreciatively at something he said, her hands lingering on the impeccably tailored sleeves of his fashionable coat as he set her on her feet and, finally, released his hold on her waist. The rapt way she smiled up into his face, the possessiveness of her hands on his arms, even the way she seemed to lean into him as she talked, clinched the matter, as far as Jessie was concerned. The man was Celia's latest lover, and she had had the appallingly bad taste to bring him home to Mimosa. The question was, why?

Whatever his name was, wherever he was from, this man was trouble. Jessie felt it in her bones in the same way Tudi felt oncoming rain.

II

"What do you suppose she's up to?" It was more a case of Jessie thinking aloud than asking a question, but Tudi answered anyway.

"Lamb, I gave up tryin' to figure out Miss Celia years ago. Don't stare so, now. It ain't nice."

Tudi's admonition was a case of the pot calling the kettle black if Jessie had ever heard one, but that moment wasn't the time to say so. Besides, Tudi had a point. It wouldn't do to be caught gaping. As the horse and buggy were led away, Jessie set the rocking chair in motion again with a gentle push of her foot against the whitewashed floor, and took another bite out of the cherry tartlet. Beside her, Tudi lowered her eyes to her lap and once again began snapping beans.

Then the stranger turned to escort Celia up the broad steps that led to the upper gallery and the family sitting rooms beyond. Jessie took one look at his face and stopped eating again. The tartlet was suspended, forgotten, in her hand as she stared in growing dismay.

Even to her critical, untutored eyes, the man was dazzling. As the pair of them came up the stairs, he was smiling down at Celia, who had tucked her hand into the crook of his arm, his long fingers covering her childlike ones where they rested on his

sleeve. His teeth gleamed white against the tan of
his face, and his features were handsome and regular. As he threw back his head to laugh at something Celia said, Jessie saw that beneath thick black
brows his eyes were very blue, as blue as the hal-
cyon sky that overlay the Yazoo Valley that day.

Some of the local planters and their sons were attractive men, and Jessie privately thought that
Mitchell Todd, whose family owned neighboring
Riverview, was very handsome indeed. But Mitch
and the rest paled before the sheer physical splendor of this man, who besides his good looks had
about him an air of excitement and danger and rakish charm that the others definitely lacked.

Jessie thought, Whoever he is, he's not from these
parts. Then they reached the top of the stairs, and
both Celia and the stranger saw Jessie and Tudi at
last. Jessie put the cherry tartlet carefully in her lap,
hoping it would not ooze all over her, and gripped
the armrests hard.

"Why, Jessie! Goodness, you do look a fright! Oh,
well, it can't be helped, I suppose. Stuart, dear, this
is my wayward stepdaughter." Celia rolled her eyes
as if to emphasize whatever she had told the man
about Jessie. He smiled at Jessie. It was an utterly
disarming smile that made him look handsomer than
ever. In response, Jessie's hands tightened on the
armrests in an involuntary gesture of physical resis-
tance to that potent charm. Her face tightened, too,
and she knew that it had assumed the familiar sullen
expression for which Tudi was forever chiding her
and which she could not seem to help when she was
around Celia. Celia, who in the most artless way
imaginable was forever calling attention to her stepdaughter's myriad faults.

Ignoring Tudi as she always did the slaves unless
she was scolding them or giving them an order, Celia
smiled at Jessie, too—unusual enough in itself to underline Jessie's forboding, if Jessie had been in any
state to notice—and pulled the man toward the end

of the porch where Jessie sat. The hummingbird, alarmed, took wing, adding the whirr of its movement to the jingle of the departing buggy. The silk skirt of Celia's fashionable afternoon dress rustled as she moved.

Celia was immaculate as always, from the top of her fetching little hat to the toes of the tiny satin slippers that just peeked out from beneath her skirt. Her dress was almost the color of the sky and the stranger's eyes—Celia had a predilection for pale blue—and in it Celia looked lovely and slender and amazingly young. Jessie wondered, uncharitably, if her new beau had any notion that Celia had turned thirty the previous winter. Then Celia, the man in tow, stopped before her. Jessie stared stonily up into the stranger's smiling face as Celia prattled on in the artificially sweet voice she affected when she was in the company of men.

"Jessie, this is Stuart Edwards. Really, dear, you do look like you've been dragged through a bush backward! And is that a sweet you're eating? You *know* you must not eat sweets if you ever want to outgrow that baby fat! You really must make more of an effort with your appearance. You'll never be a beauty, I know, but you could at least strive for presentable! Stuart, pray forgive her! Usually at least her face is clean! Goodness, Jessie, I hadn't realized until now, but you've just turned into a great gawk of a girl while my back's been turned, haven't you? You'll likely give Stuart a disgust of me and make him think I'm a dreadful stepmama and terribly old to boot, though I was decades younger than my late husband and really am of an age to be a sister to Jessie rather than her stepmama." This last was said with a frown for Jessie and a trilling laugh and a sideways glance for Stuart Edwards.

"It must be instantly clear to anyone who has the use of his eyes that you and Miss Lindsay are very much of an age," Edwards interrupted gallantly. "How do you do, Miss Lindsay?"

The smooth compliment pleased Celia, who fluttered her lashes and simpered at him, uttering a sickening "Oh, Stuart!"

Edwards smiled at her, then bowed politely to Jessie, who met his oozing charm with stony silence. Flattery might turn Celia all syrupy sweet, but it was wasted on her! Behind Edward's back Celia narrowed her eyes at Jessie in a look that promised retribution for her rudeness when they were alone. Jessie ignored the implied threat. One advantage that her size gave her over her doll-like stepmother was that she no longer had to physically fear Celia.

"Really, Jessie, have you no manners at all? You must at least say, 'How do you do?' when you are introduced to someone." Celia's tone of pretty chiding hid her real urge to box her stepdaughter's ears, Jessie knew. Still Jessie said nothing, just looked up at the pair of them in a way calculated to make known her contempt. At her expression Celia made a disgusted little noise under her breath and took Edward's arm as if to draw him away. "Pray overlook her lack of manners, Stuart! I've tried my best with her, but as you see, she pays me no mind. Perhaps now that she's going to have a father again she'll—"

"What did you say?" Jessie spoke at last as that sank in, her voice an incredulous squeak. She could not have heard correctly, or understood what she had heard. Celia looked nervously, appealingly, up at the man beside her. Jessie realized that her ears had not deceived her. She got slowly, carefully, to her feet, rescuing the cherry tartlet from her lap without even realizing that she was doing so. Shock caused her to move as if she were suddenly very old.

Celia was a shade under five feet in height and delicately made, while Jessie was a good six inches taller and very far from delicate. Standing, Jessie loomed over her stepmother, and her demeanor was something less than loving. Edwards made a move

as though he would get between them, but he did
not and Jessie ignored him. Her eyes were on Celia.
Celia, who stood with her back to Edwards looking
up at Jessie with the malice that, when they were
alone, was her usual attitude toward her stepdaughter.

"Now, Jessie, dear, I feared you'd be a little upset, but you see, Stuart and I are in love and . . ."
That artificially sweet voice grated on Jessie like fin-
gernails on a blackboard. The hand that was not
holding the cherry tartlet clenched at her side.

"Your stepmother has done me the great honor
to promise to be my wife, Miss Lindsay," Edwards
interrupted, moving closer to Celia, his voice and
eyes hard in Celia's defense. "We hope you'll wish
us happy."

Clearly his hope was destined to be unrealized.
Jessie looked from him to Celia for a long moment
without speaking while the awful news sank in. Her
stomach churned, and her face went paper-white.

"You're going to—get married again?" she
croaked at last.

"Just as soon as it can be arranged." It was Edwards who replied, although the disbelieving question had been addressed to Celia. Jessie ignored
Edwards as though he weren't there.

"Does this mean you'll be . . . going away?" Jessie still spoke to Celia in a voice that sounded as if
she were being choked. Even as Jessie asked the
question she knew the answer: Celia would never
go away.

"Of course we'll take a little wedding trip, but I
couldn't leave you for longer than that, could I,
dear? No, of course not. Your dear father left you to
my care, and I'll never violate that sacred trust,
however much you may hate me for it! Stuart will
be moving in here, to relieve me of some of the bur-
dens I've shouldered in trying to run this place as
your father would have wished, and he'll try to be

a father to you. Maybe, just maybe, his guidance will have the effect on you that mine has not. I—''

"You can't do this!"

"Oh, Jessie, why must you make everything so difficult? I only want what's best for us all. . . ." Celia's plaintive cry snapped Jessie's control.

"You—can't—do—this!" she hissed, taking a hasty step toward her stepmother. Celia squeaked and stepped just as hastily back. Jessie grabbed one of her stepmother's fragile arms and gave it a shake. "Do you hear me, Celia? You just can't!"

"Get hold of yourself, Miss Lindsay!" This time Edwards did insert himself between Jessie and Celia, his hands gripping Jessie's shoulders hard enough to hurt. Jessie yanked free, at the same time, as had no doubt been Edwards' intent, freeing Celia.

"Jessie, *dear*." Celia rubbed her arm and looked on the verge of tears. Knowing her for a fake and a fraud, Jessie scowled murderously at her.

"I believe it would be best if we postponed any further discussion until your stepdaughter is more herself," Edwards suggested, wrapping an arm protectively around Celia's slight shoulders and giving Jessie a look that mingled dislike with clear warning.

"She *is* herself." Celia sounded despairing as she turned to look up at him, her small hands grasping his shirtfront in a manner that even Jessie would have considered pathetic if she hadn't known Celia so well. "She's always like this. She's hated me since I married her father. She—she never wants me to be happy—"

To Jessie's disgust, Celia then burst into noisy tears. Edwards, of course, fell for the sickening display hook, line and sinker. Jessie watched the pair of them balefully while Edwards held the sobbing Celia close and whispered comfortingly in her ear. Tudi, who still sat in the rocking chair, eyes lowered discreetly to the beans she snapped while her ears practically stood out from her head as she drank in every word, took advantage of the twosome's dis-

traction to flash Jessie a quelling look accompanied
by a slight shake of her turbaned head. Jessie saw,
but was too upset to heed the silent message. She
felt as though she had tumbled headlong into a
nightmare.

"You can't do this," she said again. Her words
were addressed to Celia's slight back, which was
heaving as she wept noisily into Edwards' shirtfront.

"I am going to marry your stepmother, Miss Lindsay," Edwards said, his voice even, his eyes wintry
as they met hers. "You might as well accustom
yourself to the notion, and stop subjecting us to
these theatrics. I might warn you that as soon as I
am your stepmother's husband you will be under
my control, and I'm perfectly capable of dealing with
spoiled children as they deserve."

Jessie stared at him, looked deep into eyes that
were as cold and unyielding as ice, and felt such
rage and hate fill her that she trembled with it. She
was so angry that she caught her breath on what
was almost a sob. But she couldn't cry. She never
cried, and she would perish before she would sink
so low in front of him—them! Her chin came up,
belying the wet glitter in her eyes. She didn't know
it, but she looked very much a child suddenly, an
angry, lost child. The corner of Edwards' mouth
turned down impatiently as he saw the incipient
tears, and he made a move as though he would lay
a consoling hand on her shoulder. Jessie saw the
sudden pity in his eyes and bared her teeth at him.
How dared he feel sorry for her!

"Miss Lindsay . . ." His hand actually touched
her arm, gave her a little pat. Violently Jessie
knocked his hand away.

"Don't you dare touch me!" she spat, her eyes
blazing hatred at him through the tears she refused
to shed. Then with a wild cry she whirled and ran
for the steps, shoving roughly past him, past Celia—
who had recovered from her tears and was sniffing

dolefully against his chest while her eyes, peeping sideways at Jessie, gleamed with triumph.

"What the hell . . . !" The exclamation came from Edwards when Jessie shoved him, but she never once looked back as she fled down the steps and toward the stables. Thus she never had the small satisfaction of realizing that the hand she had pushed him with was the one that had held the cherry tartlet—and her action had smashed the oozing pastry all over the sleeve of his immaculate black coat.

III

It was dusk when Jessie turned down the long drive that led to the house. Beneath her, Firefly's sleek sorrel hide was flecked with black mud, and her steps were slow even though they were approaching home. Jessie felt a momentary pang of conscience over the wild gallop that had taken them deep into Panther Swamp. At the end, the mud had come almost up to Firefly's hocks, and it had been tough going making their way back out of the oozing, slimy muck. At Firefly's heels trotted Jasper, the rough-coated, enormous hound of indeterminate parentage who'd been hers since he was a pup. Jasper was even muddier than Firefly, and his tongue hung out, but he'd had a high old time of it chasing possums and squirrels, so Jessie didn't feel too guilty about him. But she did feel bad for Firefly. She should have had more sense than to take the dainty mare to the swamp. However, at the time she'd been too upset to consider consequences.

Celia was going to remarry. The notion was so shocking that it seemed unreal. Jessie had wrestled with the news throughout the course of the afternoon, but she was no nearer to accepting it than she had been when she had fled the gallery hours earlier. The idea was simply unthinkable. It was not to be borne.

The drive, a dirt lane, was two-pronged, with one branch forming a circle in front of the house and the other leading to the stable. Huge old oaks, already green with new leaves, linked branches overhead to form a canopy all the way to the stable and beyond, to the slave cabins and the overseer's house. Jessie headed Firefly toward the stable. Twin columns of smoke rose from the cookhouse next to the big house and from the communal kitchen in the slave quarters. The pungent smell of hickory smoke scented the air.

As Jessie drew closer to the house, its long mullioned windows illuminated one by one, first in the ground-floor reception rooms and then upstairs, in the family quarters. Sissie, Rosa's young daughter who was being trained to one day take her mother's place as cook, was going from room to room lighting lamps and candles, as was her job each evening. The light from the windows lent a warm glow to the whitewashed brick of which the main part of the house was constructed. Originally built as a solid brick rectangle before the turn of the century, Mimosa had been added to over the years, so that it now formed the shape of a T, with the tail of the T made of pressed cypress and the whole structure painted to conceal the marriage of brick and wood. Twelve imposing Doric columns soared past the second-story gallery to the elaborately carved eaves. Their majesty was complemented by the long flight of steps that fronted the drive and led to the upper portico.

Jessie stopped Firefly and sat back in the saddle, drinking in the familiar sights of home. She loved Mimosa, loved it with a fierceness that she was just now discovering. The plantation had belonged to her mother's family, the Hodges, for generations. When her mother, Elizabeth Hodge, an only child, had married Thomas Lindsay of Virginia, there had apparently never been any question as to where the newlyweds would live. Mimosa would in the natural course of things belong to Elizabeth one day, and the ensuing years would give Josiah Hodge plenty of time to teach his new son-in-law the intricacies of managing an operation that consisted in part of over ten thousand acres of planted cotton, a sawmill, a gristmill, a blacksmithy, and nine hundred and ninety-two adult slaves.

What no one could have foreseen was that Elizabeth Hodge Lindsay would outlive her parents by no more than two years. Thomas Lindsay had remarried a scant year after that—Celia Bradshaw was a pretty little miss he met on a trip to New Orleans—and had died little more than a year later. Still infatuated with his child bride, Thomas had written a will that left Mimosa lock, stock, and barrel to Celia with two provisos: first, that his daughter by Elizabeth, Jessica, be provided with a home for life there if she chose to make use of it; and second, that none of the slaves who belonged to the place at the time of his death be sold.

Jessie had been only nine when her father died, so the leaving of Mimosa to Celia had not bothered her particularly. Mimosa was her home, had always been, would always be, and no legal technicalities about ownership could change that. It had taken the shock of Celia's announcement that afternoon to make clear to Jessie just how uncertain her position was. Somehow she had never foreseen that Celia would remarry—though she should have. Of course she should have. But she'd never really thought about it. Even if she had, she probably would have concluded that Celia liked men, a wide variety of men, too much to settle on one. Like an ostrich with its head in the sand, Jessie had refused to see anything unpleasant. What a fool she had been! And what a fool she had been, upon hearing Celia's news, to even hope for a moment that remarriage might mean that Celia would be leaving.

Of course Celia was not going to leave Mimosa. She owned it. She could bring in a husband or lover or whomever else she chose with impunity, and turn over to him the plantation that should by right of blood and devotion belong to Jessie. Could Celia sell the place? The horrifying idea occurred to Jessie, along with the realization that she didn't know the answer. She'd never thought to inquire. With the blind trust of youth she'd believed that life would go on the way it always had forever.

She'd never even considered that things might change until the notion was thrust beneath her nose. Now she was faced with a shattering sense of loss. Mimosa, her home, belonged to Celia, and that was a fact that she was powerless to do anything about. If Celia and her Stuart wed and had children, those children would almost certainly inherit, not she. The thought was agonizing, immobilizing, and not to be borne. Indeed, Jessie didn't mean to bear it. Whatever else she was, Jessica Lindsay was no namby-pamby miss. She was a born fighter, and she meant to fight tooth and nail for her home.

Whatever it took, Jessie had decided during the course of the afternoon, she would prevent this marriage, if she had to run Firefly over the top of the prospective groom to do it. The thought of Edwards' immaculate personage trampled in the dust brought a grim smile to Jessie's lips. She would shoot him, if she had to, to preserve her home. But it was likely that nothing so drastic would be required. In all probability she had merely to tell him about Celia's proclivity for men, and he would be so shocked that he would hastily decamp. Jessie hated to be the bearer of tales, but in this case she felt she had no choice. Celia certainly did not deserve her loyalty.

Then Jessie noticed that all the lights in the house were lit, and Jasper had abandoned them to go to the stable and his dinner. With a gentle nudge of her knees Jessie set Firefly in motion again.

There was no need to despair. Celia and her beau weren't wed yet. As the saying went, there was many a slip betwixt cup and lip—and she meant to provide the necessary joggle of the elbow to cause this particular brew to spill.

Progress, thin, bent, and ancient-looking—which he had been for all the years she had known him—stood at the door of the stable, looking anxiously around as Jessie approached. His wrinkled coffee-colored face relaxed visibly when he saw her riding toward him.

" 'Bout time you was gettin' home, Miss Jessie,'' he greeted her as she drew rein beside him.

''I took her into the swamp, Progress. She's covered with mud, and I'm ashamed of myself.'' Jessie slid down from the saddle, patted Firefly's neck in contrition, and handed the reins to Progress.

''I c'n see that, Miss Jessie.'' Progress would ordinarily have expressed his disapproval with the freedom of one who had been in the family since before Jessie's mother's birth, but since he did not volubly scold her for her foolishness, Jessie realized that he must have heard of her upset. ''Don't you worry none, I'll take care of her.''

''You heard about Miss Celia.'' It was as much a sigh as a question. The news would have spread through the house like wildfire, and from there to the stable was a very short step, especially considering that Tudi was Progress's sister.

''Yes'm, I did.''

''I'm not going to let it happen, Progress.''

''Now, Miss Jessie . . .''

''I'm not! I'm not, do you hear?'' Her voice was fierce. Progress sighed.

''I hear you, Miss Jessie, I hear you. But sometimes there's not a whole lot we c'n do to prevent other folk from doin' what they take it in their minds to do.''

''I won't let it happen! I can't, don't you see? Celia never cared anything about Mimosa, and he won't either, and they might even sell it and—''

''You always were one to jump your fences before you got to 'em, Miss Jessie, even as a chile. Miss

Celia's not going to sell Mimosa! Why should she? It's the best cotton producer in the valley, and has been since your grandpa's time. Now, quit borrowin' trouble and run on up to the house and get your supper. Tudi's done been down here three times, lookin' for you. She's mighty anxious, I c'n tell you."

"But, Progress—"

"Go on, now. Shoo."

"Oh, all right. I'm going. You give Firefly a warm bran mash, you hear?"

"I will, Miss Jessie. And, uh, lookee here . . ."

"What?" Already several steps on her way, she glanced over her shoulder at him. It wasn't like Progress to be at a loss for words.

"If'n I were you, I'd go get my supper in the cookhouse and then head on up to bed. Send word down to Miss Celia that you're home, so she won't worry none, and just stay out of her way 'til morning."

"Why should I do that? I have some things to say to her."

Progress sucked his lower lip thoughtfully. When he spoke, it was with reluctance, as if he was not quite sure of the wisdom of saying what he was about to say. "He's still here—Miss Celia's beau. I don't reckon it'll do you no good to have another quarrel with the pair of 'em tonight."

"Still here!" Jessie's head snapped around and she stared up at the house, her fists clenching at her sides. "Why? Does he think he owns the place already?"

"I don't know whut he thinks, Miss Jessie. I only know that you're gonna cause a heap o' trouble for yourself if you don't . . . Miss Jessie, you keep a civil tongue in your head, now!" This last was called after her in a scolding, beseeching tone as Jessie stalked toward the house without waiting for him to finish. Muttering and shaking his head, Progress watched her go, his hand absently stroking Firefly's muzzle. Then he looked skyward as if for divine help and turned to walk the mare into the stable. Easier to stop the flow of the river than to stop Miss Jessie when she was in a mood.

Jessie completely forgot about heading for the cookhouse and supper, about her exhaustion and bedraggled appearance. She marched toward the front of the house, stride militant, jaw pugnacious. Her anger, which had cooled over the course of the afternoon, heated again. She would not let that— *interloper* make himself at home in her house without a battle!

They would most likely be in the dining room by this time, sitting down to supper. Celia would want to impress her beau, so the meal would be grand. Just thinking about its probable composition—a ham and yams, or maybe a roast chicken—made Jessie's stomach growl. Until that moment she hadn't even realized she was hungry. Except for the cherry tartlet, most of which had gone to waste, she hadn't eaten at all that day.

Jessie climbed the steps, seething, mentally rehearsing the coming confrontation. Visions of her own eloquence and power, and an even more satisfying vision of the vanquished Edwards fleeing from Mimosa never to return, floated tantalizingly in her head. Afterwards, of course, Celia would hate her more than ever, and make her life difficult, but that would be a small price to pay to keep Mimosa safe. Until the next man. . . . But she wouldn't think about that. Maybe, after seeing how horrified this one was once he learned the truth, Celia would give up the notion of remarriage. And if she didn't . . . Well, Jessie could deal with only one calamity at a time.

With the onset of darkness the air had grown cooler, and Jessie might have shivered in her worn-thin gown if she had been in any state to notice the chill. So wrapped up in her own thoughts was she that she was oblivious to the drop in temperature,

as well as to the delicate scent of mimosa that wafted
on the breeze with the hickory smoke and the aroma
of what might have been ham. The chirping of crickets and night birds went unheard. Her thoughts
were all concentrated on the coming confrontation—
on what she must do to rid Mimosa of the interloper
who threatened it.

Thus she didn't notice the bright glow of a cheroot
tip on the upper gallery, or the man who leaned
against a pillar, smoking, watching her rapid ascent
with narrowed eyes.

"Good evening, Miss Lindsay."

The unexpectedness of the soft drawl, coming
seemingly out of nowhere, made her whirl toward
its source. Since she had just reached the top of the
steps, the sudden movement threw her off balance.
Jessie teetered wildly for a moment, eyes huge as
she quivered on the brink of tumbling down the
stairs she had just climbed. Then a hand, grabbing
lightning-fast through the darkness to close over her
upper arm, saved her. She tumbled forward instead
of back, to fall against her rescuer's chest.

Her heart pounded from the nearness of her escape. Both hands and forehead rested against his
shirtfront, and for a moment she was content to stay
that way as she fought to get her breathing under
control. The steps were steep, and a fall down them
would almost certainly have caused her an injury.
He had saved her from that, but then, he had been
the cause of her near fall in the first place, so she
owed him no gratitude.

He smelled of leather and good cigars. The linen
of his shirtfront was smooth beneath her hands. Beneath it his chest felt warm and solid. She was tall,
but he was taller by a good head. The breadth of his
shoulders dwarfed her own, though she was far
from daintily made. Jessie registered all this in a
scant few seconds. Then he was releasing his grip
on her left arm, wincing and flexing his right hand
as though it pained him. Quickly she stepped back,

but his left hand, which had also closed over her arm when she careened into him, retained its grip on her.

Jessie's eyes snapped up to his as she prepared to let him have the rough side of her tongue without further delay. But something in his expression made her forget what she had been going to say. She found herself looking into eyes that were almost colorless in the shadowed gray gloom of the gallery, eyes that were hooded and watchful and as predatory as a wolf's. Meeting them, Jessie realized suddenly that this man was an enemy worthy of the name. Despite his handsome face and elegant clothes, despite the outward gentility of his manners, those eyes gave him away. This was no gentleman planter, no landed aristocrat softened by a cushion of wealth. Like herself, this man was a fighter. And, she feared, he was a far more experienced fighter than she.

"Careful." He sounded amused, probably by the wide-eyed fixity of her gaze. Brought abruptly back to reality, Jessie snatched her arm from his grip and backed another few paces away, taking care this time to stay clear of the edge of the porch.

IV

"You're not wanted here, Mr. Edwards. It would be easier on everyone if you would just get in your buggy and go away."

He stuck the cheroot back in his mouth with his left hand and looked her over for a moment without answering, resuming his indolent lounge against the pillar. His right hand hung motionless at his side, the fingers occasionally flexing as if the hand bothered him. It occurred to Jessie that the very casualness of his attitude was insulting, and her hackles rose.

"Polite little thing, aren't you? Well, I can't say Celia didn't warn me. Miss Lindsay, since we are being so charmingly frank, let me say this: I aim to marry your stepmother. What would make things easier on everyone, but most particularly on you, would be for you to just reconcile yourself to that, and spare us the histrionics."

"I have no intention of making things easy for you. In fact, I plan to make things as difficult as possible."

He sighed, and puffed at his cheroot. When he spoke, his voice was almost too gentle. "Miss Lindsay, it obviously hasn't occurred to you that after the wedding I will have some—no, a great deal of—authority over you. I would hope that our relationship can be at least marginally pleasant, but if not, you'll be the one to suffer. Make no mistake about that."

Jessie gritted her teeth. "If you are determined to marry Celia—I don't care about *that!*—why don't you take her to your property to live? I thought a man was supposed to support his wife, not the other way around."

That irritated him. Jessie could see it in the slight narrowing of his eyes. But that was the only sign of perturbation he revealed, and when he spoke, his voice was as untroubled as it had been before. "Not that it's any of your business, but my holdings do not include a property suitable for the installation of a wife. Besides, Celia is happy here, and I like the place, too—very much."

"Mimosa is mine!"

"You'll always be welcome here. Although your manners may need to be improved upon."

"You cannot really wish to marry Celia! Why, she's more than thirty!"

"A great age, to be sure. But your stepmother carries her advanced years so charmingly."

"You don't love her!"

"And how would a child like you know anything about love?"

"You can't love her! Celia is—is—you can't love her! No one could! So why do you wish to marry her?"

"My reasons, my dear, like my feelings, are none of your concern."

"You're marrying her for Mimosa, aren't you? It's not Celia you want at all, but her money! You're nothing but a dirty fortune hunter!"

There was a moment of pregnant silence. Stuart took a drag on his cheroot so that the tip glowed bright red. Then he pulled it from his mouth.

"You really are a spoiled little brat, aren't you? Let me put you on notice, Miss Lindsay. I have tolerated quite a bit from you today because I realize that you are, understandably, upset. I will not tolerate any more. Very soon I will be in the position of father to you, and I mean to exercise a father's prerogatives and discipline my new daughter. In other words, any rudeness on your part will be more rudely dealt with. Do I make myself clear?''

''You think you can discipline me? Just you try it!'' Jessie's head came up and her shoulders squared challengingly. Outrage shimmered in her eyes and in her voice. ''The people here will tear you apart! They're my people, just like this is my house! Just you try lifting a hand to me!''

''After the wedding, it will be *my* house,'' he pointed out quietly. ''And the slaves will belong to me. If you have a care for them, you won't encourage them to lift a hand against their new master.''

The point he made was so valid that Jessie nearly choked. ''You're vile!''

''And you're pressing your luck. If you keep it up, you'll regret it, I promise you.'' He took a puff of the cheroot again. ''Come, Miss Lindsay, can't we cry friends? I mean to marry your stepmother, and nothing you can say or do is going to make me change my mind. But there's no need for you and me to be at constant loggerheads. I have no intention of playing the heavy-handed steppapa unless you force me to it.''

''Steppapa! You—I . . .''

Before Jessie could find the words to adequately express her feelings, the front door opened and Celia stepped onto the veranda. She saw Stuart immediately and crossed to him, smiling. Partially hidden by the shadows, Jessie at first escaped her notice.

''You've been out here so long, Stuart! I was getting quite worried about you!''

''I've been furthering my acquaintance with your delightful stepdaughter.'' He indicated Jessie with the cheroot.

Celia looked in Jessie's direction with a notable lack of enthusiasm. ''So you're home at last, are

you? Well, you've missed supper. Sissie's already
cleared away. Perhaps in future you can contrive to
be more prompt.''

"I'm not hungry." The sullenness that Celia always seemed to conjure up was there in Jessie's
voice. Jessie heard it herself, and hated it. It made
her sound weak, when what she needed was to be
strong.

"Why, I do believe that's the first time I've ever
heard you say that! Really, dear, that's so encouraging! Perhaps, after all, we may be able to whittle
you down to a manageable size. Gentlemen don't
like ladies who are overplump, you know. But really,
you should eat something. If you run along to the
cookhouse, I'm sure Rosa will fix you a plate.''

"I said I'm not hungry!" Cheeks burning at having a stranger's attention called to her size, Celia
glowered at her stepmother.

Celia shrugged prettily. "Well, you must suit
yourself, of course. Come along inside, Stuart. It's
growing chilly out here.''

Celia took Stuart's arm. He smiled lazily down at
her, dropping his half-finished cheroot and grinding
it out with his boot as he straightened away from
the pillar at last. Jessie saw the potent charm of that
smile, the intimacy of his black head bent over Celia's fair one, and felt her temper snap. They were
dismissing her, treating her as if she were a child,
when she—she, not Celia and certainly not he—was
the rightful owner of Mimosa!

"There's something you don't know about my
stepmother, Mr. Edwards," she said coldly to their
retreating backs.

If she had expected to freeze them in their tracks,
Jessie was doomed to disappointment. They kept on
walking as if they hadn't heard, totally wrapped up
in each other.

"Mr. Edwards!"

He threw her an impatient look over his shoulder,
but it was Celia who answered.

"Really, Jessie, you are being too tiresome! If you have something to say, you may say it to me in private in the morning."

"I have something to say to Mr. Edwards." Jessie walked determinedly forward, moving into the light cast by the open door. Both Celia and Stuart regarded her with varying degrees of annoyance.

"As Celia said, Miss Lindsay, you're growing tiresome. Why don't you run along and get your supper, then go on up to bed like a good chit, before you get yourself in trouble?"

"Not—quite—yet." Jessie bit the words off, infuriated by his condescending attitude almost as much as by his actual presence. But getting the words out took some doing. Jessie started to speak, faltered, and had to take a deep breath before she could continue. Despite her anger, she was surprised to find that her hands were shaking. Telling tales on Celia was harder than she had expected, but it had to be done. Clasping her hands together, she lifted her chin high and met Stuart's gaze squarely. "If you're planning to marry her, there's something you should know."

"And what is that?" He was humoring her, she could tell. It was there in his voice, but there was patience, too. Beside him, Celia fixed her eyes on Jessie. Jessie dared not look at her. Celia could not know what was coming, because she did not know that Jessie knew about her disgusting secret life. Her stepmother would hate her forever for this.

Jessie took another deep breath. It was now or never.

"What would you say if I told you that Celia has . . . gentlemen friends?" No, that sounded as if she meant that Celia had perfectly respectable beaux. Jessie knew she would have to be more specific, but her upbringing, haphazard though it was, had not included a means of describing what she was trying to describe. Celia's eyes widened, while Stuart shook his head and looked amused. Jessie searched frantically for a way to say it, then spat it out anyhow before they could interrupt. "What I mean is, Celia is—is a—whore."

Jessie stumbled over the word, but she got it out. Celia gasped and whitened, her hand flying to her mouth. Stuart blinked once, as if it took that long for the word and its meaning to register. Then, without a word, without any indication of what he meant to do, he lifted his hand and slapped Jessie sharply across the cheek. She stumbled back, her hand flying to her stinging face.

"How dare you?" Celia choked, bright flags of color blazing in her cheeks. Her eyes burned into Jessie's, promising dreadful retribution. "You little ingrate, how dare you?"

Stuart reached out and caught her arm, hauling her back into the light. Jessie was too stunned even to resist.

"If you ever, *ever* say such a thing of your stepmother again, I'll give you a hiding you won't forget." Stuart spoke through his teeth, his eyes blazing down at her. "Do you understand me?"

"But it's true. . . ."

"You've just crossed the line of what I'm prepared to tolerate." From the expression on his face, Jessie thought he might be going to repeat the slap. She shrank back in his hold, her free hand flying up automatically to ward off the blow she feared. But to her shock, Celia intervened.

"Don't, Stuart. I'm sure she doesn't realize what she's saying. She's only a child."

Such championship from Celia was totally unprecedented, and for a moment Jessie gaped at her stepmother, uncomprehending.

"You're more tolerant of this foul-mouthed brat than I would be," Stuart said, still talking through his teeth. His hand tightened on Jessie's arm. "If you were a man, Miss Lindsay, I'd kill you for what you just said. As it is, you're getting off far more lightly than you deserve. But I'm putting you on notice: from now on you address your stepmother, and speak of her, with respect. She may be prepared to tolerate less, but I am not. And I'm the one you have to deal with, make no mistake about that.'

"But I—"

"That's enough! At this point all I'm prepared to hear from you is an apology to Celia."

"I won't apologize! I won't! You let me go, you—" Jessie, recovering from the shock of having her face slapped, was growing angrier by the second. She yanked at her imprisoned arm to no avail, her face crimson, her eyes snapping. Stuart kept his grip with no apparent effort. Only the ominous tightening of his mouth revealed just how furious he was. Celia, hands clasped in front of her bosom, stood watching the one-sided battle between her new fiancé and her stepdaughter, managing to look both angelic and mortally wounded by Jessie's accusation. Jessie, knowing that she had spoken nothing less than the truth, knew also that she had lost. Celia's secret had been the hope to which she had clung. Jessie had been sure, so sure, that no man would want to marry Celia once he knew about her men. But Stuart Edwards hadn't believed her! She had never even considered that. . . .

"Well?" His voice was ominous.

"Well, what?" Jessie's bravado, heightened by her fury at not being believed, caused his brows to twitch together.

"Celia is waiting for an apology."

"She'll wait a long time, then."

His mouth thinned. His hand tightened on Jessie's arm. But before he could say anything, Celia intervened once more.

"She'll apologize in the morning, I'm sure. Come, Stuart, don't be too harsh with her. As I said, she's little more than a child."

"A very spoiled, ill-mannered child," Stuart muttered, his eyes flickering over Celia before moving back to freeze Jessie. "Very well, then, Miss Lindsay, since Celia wishes it, you may offer her an apology in the morning. But you will apologize, make no mistake about that. In the meantime, you will go to your room. You're not to come down again before morning, and then only if you're prepared to apologize.''

"You don't give orders around here," Jessie hissed, finally succeeding in jerking her arm free of his hold. "And you never will. I'll do as I please, you—you dirty fortune hunter!"

He grabbed for her, but she had already put herself beyond his reach. Whirling, she brushed by Celia and flew down the stairs, her feet barely touching the steps. A man capable of slapping a young lady's face was capable of any degree of violence. . . . Beyond the reach of the lighted windows, the lawn was dark and full of shadows. Jessie gathered up her skirt clear to her knees and ran as if the devil himself were at her heels.

Which he was. Stuart Edwards ran down the stairs and across the lawn after her, his face black with fury. Truly frightened by the single glimpse she got of his face as she cast a quick look over her shoulder, Jessie fled into the night.

He caught her just as she reached the edge of the orchard. She'd thought to hide there amongst the hundreds of trees. But his hand clamped on her shoulder and jerked her back toward him before she could lose herself amongst the twisting black trunks and shifting shadows.

As his hand closed over her shoulder Jessie screamed, thoroughly unnerved by the chase and her capture. Spinning helplessly around toward him, Jessie watched his face twist with rage. She screamed again as he caught her upper arms and gave her a shake. He shook her again, hissing something at her. He looked furious enough to do her a real injury.

Jessie's only thought was escape. The instinct for self-preservation blazed to life inside her, and it was that which caused her to leap for him instead of jerking away, her fingers curved into talons that raked his cheeks as they strove to reach his eyes.

"You hell-born little bitch!" he bellowed, freeing her as his hands flew to his face. Jessie whirled, but before she could get away he caught her again. She kicked and screamed as he lifted her off her feet.

"Damn you, you little brat, I ought to beat you until you can't sit for weeks!"

He had her arms well secured, and was carrying her back toward the house. Jessie screamed, struggling frantically. She had actually opened her mouth to bite him when, over his shoulder, she saw a slight figure running toward them from the darkness of the orchard, hoe raised.

The sight shocked her back to her senses. More than for herself, she feared for him, for all of them who would soon find themselves in Stuart Edwards' power.

"No!" she cried. "Progress, no! I'm all right, I'm all right, do you hear? It's my fight—leave me to it!"

Stuart Edwards whirled as her cry alerted him to his danger. His eyes sought and found Progress, who had stopped running and now stood just beyond the edge of the orchard. It was too dark for Edwards to make out more than the silhouette of an old, stooped man, but the hoe was still raised, its honed edge glistening threateningly.

"Go back, please go back! I'm ordering you!" Jessie's words held an edge of desperation. To her relief, Progress visibly hesitated, then lowered the hoe. Stuart Edwards' eyes never left him. For a moment the issue hung in the balance, and then Stuart swung away again, presenting his unprotected back to Progress as he continued to carry Jessie toward the house.

This time Jessie didn't fight. She feared that to do so might cost Progress his life. For a slave to strike a white man was an offense punishable by death.

"So you care for them, do you? That's the only thing I've seen about you yet that's favorable," Stuart said. Then both of them were silent as he reached the stairs, climbed them, crossed the veranda, and entered the house. To Celia, who waited on the porch, arms wrapped around herself, forehead puckered in a frown, he said only: "Where's her room?"

Celia told him. Then Stuart Edwards carried Jessie into the house, past Sissie and Rosa, who looked on wide-eyed but thankfully silent, and up the stairs to her room. He dropped her unceremoniously on her feet just inside the door.

"You will not come out for the rest of the night, and you will apologize to Celia in the morning," he said icily.

Jessie was too shaken to manage a reply. She could only watch, knees wobbling, as he removed the key from the lock and shut the door on her. From the other side she heard the click as he locked her in.

Standing there in the dark, staring sightlessly at the closed portal, all she could think of was his face as he'd shut the door. The light from the hall had shone on it, illuminating it clearly.

Six raw gashes had bisected the smooth-shaven cheeks. She'd scratched him badly, and she didn't know whether to be glad or sorry.

V

The next time the key turned in the lock, it was full morning. Sissie had come up during the night, sent by Tudi and Rosa, to scratch on the door and inquire in a hoarse whisper if Jessie was all right. Though sorely tempted, Jessie refused Sissie's offer to release her with the skeleton key that Tudi, as housekeeper, was permitted to carry. If she was to escape—and how she would love to, just to thumb her nose at Stuart Edwards!—she would have to do it under her own steam. Unless she could come up with a means of preventing him, he would soon be master of the house and its servants. Angry as she was, Jessie did not want Tudi or any of the others to get in trouble for helping her. They were her people, her responsibility—and all the real family she had.

As the door opened, Jessie turned away from the tall window, where she had been contemplating her chances of surviving a jump without breaking her neck or a leg. She most dreaded to see Stuart Edwards, but the intruder could not be he. He had left some two hours after he had locked her in the night before, and she was almost certain he had not yet returned. Her window overlooked the drive, so unless he had ridden to Mimosa through the fields, she would know of his presence.

"I hope you slept well, Jessie."

Celia smiled unpleasantly as she walked into the room, shutting and locking the door behind her. This morning she was dressed in a charming gown of blue-striped white muslin, and her hair was arranged in girlish ringlets about her neck. Trying to appear younger for her lover, Jessie concluded with a silent sneer as Celia tucked the key into her sash, then gave it an ostentatious little pat. Jessie eyed her. Given their relative difference in size, Jessie had no doubt at all that if driven to it she could wrest the key from Celia in a matter of minutes. But Jessie had never physically challenged her stepmother, and it was clear that Celia expected today to be no different. Celia's very confidence was a deterrent. Jessie considered, hesitated, and was lost.

Not seeming to expect an answer, Celia looked with casual interest around the room, which she rarely entered. Except for the substitution of Jessie's parents' marriage bed for the original small one, the decor had not changed much since Jessie was a child. The walls were white and largely unadorned, the curtains plain muslin, the furniture good quality mahogany but unpretentious. The elegantly carved four-poster was the only object of any beauty, and Celia regarded it with a frown.

"That bed looks ridiculous in here. It's far too elaborate for a young girl."

"I like it." Try as she might, Jessie could not keep the sullenness from her voice. It made her sound very young, she knew it did, yet something about Celia invariably brought it out. Biting her lip in chagrin, Jessie fell silent, waiting to hear what Celia wanted.

"I'm sure you do. Your eye for furnishings is about as well developed as your eye for clothes. Look at that dress you have on, for instance. You're far too fat for it, and even if it fitted you perfectly, it's positively hideous." Celia sat in a small carved chair near the wardrobe, her hands complacently smoothing the skirt of her own perfectly fitting dress.

Unable to stop herself from reacting as Celia intended, Jessie glanced down at the green riding habit that was her habitual daily attire. It was too small and badly worn, true, but then so was every other garment she owned. Jessie had not had a new dress in nearly three years, not that she cared. Even if she'd had a wardrobe as extensive as Celia's, she would still have worn the beloved riding habit.

"Be that as it may, I did not come here to discuss your appearance. We need to have a little talk, you and I." Celia's eyes, bright with derision, moved over Jessie once more before fixing on her face. Trying not to fidget beneath that harsh gaze, Jessie bit the inside of her jaw so hard it bled. Of their own volition her hands slid behind her to clench on the edge of the windowsill, out of Celia's sight.

"Last night you called me a name that I never want to hear repeated." The voice Celia used with Jessie was a far cry from the honeyed lisp she affected for Stuart Edwards. Just as the coldness of her eyes and the set look to her mouth were expressions that Jessie was sure no man had ever seen. This woman sitting in her bedroom was the real Celia, the one whom no one save Jessie and the servants ever saw. The one Jessie feared and despised.

"Though that hardly bears saying, does it? I'm sure you're not stupid enough to say such a thing twice. It couldn't have been a pleasant experience, having Stuart slap you. He was so angry! I found it quite delicious, really. He's such a handsome man, and so in love with me. Fancy, he would have killed you for saying that if you'd been a man! Of course, you'll probably never understand what I'm talking about. It's quite doubtful that any man will ever fall in love with you."

Given the fact that the young men thereabouts seemed unaware of Jessie's existence, that was a fair, if unkind, statement. It hurt, though Jessie hoped

Celia didn't realize how much. Celia couldn't possibly know about Mitchell Todd. . . .

"If you were to say such a thing again, why, there's no telling how angry Stuart might get. He might beat you—or he might even send you away. Up north, to a school for young ladies, say—though you're getting a bit old for that. Still, I'm sure something could be arranged."

"You know that what I said is the truth." Jessie knew from experience that the best way to respond to Celia's baiting was to keep quiet, but she couldn't hold back the words any longer. Stuart Edwards might not know the truth, might have reacted in righteous if wrong indignation to Jessie's charge, but Celia knew that Jessie wasn't lying. She'd probably been with more men than Jessie even suspected.

Celia looked her over, smiling.

"That I'm a whore? I certainly am not," she denied briskly. "A whore takes money for pleasing men, and I never do that. What do I need with money? All this"—with a sweeping gesture, she indicated Mimosa—"is mine."

Jessie's face tightened. Celia shook her head, still smiling. The yellow ringlets bounced against her neck.

"You're such a child, Jessie! You don't know the first thing about men—or women. Men are so big, such animals, and yet a clever woman can lead them around by their noses. A man in love will do anything, anything. . . . Especially if a woman refuses to give him what he wants. That's the secret, Jessie: don't give in until you get what you want. Make them beg. . . . Your father married me because he wanted me in his bed and he knew he couldn't get me there any other way. And look what I got out of it: a year of nights spent pleasing him—and he was well enough looking—and all this. Mimosa."

"He—Mr. Edwards—doesn't have anything to offer you." Jessie could barely get the words out. At Celia's casual reference to her father, as if he were

just another in Celia's parade of men, Jessie's hands
clenched so hard on the sill behind her that her
knuckles ached. Celia was making her feel physically sick.

"Doesn't he?" Celia smiled her sly smile and
looked genuinely amused. "Stuart's so handsome,
he sends shivers down my spine. Don't you find
him handsome? Of course you must, whether you'll
admit it or not. All women do. And he's so masterful. I *do* like a masterful man." Here her eyes
drooped sensuously, while Jessie felt her face start
to heat. She'd always known Celia had a coarse
streak, but never before had her stepmother dis-
played it so openly. Despite Jessie's new maturity,
such frankness about such an intimate subject embarrassed her. The very fact that she was embarrassed embarrassed her still more. Her face turned
three shades of crimson, and she was powerless to
do anything about it.

As Celia noticed Jessie's blush, her smile broadened. "Besides his very obvious physical attributes,
he comes from a good family, and while I doubt that
he's as rich as I am, he has a nice little nest egg. He
could marry anyone, anyone at all—and yet he's
chosen me over all the sweet young things around,
and some of them quite pretty, too. Getting him to
propose was quite a coup for me—but, of course,
you wouldn't appreciate that."

"Now that you've gotten him to propose—and everybody knows it—isn't that enough? You don't
have to marry him. Why would you want to? He'll
interfere with your—your trips, and your m-men,
and . . . and . . ." Despite her embarrassment, Jessie got the words out. Perhaps if she could just get
Celia to think of the disadvantages that came with a
husband, she might yet manage to stave off the marriage.

"Much as I hate to admit it, I'm turned thirty years
old. My looks have lasted marvelously, but they're
bound to fade sooner or later. I've thought about

remarrying for some time—without a husband, a woman past a certain age is pitied—but most of the men with the right background are so boring! Or unattractive, or both! But Stuart—" She shivered delicately, the gesture saying far more than words could have. Jessie felt herself blush again at the images that shiver conjured up. "I can see myself married to Stuart. It will be exciting. *He's* exciting."

"But marriage is for a lifetime. The excitement is bound to fade, and then you might—might start getting interested in other men. From what I've seen of Mr. Edwards, I don't think he'd like having his wife step out on him." Even as she spoke, Jessie realized that her words were rolling off Celia like water off a duck's back.

"Do you know, I think Stuart just might be man enough to keep me at home. And if he isn't . . ." Celia shrugged, smiling. "I doubt he'll interfere with what I do. How can he—if he doesn't know anything about it?"

Her voice grew colder, with a steely undertone. "Of course, should anyone be foolhardy enough to tell him that there is occasionally more to my trips than shopping, or that I may have been something less than a properly chaste widow for the past few years, the consequences for that person will be extremely unpleasant, I assure you."

"You must know that he doesn't love you. He's marrying you for Mimosa." It was a desperate try, but even as she said it Jessie knew it wasn't going to work. Either Celia refused to see, or she didn't care.

Celia smiled at Jessie. "Stuart and I are going to be married two weeks from Sunday. He's quite swept me off my feet, and I see no reason to wait any longer. The Misses Edwards—they're Stuart's aunts, by the way; he's from the Charleston branch of the family, and very hoity-toity they are, too—are just thrilled that he's going to be marrying and staying in the vicinity. They are going to have a little party for us tonight at Tulip Hill. To celebrate the engagement, of course. You'll attend that, and you'll be pleasant and polite to everyone, especially Stuart. We wouldn't want anyone to think you were unhappy with the situation, now, would we? Gossip is so unpleasant! And you'll also attend the wedding. In fact, I might even let you be my bridesmaid.'' Celia's eyes narrowed as if she were momentarily considering. ''Yes, I'm sure that's a good idea. You will be my bridesmaid. And you'll smile, Jessie.''

Jessie regarded Celia with loathing. Her stepmother was leaning forward as she talked, delicate and lovely-looking as always, a little smile on her face while she gave instructions to Jessie that she must know Jessie would never follow. Threats or no, Jessie meant to shout her displeasure to the rooftops.

''And if you're not pleasant and polite, Jessie, if you don't do as I have said—'' Celia paused, her face settling into sharp lines of malice. Jessie, watching, was reminded of a beautiful rock she had once picked up that, underneath, was crawling with maggots. Discovering the difference between what Celia pretended to be and what she really was, was exactly like that. ''If you don't do exactly as I've told you, I'll have that dreadful dog you're so fond of shot, and your little mare, too. Just keep that in mind.''

''Shoot—Jasper? And Firefly? If you even try such a thing, I'll . . .'' Horrified, Jessie came away from the window, taking a quick step toward Celia, her fists clenching.

''You'll do nothing, my dear stepdaughter, because there is nothing you can do. Your father left everything on this place to me. I can do just as I please with those animals. By law, they're mine, not yours.''

''If you hurt them, I'll kill you!''

''Really, Jessie, there you go again having histrionics, as Stuart might say. Of course you won't kill me. You'll do as I say.''

With a satisfied look at Jessie's reddened, twisted face, which screamed of impotent fury, Celia got to her feet, casually shaking out her skirt.

''As far as I'm concerned, we can forget that that unpleasant scene last night ever happened.'' Celia crossed to the door and unlocked it. Opening it wide, she passed through it, leaving the key in the keyhole as if confident that there would be no need to lock Jessie in again. Jessie breathed a silent sigh of relief that she was leaving. Never in her life had she thought to hate anyone as she was growing to hate her stepmother. Then, from the hall, Celia looked back at Jessie over her shoulder, her brows lifting delicately.

''Oh, and I'll tell Stuart you've apologized, shall I?'' she breathed, smiling, and without waiting for an answer moved off down the hall.

VI

It was four o'clock that same afternoon, and Jessie was standing miserably in front of the cheval glass in the corner of her bedroom. Tudi, positioned behind her, was sticking the last of a mouthful of hairpins into the precarious upsweep of her hair. Sissie crouched at her feet, industriously sewing a gathered flounce to the hem of the made-over dress so that it would reach past Jessie's ankles. Slanting rays of sunlight poured in through the pair of windows that overlooked the side yard, bathing Jessie and her helpers in their brightness. The effect, as she viewed it in the mirror, made Jessie grimace.

Caught in the bold wash of sunlight, the deficiencies of her appearance became glaringly obvious. The demure white muslin dress, selected by Celia three years ago because it was so suitable for a young girl, had yellowed ever so slightly since then. The tiny pink sprigs with which it was adorned had faded until they were a pale shadow of the shade they had once been. The pink flounce that Sissie was adding, in the hope that it would freshen as well as lengthen the dress, looked hopelessly out of place. So did the pink satin sash, which Sissie had borrowed from Minna, Celia's maid, who had unearthed it amongst a pile of Celia's discarded clothes. The pink flounce was from the same dress that had yielded the sash,

53

and the color of both bore only a general resemblance to the shade of the sprigs.

To make matters worse, although Tudi had tried her best in the matter of the bodice, it was still too tight. For one of the few times in her life Jessie was wearing stays (she'd had to, to get into the dress), but although they whittled her waist to some small degree, they had the opposite effect on her bosom, which was pushing against the cloth covering it as though determined to escape. The once modest scoop neckline did not quite conceal the excess flesh; enough soft white cleavage showed to make the dress too revealing for a young lady of Jessie's tender years.

Tudi, scandalized, had been all for jettisoning the dress. Only the sorry fact that Jessie did not possess another in better condition stayed her hand. Borrowing a gown from Celia's vast wardrobe had been considered, but the sad truth was that no dress made to fit Celia's tiny frame could be stretched to cover Jessie. So Sissie, who at age fourteen was the most accomplished seamstress in the house, including Tudi and her mother, had come up with a compromise: she would purloin another section of the pink dress, and use it to make a ruffle around the neckline. With that addition, the gown would be perfectly respectable, if not entirely fashionable.

"Stand still, Miss Jessie." Made a trifle cocky by her new importance, Sissie admonished Jessie in a stern tone as she stood up to attach the all-important neck ruffle. Scrawny and several inches shorter than Jessie, her hair still in childish plaits, Sissie had to stand on tiptoe to do the sewing. Chafing, Jessie stood still under her determined ministrations, hoping that the addition of the pink frill would somehow magically improve her appearance.

It didn't. When Sissie stepped back, and Jessie was allowed to admire her handiwork, she looked at her reflection again and felt a sinking sensation in the pit of her stomach.

"I look just dreadful," she said with conviction.

"Oh, lamb, you do not!" Tudi protested, surveying Jessie's reflection from behind her.

"You look fine, Miss Jessie," Sissie added stoutly, but Jessie was not fooled.

"I look like a Holstein cow in a dress."

"Miss Jessie!" Tudi's protest was severe, but there was a giggle underlying Sissie's simultaneous one. Glumly, Jessie knew her pronouncement was true.

"I do. My hair's too red and my face is too round, and as for the rest of me—I'm just plain fat."

"Now you just stop thinking like that!" There was fierceness in Tudi's eyes as Jessie met them in the mirror. Tudi never could stand for anyone to belittle her lamb, as she had called Jessie when she was little. Not even Jessie herself. "You're hair's a nice, rich mahogany color, not red at all. And it curls— my, how Miss Celia would love to have your curls! Minna tells me she spends every night in curl papers. Your face is real pretty, with those big brown eyes and that cute little nose and those soft round cheeks like a young girl should have. And you've got nice skin, too."

"I'm fat as a pig," Jessie said dispiritedly, her shoulders drooping. The topknot that Tudi had spent the past twenty minutes arranging wobbled as her chin dropped, and Jessie knew it wouldn't last. Any hairstyle she attempted never did, which was one reason she never bothered. Itchy strands would be straggling around her face before the night was half over, and the topknot itself would slide into just the right position to look ridiculous. That was what always happened when she tried to get herself up.

"You're healthy, lamb, not fat. It's just that Miss Celia's such a teensy little thing, and you're forever seein' yourself beside her."

"Oh, Tudi." There was no point in arguing with Tudi, Jessie knew. Tudi, seeing her onetime charge through the eyes of love, would never admit that there might be something lacking in Jessie's appear-

ance. Looking at herself in the mirror, Jessie faced
the bitter truth. At five and a half feet, she was tall
for a female, although that was not so dreadful. But
she was also, to put it kindly, plump; or, if one
wasn't so kind, fat. The short puffed sleeves of the
dress cut into her upper arms, making them bulge
just below where the sleeves ended. Her bosom
bulged, too, straining at the bodice, and so did her
waist. She had no doubt that her hips would strain
at the skirt if it had not been cut so full.

"Here, let me put these on you, Miss Jessie.
Maybe they'll help." Sissie reached up to screw to
her lobes a pair of dangling pearl earbobs that had
belonged to Jessie's mother. Tudi fastened the
matching necklace around Jessie's neck.

When they stood back, Jessie took another look.
What she saw heartened her a little. Perhaps the
earrings and necklace did help. At any rate they
seemed to call attention to the thick-lashed brown
eyes that were her best feature, and away from her
figure, which was her worst. If only she did not have
those thick dark brown brows that slanted like sable
wings across the whiteness of her forehead, and if
only the bright pink of the added embellishments
did not clash so hideously with the reddish tinge to
her hair, she might look almost—pretty.

"Tudi, I've been calling you for this age! Really, I
don't expect to have to come looking for servants in
my own house!"

Celia's voice, coming from behind them, made all
three of them start guiltily and turn to her. Framed
in the doorway, she looked lovely, her pale hair
smoothly upswept, her dress a soft pink silk with
the skirt gathered fashionably toward the back in a
style that made the most of her fragile figure. Lace
gloves covered her hands, and in one hand she held
a painted fan, which she swished through the air
with languid grace.

"Good Lord," she said, her eyes fastening on Jessie and widening with amusement. Immediately Jes-

sie felt about two inches tall, and about as pretty as a bullfrog.

"Well, I suppose it can't be helped," Celia continued after a brief pause in which no one said anything. "I'm glad you're ready. Stuart's here to fetch us, and I don't like to keep him waiting. Tudi, I want you to be sure to take the linens for my bed outside tomorrow so that the sun can bleach them. They're getting dreadfully yellow—almost the color of Jessie's dress."

"Yas'm." Tudi's face tightened, but Celia had already turned away and did not see.

"And, Sissie, you can start embroidering those tea cloths right away, since you won't have to help Rosa with supper. I've no patience with idle hands, as you know."

"Yas'm." Sissie's voice echoed Tudi's for expressionlessness.

"Come along, Jessie. And remember what I told you, dear."

Celia was already halfway down the stairs, and her voice floated back to Jessie, suddenly as sweet as spun sugar. Jessie guessed, and rightly as it turned out, that Stuart Edwards must be waiting within earshot in the hall below.

VII

"You may kiss me, Jessica, as we're to be family now." Miss Flora Edwards presented her crumpled cheek. Jessie, doing her best not to scowl, had no recourse but to give it a peck.

"You may kiss me too, if you like, Jessica," Miss Laurel Edwards said as Jessie straightened away from her sister. Jessie took a deep breath and gave the other elderly lady's cheek a peck. Then Miss Laurel took her hands, and both ladies beamed at her while Jessie did her best to smile back. It was an effort, and she did not doubt that her smile looked halfhearted.

The picnic supper that the Misses Edwards had put on in honor of their nephew's engagement had concluded as darkness had fallen. The party, which included all the nearby neighbors and some of the ones farther away, had then moved indoors. The picnic had been bad enough, but when Jessie had discovered that dancing was the next order of the evening, she had ducked into a rear parlor to escape. There, to her horror, she had run into the old ladies, who were arguing spiritedly about whose fault it was that the ices had melted before they could be served. She'd known Miss Flora and Miss Laurel from birth, but vaguely, as one did neighbors separated by several miles. Certainly they had never expressed any particular fondness for her before this moment. But, as they proceeded to tell her in great detail, since their nephew was marrying her stepmother (dear Celia, wasn't she just the sweetest creature?), that made Jessie (more or less) their grandniece by marriage.

Frequently digressing from the point, and more frequently interrupting each other, the Misses Edwards gave Jessie to understand that their dearest wish was to see their nephew, who was their closest living male relative, settle down near them. To that end, they had invited Stuart to visit, not once but many, many times. Imagine their delight when he had at last shown up on their doorstep! And he so charming, and the spitting image of their baby brother, who had been his father!

Of course Tulip Hill would be his one day, when both Miss Laurel and Miss Flora had passed on to their reward. Although their family (except for their baby brother, who had died in an unfortunate accident at the age of forty-two, leaving little Stuart without a father during his growing-up years) was quite long-lived—their mother had lived to be ninety-one, and her mother had passed on one month short of her hundredth birthday! So Miss Flora and Miss Laurel concluded, with a titter shared between them, that it might be some few years yet before Stuart inherited, as Miss Flora was in her, um, sixties, with Miss Laurel some three years younger.

"And why aren't you dancing, miss?" Miss Flora demanded of Jessie at last with a mock frown. With her masses of silky hair, which had presumably been dark like her nephew's but was now somewhere between white and silver, she must once have been the beauty of the family. She was taller than her sister and not quite as plump, but both had silvered rather than grayed and had the fine white skin prized by all Southern women. Age had wrought fine lines in Miss Laurel's face; Miss Flora's was frankly wrinkled. But still, the sweet scent of powder and lotion emanated from their skin at close range, both complexions were carefully tended, and both ladies were beautifully dressed.

"I—I don't—" Jessie stuttered, caught by surprise. The truth was that she didn't know how to dance. Worse than that, she didn't expect to be asked. She'd grown up with the boys; she knew each and every one of them by name, and they knew her, too. As a child, she'd met them on their own ground—throwing rocks, climbing trees, giving as good as she got in everything from fist fighting to daredevil horseback riding. But now—now she was a young lady, and they were gentlemen. To them, she seemed to be invisible. With them, she had no idea how to act. As for the girls, they might as well have been from a different species. She felt even more awkward around them than she did around the boys.

The picnic had been uncomfortable enough, with all the young people polite to this near stranger in their midst but gravitating quite naturally to their particular friends. After the initial, politely masked surprise at her presence had died down, Jessie had found herself quite alone. The Misses Edwards had hustled Celia and Stuart off as soon as their carriage had arrived. (Not that Jessie was sorry about that; the ride had been miserable, with Celia fawning all over Stuart while Jessie, in the rear, had maintained a sullen silence.) Once the announcement and laughing toasts were over, the engaged pair had made the rounds of their friends together with Stuart's two proud aunts, accepting congratulations that barely masked the envy the women felt toward Celia for having carried off this matrimonial prize. Watching ladies of every age slaver over Stuart, Jessie had scarcely managed to hide her scorn. What fools they all were, not to see further than a handsome face!

She'd been quite comfortable lurking behind a bright yellow forsythia bush, observing the festivities while remaining unobserved herself, until Bess Lippman had taken it into her prissy blond head to rescue her. Bess, whom like nearly everyone else at the party Jessie had known since infancy, was a younger version of Celia: sickly sweet on the outside and hard as steel within. Jessie had never liked her, and Bess's mother had long since forbidden her carefully raised daughter to associate with such a hoyden as Jessie. So she'd been understandably surprised when Bess, rounding the forsythia with a sympathetic ''Tch-tch,'' had scolded her in a playful tone for hiding herself away and, linking their arms with a strength that belied her frail appearance, dragged Jessie out.

In fact, Jessie would have been flabbergasted had it not been for the admiration in Oscar Kastel's eyes. Of course, Bess was exhibiting her kindness for the benefit of her tall, thin beau, spectacles and incipient bald spot notwithstanding. If Bess's action helped her snare an offer at last, Jessie thought nastily, then she supposed she ought not to begrudge her interference. After all, Bess was twenty, and on the verge of being an old maid despite her pale prettiness and expensive frocks. Perhaps the young men weren't quite the fools the young ladies were, after all. Certainly, if Bess Lippman's single state was any indication, they weren't as easily deceived by outward appearances.

Once she was in public view, Jessie could do nothing but grimly endure as Bess pulled her over to the long table set aside for the young folks. Oscar Kastel had beamed in the background when Bess had gaily called everyone's attention to the forlorn one. As the others greeted her, Jessie had no choice but to force a smile and join them. In the end she had sat with them for the uncomfortable, seemingly endless meal, although no one had talked to her except to exchange the merest courtesies. She had felt miserably out of place, but at least she'd been able to occupy herself with eating some of the delicious barbecue

and the crumb cake that was the cook at Tulip Hill's
(Jessie thought her name was Clover) specialty. But
dancing—or not dancing, while everybody watched,
and labeled her a wallflower—was an ordeal she just
could not face.

"She's shy," Miss Laurel said with a twinkle in
her eyes that were more gray than her sister's.
"Don't worry, Jessica, we'll look after you. Come
along, dear."

"Please, I . . ."

But protests were useless. Miss Laurel hooked her
arm in Jessie's as though they were two young girls
together and tugged her toward the opposite side of
the house, where the pocket doors separating the
two front parlors had been opened and the huge
space that resulted cleared for dancing. A musicians' platform screened with vibrant masses of pot-
ted flowers had been erected in one corner beside
two massive French doors that led to the back portico and rear gardens. The lilting strains of a qua-
drille emanated from the platform.

Seated on little chairs set around the perimeter of
the room, soberly clad matrons of all ages chatted
quietly amongst themselves. They would pass the
evening by watching the dancers and criticizing the
girls and their beaux, taking the floor to dance with
only their own husbands or brothers. Marriage automatically relegated a woman to dull clothes and a
chair on the sidelines, leaving the pretty, bright
dresses and enjoyable flirtations to the young, unmarried girls.

The older gentlemen, to a man undoubtedly dra-
gooned into attendance by their determined wives,
congregated around the punchbowl that had been
set up along with a table of refreshments in a small
antechamber. Their voices rose and fell as they dis-
cussed, from the few words Jessie could overhear,
various hunting exploits and the falling price of cotton. In the center of the room, perhaps twenty
young couples twirled about in the movements of

the dance. Jessie knew them all, of course, had
known them since birth, but—but . . .

The girls in their soft pastel dresses bore little resemblance to the playmates she remembered from
the years before their mothers decided that she
wasn't a suitable friend for their darling daughters
after all. Every one of them looked so pretty, with
their hair all shiny and styled, not in a topknot as
hers was, but so that it was tied away from their
faces and fell down to their shoulders in fat ringlets.

And their dresses—their dresses were not like
hers, either. Their bodices were tiny and revealed
far more of their white bosoms than the inch or so
of décolletage that had so scandalized Tudi. Their
sleeves, though short and puffed, were styled so that
they fell away from creamy shoulders, baring them,
too. The effect looked rather as if the top of the dress
might fall to the wearer's waist at any moment, but
all the girls wore them and in their mothers' presence, too, so that it must not only be the fashion but
also perfectly respectable. Tiny waists were accen-
tuated by enormous sashes, sashes that ended in the
back in huge bows and trailing streamers and were
wide enough to make the sash around Jessie's waist
look like a mere ribbon. Skirts were huge and billowing, longer in back than in front, so that small
satin slippers and an occasional tantalizing glimpse
of ankle were visible as the dancers whirled.

The dresses they wore on the dance floor were not
the same garments they had worn to the picnic earlier. Jessie realized with a sinking feeling that all the
young girls except her had brought dance dresses
with them, and changed into them after supper. Her
patched-together gown looked more out of place
than ever in comparison with the frothy confections
the other girls wore for dancing. But how could she
have known that they would change? And, given
her limited wardrobe, what could she have done
about it if she had known?

Watching, Jessie felt acutely self-conscious. Her

own sartorial shortcomings were painfully obvious even to her. With her faded, old-fashioned dress rendered even more dreadful by Sissie's bright pink embellishments, Jessie knew that she looked woefully out of place. If only everyone would leave her alone, she would steal away somewhere and hide until it was time to go home. By coming, she had appeased Celia and given tacit approval to the marriage. Celia was fully occupied in exhibiting her catch, and would neither know nor care if Jessie quietly disappeared until the evening was over. If it ever *was* over . . .

But the Misses Edwards had other ideas.

Miss Flora fell in on Jessie's other side, linking her arm with Jessie's, too. Jessie had no choice but to let the two old ladies bear her off. They tugged her toward the gaiety like two small keelboats towing a paddle wheeler.

"Now, then, let's see if we can't find you a partner," Miss Flora said, to Jessie's horror, pausing in the doorway to survey the room. Unable to free herself from the ladies or think of any way to politely circumvent them, Jessie was forced to stand between them, miserably aware of how dreadful she must look in comparison. The Misses Edwards were plump but small. Neither of their silvery heads reached past Jessie's shoulder. Despite their advanced age, their gowns put hers to shame. Miss Laurel was dressed sumptuously in lavender satin, while Miss Flora was clad almost identically in mauve.

The music swelled. Laughter and chatter filled the air. Eleanor Bidswell, resplendent in an apple-green gauze gown, floated by in the arms of blond Chaney Dart. Jessie had know her as Nell when they were little girls of seven and eight, but the petite redhead on the dance floor bore no resemblance to her childhood friend. Tall and willowy Susan Latow, in blue-sprigged muslin, danced with dark-haired Lewis Russell, while Margaret Culpepper, small, dark, and slightly plump but making the most of it in a low-cut gown of palest peach, was partnered by Howie Duke. Mitchell Todd wove his way through the crowd, a full punch glass in his hand, obviously on his way to find his partner, who must be sitting somewhere on the sidelines cooling off while he fetched her a drink. Mitch, who with his soft brown curls and hazel eyes had held a special place in her heart forever. . . .

"Mitchell! Mitchell Todd!"

Jessie was horrified to hear Miss Flora screech across the dance floor to none other than the object of every single one of her adolescent yearnings. Her head swung desperately toward Miss Flora, her mouth opened to object, but it was too late.

"Yes, ma'am?" With his customary good manners, Mitch turned and lifted his eyebrows at Miss Flora inquiringly. He had to raise his voice to make it heard over the din, but it was still the velvety voice that sent shivers down Jessie's spine every time she heard it. Then his eyes left Miss Flora and he was looking at her instead and Jessie thought she would die. . . .

"Come over here, Mitchell, and dance with Jessica!" This command, boomed at the volume of a cannon firing, made Jessie long to sink through the floor. Her face turned seventeen shades of crimson as Mitch hesitated, glanced at the full cup in his hand, then shrugged and headed toward the threesome in the doorway. If a heavenly chorus had announced that the world was ending right at that moment, Jessie would have fallen to her knees and given thanks. If a killer tornado had whirled through the valley and blown Tulip Hill and all therein into the next county, she would have considered herself saved. If . . .

But there was no more time for ifs. Mitch stood in front of her. Frozen with embarrassment, Jessie couldn't even look at him, much less summon the wit to try to circumvent what was about to happen.

"I'm sorry, Miss Flora, I couldn't hear what you said," he said mildly, smiling at the old lady. His front two teeth overlapped slightly, giving him an endearing boyish quality that made Jessie's heart go pitter-pat. Evidently he'd been trying to grow a mustache, because there was a line of brown fuzz above his upper lip. This evidence of burgeoning masculinity made her palms go damp. Or maybe the cause was sheer nervousness.

"She said you should dance with Jessica," Miss Laurel interjected. Jessie cringed. Her palms grew damper.

"Why—why—" He was taken aback, Jessie could tell he was taken aback, and of course he didn't want to, but what could he say? His innate good manners would leave him no recourse. "It'll be my pleasure. If you'll take this punch, Miss Laurel. It's certainly delicious, by the way. Please give Clover my compliments on the recipe."

Miss Laurel took the punch cup with a smile while Miss Flora tittered thanks for the compliment to their cook. Mitch held out his hand to Jessie. She looked from it to his face with paralyzing mortification. What could she do? What should she say? She didn't want him to dance with her because he was forced into it.

"Well, Jessie—I mean, Miss Jessica—shall we have a go?"

He'd known her forever, of course, and as children they'd been Jessie and Mitch to each other, but now he was Mr. Todd and she— But that was precisely the trouble. She was *not* Miss Jessica. That was the name of an elegant young lady like all the other elegant young ladies. Like Eleanor and Susan and Margaret and Bess.

"Go on now, Jessica. Have a good time, and don't trouble your head about us."

Miss Flora, bless her, whether from ignorance or kindness, had ascribed Jessie's hesitation to a pretty

unwillingness to leave her two hostesses to themselves.

"I—" Jessie opened her mouth to refuse, to tell
Mitch that he was off the hook because she couldn't
dance, didn't want to dance, particularly didn't want
to dance with him, of all people, but he seized her
hand and pulled her toward the dance floor before
she could get the words out.

"Jessica's going to be our niece now, you know!"
Miss Laurel—or was it Miss Flora?—called after them
as Mitch drew her out onto the floor. Then he was
turning toward her, smiling, while cold sweat prick-
led down her spine and her feet, like her tongue,
turned to stone.

The music changed. The tempo grew livelier. A
murmur ran around the dance floor.

"A reel!" came the excited cry from all around
them. There was a flurry of applause, and then everyone scattered, hurrying to form the parallel lines
needed for this dance. Mitch looked at her with a
shrug and a smile. Jessie, near giddy with relief at
being spared the awful confession that she could not
dance, to say nothing of the spectacle she was sure
she would make of herself if she tried, managed to
smile back. It was nine-tenths pure relief, but it was
a smile.

Just when Jessie was thinking that there must be
a God in heaven after all, just when she was thank-
ing her lucky stars or her patron saint or her fairy
godmother or whoever it was who had arranged
her salvation, Mitch grabbed her by the hand and
pulled her into the forming line. Other couples,
laughing and chattering, fell in behind and beside
them. The gentlemen lined up on one side, the ladies on the other.

The reel was a general favorite, and this time the
dancers included young and old alike. On her left
was Margaret Culpepper. On her right was Lissa
Chandler, a matron of about Celia's age who was
the mother of four young daughters.

The fiddler moved to the front of the platform and lifted his fiddle high. The announcer called out, "Ladies and gentlemen, grab your partners!" Then the announcer bowed and stepped back with a flourish. The fiddler struck up, his bow moving busily across the instrument as he scraped out the rollicking rhythm of the reel.

As the guest of honor, Celia and Stuart were the first to skip through the laughing, clapping corridor. Watching, Jessie supposed that they looked well together. Certainly they were a study in contrasts, with Celia so blond and petite and Stuart Edwards so tall and dark. Celia's cream satin skirt belled out around her as she danced, swinging from side to side and lending her an air of unaccustomed vivacity. Her cheeks were flushed rosily, and her pale gray eyes sparkled. It was an evening of triumph for Celia, and she was clearly enjoying every moment of it. Certainly she looked prettier than Jessie could ever remember seeing her. As for Stuart Edwards—much as Jessie hated to admit it, and she did hate to admit it, in his elegant black evening clothes he was a sight to steal a female's breath away.

Which only went to prove the old adage about beauty being no more than skin-deep.

But she was obviously the only female of whatever age present who hadn't fallen under the spell of his good looks. Ever since he had arrived, the ladies had been following him with their eyes. The bolder ones had openly flirted with him, reluctantly acknowledging Celia's prior claim but still determined to try their luck. Even some of the older married ladies had given him more than one come-hither look. To his credit—and Jessie hated to acknowledge that there was anything that was to his credit, searching for an ulterior motive that would account for his circumspection—he had not seemed to accord any of them more than polite attention. He had stayed properly at his fiancée's side all day, deflecting female silliness with a smile and a quip, while

Celia showed him off like a hunter with a trophy, queening it over the other ladies because she had him and they only wished they did.

The sight made Jessie sick, so she tried not to watch any more of it than she had to. But Celia's silent boasting and her fiancé's deliberately charming smile were pretty hard to miss.

Celia and Stuart were cheered as they came to the end and separated, moving back into line. Nell Bidswell and Chaney Dart were right behind them. With her green dress billowing and his blond hair gleaming under the light of the chandelier, they made a handsome couple. To Jessie's surprise, Miss Flora had found a partner in the widowed Dr. Angus Maguire, and that elderly couple skipped the length of the line after Nell and Chaney with as much energy as any of the young ones. They were roundly cheered, too.

Jessie had been so caught up in the spectacle of the dance that she didn't realize it was her turn and Mitch's until Lissa Chandler high-stepped into the middle to join her husband. Seth Chandler was the heir to Elmway, and Jessie guessed that the richness of that plantation had gone a long way toward increasing the squat, balding Seth's appeal for his pretty young wife. Which meant that Lissa Chandler had married for money, just as she suspected Stuart Edwards of planning to do. But somehow it seemed different for a woman. Women were supposed to find security in their husbands, not the other way around.

Then it struck Jessie that the Misses Edwards had said that Stuart would be their heir. Tulip Hill was not nearly so large or profitable as Mimosa, or Elmway, for that matter, but it was certainly a respectable property. Maybe—and the thought made her scowl—just maybe, she had wronged Stuart Edwards when she had accused him of being a fortune hunter. Maybe the man was truly in love with Celia after all, impossible as it seemed.

"Ready, Jessie—uh, Miss Jessie?" Mitch's question recalled Jessie's wandering attention. She blinked at him across the space separating them with something very near to panic. Her thoughts had been so busy that she had almost forgotten she was in line for the reel, much less that she and Mitch were next. Unless a miracle occurred within the next few seconds, she was going to have to dance down the long corridor of clapping revelers with Mitch, of all people.

If she could even dance.

The movement was no more than skipping with joined hands in time to the music. She could manage that. She had to, or make a fool of herself by darting out of the line. And suddenly it was very important that she not make a fool of herself in front of Mitch.

The music was wonderful, the laughter infectious. Mitch was the boy she had swooned over in secret for years. Maybe, maybe, he was going to notice her at last. He had not seemed adverse to dancing with her, and he was smiling at her now.

Suddenly the world did not look bleak, but bright.

"Ready," Jessie answered, and with a beaming smile she stepped out into the center to clasp hands with the boy she'd been silently, hopelessly, in love with for years.

VIII

Mitch's hands were warm, his skin soft and dry. He clasped her hands strongly, smiling down into her eyes. (Funny that she'd never noticed before how much taller he was than she; perhaps he'd grown.) Just the feel of his hands holding hers made her go all shivery. Jessie flushed rosily, beamed, and somehow made it down the clapping corridor to the end of the line. The only embarrassing moment came when it was time for them to part; Jessie was so enraptured that she forgot to let go.

The rest of the dance passed in a blur for her. She smiled, and clapped, and skipped down the corridor on cue, but her focus was entirely on Mitch. Caught in the throes of first love, she scarcely knew whether she was on her head or her toes. All she knew was that the day that had started so horribly had turned into a wonderful, magical evening. She wanted it never to end.

When the reel concluded, she braced herself, sure that he would leave her. Instead he offered her his arm and led her to a chair near the French windows, which had been opened to let in the night air. The band played another tune, and couples whirled about the floor. Jessie watched them, smiling idiotically. Mitch had stayed by her side, not speaking much but *there*. Jessie was tongue-tied but happy.

She supposed, dizzily, that he was in much the same state.

She dared a sideways glance at him, desperate for some brilliant conversational gambit that would dazzle him. Nothing occurred to her—but he smiled at her anyway.

"Shall I fetch you some punch?" he asked, getting to his feet. Jessie looked up at him, her eyes vulnerable with happiness, her smile wide. Truthfully, she was loath for him to leave her, but on the other hand, if he fetched her punch he would certainly return, and maybe while he was gone she could think of something to say. If she didn't talk soon, he would think her a complete ninny.

"That—that would be nice," she managed, her fingers twisting in her lap. He grinned at her, nodded once, and was gone. Jessie watched him make his way across the crowded dance floor toward the punch bowl, and practically sagged with relief. Thank the dear Lord, she had a few minutes to come up with something to say!

What did men like to talk about? Desperately she recalled the male conversation she had overheard in the minutes before dear, darling Miss Flora had summoned Mitch to her side. Could she talk about hunting, or the price of cotton?

". . . can't believe you let that child come out in that—that getup. She looks ridiculous!"

"Really, Cynthia, what do you expect me to do? She's eighteen, you know—oh, yes, she is!—and she has a closet full of lovely dresses that she absolutely refuses to wear. I certainly can't force her—why, she's twice my size and, though I hate to tell such tales of my own stepdaughter, possessed of a violent disposition that makes me quite fear her! 'Tis nothing short of a miracle that I got her to come tonight at all. I had to twist her arm, I promise you!"

"Well, you'll certainly never marry her off while she's tricked out like that! If her mother could see her, she'd spin in her grave!"

The speakers were Celia, of course, and Mrs. Latow, Susan's mother. They were strolling together along the edge of the dance floor and obviously had not seen Jessie sitting in her corner. Jessie had only just realized herself that she was in a corner, partially shielded from view by the musicians' platform on one side and the tall window's billowing curtain on the other. Certainly Mrs. Latow had not seen her, and Jessie didn't think Celia had, either. Although they had only to turn their heads, and they would spy her instantly.

The knowledge that Celia was telling lies about her did not bother her as much as Mrs. Latow's comments about her dress. Celia had lied about her for years; Jessie had given up trying to do anything about that. To defend herself from Celia's particular brand of malice was like boxing with shadows; one can't hit what one can't see. At first she'd been surprised when the neighbors had started to give her the cold shoulder, and later, when the cause became clear, hurt that they would believe Celia's tales. But then it had simply ceased to bother her. She didn't need them, any of them. She was happy with her animals and the servants for company.

But Mrs. Latow had said she looked ridiculous. That hurt. Jessie looked down at herself, at the faded, too-tight sprig muslin with the garish ruffles at neck and hem, and knew in her heart that Mrs. Latow spoke nothing less than the truth.

Although Mitch hadn't seemed to think so. Unless he'd merely danced with her to be kind. But she wouldn't think about that. She wouldn't.

Celia and Mrs. Latow were still gossiping as Jessie stood up, moving carefully so as not to scrape the chair against the floor or otherwise call attention to herself. This once, she was determined not to let Celia spoil things. She was having a marvelous night, a night beyond anything she could ever have dreamed of. Mitch would be coming back soon with the punch, and she wanted to get out of Celia's way before he returned. Suppose he overheard Celia's poison, or suppose Celia joined them, as, suspecting her stepdaughter had found an admirer, she might very well do? Celia would somehow find a way to destroy Jessie's pleasure. She always did.

One cautious sideways step, then another and a third, and Jessie was sliding out the French window, into the cool darkness of the rear portico. Inside, the curtain fluttered, concealing her exit. She leaned against the rough brick of the rear wall of the house and, peering around the curtain, watched through the window for Mitch. Once he came, she would step back inside. Determinedly she tried to dismiss Mrs. Latow's criticism from her mind. Perhaps Mitch was more discerning than most of the others present; perhaps he hadn't even noticed what she, or any of the rest of them, wore.

Just as Celia and Mrs. Latow moved on, Mitch returned with the punch. What perfect timing! Jessie smiled and almost stepped through the window again.

Then she saw that he was not alone. Jeanine Scott was with him.

"See, what did I tell you? She's gone. She was probably as horrified to have to dance with you as you were to get stuck with her. I'll bet she was glad to get a chance to escape."

"She wouldn't just run off. She has to be around here someplace." Mitch looked around as though Jessie might be hiding under a nearby chair. Jeanine giggled.

"She couldn't very well hide there. She's too big."

"That's not very nice, Jeanine." Mitch looked reprovingly at the slender brunette. Jeanine made an apologetic grimace.

"Oh, you're right, of course, and I'm sorry. But it was so embarrassing! There I sat, refusing all offers to dance because I said I had promised you, and then there you were, dancing with her! I had to sit the reel out, and you know it's my favorite."

"I know." Mitch sounded remorseful. "I told you, I couldn't help it. When Miss Flora practically ordered me, what could I say?"

"You're such a gentleman, of course. But then, I guess I wouldn't like you so much if you weren't." Jeanine fluttered her eyelashes coquettishly. Pressed tightly against the outside wall, Jessie clenched her fists against the pain. Her every instinct screamed for her to walk away so that she wouldn't have to hear any more, but she couldn't move.

"You're a flirt, Jeanine." Mitch didn't sound disapproving at all.

"And you love it, you know you do."

"I can't imagine where she could have got to." With a faintly harassed air, Mitch glanced around again as if expecting Jessie to materialize out of thin air.

"Maybe she had to retire for a few minutes. Or maybe some other gentleman asked her to dance." Jeanine sounded impatient. Mitch looked at her as she said that last, his expression clearly skeptical. Then they both laughed.

"All right, I grant you that's not very likely. But the fact remains she's gone, and that lets you off the hook, my charming Sir Galahad. And they're playing a turkey trot. My second favorite."

Mitch laughed again and set the cup of punch down on a chair. Then he offered his arm to Jeanine with a burlesqued bow.

"May I have the honor of this dance, Miss Scott?"

"You may." She dimpled, curtsied, and took his arm. Without a backward look, he led her onto the floor.

Jessie stayed where she was, profoundly thankful for the darkness that hid her. Suddenly the unaccustomed stays were far too tight, constricting her rib cage like iron bands. She could not catch her breath no matter how she tried. The world seemed to spin, and she rested her forehead weakly against the cool brick wall. Her heart pounded, ached. With commendable detachment she thought that this must be what it was like to feel it break.

Then, from behind, two hands closed over her upper arms. A voice that she instantly recognized growled in her ear.

"If you're going to faint, for God's sake don't do it here."

IX

Stuart Edwards' touch, his words, stiffened her spine enough to keep her from either fainting or throwing up, which seemed the more likely of the two fates that threatened her. He kept his grip on both her arms as he pushed her ahead of him off the portico, out of the sight of several amorous couples who had chosen to retire there for privacy and who watched the interplay between Jessie and her stepfather-to-be incuriously. Shifting his hold to one arm, he practically dragged her down the shallow flight of stairs that led to the garden, then along the cobbled path that wound through it to a secluded iron bench in the grape arbor. The bench was hidden from the view of anyone not standing directly in front of it by a trellis curtained by festoons of lacy, sweet-smelling vines. He pushed her down on the bench without ceremony, then stood in front of her, fists on hips, mouth tight and angry-looking. Jessie stared up at him, heart aching, and winced at the grimness of his face. Although if he'd been kind to her she might very well have disgraced herself forever by bursting into tears.

Though she did not know it, her eyes, darkened to the color of bright polished walnut by hurt and incipient tears, looked huge and lost. Her face was as white as the pale moon that floated overhead.

79

Her hair, as she had predicted, had been loosened from its precarious topknot by the vigor with which she had participated in the dance. It tumbled in thick disorder around her face and down her back, while individual curls caught stray moonbeams and reflected them with a glint of red. Her lips trembled, then were quickly compressed before he could detect this shaming sign of weakness. Still he scowled at her, and such obvious dislike on top of everything else was too much. Jessie shut her eyes, leaning her head against the garland of intertwining iron roses that formed the back of the bench.

"Put your head between your knees," he ordered grimly.

Trying her best to block out the memory of Jeanine and Mitch—Mitch!—laughing at her, Jessie barely heard him. With an impatient sound, he stepped toward her, spread his hand flat against the back of her head, and thrust it down past her knees. Despite her instinctive recoil, he kept her in that position by the simple expedient of curling his hand around the nape of her neck and refusing to let go.

"Let me up! What do you think you're doing?" Taken by surprise by such rough-and-ready ministrations, Jessie tried to squirm free. But his grip was unbreakable.

"Quit talking and breathe."

Jessie gave up. At the moment she didn't have the strength to fight him, didn't even particularly want to fight him. Instead she went limp, obediently allowing her head to droop almost to the ground, her hair puddling on the cobblestones in front of the bench. The unruly mass of curls covered the toes of his polished boots like a mahogany blanket. The sight was curiously disturbing, and as she saw it Jessie came to life again, jerking her head up as far as she could, trying once more to break free.

"I said breathe!"

His hand on the back of her neck pushed her head down again. Clearly he meant to hold her there until she did as he said. Furious, Jessie quit worrying about her hair touching his boots, indeed quit thinking about anything except how much she detested this autocratic man whose prisoner she seemed to be.

She did as he said, taking deep gulps of the crisp night air. In a matter of minutes she was feeling better. Well enough, at least, to wish him at the devil. Of all people to witness her humiliation, why, oh, why had it had to be he?

"I'm fine now, Mr. Edwards. You can let me up." Her voice was chillier than the night.

He removed his hand. Jessie sat up, shaking her head so that she could see through the tangle of curls. The last of the pins went flying, and her hair spilled down her back in a riotous mass that reached past her hips. The stays did not feel quite so suffocatingly tight now. To her relief, she was able to breathe normally. She sat still for a moment, fingers curling around the cool iron fronds at the edge of the seat, thankful for the shadowy darkness that concealed her expression from him. She felt bitterly ashamed. She had made a complete fool of herself tonight, first by even imagining that Mitch might be interested in a great gawk like herself, and second by wearing her heart on her sleeve. To top off her folly, she had been absurdly hurt when she had learned the awful truth and had let this man whom she detested see her pain. Now she had to think of something to say to save face, in front of him. How much of what had occurred to overset her did he know? Could she perhaps convince him that she was suffering from nothing more than a passing attack of illness?

"I should never have eaten those chitlins," she said in as light a tone as she could muster, darting him a quick, assessing look as she spoke. His mouth curled.

"Come now, Miss Lindsay, you take me for a flat. I was blowing a cloud on the porch when you came

sliding out the window. I threw my cigar away and
came up behind you to escort you back inside, and
I was privileged to hear every disgraceful word that
puppy said. If you like, I'll call him out for you."

He sounded perfectly serious. Jessie's eyes widened as she looked up at him. Of course, as her
stepmother's prospective husband, he was the nearest thing to a male protector she possessed. Unbe-
lievable as it seemed, it was now his prerogative,
indeed his obligation, to defend her honor. But her
honor had not been damaged, only her heart. Did
men really shoot each other over such incidents? At
the thought of Stuart Edwards blowing a hole
through Mitch—that the outcome might conceivably
go the other way never even occurred to her—she
hurriedly shook her head.

"No. Oh, no. Thank you."

"As you wish." He fished a flat cigar case from
his pocket, opened it, extracted one of his everlasting cheroots, then pocketed the case again. Lighting
one of the squared ends, he took a deep drag. The
tip glowed brightly, the strong scent of burning tobacco filled the air, and then he pulled the thing
from his mouth.

"The boy's a bigmouthed fool, and the girl he was
talking to is an empty-headed flibbertigibbet. You're
being absurd if you let yourself be hurt by anything
either of them has to say."

"I wasn't hurt." Pride stung, Jessie protested a
little too quickly.

He considered her for a moment without speaking, shrugged, and stuck the cheroot back in his
mouth. "Of course you weren't. My mistake."

Her protest had been nothing short of idiotic, Jessie knew. Having witnessed her physical symptoms,
he knew just how hurt she'd been.

"All right, maybe I was. A little. Anyone would
have been."

He pulled the cheroot from his mouth. "It always

hurts when we care about people who don't care about us.''

Jessie snorted. ''How would you know? Ladies fall all over themselves to get to you. I bet they've been making cakes of themselves over you since you were first breeched.''

He grinned unexpectedly. It was a wry, oddly disarming grin, and Jessie was surprised at the charm of it. ''Not quite that long. As a matter of fact, when I was a boy of about fifteen—a little younger than you are, but not much—I fell head over heels in love with an elegant young lady from a fine old family. I used to see her about the streets as she'd go marketing with her mammy, and I'd follow her. She looked at me once or twice, and smiled, and batted her eyes as young ladies do. I was sure we were madly in love. Then I overheard her laughing with her mammy about that dirty bowery boy who followed her everywhere. I slunk off like a whipped pup. I can still remember how much that hurt. But as you see, I survived, and quite handily too.''

It was nice of him to share that long-ago humiliation with her, though Jessie doubted that it was true. First, it was inconceivable to her that any female in her right mind would give a man who looked like Stuart Edwards the cold shoulder. Even as a boy he must have been extraordinarily attractive. Second . . .

''That's a lovely story, but you're bamming me, I know. How could any girl mistake an Edwards for a dirty bowery boy?''

For the barest moment, he looked almost startled. Then he laughed, and took another drag on the cheroot. ''I have no idea how she could have made such a mistake, but she did, I promise you. Perhaps in my jaunts about the streets I got a little dirtier than she might have expected an Edwards to be.'' His hand holding the cheroot dropped to his side, and he turned so that he stood with his shoulder to her, looking back toward the house. His expression was thoughtful. After a moment he glanced her way again.

"You're going to have to go back in, you know." It was said mildly, but the very image he conjured up made Jessie shudder.

"Oh, no. I can't."

"You have to. Otherwise people will talk about you, and that's never pleasant for a young lady. You were having such a good time dancing, and then you disappeared. How does that look? Your beau might even have enough brains to put two and two together and figure out that you overheard him talking to that fish-faced young lady. You surely don't want him to know that he hurt you enough to make you run away?"

"No!" The idea of that was even worse than the idea of facing the ballroom full of people again. Then the rest of his words registered. Despite her misery Jessie had to grin, though it was a trifle wobbly. "Do you truly think Jeanine Scott is fish-faced?"

"Absolutely. And believe me, I've had enough experience with ladies to know fish-faced when I see it."

"Oh, I believe you!" Her grin firmed, and as it did, some of her heartache eased. Though he was probably saying it just to be kind, of course. Still, it was what she needed to hear.

"Do you, now? And you're laughing at me to boot. Come on, then; on that cheerful note it's time to take you back inside."

He threw his cheroot away and held out his hand to her. Jessie looked at that long-fingered hand and felt her stomach turn over. The idea of going back inside—back to where people were spreading lies about her and laughing behind their hands and pitying her—made her feel physically ill.

"Please, can't we just go home?"

She asked the question in a tiny, shamed voice that said volumes about how hard it was for her to admit to such weakness. Her eyes rose to his beseechingly. If she hadn't bit down hard on her lower lip, it would have trembled.

"Jessica." He said her name in a way that was both impatient and impossibly gentle.

She just looked at him without speaking. With a lithe movement he hunkered down in front of her and took her hand in both of his. His hands were large, far larger than hers, and strong, and warm. Jessie hadn't realized how cold her hands were until she felt the warmth of his.

"What do you want me to do? Go in there and fetch Celia away from the party while you hide out here, then bundle the both of you home?"

"Please don't—tell Celia." It was a wretched whisper. His mouth tightened, and Jessie thought for a dreadful instant that she had made him angry with her. It was surprising how much she suddenly disliked the idea of making him angry. For a few minutes, out here in the dark, they'd almost become . . . friends.

"If I fetch her away from the party, I'll have to tell her something."

"Couldn't you just say that I was ill?" Not that Celia would care, Jessie knew. Celia would be livid at having her engagement party interrupted—and Jessie would pay for the interruption later.

"Celia's your stepmother, Jessie. She's the best one to help you deal with all this. Not me."

"Please don't tell her. Please." Her hand twisted in his, closed urgently around his fingers. He looked down at their entwined hands, then stood up suddenly, freeing himself.

"All right. I won't tell her. Though I think it's a mistake."

"Thank you." Relieved, she smiled at him. He looked down at her again, his hands thrust into his pockets, his expression impossible to read.

"But my silence is going to cost you. If you want me to keep secrets from my wife-to-be, you're going to have to do something for me in return."

"What?"

"Walk back in there like the fighter I know you to be, and pretend to be having a good time until Celia's ready to leave. It'll be hard, but you can do it. And it's for your own good. You don't want that boy you fancy to guess you've been out here sniveling in the dark because he's not interested, do you?"

"No!" The very notion was hideous.

"Well, then, do we have a deal?"

"Yes." But Jessie's eyes flickered, and she chewed the inside of her cheek as she considered the enormity of what she was about to do. To go back inside and pretend that the world was just as it had been fifteen minutes ago would be the hardest thing she had ever done in her life. To face Jeanine Scott, and Mitch . . .

"Mr. Edwards?" Her voice was tiny. He regarded her with eyebrows raised inquiringly. She rushed on before she completely lost her nerve. "When we go in, may I—may I stay with you? I don't really know any of them, and it's so awful, and I look awful and I know it, and—and I don't want anyone thinking he has to dance with me." Her voice trailed off, and she looked miserably at the cobblestones. "If you want to dance with Celia, or anyone, of course I don't mean you can't, but—but the rest of the time." As she finished this garbled speech, her face felt as hot as if she'd stood in front of a roaring fire for an hour. Jessie knew that if there had been enough light to allow him to see properly, her cheeks would have looked as red as the stones at her feet.

She thought that if he laughed she would die, but to her relief he didn't even smile.

"Don't worry, Jessie, I'll look after you," he promised gently, and held out his hand.

Jessie hesitated only a few seconds before she put hers into it and allowed him to pull her to her feet.

X

"Hold on a minute. We're forgetting something. You can't go back in there with your hair like that. God only knows what they'll imagine you've been doing."

He had drawn her into the full spill of moonlight before suddenly frowning at her. At his words Jessie tugged her hand from his and raised both of them, self-consciously, to the wayward bulk of her hair.

"Where are your pins?" He sounded resigned.

"Here's one—and another. . . ." Jessie found several still valiantly clinging to long-since-liberated curls and pulled them out. "But I don't have a mirror, or a brush."

"Give them to me." He held out his hand. Jessie dropped the half-dozen hand-whittled hairpins she had recovered into his palm.

"Is that all?"

"It's all I can find."

"They'll have to do, then. Turn around, and I'll see what I can contrive."

"You?" The single word was tinged with disbelief.

"At least I can see what I'm doing. Besides, this won't be the first time I've pinned up a lady's hair. Turn around."

As Jessie was slow to respond, he put his hands

87

on her shoulders and turned her to suit him. His
palms were warm and abrasive against her bare skin.
The masculine strength of his hands sent a little
shiver down her spine. The feeling was not unpleasant, but nevertheless she pulled away.

"Hold still, damn it."

From the way he talked, his mouth was full of
hairpins. Both his hands were occupied in gathering
up the masses of her hair. It was long as a horse's
tail and twice as thick, strong curly hair that had a
mind of its own and adapted only with great reluctance to the demands of fashion.

Jessie held very still as he ran his fingers through
her curls to work out the worst of the tangles, then
pulled her hair straight back from her scalp, twisting
it into a long rope. With what she considered surprising deftness for a man, he coiled it on top of her
head.

"Hold this," he directed, taking her hand and
laying it flat on top of the coil. Then, when she did
as he directed, he strategically inserted what few
hairpins remained.

"Ouch!" One stabbed into her scalp, and she
jumped.

"I said hold still! You'll make the whole thing
fall."

Jessie held still.

"All right, you can let go."

Cautiously Jessie let her hand fall to her side, certain that at least half her hair would follow. But to
her amazement the coil stayed in place, and felt at
least as secure as the topknot had earlier.

"Thank you," she said, sounding surprised as she
turned to face him. "Wherever did you learn to do
that?"

"I've groomed a few fillies in my time." He
grinned wickedly, his expression such that Jessie
was not sure whether he meant horses or females.
While she looked at him suspiciously, he offered her

his arm. The gesture was more automatic than gallant, but still . . .

No gentlemen had ever offered his arm to Jessie before.

Hesitantly, she placed her hand in the crook of his elbow. Her fingers tingled with the feel of smooth superfine overlying hard muscles, but he was already walking her back toward the house as though nothing was out of the ordinary. Of course, he must walk with ladies this way all the time.

To him, such a courtesy was commonplace. But Jessie, for the first time in her life, felt like a real young lady. Not like an unattractive, oversized tomboy at all.

"If anyone should be so impertinent as to ask, you can say you slipped away to repin your hair," he was saying. Jessie nodded, once again unable to think of anything to say.

Faint strains of music from the house drifted out over the gardens. The scents of roses and lilacs vied with each other to form a thick, heady perfume. A raindrop fell, then another.

"Let's get you inside. It's going to rain."

Ruthlessly hurried, Jessie scarcely had time to worry about how she would react if she came face-to-face with Mitch or Jeanine Scott before he had whisked her onto the portico under the sheltering overhang. No sooner had they gotten under cover than it began to rain. In moments the gentle spattering had turned to silvery sheets, and the smell of rain overrode the perfume of the flowers.

"God, I hate that smell," Stuart Edwards muttered, and with a hand in the small of Jessie's back he urged her through the open French window.

XI

Inside, nothing had changed. Jessie hesitated, moving imperceptibly closer to Stuart Edwards' side as her eyes grew accustomed to the bright glow of the chandeliers. The band still played gaily. In the center of the floor, couples laughed and twirled. The gossiping matrons still sat in their chairs along the wall, the gentlemen held court by the punch bowl, and Miss Flora and Miss Laurel huddled near the opposite wall in the throes of what looked like a spirited argument.

Jessie glanced up at the man beside her. The candlelight played across his face, and for the first time that day she really noticed the scratches she had inflicted. They ran three abreast down each lean cheek from just below his eyes to his mouth, not as raw and red as they had been the night before, but definitely there. She wondered how he had explained them away.

He must have felt her eyes on him, because just then he looked down at her. One corner of his mouth quirked up. The skin around those sky-blue eyes crinkled, and he smiled. Despite the scratches, the man was devastatingly handsome when he smiled.

"The rain's made your hair curl all around your

face. It looks charming.'' It was a conspiratorial whisper, designed to hearten her, Jessie knew.

"It always curls. It's the bane of my life.'' Jessie was speaking at random, grateful for his effort but too nervous to take any pleasure from the compliment. Her eyes searched the crowded room. Celia danced by in the arms of Dr. Maguire, wiggling her fingers at Stuart and giving Jessie an appraising look that suddenly turned hard. But Jessie, preoccupied, scarcely noticed Celia. She was looking for Mitch, and found him, as she had expected, dancing with Jeanine Scott. Mitch saw her at the same time that she saw him. Lifting a hand in greeting, he bent his head to whisper something in Jeanine's ear. Jessie shuddered.

"I think they're coming over here,'' she muttered frantically, clutching at Stuart Edwards' sleeve.

"Then we'll just have to move, won't we?'' he said cheerfully, and before Jessie knew what he was about, he had her right hand in his and his arm around her waist and was sweeping her onto the dance floor.

"What are you doing?'' she hissed, effectively distracted from Mitch's doings as she stumbled over her rescuer's booted feet and all but fell to her knees. Only his arm around her kept her upright.

"It's called the waltz, I believe,'' he said, straight-faced. Luckily his hold on her was viselike for all its deceptive ease. She had no choice but to follow his movements. To her shock, she found herself being twirled across the floor in what she hoped was an approximate duplication of the other dancing couples' movements.

"Mr. Edwards, I can't dance!''

"Since we're soon to be closely related, I suggest you call me Stuart. And I may be mistaken, but you seem to be dancing quite adequately.''

He smiled down at her charmingly. She stepped on his toe.

"Careful.'' He'd said the same thing to her in ex-

actly the same tone once before. The memory threw
off her budding attempts to match her steps to his.
She stepped on his toe again, muttered a shamefaced apology—and found herself whirled about in
a series of breathtaking turns that left her so dizzy
that all she could do was cling to him, praying that
she did not look as disconcerted as she felt.

She was as close to him as she had been that first
night on the veranda when he had saved her from
falling down the steps, and her perceptions of him
were every bit as acute.

Tonight he smelled of rum punch and rain. His
shoulder beneath her hand was wide and strong.
Her eyes were on a level with his neck. It was very
brown against the whiteness of his cravat. A faint
black stubble shadowed the strong lines of his chin
and jaw. His mouth was beautifully shaped, his lips
a brownish shade of rose and firm-looking. His nose
was straight, his cheekbones rounded and high.

Preoccupied with her inventory of his features,
Jessie let her gaze drift higher. With a shock she saw
that he was watching her, his sky-blue eyes twinkling with amusement. Jessie blinked, embarrassed
to be caught looking at him, and hastily dropped her
eyes. Her loss of concentration caused her to stum-
ble over his feet again. His arm tightened around
her waist, holding her upright.

And it was then that Jessie made an appalling dis-
covery.

Celia had said that Stuart Edwards sent shivers
down her spine. Suddenly, vividly, Jessie knew just
what Celia meant.

She dared not raise her eyes above his chin, terrified that her new awareness of him must be written on her countenance for him to read. Stiffening
in his arms, she held herself as far away from him
as she could, only to have him pull her closer impatiently. There was still the prescribed amount of
space between them, but Jessie was acutely conscious of the strength in the arms that held her, of

the hard muscles that lay beneath the immaculate linen shirt, of the sheer overwhelming masculinity of the man.

Forever afterwards, when Jessie remembered that dance, she remembered it as the time when she truly began to grow up.

"Smile, Jessie, or you'll have everyone thinking you don't like me," he chided in her ear, and twirled her about in the first of another series of dizzying turns.

What else could she do? Jessie smiled.

XII

Veni, vidi, vici: I came, I saw, I conquered. Julius Caesar had said the words once, and Clive McClintock repeated them with silent satisfaction as he stood solemnly before the flower-bedecked altar of the small church, watching his soon-to-be bride walk down the aisle behind her stepdaughter. The wedding march swelled, the spectators leaned forward the better to see Celia in her bridal garb, and Clive smiled. Everything he had always wanted was headed his way.

As prizes went, Celia Lindsay and her plantation did not quite equal the riches of ancient Rome, but she'd do. Oh, yes, she would do very nicely. She was lovely, well bred, malleable, a lady. And rich. Very rich. Land rich. Without Mimosa as an incentive, Clive would never have offered marriage. Bed, maybe, but not marriage. He supposed, in a way, that the stepdaughter had been right when she had called him a fortune hunter. But he meant to see that Celia did not lose anything in the deal. Or the stepdaughter, either, if it came to that. He meant to do his damnedest to make Celia a good husband, and if ever a chit had needed the proverbial iron hand in the velvet glove, it was Jessica Lindsay. They'd both benefit from having him take control of their plantation and their lives.

The way things had worked out was nothing more
or less than poetic justice. He'd vowed, that never-
to-be-forgotten morning on the deck of the *Mississippi Belle*, that someone would pay for stealing his
money. And that someone had turned out to be Stuart Edwards, who had unwittingly repaid what he
had stolen by giving Clive something he no longer
had any use for—his identity. And the unused por-
tion of his life.

Assuming Edwards' identity was not something
that Clive had originally set out to do, of course.
Hoping to find anything that would lead him to Hulton and his money, he had shrugged off all offers of
treatment for his hand to conduct a furious search
of Edwards' belongings. He'd found a little cash, a
few mementos—and a letter. The letter he'd pocketed for its address: Tulip Hill Plantation in Yazoo
Valley, Mississippi. Perhaps Hulton was headed
there.

Then Luce, with a doctor in tow, had found him
and insisted that he let the man look at his hand.
For days after that, Clive had done nothing but curse
the heavens, drink, and search for Hulton and his
money, both of which seemed to have disappeared
off the face of the earth.

When Clive finally got around to reading the letter
and learned that it was from Edwards' two elderly
(and slightly dotty, from the sound of them) aunts,
he'd nearly crumpled the thing up and tossed it
away as useless. But for some reason he'd kept it.
Only later, after the best doctors in New Orleans
had assured him that they'd done all they could, but
that it was doubtful he'd ever recover full mobility
in the fingers of his right hand, did he remember
Edwards' aunts.

The knife thrust had severed nerves, muscles, tendons. He would suffer some degree of paralysis in
that hand for the rest of his life.

A gambler's hands were his livelihood. Since boy-
hood Clive had been able to do anything with cards;

sleight of hand was something at which he'd excelled. The quick dexterity of his fingers had enabled the onetime "dirty bowery boy" to provide himself with the trappings of a comfortable, sometimes even luxurious, existence. A few more years, and he would have been set for life.

But no longer. His means of earning a living had been stolen from him along with his money. Losing the mobility in his right hand was far worse than being robbed.

It was only after weeks spent alternating between drunken self-pity and even more drunken rages that the idea had come to him. He had searched frantically for the letter and read it again, carefully this time.

Edwards' aunts owned a cotton plantation, which undoubtedly meant that they were rich. And they were prepared to leave the whole kit and caboodle to their nephew if he would only come and visit them. They were old and lonely, and he was their last surviving male relative. They loved him already, although they hadn't seen him since he was a babe in arms.

There was more on that subject, three pages worth with the lines crossed and recrossed so many times that it made making sense of the letter difficult. But Clive managed to grasp what to him were the essential facts: two not-quite-sane old ladies, with no other relatives in the world, were prepared to leave their (vast) worldly goods to their nephew if he would only visit them.

Unfortunately for them, their nephew was dead. But Clive was not. Stuart Edwards had robbed him of forty-five thousand dollars and his livelihood. Stuart Edwards owed him.

Clive never let a debt go uncollected if he could help it.

That there would be a few unanticipated problems in the execution of his scheme Clive never doubted, but he also never doubted that he could overcome

them. In his many years of living by his wits, he'd
learned, by and large, that people saw only what
they expected to see, and believed most everything
they were told. If he were to present himself to the
two doddering old ladies at Tulip Hill Plantation as
their prodigal nephew, who was there to say him
nay?

Racking his brain for what he could remember of
the dear departed, Clive recalled that Stuart Edwards had been tall, with black hair. Clive had no
idea of the color of the fellow's eyes, but if the old
ladies hadn't seen their thieving nephew since he
was an infant, they probably wouldn't know that
detail, either. Besides, the chances that Edwards'
eyes had been blue were fifty percent. Not bad odds,
if it came to that.

And if there should by chance be any question
about his identity, Clive had the letter, addressed to
himself as Stuart Edwards in Charleston, South Carolina, as proof that he was whom he claimed to be.
That and an agile brain, which had never in twenty-
eight years failed him. Deceiving two old ladies
should be ridiculously easy. Besides, he'd probably
make them a better nephew than Stuart Edwards,
thief and would-be murderer, ever had.

Clive had planned to visit with them for a while,
establish himself in the neighborhood as Stuart Edwards, and then, when the old ladies passed on to
their reward (from the sound of their letter, it
couldn't be too long), come back and collect his inheritance with the entire community to vouch for
who he was.

The best plans were always simple ones.

Indeed, everything had gone even better than he
had expected. Miss Flora and Miss Laurel had fallen
on his neck from the moment their majordomo had
announced who he was, and accepted him instantly
as their nephew. Not a single question had been
raised as to his identity.

The only catch was that the two old ladies, for all

their dottiness, seemed to be in the best of health. It was brought home forcibly to Clive (from the Misses Edwards' chatter about their long-lived antecedents) that it might be a considerable number of years before his scheme could come to ultimate fruition.

Not that he wished the old ladies any harm, but . . .

And then he had met Celia Lindsay, wealthy widow.

Until her exact marital and financial status had been made clear to him by Miss Flora, the cannier of his two aunts, Clive had paid her scarcely any attention. Her looks were well enough, but certainly nothing to catch his eye amongst a bevy of dewy-fresh debutantes.

But a wealthy widow had much to recommend her. And a wealthy widow who was doing her utmost to lure him into her bed made it almost ridiculously easy.

Clive was nothing if not adaptable. Instead of waiting for the Misses Edwards to pass on to their reward, he would change his plans. He would turn his much-heralded charm on Mrs. Lindsay, sweep her off her feet, and wed her and her plantation without further ado. Thus would he acquire the land he had always dreamed of, and a way of life he had never even thought to aspire to.

He quite liked the idea of Clive McClintock—no, make that Stuart Edwards—Esquire, gentleman planter.

XIII

"Dearly beloved . . ."

Jessie stood a little to the left and behind her stepmother, clutching Celia's bouquet of white roses and lilies of the valley with fingers that were not quite steady. The sweet scent of the flowers teased her nostrils as she listened to the words that would give Mimosa over into Stuart Edwards' keeping.

In truth, she didn't know what she felt. Less than a fortnight ago, she would have sworn that she would have shot the man rather than see him take title to all that should have been hers. But that was before they had become friends, at least after a fashion. Before she had discovered a kindness in him that was completely foreign to Celia's nature.

The bitter truth was that Mimosa wasn't hers, but Celia's. And in the many sleepless nights she had passed since the disastrous engagement party, Jessie had come to believe that Stuart Edwards would be a far better steward for the property and the souls who came with it than Celia had ever been.

It was also possible that he would continue to be a friend to her. Jessie had discovered that she very badly wanted Stuart Edwards for her friend.

So here she was, acting as her despised stepmother's sole bridesmaid, tricked out in a voluminous silk gown in the same hideous shade of pink as the ruf-

fles Sissie had sewn on her old muslin dress. The
gown was new, but that was all Jessie could say for
it. Celia had personally selected the style and the
material, and Jessie could only suppose that she had
chosen both with an eye to making her stepdaughter
look as unattractive as possible. Flounces cascading
down from her shoulders to her hem, with only a
wide sash to announce that she even had a shape,
certainly did nothing to flatter Jessie's figure. In fact,
when she had looked at herself in the cheval glass
in her bedroom before heading for the church that
morning, she had decided that she resembled nothing so much as the beruffled pin cushion on Celia's
dressing table. The shape and the color were the
same.

She had also decided that violent pink was not a
good color for a female with glints of red in her hair.

Celia, on the other hand, looked lovely. Her petite
figure was shown to best advantage in a shoulder-
baring satin gown in the shade of ice blue so pale as
to look almost white in some lights. Her blond hair
was dressed in an elegant knot of curls that cascaded
from beneath the brim of her wide picture hat. As a
second-time bride, Celia was not permitted the ro-
manticism of a white gown and veil, but there was
a wisp of veiling beneath the ribbons and flowers on
her hat, and her dress was lavish with lace. On the
whole she looked very bridal.

And, though Jessie hated to admit it, very young
and very pretty.

"Do you, Celia Elizabeth Bradshaw Lindsay, take
this man . . ."

They were saying their vows. Jessie watched, trying not to look as anxious as she felt, as Celia swore
to love, honor, and obey her new husband.

Then it was Stuart's turn.

"Do you, Stuart Michael Edwards . . ."

His voice was very steady, low and perfectly clear,
as he promised to love and cherish Celia for the rest
of her life.

"The ring, please."

Seth Chandler had agreed to stand up with Stuart, and he fumbled in his pocket for a minute before finding the ring and handing it over.

Stuart slid the ring onto Celia's finger. His hand was large and long-fingered, brown and strong-looking, its masculine beauty marred only by a reddish puckered scar that sliced diagonally across both its back and its palm. Her hand was slender-fingered, delicate, and lily-white, tiny compared with his. Looking at those two joined hands, Jessie felt a spurt of what could only be described as longing.

But what she longed for she couldn't have said.

"I now pronounce you man and wife. You may kiss the bride."

Stuart kissed Celia, his dark head bending over her fair one. She clung to his shoulders for an instant, her nails digging intimately into his dove-gray coat. Then he was straightening, and she was looking around, laughing and rosy as triumphant music filled the air. Again Jessie felt that stab of longing.

Then she was handing Celia her bouquet, and Celia and Stuart were retreating down the aisle arm in arm, the epitome of the happy bride and groom.

Just how it started Jessie never knew. When she arrived on the church stoop on Seth Chandler's arm, the guests spilling out behind her, the scene was already in progress.

"She's mine! I tell you, she's mine! She gave herself to me—she promised me—!"

"Why, that's Mr. Brantley, our overseer," Jessie said, shocked, to no one in particular. Stuart and Celia, seemingly frozen in place, stood poised at the top of the steps leading down into the churchyard. Stuart heard her words; Jessie saw him stiffen, and as she realized the significance of what was happening she felt her stomach clench.

Celia's sins had just caught up with her in the person of Ted Brantley. She had been sneaking

down to the overseer's cottage for years. Jessie had
even seen her headed that way in the evenings after
supper. The only thing that surprised Jessie about it
was that she hadn't tumbled to the meaning of those
solitary walks before this. But then she'd thought
that Celia, who was at least as intelligent as a bird,
had enough sense not to foul her own nest.

Apparently she'd been wrong.

The churchyard was filled with people from Mimosa and Tulip Hill. Only the most favored of the
house servants had been allowed to occupy the rear
pews of the church. The rest of them had waited
outside to cheer the bride and groom when they
emerged. Most had come on foot, but there were a
few wagons drawn up outside the gate.

"She's mine! She's been mine for years!"

Mr. Brantley was on horseback. Surrounded by a
sea of mostly black faces of well-wishers on foot, he
was as visible as a mountain on a flat plain. He was
weaving in the saddle, clearly drunk, so drunk he
could barely keep his seat on the horse, so drunk he
was crazy with it.

But not too crazy not to recognize Celia on the
steps of the church.

"Celia! Celia, my darlin'! What about me? You
love me, not him! You said so!"

Celia stood without moving, white-faced and silent, clutching her new bridegroom's arm as she
stared out over the crowd at her erstwhile lover.

"He's insane," she said disdainfully. Then, more
quietly, "Get him out of here."

The slaves nearest Brantley shifted uneasily, looking up at him and trying with gestures and low-
voiced pleas to shut him up. But none of them, even
the ones most loyal to Mimosa, dared to lay a hand
on the white overseer. None of them cared enough
for Celia to take the risk.

Behind Jessie, the crowd continued to swell out of
the church, milling about on the stoop and, for those
who couldn't get out, in the vestibule, standing on

tiptoe as they tried to peer over their neighbor's
shoulder to get a look at what was going on.
Shocked murmurs rose on all sides.

"Insane, am I? You bedded me, said you loved
me! You can't deny it! What about those times you
came to me, those things you said? You're mine,
mine, mine!"

Everyone watched and listened with fascination.
The crowd was alternately appalled and titillated de-
pending upon the hearer's individual disposition,
but no one seemed to know what to do to bring the
dreadful scene to an end. Until Stuart, his face utterly expressionless, freed himself from Celia's hold
and ran lightly down the steps toward the burly,
ginger-haired drunk.

The crowd parted like the Red Sea before Moses.
Stuart gained Brantley's side, reached up, and
grabbed the man by the coat.

"Hey, what the hell . . . !" Brantley sputtered as
he was dragged from the saddle. Then, apparently
recognizing his danger, he swung a haymaker at
Stuart that would have taken his head off if it had
connected.

But it didn't. Stuart answered with a punch to the
man's face that snapped his head back and sent
bright droplets of blood spurting from his nose to
shower those nearby. That one punch left Brantley
dangling limply in Stuart's hold.

"You there, haul this trash out of here," Stuart
said to a nearby field hand, dropping the uncon-
scious Brantley to the ground as if he were no more
than the garbage Stuart called him.

"Yes, suh," the worker replied, wide-eyed as he
looked from his new master to the fallen overseer.
Then the wagon was brought and Brantley, still un-
conscious, was lifted into it.

The buzz of conversation behind Jessie had risen
to feverish heights. It quieted abruptly as Stuart
swung around and came back toward the stoop and
his bride.

Instinctively Jessie drew closer to Celia. She was less than fond of her stepmother, but they were family, nevertheless. Despite the years of antipathy between them, Jessie could not stand by and watch Celia be publicly humiliated, or worse. Any scandal involving Celia would inevitably involve Mimosa, too.

Watching her new husband approach, Celia stood as white and unmoving as a marble effigy. Jessie knew that Celia was frightened. She could see it in her widened nostrils, smell it in her sweat.

And who wouldn't be frightened, under the circumstances? Jessie knew that if she had to face Stuart Edwards' wrath, she would be petrified.

But Stuart surprised them all. He neither shouted nor hit Celia nor renounced the vows he'd just sworn.

"What is it about you that drives men insane for love of you, I wonder?" he said lightly as he rejoined Celia on the stoop. "I'd better take care lest I succumb to that fate myself."

Then he smiled at her as if he had not the slightest notion that there had been any truth to Brantley's claims, and signaled for Progress to bring round the buggy.

For a few minutes Jessie was fooled. She felt the tension of the crowd ease, and everyone gathered closer, exclaiming over what had occurred as if it were some kind of tribute to Celia's beauty.

Celia, for her part, rose to the occasion magnificently. Jessie watched her stepmother and Stuart receive the good wishes of the crowd and parry the inevitable jests, and marveled. Celia had come within a hairbreadth of a scandal over her virtue that would have ruined her name forevermore. And her new husband, the man most intimately concerned with her virtue, or lack of it, had rescued her from the brink of the abyss without even appearing to realize just how close to the edge she had been.

Which left Jessie wondering if perhaps, just per-

haps, Stuart truly did believe that Brantley's boasts
were nothing more than the empty bombast of a
lovelorn drunk.

Until he'd handed Celia into the carriage and
looked around to meet Jessie's eyes.

In those icy blue depths she read the truth: before,
when she'd called her stepmother a whore, he'd
slapped her face for being a liar. Now he was willing
to consider the possibility that perhaps, just perhaps, Jessie had been telling the truth.

XIV

The wedding trip lasted a mere three weeks. It was to have been twice as long, but near noon on the first day of July, Jessie was seated on the upstairs gallery with Tudi and saw the now familiar buggy bowling briskly along the road toward Mimosa. The scene was an uncanny repeat of the first time she had set eyes on Stuart Edwards. Only this time, instead of uneasiness, she felt a burgeoning pleasure.

Absurd to think she might have missed a man she barely knew, a man whom by all rights she should still consider her enemy.

"You're all lit up like a Christmas tree," Tudi observed, looking up from the mending in her lap.

"They're back." Jessie got to her feet to stand leaning over the railing, watching the buggy approach.

"You ain't never that eager to see Miss Celia," Tudi exclaimed with a combination of surprise and disbelief.

"Things will be different now that Mr. Edwards is in charge," Jessie said earnestly, looking back at Tudi over her shoulder. "He's not like Celia. Truly he's not."

"Well, that bird sure changed its tune mighty fast," Tudi muttered, but Jessie paid her no mind.

It was all she could do not to run down the steps to greet the new arrivals as the buggy rocked to a halt on the drive.

She managed to restrain herself, barely, and instead hung over the railing, watching.

The yard boy, young Thomas, Rosa's baby, came running out to hold the horses. Stuart climbed down. He was nattily dressed in a pale gray cutaway coat and bone breeches, with a pale gray bowler on his head. The crisp black waves of his hair gleamed with blue highlights in the sun. Despite the hundred-degree heat, he didn't look as if he knew what it was to sweat.

Jessie dabbed at droplets on her own upper lip and forehead with the let-out hem of the ancient white muslin dress she wore, then waved, but he didn't look up.

Instead he went around to help Celia from the carriage. Celia allowed him to help her down, but released his hand the moment her feet touched the ground. Even twelve feet above them, as Jessie was, she could sense the animosity in the air.

A third person alighted from the jump seat. The visitor was a man, tall and gangly with light brown hair. He was dressed almost as elegantly as Stuart, but without the dazzling effect.

Celia said something to him, and he nodded. Then the three of them started up the stairs, Celia in the lead and the two men trailing behind.

"You're back early."

Jessie had seated herself on the railing and turned to greet the new arrivals. For her stepmother she had an appraising look. Celia was beautifully dressed as always in a smart traveling costume in a delicate shade of apple green, with a cunning hat tilted low over her forehead. But she bore little resemblance to a bride just back from her honeymoon. Her face was pale, and there were faint shadows beneath her eyes. As she glanced at Jessie, her mouth was tight.

"Stuart didn't like the idea of leaving the place without someone who was familiar with things to oversee it, so we had to come back. Though why we couldn't just send Graydon on ahead and finish our honeymoon as planned, I don't understand." Celia sounded thoroughly put out. As she finished speaking she slanted an angry look at her husband, who had just stepped onto the veranda with the man Celia had called Graydon.

"We've been over this a dozen times, Celia. Until your cousin learns the ropes, he can't be expected to run an operation the size of Mimosa without guidance. Besides, I want to go over the books, see for myself how things stand." Stuart's reply was courteous, but it was clear that his patience was beginning to fray.

"And I told you that Graydon's handled everything at Bascomb Hall for the past six years. He's experienced, for God's sake. You're just being difficult to get back at me."

"I think this discussion would be better finished in private, don't you?" Stuart's tone was still pleasant, but his eyes were suddenly as hard as steel. Celia flashed him an almost hating look.

"I'm going to go lie down. My head hurts. If you had any sensitivity at all, you wouldn't have asked me to travel in such heat."

Without waiting for a reply, Celia walked into the house, removing her hat and calling in a fretful voice for Minna as she went.

Jessie looked at Stuart with a combination of surprise and heightened respect. She didn't know how he'd managed it, but there was already no doubt about who was running that marriage. As hell-bent on having her own way as she knew Celia to be, to get the upper hand so quickly must have required some doing on his part.

"Hello, Jessie." Stuart watched Celia go, then turned to smile rather wearily at Jessie.

"Hello." Her answering smile was shy. Then,

feeling she had to say something to ease the tension
that still lingered in Celia's wake, she offered: "Celia's always been a poor traveler."

"Many ladies are, I believe." His answer was perfectly bland, but it couldn't have been more plain
that he didn't care to discuss the subject. Then his
eyes moved to Tudi. "And you're . . . ?"

"Tudi, Mr. Edwards, sir." Tudi had stood up re-
spectfully as her new master had climbed the steps.
Her hands were clasped in front of her, the mending
she had been working on bright against the white of
her apron. Her eyes had been discreetly lowered
during his exchange with Celia. She lifted them now
to look him full in the face. Her tone was respectful,
but no more. Tudi was a slave, but she was also a
force to be reckoned with at Mimosa.

"Tudi. I'll remember in future." His faint smile
acknowledged her importance. Then his eyes swung
back to Jessie. "Jessie, this is Graydon Bradshaw.
He's Celia's cousin, and Mimosa's new overseer.
Graydon, this is Miss Jessica Lindsay, Celia's stepdaughter."

"How d'ya do, Miss Lindsay?" Graydon Bradshaw
bowed in Jessie's direction. Jessie, instinctively wary
of any cousin of Celia's, merely nodded by way of
reply.

Stuart looked at Tudi again. "Is there someone
who can take Mr. Bradshaw to the overseer's house
and help him settle in?" If he was hoping to get on
Tudi's good side, then he was going about it the
right way, Jessie thought, faintly amused. His tone
was almost deferential.

"Yes, sir, Mr. Edwards. I'll have Charity do it.
She used to see to Mr. Brantley." Tudi's eyes widened as this last slipped out. From her suddenly self-
conscious look, it was clear she felt that she might
have said the wrong thing.

But if he noticed anything amiss, Stuart gave no
sign of it.

"That'll be fine." He nodded. Dropping her

mending in the basket by the chair, Tudi turned to Graydon Bradshaw.

"If you'll follow me, Mr. Bradshaw."

"It was a pleasure making your acquaintance, Miss Lindsay," Bradshaw said as he left, and Jessie nodded again.

Left alone with Stuart, Jessie felt suddenly awkward. After all, it was possible that their newborn friendship had not survived what had obviously been a rigorous honeymoon.

"God, it's hot," he said, dropping into a chair. "Hell couldn't be hotter than Mississippi in the summer."

He took off his elegant hat and fanned himself, his eyes on the baggage which Thomas and Fred, the other yard boy, were hauling out of the buggy and piling on the grass near the drive.

"It's not nearly as hot as it will be in August."

"God forbid," he said piously, and they both laughed. Then, still smiling, he looked up at her where she perched on the porch rail.

"And what have you been doing with yourself these past weeks?"

"Nothing much. Riding. And playing with Jasper, mostly."

"Jasper?"

"My dog."

"You don't mean that that enormous, flea-bitten hound I've seen hanging around the stable belongs to you, do you?"

"He's not flea-bitten!" In defense of her pet, her tone was indignant. Stuart grinned.

"But you admit to everything else. Don't look so het up. I like dogs."

"Oh." For a minute there, she had been afraid he was an animal hater like Celia. Of course, she should have known that he wouldn't be. The friend whose acquaintance she had made that night in the garden at Tulip Hill couldn't dislike dogs.

"I brought you a present." He tossed the words

at her casually, but his eyes were smiling as they watched for her reaction.

"You—what?" To say that his words were unexpected was an understatement. Not since her father died had anyone but the servants thought to give Jessie a present. Her eyes went wide. "Did you really?"

"Cross my heart."

"What is it?"

He shook his head. "Wouldn't you rather wait and see it? It's in with the baggage. In fact, if I'm not mistaken, it's in the box those boys just lifted out from under the seat."

"Oh, can I go look?" She practically clapped her hands with excitement. Stuart regarded her indulgently.

"Go get the box, and open it up here where I can watch."

Jessie didn't need any second telling. She flew down the stairs, practically running despite the heat, and hovered over the box for a delicious instant before lifting it into her arms. It was a large box, and flat, but not particularly heavy.

What could it be?

Her steps were slower as she climbed back up to the gallery, where he waited, smiling. Anticipation was a sensation that was as new as it was pleasant.

"Well, go on, open it," Stuart directed impatiently as Jessie set the box on the floor and knelt beside it, admiring its gay silver ribbon.

She looked up at him then, a shy smiling look, and slid the ribbon off one end of the box.

XV

Jessie lifted the lid off the box, then sat motionless for a moment staring at the contents. What lay within was folded, so that she couldn't be sure, but it appeared to be an afternoon dress. She touched it almost hesitantly. The material was the finest India muslin, and the color was a soft primrose yellow.

"Take it out and look at it," Stuart said. He was rocking a little in the chair, smiling as he watched her hover over her present.

Jessie lifted the dress from its box and stood with it, holding it out at arm's length so that she could see it better. It had a simple, fitted bodice with short puffed sleeves and a modest neckline that nevertheless would leave most of the wearer's shoulders bare. The waist was fitted, and below the waist the skirt formed a bell shape that ended in a single flounce of cream-colored lace. More lace edged the sleeves.

"The sash is in the box," Stuart said. Jessie looked down to behold a cream satin sash that must have been six feet long still folded into the box. She looked from the sash to the dress and then over at Stuart.

"Well?" he asked, though from the grin that lurked around his mouth he already knew the answer.

"It's beautiful. Thank you. I never expected—you

115

didn't have to bring me a present.'' This last was almost gruff.

''I know I didn't have to. I wanted to. After all, we're family now. Besides, the dress is as much from Celia as from me.''

Jessie knew that wasn't true. Celia went on trips several times a year and had never yet brought her back so much as a hair ribbon. The idea that Celia would remember her unloved stepdaughter on her honeymoon was ludicrous. But she didn't say so. Hard as it was to remember, Celia was now Stuart's wife. If he had not liked hearing the unpleasant truth about her before, he would undoubtedly resent it more now. And she didn't want to make Stuart mad at her. More and more, Jessie was beginning to realize how starved she had been these past years for a friend.

''Wherever did you get it?'' Jessie didn't reply to his last statement directly. Instead she looked at the dress again. It really was gorgeous. If only it looked half as lovely on her as it did by itself. . . .

''In Jackson. Celia took me through so many shops that I couldn't tell you which one.''

''How did you know how—how big to tell them?'' The awful suspicion that the garment would be too small occurred to Jessie. If Celia had really had any say in its ordering, it certainly would be. Giving Jessie a lovely present that she couldn't possibly wear was just the kind of thing Celia would do. Of course, unless the fit was impossible, Sissie could always let it out.

''I told the dressmaker that you were yea big—'' Stuart demonstrated a certain height and girth with his hands, grinning widely as Jessie, watching, turned pink. ''No, I didn't. Actually, though I hesitate to admit it to a young lady of your tender years, I'm a pretty fair judge of female sizes.''

''From experience, I take it?'' Jessie responded with spirit, refusing to surrender to his teasing despite her blush. Stuart leaned back in his chair with-

out answering, but his knowing look was all the
answer Jessie needed. Her straight little nose lifted
reprovingly, and she turned her attention back to
the dress. Reversing it, she held it close to her body
with her arm pressed against its waist to approximate the manner in which it would be worn. In
length, if in nothing else, it looked as if it would fit.
Perhaps if Tudi put insets in the sides . . .

'' 'Scuse me, Massah Edwards, but where you
wantin' me to be puttin' your things?'' The speaker
was Thomas. He stood at the top of the stairs, a
valise in each hand. More luggage was piled at the
bottom. Fred had vanished with the carriage. Jessie
wondered, amused, how Thomas had managed to
get the coveted task of carrying in the bags. She was
pretty sure that Thomas would find his way to the
cookhouse before the job was done, where Rosa
would reward him for his hard work with a slice of
whatever pie she had on hand. Both boys had notorious sweet tooths, and once Fred had even gone
so far as to steal and eat a whole pound of sugar.
He'd been punished, of course, but the bellyache
he'd suffered as a result of his misdeed had been far
worse than the whipping Rosa had given him.

''In Miss Celia's room. Get somebody to show you
if you don't know where it is.''

''Oh, I know.'' Thomas grinned. ''I know every-
thin' about this here house. I was born down in the
front hall.''

''Were you really?'' Stuart sounded suitably im-
pressed.

''Yes, he really was. Rosa—she's our cook—is his
mother, and she couldn't make it to the infirmary in
time. This is Thomas.'' Jessie performed the intro-
duction as an afterthought. Thomas bobbed his
head.

''I'm glad to make your acquaintance, Thomas.
Since you know where to put the bags, you can take
them on in.''

''Yes, suh. In Miss Celia's room.'' Thomas, his

slight body bearing up manfully under his load, maneuvered through the door to the house and disappeared. Stuart's attention turned back to Jessie.

"Go try it on."

"Oh, I . . ." she demurred, suddenly afraid that the dress would be too small and she would have to admit as much to him. She would die of embarrassment.

"Go on. Scat. Or you'll make me think you don't like my present."

"I do! Of course I do!"

Jessie knew when she was defeated. Gathering up the box and the sash, with about as much pleasure as she might have a rope with which to hang herself, she turned toward the door.

"Come back here and let me see it when you get it on," he called after her as she went inside. Jessie didn't answer. If the dress looked dreadful, wild horses couldn't drag her out where he could see her.

Despite Jessie's fears, the dress turned out to be a reasonable fit. Apparently Stuart really had a great deal of experience in judging women's sizes. Oh, it was a trifle snug through the waist, but Sissie, whom Jessie had summoned to assist her, assured her that that was because it was designed to be worn with stays. Jessie hated the only pair of stays she possessed worse than she hated poison ivy, but under the circumstances . . . She struggled out of the dress and let Sissie lace her into the stays.

"Take a deep breath," Sissie instructed, her fingers twined in the laces. Jessie did. Sissie jerked so hard that Jessie thought her ribs might break.

"I can't breathe!" Jessie moaned, but Sissie was having none of that. She yanked on the laces again, then tied them in a knot so tight that Jessie feared she'd suffocate if she wore the stays for longer than a few minutes.

"Now let's put on that dress," Sissie said militantly, gathering it up. Flinging it over Jessie's head, she pulled the skirt down and twitched the bodice

into place. Then she did up the hooks that fastened
the back. Finally she came around in front of Jessie
to adjust the neckline, and tied the sash in a big bow
in the back.

Only then was Jessie permitted to stand in front
of the cheval glass.

The young lady she saw looking back at her was
a revelation. She was certainly tall, but not by any
stretch of the imagination could she be described as
fat. She was full-bosomed, yes, and round of hip,
but with the constriction of her waist the effect was
nothing short of femininely voluptuous. Instead of
digging into her flesh around the edge of sleeves
and neckline, as most of her too-small summer
dresses did, the sleeves and neckline of this dress
gently hugged her curves. Without the little rolls
caused by too-tight sleeves, her arms looked entic-
ingly firm. And her bosom—in every other dress she
possessed it was either smashed flat or pushed up
so that it spilled over. Neither effect was particularly
attractive. But in this dress her bosom looked soft
and shapely, full but not overfull.

"Sissie—Sissie, what do you think?" Jessie
croaked, staring at herself as if she were afraid that
the young lady in the mirror might turn out to be a
mirage, and vanish as soon as she looked away.

"Why, Miss Jessie, who woulda thought it? You
look real pretty," Sissie breathed, staring at Jessie's
reflection with the same wide-eyed awe that was on
Jessie's face. "Real pretty."

There was no mistaking Sissie's sincerity. Jessie
ran her eyes over the young lady in the mirror again,
still not quite convinced that what she saw was not
some trick of wishful thinking—or of the light.

But the creamy shoulders she saw rising out of the
demure yellow neckline were definitely hers. Just to
make sure, she touched them, and watched her reflection do the same thing. The small waist tied with
the wide sash of creamy satin was hers, too, as im-

possible as that seemed. No wonder all the ladies
wore stays, if this was what it did for their figures!

The pale yellow color did wonderful things for her
skin, making it look as creamy smooth as the satin
sash. Her eyebrows were the same slanting dark
slashes against her forehead that they had always
been, but they no longer seemed to be the defect
that Jessie had considered them. If one wanted to
look on the positive side, then one might even think
that their darkness made her skin look creamier by
contrast. Her eyes were their usual soft brown, but
they were shining with excitement and pleasure and
looked far more interesting than usual. For the first
time Jessie noticed the thick sweep of her own
lashes, and she lowered them experimentally, then
raised them again. Why, her eyes were pretty, despite the fact that they were ordinary brown! Excitement had brought rosy color to her cheeks and a
smile to her lips. Both were becoming, and as Jessie
studied her reflection, her smile widened.

"I do look . . . almost pretty, don't I?" she asked
Sissie shyly, hungry for reassurance.

"Miss Jessie, when Miss Celia sees you she's
gonna pitch a fit," Sissie said with conviction. Jessie
looked around at Sissie, her eyes widening at the
prospect. Then both girls grinned.

"I hope so," Jessie said. Turning back to her reflection she lifted both hands to her hair.

Her impossible, unruly hair. The only incongruous note in an otherwise unexceptional picture of a
fashionable young lady.

"There's so much of it." Sissie assessed the problem with a frown. "Miss Jessie, if I had a head of
hair like that, I'd take some scissors to it."

Jessie stared at her hair, which had been twisted
up on top of her head that morning more for coolness than for fashion's sake. The pins were worked
loose, as usual, and the heavy knot had slid around
until it dangled just over her left ear. Yard-long tendrils escaped every which way. The only reason they

didn't itch, or obscure her vision, was because Jessie
was used to them.

"Would you really?" she asked doubtfully. Her
hair was a disaster, but to cut it short . . .

"I would." Sissie was firm. Jessie suddenly took
fright at the whole idea and shook her head.

"Just put it up again for now, Sissie. I'd probably
end up looking like Jasper if you started cutting on
it."

"Not me, Miss Jessie. A proper hairdresser," Sissie said impatiently, already starting to pull the remaining pins from Jessie's hair. "Look how Miss
Celia's always having the latest styles done in Jackson. You could go there."

The idea of going to Jackson to shop and have her
hair styled in the latest fashion had never occurred
to Jessie. Indeed, before the last few minutes she
would have sworn up one hill and down the other
that she was about as interested in clothes and feminine fal-lals as she was in the life cycle of the boll
weevil. In fact, she probably would have said the
boll weevil actually interested her more. After all,
the weevil had to do with cotton, and Mimosa was
a cotton plantation, so knowing about the pesky in-
sect might prove useful sometime or other. There
was utterly no use to fashion that she could see.

At least, she'd thought that before she had beheld
the amazing transformation in her looks wrought by
the yellow dress.

Sissie had brushed her hair out and was pinning
it doggedly back into place. Both girls knew that the
effort was likely to be wasted. Her hair would escape from its pins before an hour had passed.

But even knowing that, Jessie was dazzled by what
she saw as she looked into the mirror one last time
before hurrying out to the gallery to show Stuart.

The ugly duckling had become, if not quite a
swan, at the very least an attractive little duck.

XVI

Stuart was still sitting where she had left him, lazing back in a rocking chair on the upper gallery. Someone had brought him a mint julep, which he sipped at intervals. His hat lay on the floor by the chair.

He didn't hear her step out on the gallery. For a moment Jessie stood still, undecided. Should she run back inside without showing him the dress after all? Had he expressed an interest in seeing her in it just to be kind?

But he had bought the dress for her. Surely that meant he liked her at least a little.

"Why, Jessie."

He turned his head and saw her. Jessie felt a funny nervousness start in the pit of her stomach, but there was no turning back now. She took a deep breath and walked bravely toward him.

He watched her without speaking, his face expressionless, his eyes unreadable.

It was the most unnerving thing he could have done. Jessie stopped walking, her arms crossing over her bosom in an instinctively defensive gesture.

Still he didn't say anything, just looked her over with those sky-blue eyes that were as fathomless as glass.

"Well?" Jessie squeaked at last, sure that she had

made a dreadful fool of herself and that she really
looked awful and that the transformation she had
seen in her mirror had indeed been the result of either wishful thinking or the light.

"You look lovely," he said then, and smiled.

The butterflies in Jessie's stomach stopped doing
acrobatics. She smiled back with shy pleasure. Then
her gaze dropped, and she smoothed her skirt with
her hands because she didn't know quite what else
to do with them.

"It's the dress. It's beautiful." She had recovered
her poise enough to look at him again.

Stuart shook his head. "No, Jessie, it's not the
dress. It's you in the dress. You look lovely. You
mustn't sell yourself short."

Jessie's throat tightened. For some absurd reason
his compliments brought her to the verge of tears.
Kindness was a rare and precious commodity in the
world she'd grown up in, and she treasured it like
a miser might gold.

"I'm glad Celia married you," she said suddenly,
fiercely. Then, before she could embarrass herself
any further, she turned and walked swiftly toward
the door.

"Jessie . . ."

But what he intended to say she never knew. Celia
came through the door at that precise moment, a
half-full glass of tomato juice in her hand. When she
saw Jessie, she stopped dead. Her eyes swept Jessie
once, twice. They widened, then narrowed, then finally lifted to Jessie's face. Jessie waited, helplessly
vulnerable, for the broadside she knew would come.

"Well, I'm glad to see you can fit into that dress
that Stuart insisted on having made up for you,"
she said. "It's a pity the shop had to use so much
more material than usual to fashion it in your size,
but still, I suppose it looks well enough."

Before Jessie could have her pleasure in the dress
totally deflated by Celia's malice, Stuart got to his
feet and came over to stand behind her. His hands

rose to rest comfortingly on Jessie's shoulders, and he met his wife's eyes over the top of Jessie's head.

"She looks charming, Celia, and the shop didn't have to use any more material than they would have for any female of average size. Being so petite yourself, you forget that most of the rest of the world is a deal bigger."

Jessie could have told him from experience that the best defense against Celia's tongue-lashings was feigned deafness and silence. To contradict her in any way only made her look for other, more deadly weapons to use on her quarry. But either Stuart had not yet learned that basic tenet of life with Celia, or he did not care.

Celia's eyes hardened as they touched pointedly on Stuart's hands. Something about the expression on Celia's face made Jessie's cheeks heat. With nothing more than a look, Celia had managed to make Jessie feel unclean.

To Stuart's credit, he didn't remove his hands, although he must have been aware of Celia's silent insinuation.

"Did you want me for something, Celia?" he asked coolly. His voice gave no hint that he was not perfectly calm. Only Jessie got an inkling of his rising anger, and only because his fingers had tightened fractionally on her shoulders.

Calm disregard of her verbal assaults tended to act on Celia like kerosene on a fire. Jessie was not surprised to see Celia's eyes flash with fury as she raised them from where Stuart's hand still rested on Jessie's shoulders to his face.

"Indeed I did. I had intended this discussion to be private, but since you and my stepdaughter are on such intimate terms, I suppose I might as well say my piece and have done with it."

"Please do, my dear." Stuart sounded almost bored, but his hands tightened still more on Jessie's shoulders. Embarrassed by the marital quarrel that was obviously on the verge of exploding, Jessie

would have slipped away. But she couldn't, because
Stuart, whether consciously or not, held her fast.

"Very well, then. I would prefer it if you would
keep your belongings in the room where you are to
sleep, rather than instruct the servants to dump
them in my chamber."

Stuart's fingers dug in until Jessie thought she
must wince. Valiantly she fought the impulse. It
would never do to let Celia know that Stuart's un-
ruffled facade was just that.

"Somehow I rather thought that your room was
my room. We are married, you know."

Celia smiled unpleasantly. "Oh, yes, I know. I
know all too well. However, I prefer that we have
separate chambers for sleeping. Though, of course,
I won't deny you your marital rights, if you insist
on taking advantage of them."

Jessie did wince then as Stuart's fingers went almost to the bone. She blushed, too, at being privy
to such intimate talk. Feeling her wince, Stuart released her, and gave her a little shove toward the
door.

"Go on inside, Jessie."

She needed no second urging. She edged past
Celia—

"Oh, no!"

"You clumsy creature! You've made me spill my
drink!"

Both cries were simultaneous as Celia's glass up-
ended all over Jessie's dress. The bright red tomato
juice ran down the yellow skirt and was greedily
absorbed by the muslin. Horrified, Jessie tried to
brush the worst of the mess off with her hands, but
to no avail. She had a dreadful feeling that the dress
was ruined.

"You did that on purpose!" Jessie looked up from
her damaged skirt to glare at Celia.

"I certainly did not! 'Twas your own fault, you
bumbling ox! You jostled my arm!"

"I did not!"

Jessie's fists clenched, and she closed her jaw so tightly that it quivered. Celia was gloating, pleased with herself and her triumph, Jessie could tell. For once in her life, Jessie knew the urge to kill.

"Go inside, Jessie." Stuart's hands closed over her upper arms, preventing her from flying at her stepmother before she even knew for sure that that was what she had meant to do.

"My dress!"

"I know. Go inside."

"But . . ."

"Do as I say."

Jessie went. Furious and sickened, she fled toward her room, where she practically ripped the dress to shreds getting out of it. Damn Celia, damn her, damn her! She would hate her until her dying day!

On the gallery, Stuart fixed his wife with glittering eyes.

"Why did you do that?"

She smiled. "It was an accident. Surely you don't think I'd damage the silly chit's dress on purpose."

"I know you would."

"Thus speaks a loving husband."

Stuart's mouth tightened. "Be warned, Celia, that I'll not stand by and watch you hurt Jessie or anyone else. You married me, for whatever reason, for better or worse. And I have it in my power to make your life a great deal worse."

"I hate you!"

"I'm sorry to hear it."

"I must have been insane to marry you!"

"Funny, I was thinking the same thing myself."

"If you think you can come in here and just take over, tell me what to do with my stepdaughter, take charge of my property and—"

"That's exactly what I think. In fact, I know I can. I'm your husband, my love. Everything you once owned now belongs to me. Or in your haste to get me into bed did you overlook the fact that married women aren't allowed to own property?''

"You're vile!''

"Not yet,'' Stuart said grimly, and reached out to catch her by the arm.

"Keep your hands off me! I hate you!'' Celia batted his hands away, then ran inside, sobbing hysterically. "I hate you, I hate you, I hate you!''

"And I,'' said Stuart bitterly to the still vibrating door, "hate you. God help me, I do.''

Downstairs in the keeping room, Tudi heard the commotion abovestairs and lifted her head. She listened for a moment, then as the sounds died away shook her head.

"Look like there be trouble in paradise,'' she muttered, then turned her attention back to the task at hand.

XVII

Over the next few weeks, life at Mimosa settled into a routine that was comfortable on the outside while seething with tension beneath. Celia alternated between attempting to cajole Stuart and loudly hating him. Stuart seemed impervious to both approaches, impervious to Celia. If there had ever been any love in that marriage, it had vanished soon after the ceremony. It was common knowledge amongst the house servants that Mr. Stuart never went near Miss Celia's bed. And what the servants knew, Jessie learned soon after, whether she wanted to know it or not. She found the idea of Celia's estrangement from her husband in all its accompanying detail both embarrassing and, to her shame, reassuring. Maybe because she was increasingly beginning to think of Stuart as hers.

He had rapidly become father, brother, and friend, all in one impossibly handsome package. Jessie had never realized how much she had missed having such until Stuart became a fixture in her life. He was unfailingly kind to her (strange as it seemed that anyone who would marry Celia could possess a kind heart), treating her with a careless affection that Jessie soaked up as eagerly as a sponge might water. It was all she could do not to tag after him like a puppy with its master. The only thing that held her back was her pride—and Celia's tongue. With her marriage a disaster, Celia's bitterness spilled like acid over everyone at Mimosa. Although she minded her tongue to a certain degree in Stuart's presence, when he was not around, Celia made Jessie her favorite target.

Under the circumstances, Jessie spent a great deal of time away from the house. She rode Firefly daily, roaming the nearby piny forest with Jasper at her heels from dawn to dusk. Usually she would take care not to come home until after supper was served, and would then take her own meal in the cookhouse with Rosa. Considering the forbidding atmosphere that permeated the dining room each night, Jessie was not sorry to content herself with the leavings of the main meal. According to Sissie, who most often got the thankless task of waiting at table, the master sat at one end of the long table and the mistress sat at the other, eating in grim splendor separated by acres of polished wood while neither said anything more to the other than was absolutely necessary. The swishing of the intricately carved mahogany punkah fan overhead and the rattling of dishes as Sissie served were the only sounds that broke the tense silence.

Often Jessie did not even bother returning to the house for luncheon, when Stuart would invariably be absent and Celia would be waiting to pounce on her stepdaughter like a spider on a fly with some imagined (or occasionally not so imagined) misdeed. Instead Jessie took to carrying with her an apple and a chunk of bread, and found that she did not miss the heavier meals that had once been the highlights of her days.

This method of snatch-as-snatch-can eating, coupled with the extra hours she was spending in the saddle, was having a markedly beneficial effect on Jessie's appearance. So gradually that she hardly noticed it, she was slimming down.

Every morning Stuart worked with Graydon

Bradshaw in the plantation office. Most afternoons he spent riding around Mimosa, educating himself about everything from picking cotton to pruning fruit trees to how the field hands' children were cared for in the nursery down in the quarters. Pharaoh, the slave foreman who had labored under Brantley for years, could usually be found at Stuart's side. Pharaoh was a big man, dark as ebony and brawny with muscle. He was also as knowledgeable about the plantation as ever Brantley had been. Had he not been a slave, Mimosa would have had to look no further for her new overseer.

As Stuart learned the intricacies of running a plantation, Graydon Bradshaw nominally oversaw things, while rarely venturing out into the blistering heat of the fields. Jessie saw little of the dapper new overseer, but she heard much through the servants. Celia was apparently spending a considerable amount of time helping her cousin settle in. Knowing Celia, Jessie did not quite like the sound of that. Although, she thought hopefully, surely even Celia would not go so far as to play her new husband false right under his nose with an overseer who also happened to be her first cousin.

Or would she? If she was capable of such depravity, Jessie hoped devoutly that she would be discreet. The explosion that would certainly ensue should Stuart catch her at her favorite game was frightening to contemplate. For all his kindness and charm, Stuart was very much a man, and Celia, whether he disliked her or not, was his wife. Jessie knew as well as she knew anything that Stuart was not the kind of man to tolerate being made a fool of. She herself had witnessed his temper. Should Celia play him false and he discover it, Jessie had no doubt that her stepmother would greatly rue the consequences.

Sometimes Jessie could not resist the temptation and, Jasper at her heels, joined Stuart as he rode up and down the fields. He accepted her companion-

ship and that of the big dog without comment, and
even asked her questions about topics ranging from
soil conditions to the number of bales a field hand
should be expected to pick a day. Jessie surprised
herself with how much she knew. Most of his questions she was able to answer with at least a reasonable degree of intelligence.

"Shouldn't you be wearing a bonnet?" he asked
her one day, his attention arrested by the pinkened
condition of her nose and cheeks. It was a hot day
in the middle of August, and the sun was beating
down relentlessly. As far as the eye could see
stretched acres of cotton ready for picking. Their
fluffy white bolls reflected the sun, making the scene
seem dazzlingly bright. The field hands were also
dressed in white from the waist up, loose cotton
shirts that protected them as much as any clothing
could from the sun and the heat, with woven black
trousers beneath. Each field hand picked a row at a
time, his back bent and his fingers flying as he
worked. The men sang hymns and spirituals to make
the work go faster. The low, melodious sound of their
chanting was as much a part of the summer as the
buzzing of the bees.

"I never bother to wear a hat," Jessie admitted
with a shrug, more interested in who would win the
race to finish his row that two young field hands
seemed to be having. Their fingers moved with
lightning speed as they stripped each plant and
threw the bolls in the bags slung over their shoulders.

"In future, I wish you would. In the meantime,
take this. You'll be getting freckles if you're not
careful, and we can't have that." He was wearing a
wide-brimmed straw hat. Despite the jocular tone of
that last, he removed it to plop it down on her head.
Jessie was both surprised and touched by the gesture. She was not used to having anyone consider
her comfort at the expense of his own.

"I don't need it. I'm used to the sun, really I am.

And I never freckle.'' Self-consciously she lifted a
hand to the hat, meaning to remove it and hand it
back to him. He stopped her with a gesture.

"Wear it. You have beautiful skin. It'd be a shame
to spoil it.''

Jessie's hand fell, and her eyes widened at the
compliment. Stuart was no longer looking at her.
His eyes swept the fields. His expression was unreadable. Had he meant what he said? Did he truly
find her skin beautiful? The notion dazzled her. Of
their own volition her fingers rose to touch her
cheek.

Her skin rarely burned, and never freckled. Despite its pale creaminess and the reddish tint to her
hair, it was remarkably impervious to the sun. His
skin was far darker than hers, yet he probably
needed his hat more than she did. After all, he had
not had a lifetime to grow accustomed to the shimmering heat of Mississippi in August.

Whether he protested or not, she should give his
hat back.

But its wide brim did provide comfortable shade
for her eyes. And just the idea of wearing something
that belonged to him sent a guilty quiver of pleasure
down her spine.

"Thank you. That does feel better,'' she said just
as meekly as could be, and wondered at herself.
Meekness was not normally one of her attributes.
Nor was feminine flirtatiousness, which that remark
had come dangerously close to qualifying as.

"You're welcome.''

He was looking at her again, unsmiling. The sun
beating down on his bare head picked up blue highlights in the glossy black waves. The highlights
matched almost exactly the glinting shade of his
eyes. Against the swarthiness of his skin and the
darkness of his brows and lashes, those eyes looked
impossibly blue, bluer even than the cloudless sky.
The lean, chiseled regularity of his features could
have graced a coin. The width of his shoulders in

the white linen shirt gave silent testimony to powerful muscles discreetly hidden. In deference to the suffocating heat, the collar of his shirt was unbuttoned, allowing Jessie a tantalizing glimpse of crisp black chest hair. Unconsciously her eyes went lower, to his flat stomach and long, hard-looking legs in their snug black breeches and boots. Then they rose again to his face. His mouth drew her eyes. It was perfectly carved, the lower lip just a bit fuller than the upper, though at the moment both lips were slightly compressed. Jessie was mesmerized by that unbelievably beautiful mouth. She stared at it without even realizing that she was doing so, her own lips parting as a tiny shiver started up her spine.

Then Jasper, who'd been quartering the field for some minutes, put up an earsplitting combination of howls and barks as he caught sight of a rabbit and hared off in hot pursuit. The sudden onslaught of noise made the horses sidle restively, and brought Jessie back to herself with a start. She realized that she'd been staring, quite blatantly, at her stepmother's husband's mouth, and with a rush of embarrassment she wrenched her eyes away.

"You can't be cold." His words were abrupt.

"No." Despite her embarrassment, this remark out of the blue made her look at him in surprise. Jessie could only suppose that her shiver had been as much external as internal—but his attention was fixed on the front of her dress.

Puzzled, Jessie followed the direction of his eyes. She was wearing a simple linen shirtwaist and skirt, the weather being far too hot for her favorite riding habit, with only a chemise and a single petticoat for decency's sake beneath. The shirtwaist was an old one, thin from many washings, but it was clean and securely buttoned and not nearly as snug as it once had been. The skirt was a faded blue, and if it was a trifle short for riding sidesaddle, there was nothing of her legs on view, only scuffed black boots. Seeing nothing in particular about her appearance that might account for the set expression on his face, she looked back at him questioningly.

"That shirtwaist is too tight." He sounded as disapproving as he looked.

"It is not," Jessie answered, surprised. Indeed, both the shirtwaist and the skirt had once been far tighter, so tight that she'd all but given up wearing them. It was amazing how much more comfortable clothes felt when they were a trifle loose.

"Oh, yes, it is," Stuart replied, and there was a grim note to his voice that made Jessie's eyes widen. What could she possibly have done to make him sound so angry all of a sudden? He looked pointedly down at her front, his mouth tight. Again Jessie followed his eyes with her own. But this time she saw what had elicited his disapproval. A scalding blush started to rise from her neck to her face.

If the rest of her was slimmer, her bosom was not. With her skin damp with sweat, the thin linen molded itself to her shape. The full, rounded contours of her breasts were revealed rather than concealed by the clinging cloth. But the worst part, the shaming part, was the way her nipples thrust forward, hard and cylindrical and plainly visible through the twin layers of shirtwaist and chemise.

Jessie was an innocent, but she knew enough about her own body to know what those engorged nipples meant. That delicious little shiver that had come from looking at Stuart's mouth had had an unwelcome physical accompaniment. One that was too horribly plain to see.

"Don't look at me," she said in a strangled voice. Her arms crossed over her breasts and her shoulders hunched, trying to shield her shame from view. If she knew what the change in her body signified, so must he. Crimsoning, Jessie felt the most hideous embarrassment she had ever known in her life engulf her.

"When was the last time you had some new clothes?" He looked, and sounded, merely irritable.

Maybe, just maybe, he didn't realize the awful significance of what he'd seen. Maybe he truly thought that her nipples always looked like that, and he'd only just now noticed because her shirtwaist was too tight.

Please, God, let that be what he thought!

"At—at the wedding—and the yellow dress, the one you brought me." If she could just keep her wits about her, maybe she could keep him from realizing that her shameful response was a reaction to him. Just finding himself in her presence would embarrass him if he knew. He would begin to avoid her, and Jessie didn't think she could bear that. She'd grown to depend on him in ways that were far more important to her than the physical effect he had on her body.

"Besides those."

"When I was fifteen. Three years ago."

The heat of her spreading blush felt far more intense than the heat of the sun on her skin ever had. Jessie willed it to recede. To turn a thousand shades of crimson would only make him suspicious.

Stuart's lips tightened as his eyes moved over her again. Jessie held her breath, and forced herself to look fearlessly back at him even as her crossed arms shielded her telltale breasts.

"Celia's been remiss. I'll see that you get what you need."

Jessie started to reply, but before she could say anything Pharaoh rode up, and Stuart's attention switched to the big foreman.

"Mr. Stuart, it's comin' on to rain. We oughta be seein' about gettin' what's done been picked under cover."

Stuart nodded. "See to it. I'll be with you in just a minute."

Pharaoh touched his forehead and rode off. Stuart looked at Jessie again.

"You go on back to the house and change out of

those clothes," he said, and there was no mistaking that it was an order.

"Yes, Stuart." If she'd sounded meek before, it was nothing compared with how she sounded now. She was in a fever of anxiety to get away from him. His eyes met hers, narrowed. Then he touched his heels to his horse's sides and was off in a cloud of dust.

"Your hat . . . !" He would need it. Distant rumbles of thunder heralded a coming storm. But if he heard her, he gave no sign. Jessie sat and watched as he rode away. Then, still burning with embarrassment, she went to change her clothes.

XVIII

Two days later, Miss Flora and Miss Laurel came
to call. Celia was having an "at home" day, and
several of her particular friends were already taking
iced tea with her in the front parlor. But when her
husband's aunts drove up, she excused herself and
hurried out to greet them, all smiles. Jessie, who had
been playing with Jasper in the orchard and had
chosen that unfortunate moment to throw a stick for
him that sent him galloping onto the front lawn,
watched as Celia's smile changed to a forbidding
frown as she listened to the old ladies.

Nervous that Jasper's boisterous presence might
have something to do with Celia's annoyance, Jessie
summoned him from his snufflings at a molehill (the
stick quite forgotten) with a low, two-note whistle.

Jasper's head came up, his tail wagged, and at the
last minute he snatched up the stick before bounding back to his mistress. The gazes of Celia and the
aunts followed Jasper's progress until all three pairs
of eyes rested on Jessie, partially hidden by the
dense trees.

"Jessica, dear, come here," Miss Flora trilled,
beckoning.

There was no help for it. Her skirt stained with
grass and mud from kneeling in play with Jasper,

her hair tumbling every which way, and her face no doubt smudged, Jessie emerged from the orchard.

"Hello, dear," Miss Laurel said, not seeming to notice Jessie's disgraceful appearance.

"Hello, Miss Laurel, Miss Flora." Jessie dutifully kissed the two cheeks that were presented to her. She was growing resigned to the ritual.

"These dear ladies have a—a proposition to put to you." Celia's voice was sugary sweet. Looking quickly at her stepmother, Jessie was quite, quite sure that whatever the proposition was, Celia was not in favor of it.

"Proposition, my grandmother!" Miss Flora said roundly. "We've come to spirit Jessica away with us to Jackson."

"Dear Stuart says she hasn't a stitch to her name," Miss Laurel chimed in.

"To Jackson!" Horrified, Jessie looked from one old lady to the other.

"Of course I told them that you can't possibly just pick up and go," Celia said. For once, Celia's sentiments coincided perfectly with Jessie's.

"Of course Jessica will come with us," Miss Flora said.

"Run into the house and change your clothes and pack a bag, dear. You don't need to bring more than a change of dress. We'll get you outfitted when we get to Jackson." Miss Laurel echoed her sister.

Jessie looked from one to the other of them. "That's very nice of you, but really, I—"

She was silenced by Miss Flora's "Pish-tush."

"Celia is far too busy getting readjusted to married life to worry about your clothes, you know. And we are your aunts now. You may quite properly come with us."

"But really, I . . ." Jessie's protest trailed off in the face of Miss Flora's determined expression. The idea of accompanying Miss Flora and Miss Laurel on a shopping expedition of some days' duration was too dreadful to contemplate. The old ladies seemed well

meaning enough, but Jessie scarcely knew them. She
was sure she would go mad if she had to endure their
chirping presences for hours on end. The idea of ac-
quiring new dresses was briefly tantalizing (the memory of how she had looked in the late, lamented yellow
gown still warmed her), but not if she had to travel to
Jackson to do it. The truth of the matter was, Jessie
had never in her life spent a night away from Mimosa.
The idea frightened her a little.

"It's all been decided," Miss Flora said sternly.

"Dear Stuart asked us to take you," Miss Laurel
added, as if that clinched matters. And to Jessie's
dismay, it did.

Despite her misgivings, the trip turned out to be
fun. They were gone for just over two weeks, and the
time passed in a whirlwind of shopping. To Jessie's
delighted surprise, Miss Flora turned out to be possessed of an infallible eye for color and style. Jessie,
who trusted her own instincts in neither case, let Miss
Flora decide what she needed. The only outfit that she
chose for herself was a reading habit of bright peacock
blue cut in the military style that Miss Flora assured
her would be vastly becoming. Trying the dress on for
its final fitting just before they began their journey
home, Jessie had to admit that Miss Flora was right
once again: the riding habit complimented her figure
as nothing else in her life ever had.

Miss Flora had decreed brilliant jewel colors for Jessie. Jessie had silently questioned the old lady's judgment when that pronouncement was handed down,
but at the end of a fortnight's shopping she was
thrilled with the results. Something about the clear
intensity of sapphire blue and emerald green and ruby
red did wonders for her eyes and skin. The colors
made her eyes appear larger and brighter, a deep
glowing sherry brown, while her skin took on the
white smoothness of a magnolia blossom. Awe-
stricken when she studied her own reflection, Jessie
thought that her skin looked almost velvety to the
touch. Unbidden, she remembered that Stuart had

called her skin beautiful. She could hardly wait for him to see it against the foil of the new clothes.

Jessie was also thrilled to discover that she was much slimmer. It wasn't her imagination, or a trick of the light. She was actually almost slender. Over the course of the summer she'd added about half an inch to her height, while her belly and hips and especially her waist seemed to have reshaped themselves almost magically. Jessie wasn't quite sure what had brought about the change (she did wonder at first if perhaps the dressmaker had a special slimming mirror to aid in the selling of her designs), but somehow, somewhere, she had acquired a lovely woman's figure. Certainly she could no longer by any stretch of the imagination be described as fat.

"Why, Jessica, you've turned into a real beauty," Miss Laurel said with mild surprise as Jessie emerged from the encounter she'd dreaded most of all, that with a hairdresser's scissors.

"I knew she would," Miss Flora replied with satisfaction. "She's the image of her mother. Don't you remember, sister, that Elizabeth Hodge turned away beaux from as far away as New Orleans before she settled on Thomas Lindsay?"

"That's right, she did." Miss Laurel nodded.

Jessie, who'd been busy trying to catch a glimpse of her new hairstyle in every shop window that they passed, stopped craning her neck at her own reflection for long enough to smile rather tremulously at Miss Flora and Miss Laurel.

"Do I truly look like my mother?" Jessie's memories of her mother were of a dark-haired, beautiful lady who always seemed to be smiling. Impossible to imagine that she could ever look like that.

"Anyone who ever knew Elizabeth would know you for her daughter," Miss Flora answered softly. To Jessie's distress, she felt her throat begin to tighten. Suddenly her heart ached for her mother, ached as it hadn't ached in years.

"But enough of this," Miss Flora added briskly,

seeing the sudden emotion on Jessie's face. "Stand still, child, and let us look at your hair. It's certainly an improvement. At least it's out of your face."

Grateful for the diversion before she could make a fool of herself on a public street, Jessie obediently stopped and turned her head this way and that for the aunts' inspection.

"Do you really like it?" she asked after a minute. The hairdresser had taken scissors to her hair with ruthless abandon, and Jessie had been silently appalled at the length and number of curling locks that had dropped to the floor. In back the length was much as it had been, reaching down to well past her waist. The whole unruly mane had been shaped and thinned, but the locks around her face had been ruthlessly pruned to form a profusion of short curls. Madame Fleur, the hairdresser, had shown Jessie how to pin it up in back, so that the heavy mass of it formed a soft roll at the crown of her head. The shortened curls in front framed her face like a tousled halo. The effect was charming, and Madame Fleur assured her that if the hair was pinned properly, the style should last through anything, up to and including a hurricane. Jessie could also, Madame Fleur advised her, wear it down, with the hair at the crown pulled away from her face and secured by a bow. But Miss Fleur very much suggested that such a style not be attempted in the middle of summer. In such heat the remarkable thickness of Jessie's hair would act as a blanket, and Mademoiselle would be very likely to suffocate.

"You look lovely," Miss Laurel said, beaming after admiring Jessie's new hairstyle from every angle.

"Most becoming," Miss Flora agreed. And Jessie, who sneaked many another admiring glance at her reflection in the shop windows as they made their way back to their hotel, decided happily that Miss Flora and Miss Laurel were right.

Despite all her misgivings, Jessie enjoyed herself so much in Jackson that she was almost reluctant to leave.

But the nearer the carriage drew to Mimosa, the more eager she was to reach home. In the final few miles she was finally afflicted with the homesickness she had dreaded. She could barely wait to get home again. It was hard to say whom or what she had missed most: Tudi, or Sissie, or Firefly and Jasper—or Stuart.

But when the carriage rocked to a halt in front of Mimosa's front door, Jessie discovered, to her own surprise, that she was going to miss the aunts. Quite dreadfully.

"We won't get down, dear," Miss Flora said briskly. Jessie looked from her to Miss Laurel, all at once hating to part from them. Impulsively she leaned over to hug Miss Laurel, and then, fiercely, Miss Flora.

"Thank you both," she said around the sudden lump in her throat, and meant it.

Miss Flora pish-tushed, while Miss Laurel patted Jessie's shoulder.

"Don't forget that we're family now. You must come see us," Miss Laurel told her.

"I won't forget," Jessie promised. Then as Ben, Miss Flora and Miss Laurel's elderly driver, who had safely conveyed them all the way to Jackson and back, opened the door, Jessie smiled at them one last time and stepped out of the carriage.

"Good-bye, Jessica!"

"Good-bye!"

Thomas and Fred were already gathering up the dozens of boxes that Ben had slung down from the top of the carriage. The pair of them greeted Jessie vociferously. She returned their greetings, genuinely glad to see them, to be home, but inside she was torn. She, the girl who never cried, was battling the awful urge to sniffle. As the carriage bearing her new aunts swept down the drive and along the road toward Tulip Hill, Jessie felt her eyes sting. If she hadn't had Jasper's bounding attack to distract her, she might not have been able to hold back the threatening tears.

XIX

September came, and with it came Seth Chandler's birthday. Everybody in the valley knew the exact date—the fourteenth—because every year on that date Elmway was the site of the biggest party of the season. Lissa was an excellent hostess, and guests came from miles around for barbecue, fireworks, and an evening of dancing. Many from the more distant plantations stayed overnight with the Chandlers, and many more, relatives mostly, stayed as long as a couple of weeks. In fact, Miss May Chandler, Seth's unmarried cousin, had come for the party three years before and never left. Nobody thought much of it. It was the custom in the South for menfolk to offer the protection of their homes to their unmarried female relatives. And anyway, Miss May helped with the children.

Jessie had never attended Seth Chandler's birthday party, or at least not since she was a little girl and had gone with her parents. It never would have occurred to her to go this year, either, if Stuart hadn't insisted.

"Of course she's going," he said impatiently when Celia, sweeping downstairs on the morning of the party, told him that Jessie never went. Both Celia and Stuart were already dressed, and Minna followed Celia with her dance dress, carefully stuffed

with tissue and folded so that it would not wrinkle,
carried over her arm. Stuart inquired as to Jessie's
whereabouts. Upon receiving an answer that displeased him, he swore and went to fetch her himself. He found her in the stable, just getting ready
to set out for her morning ride. She was already
mounted on Firefly when he strode through the wide
door. Clad in the new blue riding habit that did marvelous things for her coloring while at the same time
making her waist look impossibly slender, her hair
only a shade or so darker than the sorrel mare on
which she perched sidesaddle, she made a pretty
picture. From the tight set to Stuart's mouth as he
looked her over, it was clear that he was in no mood
to appreciate it.

"Did you want me?" Jessie asked innocently after
a moment's silence. She nudged Firefly forward so
that the mare stood directly in front of him. Jasper
had bounded ahead upon setting eyes on Stuart,
who was a great favorite of his, and done his best
to express his welcome in the age-old way of dogs.
While Stuart, swearing, held Jasper away from his
immaculate waistcoat and breeches by the simple expedient of catching a huge front paw in both hands,
Jessie realized that for once she had the pleasure of
looking down at Stuart. Savoring the unaccustomed
advantage in height, she watched with a lurking
smile as he admonished Jasper sharply, dropped the
dog's paws to the ground, and kept him earthbound
by placing a precautionary hand on the animal's
head. Jasper took that as an incipient pat. Immediately he groveled for more, dropping to his belly and
rolling onto his back with his paws waving in the
air. It was a blatant invitation to Stuart to scratch his
belly. Jessie laughed. Stuart looked up at her. It was
clear from his expression that he, at least, was not
amused.

"Get down," he said.

"I'm getting ready to ride," she answered, not so
much arguing as surprised.

"You are going to the Chandlers' party." Aggravation was as plain in his voice as it was in his eyes. His fists rested on his hips, and his booted feet were planted wide apart in an aggressive stance.

"I never go."

"Well, you're going this time."

When she just sat there looking at him, he muttered something that she couldn't quite hear but that she was sure was distinctly uncomplimentary. Then, stepping forward, he reached up to catch her around the waist and haul her bodily out of the saddle. Jessie gasped, Firefly sidestepped nervously, Jasper leaped to his feet and barked, and Progress stepped quickly forward to hold the mare's head.

"But I don't want to go," Jessie protested, her hands closing over Stuart's upper arms to steady herself as he set her on her feet in front of him. The muscles of his arms felt hard and very strong beneath her hands, even through the cloth of his coat and shirt. Of their own volition Jessie's fingers lingered on that breath-stopping hardness. Almost immediately ashamed of herself, she curled her hands into fists and lifted them away. Ever since that day in the cotton field when her body had betrayed her so embarrassingly, Jessie had forced herself to think of Stuart strictly in an avuncular light. Besides the fact that he had become both friend and mentor, he was her stepmother's husband, for goodness' sake! The wayward images of him that sometimes flitted unbidden through her brain were nothing short of evil.

She would not recognize the tingle that his hands on her waist had ignited along her nerve endings. She would not.

"You're going," Stuart said. Grateful to focus on his words instead of his hold on her waist, she clasped her wayward fingers in front of her bosom and looked up at him.

It was a mistake.

He was scowling down at her, but his eyes were

so blue that his expression scarcely mattered. His face was lean, brown, and heart-poundingly handsome beneath the crisp black waves of his hair. His mouth was tight with annoyance, but it was still a beautiful mouth.

His hands were large, and they gripped her waist securely. Her waist had grown small enough so that his thumbs almost met just above her belly button. At the feel of them pressing, ever so gently, into her soft flesh, Jessie felt her insides heat. She bit down, hard, on her lower lip. While she still had the will to do it, she pulled back from him, away from the seductive touch of his hands.

"I don't want to go," she managed, willing her contrary bones to solidify again. Afraid he might read her reaction in her eyes, she averted them from him.

"Look at me." His voice was impatient. Reluctant, Jessie nevertheless did as he bade her. She was afraid that if she did not, he would touch her again.

Something in her face must have tempered his annoyance. When he spoke, his voice had gentled.

"Listen to me, Jessie. It's nothing short of insane for you to turn yourself into a recluse, and I'll be damned if I'll allow it. Have you never given any thought to the future? Don't you want to marry and have children someday? Of course you do. All women want that."

Jessie shook her head, and opened her mouth to deny—with some truth—any such urge. Before she could speak he was grasping her shoulders, clearly near to shaking her.

"Celia's at fault for letting you grow up as you have, but you're at fault, too. Damn it, Jessie, you're not a child anymore! You're a lovely, desirable young woman, and you'll have scads of boys panting after you if you'll just give them a chance to make your acquaintance. And you *are* going to give them a chance. You're going to this party if I have to sling you over my shoulder and carry you every step of the way!"

He had said she was a lovely, desirable woman. Did that mean that *he* found her lovely and desirable? His hands on her shoulders seemed to burn through to her skin. Jessie swallowed, and fought the urge to close her eyes.

"All right," she said, and pulled away from him again. It was either that or step closer, into his arms.

"All right?" he repeated, his hands dropping to his sides, his voice tight with exasperation. Clearly he had no idea of the effect he had on her. Thank goodness he had no idea! "What does that mean?"

"All right, I'll go to the party." If her capitulation sounded ungracious, it was because she felt ungracious. She felt taut as a bowstring and as ready to quiver, and she needed to get away from him at once. Turning on her heel without waiting for anything else he might say, she swept across the lawn to the house, leaving him staring after her.

Later, as she rode beside Celia in the backseat of the open carriage, Jessie wondered at herself for capitulating so easily. She didn't want to go to this party. Since her father's death she'd gone her own way, with not even Celia to tell her what to do. Her willfulness was well known around Mimosa, and even the servants, who loved her, had learned long ago that it was best to let Miss Jessie do as she pleased.

But Stuart—much as Jessie hated to admit it, she was clay in his hands. She wanted so much to please him that she would bend over backward to comply with his demands. Which was, when she thought it over, quite a disturbing admission. That he affected her physically there was no point in denying, at least to herself. But there was a great deal more to her wish to please him than that. Jessie decided, finally, that she succumbed so meekly to his bullying because they were friends. But, though she refused to explore it, she knew that the relationship that had developed between them was far more complex than mere friendship.

It was strange that a man she'd known for less than half a year (and hated at the outset) should have assumed such importance in her life. Was it simply that he was so kind to her, so genuinely interested in her well-being, that she gravitated to him as a hungry man might to food? Rarely since her father's death had anyone save the servants even bothered to talk to her, except to scold or ridicule. Was it any wonder, then, that she was dazzled by Stuart and the whole world of friendly companionship that he had opened up?

At least she was not the only one whom he had cozened into practically eating out of his hand. Thomas dogged his footsteps almost constantly when Stuart was walking about the grounds, and Fred vied with Thomas to fetch and carry for the master. Tudi and the rest of the house servants had long since started addressing him as the familial "Mr. Stuart," an honor that had not been accorded Celia until she had lived at Mimosa for more than three years. (Even after ten years as mistress of Mimosa, she was still mostly addressed simply as "ma'am." Celia, who had not been born to plantation life, never seemed to be aware of the subtle snub.) When even Progress unbent enough to give "Mr. Stuart's" horse, Saber, his own special bran mash to buck him up, Jessie knew that the plantation had fallen: Stuart had conquered it with scarcely a battle. And the funny thing about it was that she was glad.

"Are you ladies doing all right?" Stuart rode up beside them to ask. He was astride Saber, while Jessie, Celia, Minna, and Sissie rode in the buggy with Progress up on the seat driving. Minna and Sissie faced backward, each charged with the care of a carefully wrapped dance dress. Sissie, who had been recruited to act as Jessie's maid for the occasion, was

puffed up with her own importance. Upon being
told what her assignment for the day would be, she
had donned a clean apron and turban. Her back was
ramrod straight, and her face was as solemn as a
judge's as she sat clutching the parcel holding Jessie's dance dress.

"We'd be better if you'd had the courtesy to order
up the closed carriage," Celia said pettishly.

Jessie winced a little, but Stuart seemed unper-
turbed by his wife's rebuke. "I thought you'd enjoy
some fresh air for a change," he replied and, setting
his heels to Saber's side, cantered on to join Ned
Trimble, who was on horseback escorting his family
just ahead.

Elmway fronted on the Yazoo River. It was a low,
sprawling house made of clapboards and stone that
did not look from the outside nearly as big as it actually was. It was situated so that the rear faced the
road. As their carriage rounded the bend that
brought Elmway into view, Jessie saw that the drive
was already lined with carriages waiting to dis-
charge their occupants. Remembering the reception
that had been accorded her at the engagement party,
Jessie felt a flutter of nervousness. Would she be a
social pariah this time, too?

She looked infinitely better than she had at the
engagement party, Jessie knew. Her dress was blue-
sprigged white muslin (white was practically the
only color considered suitable for a girl of Jessie's
age for afternoon wear), but it fitted her perfectly. It
was trimmed by knots of sapphire-blue ribbon, and
even that small amount of vivid color flattered her
eyes and skin. A wide sash in the same shade of
blue wrapped around her waist. Her hair she wore
up in deference to the heat, which was still sum-
merlike. The cunning tendrils that Madame Fleur
had scissored into existence formed a soft cloud
about her face.

"Hello, Jessie! Hello, Mrs. Edwards!" Nell Bidswell and Margaret Culpepper were riding together

in Nell's mother's carriage, with Mrs. Bidswell for
chaperone and Mr. Bidswell riding beside them.
They pulled into line behind the ladies from Mimosa. Jessie, surprised to be hailed, turned and
waved. Celia did too, smiling for what, to Jessie's
knowledge, was the first time that day.

Another flurry of greetings was exchanged as
Chaney Dart and Billy Cummings rode up to the
Bidswell carriage. Mitchell Todd was not far behind
them. As Jessie saw his approach, she quickly turned
so that she was facing forward again.

"I thought Mitchell Todd was your particular
beau, Jessie," Celia said snidely, a malicious glint in
her eyes. Celia had never said anything, not a single
word, about the transformation in her stepdaughter's appearance, which had brought a slew of compliments from everyone else at Mimosa. Jessie had
known for a long time that her stepmother disliked
her, but lately Celia seemed to take particular pleasure in doing anything she could to cause Jessie
pain. When Stuart was not around, of course.

Before Jessie could say anything by way of reply
to that, she was surprised to hear Mitch call out her
name. Embarrassed, she pretended not to hear. But
then to her consternation he rode up beside the carriage.

"Good afternoon, Mrs. Edwards. Hello, Miss Jessie."

Mitch greeted Celia politely and Jessie with more
warmth. Seeing no help for it, Jessie turned to face
him. Her answering hello was, she hoped, perfectly
composed. But the memory of the last time she had
seen him was still strong. The remembered humiliation of that awful night made her cheeks heat.

"Why, Miss Jessie, you went and turned into a
beauty while my back was turned!" Mitch exclaimed, looking her over with transparent surprise.
There was a teasing note to his voice, but there was
also no mistaking his underlying sincerity. Jessie
stammered, turning pink with embarrassed plea-

sure. Celia looked on with a smile. Jessie wondered
if she was the only one who could tell how much
effort that smile cost her. Celia was seething with
jealousy, Jessie realized suddenly. She hated for her
despised stepdaughter to be the recipient of masculine attention, while she herself was relegated to
the ranks of the matronly chaperones.

It was amazing what a difference a fashionable
dress and a becoming hairstyle could make to one's
pleasure, Jessie thought hours later, after the barbecue was over and the ladies had retired to change
into their dancing frocks. Nell and Margaret had
complimented her on her beauty and asked her to
sit with them while they ate. They were popular with
the young men, so Jessie, for the first time in her
life, knew what it was to be surrounded by a positive swarm of admirers. And that the gentlemen
found something to admire in her altered looks she
did not doubt. It was obvious in the way they gazed
at her, in the teasing manner of their talk. Before,
they had been merely polite, as if she were a kind
of elderly aunt, if they'd bothered to address her at
all. Now they were almost flirting with her. For the
most part Jessie kept her eyes on the plate of barbecue she balanced in her lap, too unsure of herself
to indulge in the easy repartee that seemed to come
so easily to Nell and Margaret. But the gentlemen
did not seem to find her shyness off-putting. If anything, they redoubled their efforts, showering her
with outrageous compliments and telling her droll
stories in an effort to make her laugh.

Despite the rekindling of the childhood friendship
she'd had with Nell and Margaret, and the kindness
of the other girls, Jessie was still not quite easy in
their presence. With Sissie's help, therefore, she
dressed quickly, and went downstairs alone. She
needed some breathing space before she had to deal
with the intricacies of polite socializing again.

The ladies were all above stairs, with the exception of Lissa, who was looking harassed as she con-

ferred with her cook at the end of the hall, and Miss May, who was out on the front lawn directing the gang of children who'd come for the day in a game of hide-and-seek that entailed much shrieking and running about. Jessie listened briefly to the children's noise. She could remember playing so, once, in the warm dusk of Indian summer. But the memory was vague, and mixed up with recollections of her parents. She shook her head, refusing to allow herself to dwell on it. To become maudlin would serve no earthly purpose.

Most of the gentlemen were apparently on the long portico overlooking the river, talking politics and blowing a cloud. To avoid them, and the rambunctious children, Jessie slipped out a side door. It was obvious that this particular section of lawn was used for the homeliest of purposes: a well-tended herb garden flourished to the left of a path of crushed stone, while a compost heap moldered to the right. Wrinkling her nose at the smell of the compost, Jessie walked along the path. She picked up her skirt carefully, not wanting to soil the fragile silk. The possession of lovely clothes was still new to her, and the garments were precious because of it.

It was twilight, and the fireflies were blinking above the brightly colored wildflowers that grew alongside the path. In the distance an apple orchard added its sweet scent to the spicy aroma of the flowers. Crickets chirped as night drew closer. The air was just starting to chill.

A greenhouse stood beside the path a little way farther along. It was small, probably for the cultivation of the prize roses Lissa grew. Jessie would have paid it no particular attention if she had not seen the silhouette of an embracing couple through the translucent glass.

Though she tried not to look, Jessie could not help herself. Whoever they were, their behavior was really quite shocking. They were clearly kissing pas-

sionately. The woman's arms were locked around
the man's neck, and the shadows of their heads and
bodies merged so that they might almost have been
one.

With a pang of envy, Jessie wondered what it felt
like to be kissed like that. For years, when she had
imagined permitting a gentleman to kiss her, Mitch's
face had arisen in her mind's eye. She would close
her eyes very tightly, and pucker up her lips . . .

But to Jessie's horror, as she suited action to
thought, Mitch's face was not the one she saw
against her closed lids.

"What the devil are you doing?" Stuart asked
from somewhere behind her. He sounded amused,
as well he might. Jessie whirled. Her eyes flew open
and her mouth unpuckered to form an O as the very
face she had been dreaming about materialized before her.

"Uh, uh—what are you doing out here?" Unable,
in her embarrassment, to come up with a satisfac-
tory explanation for why she was standing in the
near dark kissing an imaginary partner, she tried to
change the subject.

Stuart merely grinned at her.

"Looking for Celia," he said, his eyes twinkling
in a way that told Jessie as clearly as any words could
have that he knew perfectly well she'd been playing
at kissing. "Aunt Flora sent me to find her. She
wants a recipe for a potion to fight the wrinkling of
skin that she swears Celia has."

"I haven't seen her," Jessie managed, while her
blood ran cold. Because she suddenly knew, as
surely as if the glass had been clear rather than
milky, just who it was who was kissing her lover
inside the greenhouse only a few yards away.

Celia, the fool, was up to her old tricks again.

XX

"So who were you kissing, anyway?"

Under the circumstances, the question should have reduced Jessie to tongue-tied embarrassment. But because her mind was racing, it barely fazed her.

"I wasn't kissing anybody."

"I know kissing when I see it."

Stuart was grinning as he walked forward to catch Jessie's chin in his hand and tilt her face up for his inspection. The light was growing dimmer by the second, for which Jessie was thankful. If it grew dark enough quickly enough, it might just keep Stuart from realizing that there was anyone in the greenhouse at all. And maybe it would keep him from recognizing the panic in her eyes as well.

Thinking fast, Jessie managed an artistic shiver.

"Let's go in. I'm cold."

"Not 'til you tell me who your fantasy beau is."

He was still holding her face tilted up to his. Jessie was too agitated to take even guilty pleasure from his touch. She pulled her chin free and caught his hand instead.

"Celia's probably around at the front of the house with the children."

"I doubt it. She detests children. She told me so."

Jessie walked around him, heading back in the direction of the house. She still held his hand, and he

obligingly swiveled with her, but other than that he
didn't budge.

"What's that boy's name? Mitchell? You could do
better, you know."

"I'm not even interested in him," Jessie snapped,
and because she was so nervous her voice carried
the ring of truth.

"So who were you kissing?"

"I was *practicing*, for goodness' sake! Will you
please stop yammering on about it and come inside?"

She tugged at his hand again. He was as immovable as a mountain.

"That dress is mighty fetching. You could be out
here practicing on Mitchell if you wanted."

Her dance dress was made of yards and yards of
deep gold silk with a low-cut bodice that left her
creamy shoulders bare and a wide skirt ending in a
triple flounce that reduced her waist to nothingness.
It was a lovely dress, and Jessie had been more than
pleased with her reflection in the cheval glass upstairs. At the moment, however, not even Stuart's
compliment could distract her from her purpose. She
had to get him away from that greenhouse at once.

"I don't want to practice on Mitch. I don't want
to practice on anyone. I want to go inside."

Stuart's eyes glinted with amusement. He hadn't
finished teasing her by a long shot, Jessie could see.
His boots remained obstinately planted as she tried
to urge him along the path toward the house. Jessie
practically stamped her foot with vexation. How was
she ever to get him away from that spot?

"Tell the truth, Jessie: you're practicing for your
first kiss. Who's the lucky fellow going to be?"

"Would you quit being so idiotic and move? Mos-
quitoes are eating me alive!"

"Funny, none are biting me. I think you're just
shy."

"I am not shy!"

"Don't let whoever he is have more than one little

peck, now, or he'll think you're fast. And keep your lips closed tight.''

"What on earth are you talking about?"

"Kissing.''

"I don't want to talk about kissing. I . . .''

But it was too late. Jessie's words died in her throat and her eyes widened with horror as Celia emerged from the greenhouse, laughing over her shoulder. Jessie could not see Celia's companion. He still stood just inside the open door.

Her shocked expression must have alerted Stuart, because he glanced around. When he saw Celia he stiffened. His fingers clenched on Jessie's hand.

Her hand tightened instinctively around his. From the tide of red that flooded his cheekbones, Jessie knew that he was not going to take discovering his wife in a secluded spot with another man lightly. She only thanked God that he had not seen the embrace.

"What the hell . . . ?'' His exclamation was low, and ugly. Jessie tried to cling to his hand, tried to hold him back, but he shook her off and strode toward his wife.

"Stuart!'' Celia's voice was little more than a squeak. She glanced quickly over her shoulder as Stuart approached her, looking, to Jessie's mind, the very picture of guilt.

Seth Chandler stepped out of the greenhouse. When he saw Stuart he stopped in his tracks.

"I, uh, we, uh—'' Chandler stuttered, his eyes bulging. He tugged at his high collar as if it were suddenly too tight.

Stuart didn't even give him time to finish. He walked up to Chandler and, without saying so much as a word, sucker-punched him with a right to his jaw that sent the man crashing back through the greenhouse door.

Celia screamed. Jessie ran toward the greenhouse and Stuart.

Stuart caught his wife by the arm and jerked her

close against his body. His eyes as they bore down into Celia's blazed murder. Celia cringed. Afraid of what he might do, Jessie ran up and caught his free arm, tugging.

"Don't hurt her," she said urgently.

"You goddamned slut." The words were very quiet. Stuart ignored Jessie entirely. His attention was all for Celia.

The insult seemed to stiffen Celia's spine. She reddened, and tried without success to jerk her arm from her husband's grasp. When she couldn't, she stopped struggling and stood glaring up at him. Celia was tiny, and Stuart was tall and muscular. Both were flushed with anger. In any physical dispute between them, it was obvious who the victor must be. Gazing at Stuart towering furiously over his wife, Jessie wondered that Celia had the nerve to defy him. He looked as if he could break her in half without any effort at all.

"Slut, am I?" Celia hissed. "For no more than talking in private to an old friend of my late husband's? If merely being private with a man makes a woman a slut, then what about our Jessie, out here all alone in the dark with *you*?"

"Leave Jessie out of this." It was a growled warning.

Celia laughed angrily. Her eyes flashed over Jessie, then returned to Stuart. At the insinuation, Jessie had immediately dropped Stuart's arm and taken a step back from him. Now she flushed. The look in her stepmother's eyes made her feel unclean.

"See there? Look at her! The picture of guilt! Come now, husband mine, confess: you've been playing fast and loose with sweet little Jessie." Celia's voice dripped venom.

Stuart's face tightened so that muscles stood out in his jaw. His hand around Celia's arm must have tightened, too, because Celia gasped and winced.

"Two nights after we were wed, I caught you in

the hay with a bloody stableboy. You weren't worth killing then, and you're not now."

"Christ, man, it's not a killing matter! There was nothing—nothing much . . ."

Seth Chandler made the ultimate mistake of getting back on his feet and staggering through the doorway. He almost barreled into Stuart, and in fact tried to steady himself with a hand on Stuart's shoulder. At his touch Stuart whirled and caught him by the lapels of his elegant coat, lifting him almost off his feet.

Chandler was a stocky, muscular man, but in the face of Stuart's wrath and his own knowledge of wrongdoing he was as meek as a whipped puppy. Watching with her hand pressed against her mouth, Jessie thought that even if she hadn't seen that furtive embrace, Chandler's very demeanor screamed guilt.

"We were just talking—it was perfectly innocent," Chandler babbled, his hands scrabbling at Stuart's where they were entwined in his coat.

"You *talk* to my wife again, and I'll beat you to a pulp." It was more of a promise than a threat. "Understand?"

Chandler nodded jerkily, fear plain in his eyes.

Stuart's lip curled. Abruptly he released his grip on the coat. Chandler's knees sagged, and he stumbled backward. He managed to catch hold of the greenhouse doorjamb, and that was all that saved him from measuring his length on the ground again.

"Get out of my sight," Stuart growled. Rubbing his sore jaw, Chandler shakily complied.

Celia had not moved, watching the demolishment of her lover's dignity with contempt plain in her eyes. As Stuart turned back to her, she stood her ground. Jessie thought her stance conveyed a kind of triumph.

"What do you care if I amuse myself, anyway? You only married me to get your damned hands on my money!"

"And you only married me to prove that you could, so I'd say we deserve each other."

Stuart reached out suddenly and caught one of Celia's bouncy ringlets, curling it around his fingers and then giving it a sharp tug.

"For whatever reason we married, the fact remains that we *are* married. I won't be made a laughingstock by my wife."

"And I won't be made a slave by my husband!"

Stuart smiled, a cold and sinister smile that was evil enough to scare Jessie, at least.

"Understand this: you've had your warning. If I catch you fornicating a second time, I'll kill you."

He let go of her hair, untangling his fingers from the clinging curl with a roughness clearly designed to hurt. Celia yelped and stepped quickly back, her hand flying to rub her abused scalp.

"I hate you," she spat.

"Good." The word was brutal. Celia threw him a murderous look, then turned on her heel and flounced off toward the house.

"Bitch," Stuart muttered. His face was dark with anger. Slamming his fists into the pockets of his coat, he swiveled in the opposite direction from Celia and started walking away from the house.

Undecided, Jessie watched him go. Should she leave him alone? The utter vileness of what she had just witnessed had left her sick to her stomach, and Stuart certainly had not looked in the mood for company. But seeing that stiff, proud back disappear into the gathering darkness, Jessie realized that she really did not have a choice in the matter after all. She could not bear for him to be alone. Biting her lip, she hurried after Stuart.

When she caught up to him, he was leaning against a waist-high stone wall that bisected a field. Jessie was almost upon him before she saw him, so well did his dark blue coat blend with the coming night

As she moved to stand beside him, Jessie said

nothing. She continued to say nothing as he stared off into the field on the other side of the wall. Neither by word nor by gesture did he give any indication that he was aware of her presence. And yet Jessie knew that he knew she was there.

It was some few minutes before he spoke.

"I'm sorry you had to witness that," he said at last.

"It doesn't matter."

He looked at her then, fleetingly, before his eyes returned to the mist that was just floating in. "You told me the truth about her, didn't you? And I slapped your face for your pains. I've never apologized for that. I do now."

"It doesn't matter," Jessie said again. The response was inadequate, she knew, but his pain was so palpable that she was hurting, too.

"I don't love her. I never loved her."

"I know."

"You were right. I married her for Mimosa."

"I know that, too."

"But I thought I could make it work. I thought *we* could make it work. God in heaven." Stuart shut his eyes for a moment, then opened them again to stare unseeingly in front of him. Hundreds of fireflies flitted across the dense blue velvet darkness that now covered the vastness of the rolling fields. Their lights flickered constantly. The sight was eerily beautiful, like a fairy dance.

"We've been married only a few months, and I hate her. I hate her enough to kill her, so help me God I do." Stuart leaned more heavily against the wall, his hands braced on its rough top, his head bowing. Jessie put a gentle hand on his sleeve, her throat tight with threatened tears. He hurt, and so she hurt. The knowledge with all its ramifications was scary.

"God, I've made a mess of things," he muttered, lifting his head suddenly. His hand lifted, too, to form a fist and pound down on the top of the wall.

Jessie started. Though it was leashed, the sheer desperate violence of the action made her heart leap with sudden, instinctive fear. Then she saw that he had straightened and was shaking and flexing his right hand. His scarred hand. The hand he'd used to punch Chandler and hit the wall.

Reaching out, fear forgotten, she caught that much-abused hand in both of hers and began to gently knead the puckered palm.

XXI

"That feels good."

He was looking down at her bent head as she worked on his hand. Jessie knew he was; she could sense it. But she refused to look up. Her attention focused exclusively on that poor maltreated hand—because she was afraid to let it focus anywhere else.

"How did you get the scar?" The question was meant to cover a myriad of conflicting emotions. His hand, with its broad palm and long fingers, was large compared with hers. The skin at the base and tips of his fingers was slightly roughened with calluses. Against the softness of her own skin as she gently rubbed his fingers, the calluses felt abrasive. His hand was warm, shades browner than hers, which looked ridiculously white in comparison, and its back was sprinkled with black hair. The scar in the center of his palm was ugly, circular, and red. His fingers had drawn in toward his palm as if from an involuntary muscular contraction. Jessie massaged the knotted tendons beneath the distracting flesh and thought she felt them ease slightly. Still she didn't look up.

"Knife fight. Some months back."

At that she did look up. "A knife fight?" There was a note of incredulity in her voice.

His mouth twisted wryly. "Does that surprise you?"

Jessie considered, then shook her head. "No. Not really. Now that I think about it, getting into a knife fight seems perfectly in character for you. I thought when I first saw you that you looked dangerous."

He smiled a little at that. "Did you, now?"

"Yes."

Looking up had been a mistake, just as she had suspected it would be. He was close, too close. So close that she could see every little whisker in the stubble that already darkened his jaw, though he'd been freshly shaven when they'd left Mimosa. So close that she could feel the heat of his body, smell the faintly musky odor of man.

"I think, Jessie, my girl, that you must be learning how to flirt." He sounded faintly surprised and at the same time a little bemused.

"I'm not flirting." Though she meant it literally, she could see from the flicker in his eyes that he took it quite another way. His lids dropped, briefly, to consider her small hands as they rubbed and cradled his.

"Aren't you?" His eyes lifted to hers again. There was an unaccustomed intensity in his gaze that Jessie found both unnerving and electrifying.

"No." It was a mere breath. Her hands had stilled their movements seconds before, but still they clung to his fingers.

"No?"

"No."

"Ah." It was a curiously unsettling sound. Stuart smiled slightly, crookedly, and his head dipped toward her. Jessie felt her own head start to whirl. Her hands tightened over his, her nails dug into his flesh, and she wasn't even aware of the possibility that she might be hurting him. Her breath stopped, and she wasn't aware of that, either. All about her the night seemed to freeze. The flickering fireflies, chirruping insects, swaying foliage, ceased to be.

Every nerve ending in her body was concentrated
on the darkly handsome face that was descending
toward hers; on the beautiful, masculine mouth that
in just milliseconds must touch her own.

His free hand, the hand she wasn't clutching as if
she'd die if she didn't, rose to encircle the back of
her neck.

Jessie's heart pounded. She felt as though it might
jump through her chest and take off leapfrogging
across the field like a startled rabbit. She swayed,
and closed her eyes. . . .

And his mouth just brushed her lips.

It was a soft caress, barely felt. Yet heat shot
through her body in its wake, heat so intense that
her bones seemed to liquefy. Her lips parted, and
she drew in a shaken breath. She felt the need to
almost gasp for air. His hand tightened briefly on
the back of her neck, then withdrew. Jessie realized
with the part of her mind that was still capable of
functioning rationally that he must be looking down
at her bedazzled face.

She forced her eyes open.

He *was* looking at her, his expression inscrutable,
his eyes impossible to read in the darkness that now
enveloped them. He was close, closer even than he
had been before, so close that her full skirt puddled
over his boots, so close that her suddenly highly
sensitized breasts were only inches away from his
broad chest. Her hand still clung to his injured one,
she realized, and though she knew she must, she
could not quite force her fingers to open and let his
go.

"You did it quite well."

"What?" She had no idea what he was talking
about. His voice was light, too light for the smol-
dering heat that coursed through her veins, too light
for her to make sense of what he said. She was on
fire, burning up, and he sounded as though nothing
had happened at all.

"Your first kiss. It was your first, wasn't it?"

This was a nightmare. It had to be. He might talk
so to her about any of a dozen mundane subjects.
But that kiss had been far from mundane. For all its
gentle brevity, it had been the most shattering experience of Jessie's life. She was still shaken in its
aftermath. But gradually, gradually, it occurred to
her that perhaps he had not been quite so affected
as she. After all, he was a grown man, not a boy, a
married man with what she had no doubt was a vast
amount of experience kissing women. What had
been an earthshaking experience for her had meant
nothing at all to him.

"Jessie?"

Looking him in the eye and keeping her voice
steady were two of the hardest things she had ever
done in her life. But she did it, because she had to.
If she let him know just how that throwaway kiss
had affected her, she would never be able to hold
up her head in his presence again. Though her foolish heart hungered for his kisses, the rest of her
feared the loss of his friendship. Her life would be
bleak indeed without that.

"Jessie, are you all right?" There was a sudden
roughness to his voice, and his eyes narrowed as
they scrutinized her. The hand that she'd been desperately clutching throughout turned in hers to grip
her fingers, hard.

"Yes, of course." To her everlasting credit, Jessie
even managed a little laugh. She felt as though she
were enveloped in a mist that muted all her senses
except the hot tingling of her flesh, but she meant
to hide her reaction if it killed her. To preserve her
pride she had to make him think that that butterfly
kiss had meant no more to her than it had to him.
"Though as a first kiss, it was not *quite* what I had
expected."

His eyes widened. "Are you saying that you're
disappointed, minx? You *are* learning to flirt." His
grip on her hand relaxed. As her hand freed his at
last, Jessie thought that some of the tension left his

shoulders. "Were I Mitch, or any one of the other boys who might have managed to lure you out here alone, that would be my cue to sweep you up in my arms and give you a kiss you wouldn't dismiss so easily. Then, of course, you would be obliged to slap my face."

"Now *that* would be a pleasure," Jessie murmured through clenched teeth hidden behind a fixed smile. The saving grace of anger was starting to set in, thank the Lord. Being furious with him was better than feeling as if she'd been kicked in the stomach by a horse.

At her unintelligible reply Stuart frowned.

"What?"

"I said I might not slap Mitch's face. Or whoever's."

"Then, my dear, they'd likely think you no lady."

"Should I slap yours, then?" How her palm itched to!

"For that little peck? It was no more than a thank-you for your gentle care of me. Quite permissible between relatives, I assure you."

"Indeed?" Jessie smiled brilliantly and clenched her fists at her sides behind the sheltering folds of her skirts. "I'm glad I was able to be of service. The next time Celia upsets you, do be sure to call on me."

He paused in the act of reaching inside his coat for his cigar case to look at her more closely.

"Good God, you're angry! At me?"

"I am not," Jessie said through that brilliant, clenched smile, "angry. But I am rather cold. If you'll excuse me, I think I'll go back to the house."

She inclined her head at him quite regally, turned on her heel, picked up her skirts, and swept back in the direction from which she'd come.

"But, Jessica." His voice, floating after her, was both plaintive and, she was enraged to discover, laced with laughter. "Isn't that a rather extreme reaction to such a disappointing kiss?"

XXII

Rage was an excellent beautifier, Jessie discovered. When she caught a glimpse of herself in the long mirror over the Chandlers' sideboard, she was startled at the color it brought to her cheeks and the sparkle it lent to her eyes. Indeed, so determined was she to show Stuart—and herself—that his kiss had meant nothing to her, absolutely nothing at all, her manner gained a vivacity that was absolutely foreign to her nature. For the rest of the evening she laughed and flirted and even danced, buoyed by enough fury-inspired confidence to trust that her inexperience on the dance floor would not be an embarrassment. And she felt that she acquitted herself quite well. Certainly she never lacked for partners, and by the time Stuart dragged her and Celia away from the celebration, no fewer than four gentlemen had begged leave to call on her at Mimosa. Graciously she granted all four requests.

She also, for the first time in her life, drank brandy. Mitch gave her the first sip when she clamored prettily to taste what was in his glass.

"You won't like it," he warned her, but when she persisted he held his snifter to her lips. With a sidelong glance at Stuart, who had joined the men by the refreshment table nearby, Jessie took a sip. As Mitch had warned her, the stuff tasted dreadful. But

171

Stuart frowned at her as she drank, and that was all
the goad Jessie needed. Defiantly she proclaimed her
liking for the beverage, and weedled Mitch's glass
from him as she took a stroll about the room on his
arm.

Half a snifter later, just as a particularly lively qua-
drille was striking up, she found Miss Flora by her
side.

"My dear, ladies drink only ratafia," Miss Flora
whispered urgently for Jessie's ears alone.

Looking over Miss Flora's diminutive shoulder,
Jessie encountered Stuart's eyes as he scowled at
her from across the room. Obviously he had sent his
aunt to remonstrate with her. Well, she was clay in
his hands no longer, and so he would soon discover!
Smiling defiantly, she inclined her head at him, then
took another, too-large gulp of brandy. It was all she
could do not to choke as the pungent liquid filled
her mouth, but she managed to keep her countenance, and even to swallow. The liquor burned her
tongue and throat going down, but after another,
more prudently sized mouthful Jessie decided that
it truly wasn't so bad. Stuart was positively black-
browed as he watched her, which spurred her on to
swallow what was left in that snifter and ask for
more. She abandoned the notion only because Mitch
refused to fetch her another, instead pulling her onto
the floor to dance.

After that, whenever she felt Stuart's eyes on her,
she'd beg another sip of brandy or whatever else her
partner of the moment happened to be drinking.
Wine was slightly more palatable than brandy, she
discovered, while bourbon whiskey was almost
completely undrinkable. She took only a taste here,
a swallow there, while the gentleman she was with
watched with an indulgent smile. Stuart's countenance grew steadily blacker. Jessie almost purred. If
she had found a way to make him angry, then she
was glad!

The alcohol's only effect on her, she felt, was to

make her livelier and more charming than she'd ever been in her life. Certainly she was charming the boots off Mitch. Clearly entranced, he danced with her twice, and hovered in her vicinity even when she took to the floor with other men. To dance more than twice with a particular partner who was not a close relative was considered improper; otherwise Jessie was sure he would not have let her out of his arms at all. His attentions to Jeanine Scott were no more than perfunctory. The slender brunette was obviously upset by Mitch's defection. Jessie would have been less than human if that had not pleased her to no end.

All in all, Jessie's evening was a triumph. So why, beneath the dimpling smiles and flirtatious giggles, did she feel so bad?

It was not yet one o'clock, and the party was still in full swing, when Stuart came up behind her as she chatted gaily with Oscar Kastel. Bess Lippman was casting the two of them furious glances from the corner of the room, where she sat with her mother. Bess Lippman, the spiteful cat, was a wall-flower, while her beau ogled plain little Jessica Lindsay! Jessie glowed with triumph until she felt a hand grip her upper arm. Smiling as she looked over her shoulder, expecting to see Mitch or one of her multitude of new admirers, Jessie discovered Stuart instead, and her smile faded. His urbane smile did not quite conceal the displeased glint in his eyes. So he did not like the way she was behaving, eh? Good!

"Good evening, Mr., uh, Kastel, isn't it?" His voice was pleasant, but the hand on her arm was hard.

"Yes, sir. Hello, Mr. Edwards. I hear you've got yourselves quite a cotton crop at Mimosa this year."

"Yes, we do indeed. Jessie, Celia's been taken ill. Much as I dislike spoiling your evening, we'll have to leave."

"Celia—" Jessie started to protest, started to call him on what she knew full well was a lie, but the warning look he gave her and the tightening of his grip on her arm dissuaded her. Making a public scene would serve no purpose but her own humiliation, she knew. She did not doubt for a moment that Stuart would not hesitate to pick her up bodily and carry her from the premises if she refused to go with him.

So she smiled at him, quite as falsely as he was smiling at her, and said, "Oh, dear."

"Quite." His eyes moved back to Oscar Kastel. "If you'll excuse Jessie and me, Mr. Kastel?"

"Oh, yes. Of course. Miss Jessie, I hope to see you soon."

"Good-bye, Mr. Kastel."

Jessie allowed Stuart to drag her away. There didn't seem to be much alternative.

When the cool night air hit her, Jessie swayed. Stuart's hand tightened on her arm.

"Tipsy, are you? I suspected as much." He sounded disgusted.

"I certainly am not," Jessie said with dignity, and to prove it pulled away from his hold and walked to the carriage by herself, without swaying once.

Celia was already inside, as were Sissie and Minna. Progress sat on the box. Disdaining to wait for Stuart's help, Jessie hoisted her skirts almost to her knees and clambered into the carriage. Celia greeted her with a virulent look. Clearly she was unhappy about their early departure and blamed Jessie. Or maybe she was still angry because of the scene Jessie had witnessed earlier. Who knew?

At any rate, Jessie didn't much care. For once Celia's mood meant nothing to her. She was too angry herself, too tired, too fuzzy-headed, and too heart-sore to care what Celia was or was not angry about.

"Your behavior tonight was a disgrace!" Celia hissed as the carriage got under way.

"Rather a case of the pot calling the kettle black, isn't it, Celia?" Jessie asked sweetly. Celia's eyes widened. It wasn't like Jessie to fight back. Then they narrowed again. But with Minna and Sissie as silent witnesses to whatever she or Jessie might say, Celia chose the prudent course and said no more. Jessie guessed that what kept her tongue between her teeth was the fear that her stepdaughter might reveal her guilty liaison with Seth Chandler.

Stuart had ridden on ahead, so that Jessie didn't see him until they got back to Mimosa. But when the carriage stopped, he was waiting for them on the veranda, smoking one of his everlasting cheroots. He made no move to help the ladies alight, leaving that to Progress. Celia climbed the steps and brushed by him without a word. But when Jessie would have followed her example, he stopped her with a hand on her arm.

"I'd like a word with you, if you please," he said quietly.

"I'm tired." Jessie tried to pull her arm from his grip as Sissie and Minna, each clutching parcels containing the afternoon's finery, slipped by.

"Nevertheless."

He was courteous, perfectly so, but the fingers circling her arm could have been forged from iron. Clearly he meant to have his own way. Jessie scowled, then capitulated with a jerky nod. If he thought to rake her over the coals, then he was in for a surprise! Her blood was up, and she meant to give as good as she got.

XXIII

The library was a small room toward the back of the first floor, little used until Stuart had taken up residence at Mimosa. He had claimed the book-lined room for his own, had it dusted and aired and furnished with a massive mahogany desk and comfortable leather chairs. It was to the library that he led Jessie, standing back courteously to allow her to precede him into the room, then closing the door behind him as he followed her in. With the candle he had taken from a stand near the front door, he lit the tapers on either side of his desk. The flickering light that resulted sent dancing shadows into every corner of the room and, as he turned to face Jessie, also hid his expression.

"Have a seat." He indicated the chair closest to where Jessie stood in the center of the room.

"Thank you, but I prefer to stand. I'm assuming that this won't take long?"

She faced him defiantly, chin up, eyes bright. He looked her over for a moment without saying anything more, moving to sit on a corner of his desk with one long, booted leg swinging idly. The highly polished black leather gleamed as it moved. Jessie's eyes were caught by that gleam. Swiftly they traveled from that swinging boot up over the formidable length of the man wearing it. As always, he was immaculately turned out. Despite the vicissitudes of his day, his breeches were creaseless, the biscuit-colored knit clinging to the powerful muscles of his legs as if they'd been painted on. His brocade waistcoat fitted his wide chest and slim midriff without a wrinkle. His long-tailed coat of blue superfine hugged his broad shoulders lovingly. Nary a spot marred his impeccably tied neckcloth, and his shirt points were as crisp as they had been when he'd donned the garment that morning. If his hair was a trifle disordered by the wind, the disorder was highly becoming. A tousle of blue-black waves fell over his forehead, framing the classically handsome face. In the candlelight his eyes glinted very blue.

Conscious of her own disorder—despite Madame Fleur's promise, the wind in her hair on the drive home had contrived to loosen long curls that now straggled down her back, and the front of her lovely gown bore a definite spot—Jessie viewed his sartorial perfection with something less than pleasure. In fact, she scowled at him.

"Since you've brought me in here to scold me, you might as well get it over with so that I can go to bed."

Something, either her words or her snappish tone, amused him. The resulting wry twist of his lips maddened her.

"You must not drink spirits at parties, you know. The good folks hereabouts will say you're fast."

If he had been angry with her at the Chandlers', his anger seemed to have faded. His voice was no more than gently chiding. In fact, he sounded very much like a fond but weary parent scolding a wayward child. But she was no child, not anymore, and he was definitely not her parent!

"Don't you dare criticize me! I wouldn't even have gone to the stupid party if you hadn't insisted. And it seems to me that your behavior tonight was far more reprehensible than mine. After all, I didn't knock my host down—or kiss my stepdaughter!"

She hadn't meant to say it, but her anger was such that it had just bubbled out. The words lay between them like a gauntlet.

Stuart's lips tightened fractionally. It was clear that her unexpected counterattack both surprised and displeased him.

"No, you didn't, did you? You merely flirted madly with all the halfway eligible men present, and got yourself royally tipsy in the bargain. Pretty behavior, for a wet-behind-the-ears miss!"

"No worse than yours! Or Celia's! And don't you call me a wet-behind-the-ears miss in that patronizing tone!"

"Certainly no worse than Celia's—and I'll call you what I please," he said, sounding placid enough, although his eyes belied his tone. They were beginning to show a decided glint, and Jessie realized that she was making him angry. Good! She wanted him angry! As angry as she was!

"What business is it of yours what I do, anyway? You'd do better putting all this effort into keeping track of your wandering wife! She's the one you found in the greenhouse, remember, not me!"

"I didn't bring you in here to discuss Celia."

Jessie laughed. The glint in his eyes flared.

"You take entirely too much upon yourself, Stuart. I neither want nor need you to tell me how to behave!"

"Really? From the way you were making eyes at that Todd boy, I half expected to find the two of you sneaking off into the dark together. Just like your stepmother would do."

"You're vile."

He smiled then, unpleasantly, and stood up. He looked very large suddenly in the small room. "Not nearly as vile as I can be, I assure you. Nor as vile as I will be if I find you in a situation remotely like the one in which we discovered Celia—or if I hear of you drinking spirits again."

"Don't you dare threaten me!"

"You're trying my patience, Jessie."

"Good!"

His lips tightened. Crossing his arms over his chest, he cocked his head to one side and surveyed her narrowly. Jessie could see that he had got control of his temper again and was trying very hard to retain it.

"This little tantrum of yours is all because I kissed you, isn't it?"

"Certainly not! And I am not having a tantrum!"

"Aren't you? You've been having one all night. The flirting, the spirits—it was all to get back at me, wasn't it?"

Jessie felt her face grow red, but whether it was from rage or embarrassment or some combination of the two, she was too upset to guess. He stood there, leaning back against the desk, looking oh-so-superior, while she gibbered like an idiot and he probed unfeelingly at the darkest secrets of her heart. Her teeth clenched, and in that moment she came close to hating him.

"You flatter yourself!"

"Do I?"

Then he smiled, kindly, and that pitying smile was his undoing. With an inarticulate cry of rage she rushed toward him, meaning to claw the smile from his face.

"Hey!"

He caught her flailing wrists, holding her off from him while she squirmed and kicked and called him every bad name she had ever heard. But her kicks did no more than scuff his boots, and her insults made him laugh. His laughter maddened her, and finally he had to pin her back against his body to subdue her.

"Let me go!"

"Behave yourself and I will." He was grinning still.

"I hate you!"

"Temper, temper."

"Maw-worm! Clod!"

"My mother always told me to beware of red-headed women. Hotheaded, she said."

"I am not redheaded!"

"Yes, you are. And you've got the temper to prove it. Calm down, Jessie, and I'll let you go."

Jessie took a deep breath and stood very still. She stood with her back to him, her posterior pressed against his thighs, her arms crisscrossed over her bosom while he held fast to her wrists. From the corner of her eye she could see his wide grin.

"I don't think one tiny little kiss is worth all this, do you?"

His tone was almost teasing. Mentally Jessie called him a word so bad that ordinarily she would blush to hear it. But aloud she said, sweetly, "Will you please let go of my wrists? You're hurting me."

"Behave yourself, now."

He gave her wrists a warning squeeze, then slowly released his hold on them. Jessie was no sooner free than she whirled on her heel and slapped him hard across his smirking face.

"That's what I think your kiss is worth!"

"Ow!"

He stepped back a pace, clapping a hand to his cheek. His eyes widened with astonishment. For a moment he merely looked at her, his expression so comical that she forgot to be afraid. She smiled at him in malicious triumph. And in so doing made her own grievous mistake.

"You—little—brat!" he said through clenched teeth, and reached for her.

"Oh!" His hands clamped over her upper arms, dragged her close. For a frozen moment Jessie glared up into eyes that blazed as cold and bright as diamonds. Then with a sound that might have been a growl or a curse Stuart bent his head.

This time when he kissed her, it bore no resemblance at all to the soft sweetness of his previous effort. This kiss was fierce, and rough, designed both to vent his anger and teach her a lesson. Eyes wide, Jessie tried to jerk her head free, but he thwarted her movement by twisting her in his arms so that her head was imprisoned against the unyielding hardness of his shoulder. His mouth clamped down on hers, crushing her lips against her teeth until her mouth was forced open. Then, incredibly, his tongue thrust its way inside. It staked bold possession, stroking the roof of her mouth, the insides of her cheeks, her tongue.

The hot, wet invasion frightened her, made her whimper and squirm in protest. To her unutterable relief, Stuart stiffened suddenly and lifted his head. For a moment they stared at each other, Jessie's eyes wide and fearful, Stuart's clouded with emotions she couldn't name.

Then, all at once, he released her and stepped back.

"*Now* you slap my face," he said quietly.

Acting blindly, more out of instinct than because he told her to, Jessie drew back her hand and dealt him a blow that resounded through the small room and rocked his head. Then she stepped quickly out of reach.

He stood looking at her, just looking at her, for countless seconds as long fingers rose to probe experimentally at his face. Dark blood rushed to fill in the mark she had left; the imprint of her hand was clearly visible on his cheek. Jessie's fingers rose to her mouth. Lips trembling, she watched him without speaking.

Finally he broke the silence. "Go to bed, Jessie." His voice was devoid of emotion. His face looked empty, too, as he met her eyes. His fingers still rested against the reddened cheek. Jessie guessed that it had begun to throb and sting. Every instinct she possessed urged her to go to him, to apologize, to find some way to make up for the blow she had dealt him.

Then she remembered that hateful kiss.

Without a word Jessie turned on her heel and fled.

XXIV

Over the next ten days the domestic situation at Mimosa deteriorated badly. Jessie spent most of her time avoiding Stuart, whom she suspected of also doing his utmost to avoid her. Celia alternated between bouts of bitter sarcasm and sullen silence, lines of discontent springing up almost overnight to age her once youthful face. Though Jessie's bedroom was in the original structure at the front of the house, and Celia and Stuart had separate but adjoining rooms in the newer rear wing, they quarreled so violently late at night that Jessie could not help but hear them. Or at least, she heard Celia, screeching furiously at her husband. Stuart's replies she usually didn't hear, although once he shouted, "I said get the hell out of here, you bitch!" loudly enough to startle Jessie out of a near sleep. On another occasion she heard a resounding thud as though something heavy had fallen or been thrown, followed by Celia's scream.

The sounds both upset and frightened Jessie, so she buried her head beneath her pillow and pretended not to hear them. Because the slaves all slept with their families in the quarters, Jessie was the only witness to this almost nightly violence. With the coming of the sun, and the servants, things went on pretty much as they always had, except for the

tension that lay over the house. It was so thick that
Jessie could feel its weight like a blanket whenever
she was indoors. The servants felt it, too. Tudi, Rosa,
Sissie, and the rest went about their duties in unaccustomed silence. All of them, Jessie included, had
a tendency to start when Celia appeared.

On the brighter side, Jessie now had a positive
surfeit of beaux. In the days following the Chandlers' party Oscar Kastel, Billy Cummings, Mac Wil-
der, Evan Williams, and Mitch Todd all came to call
more than once. Jessie sat with them on the veranda, or walked with them along the drive, or went
riding in their buggies, with Tudi or Sissie along for
propriety's sake. There was a time when Jessie
would have been deliriously happy to have Mitch,
in particular, paying court to her. But she was so
distracted over the general unhappiness at Mimosa,
and the state of her relationship with Stuart in particular, that the realization of a dream she'd held
close for years—having Mitch Todd as her beau—did
not give her the pleasure she'd always thought it
would. To her dismay, Jessie found herself smiling
at his quips and lowering her eyes at his compliments, while all the while she had to make a conscious effort to keep her thoughts from wandering.

And that, she knew, could be laid squarely at
Stuart's door.

If Stuart was aware of her newfound popularity,
Jessie couldn't say. He spent each day in the cotton
fields as the hands labored to get the rest of the crop
picked before the first of the autumn frosts. The cotton flowers had long since turned from pink to purple. When the blooms withered, signaling that the
plants were mature, every available man, woman,
child, and mule at Mimosa took to the fields, where
they swarmed over the acres of white-speckled
plants like an army of ants. The distant hum of rich
spirituals floating in from the fields joined with the
rush of the nearby river to form a background sound
so familiar that Jessie scarcely heard it anymore.

Only she, Celia, and the house servants were exempt from laboring in the fields.

When not occupied with her callers (who soon grew to be as much nuisance as pleasure, since their arrival meant that Jessie had to entertain them), she spent most of her time in the saddle. Twice she rode to Tulip Hill to spend the afternoon with Miss Flora and Miss Laurel, to whom she was growing steadily more attached. Almost always, she took care to return long after supper, which Celia and Stuart still ate together in grim silence. One place she no longer rode to was the fields to join Stuart.

Chaney Dart finally asked Nell Bidswell to marry him, and the Bidswells hosted a dinner party to make the gala announcement. To Jessie's surprise, Celia turned down the invitation. Stuart also declined to attend on the grounds that he had too much work to do getting in the cotton. On her own initiative, sparked by a desire to show him that she was not as backward socially as he thought, Jessie went alone, attended by Tudi and Progress, and to her surprise she had a good time. She suspected that Celia's unaccustomed refusal to take part in a neighborhood gathering had been engineered by Stuart, who she guessed was bent on avoiding a repetition of Celia's indiscretion with Seth Chandler. Though, to Jessie's thinking, such precautions on Stuart's part were a waste of time. Celia had men in her blood, and if she didn't find a willing partner in one place, she would in another.

Like on her own property during the long, hot afternoons.

October came. The weather cooled. Mitch Todd rode over with Billy Cummings late one day, surprising Jessie just as she was getting ready to slip away from the house. Celia had vanished as she usually did after luncheon, not to return until it was time to dress for dinner. Jessie wanted to make sure that she was out of range of Celia's verbal arrows before her stepmother got back to the house. Lately

Celia was lashing out at everything and everyone with increasing viciousness. Besides Stuart, Jessie was her favorite target.

"Will you be going to the Culpeppers' next week, Miss Jessie?"

Jessie was seated on the topmost of the steps leading to the upper veranda. Billy Cummings, a lanky blond twenty-year-old, sat some two steps below her. He was looking up at her eagerly as he spoke.

"Well, I . . ."

"You have to come. The dance won't be any fun if you don't." Mitch flashed his lopsided grin, and Jessie wondered why it no longer made her heart go pitty-pat. He sat on the same step as Billy Cummings, on the extreme left of the stairway instead of the extreme right. With Jessie positioned above and between them, she could converse with both equally well. Looking down at them, she wondered that she had ever been in awe of these two. Both were handsome, tall, upright young men, and both were older than she by a year or two, but still, they were no more than boys. She felt older than they by far.

"You know as well as I do that I'm no great shakes on the dance floor, Mitchell Todd." Jessie spoke pertly, with a glimmering smile for the boy who had once owned her heart. His grin broadened.

"Who cares how well you dance?" he answered. "What matters is how pretty you look doing it."

"And you sure do look pretty," Billy chimed in, anxious not to be outdone by his rival. Jessie smiled at both of them. She was wearing a short-sleeved, tight-to-the-waist afternoon dress of white muslin trimmed in emerald green. The neckline was edged with a cunning stand-up frill of white lace, and more white lace trimmed the sleeves and hem. Her hair curled down her back to her hips, and was caught away from her face with an emerald-green satin bow at the crown. The dress was lovely, the color flattering, and she did look pretty, she knew. That knowledge enabled her to reply to the compliment with a laugh instead of a blush.

"You tell the biggest fibs, Billy Cummings," she said in the same teasing voice she'd heard the other girls use. Billy protested, a hand pressed to his heart to underline his sincerity. Jessie laughed at him.

"Entertaining, Jessie?" Celia stepped out onto the veranda from inside the house, which she must have entered from the rear. Jessie looked around at her stepmother, her gay smile faltering. Celia's behavior of late had been unpredictable, but surely she wouldn't embarrass Jessie in front of the sons of her neighbors.

"Afternoon, Mrs. Edwards." Mitch spoke up, saving Jessie from answering. Billy echoed the greeting as both boys rose politely to their feet.

"Hello, gentlemen." Celia was already dressed for supper in a lavender-blue gown whose flattering hue eased some of the new hardness from her face. She smiled at the visitors, waved them down again, then turned to Jessie. As she looked her stepdaughter over, Celia's smile stayed in place, but her eyes chilled.

"Where's Tudi? Or Sissie?"

"Inside, I would imagine." Jessie's tone was guarded. She'd heard that brittle note in Celia's voice before, and it usually presaged trouble.

"You should not be receiving guests on your own, you know, dear. These gentlemen will think you have the manners of a ragamuffin." Celia smiled her crocodile smile at the young men, who were beginning to appear uncomfortable. Inwardly Jessie cringed. Celia was not going to be deterred by the presence of guests after all.

The big bell on the plantation began to ring, signaling the end of the workday and saving the situation at the same time. No sooner had the first peal reverberated over the landscape than Stuart rode up with Graydon Bradshaw. At the sound of the horses, Jessie looked around. In the distance she could see the fields emptying, and the long column of the slaves as they walked and rode muleback down the road toward home. The volume of the spirituals swelled as the weary singers drew closer, then turned off on the other side of the orchard to head for the quarters and their evening meal.

Stuart and Graydon Bradshaw dismounted. Thomas ran up to take the horses. The two men started up the steps as Thomas led Saber and Bradshaw's mount away. This time Jessie stood up along with Mitch and Billy to get out of Stuart's way as he climbed. Though she despised herself for it, her eyes greedily drank in the first sight of him she'd had in days. He was sweaty, his black hair curling damply around his head where he'd taken off his hat, his stubble darkening cheeks that had been tinted the color of teak by the sun, his white shirt sporting a long smear of dirt, his black breeches and usually immaculate boots dusty. It was one of the few times she had ever seen him disheveled. Curiously, it didn't detract from his dazzling attraction one whit. Behind him, Graydon Bradshaw was in a like state, but Jessie had eyes for no one but Stuart. For her, Bradshaw might not even have existed.

In the distance the bell pealed one last time and stopped. The spirituals faltered as one after the other of the singers dropped out, then finally died away altogether.

"You're going to be late for supper, as usual." Celia was looking at Stuart, who had just stepped onto the veranda. Her voice had an edge to it that Jessie hoped only those who knew her well would catch.

"I'll be changed in a minute. Gray, you're welcome to join us if you'd like. Jessie, did you invite your friends to eat?"

The very idea of sitting in the dining room with Stuart and Celia taking potshots at each other while she strove to distract Mitch and Billy made Jessie squirm, but there was no help for it now. So she forced a smile at Stuart, then turned to the young men, who stood behind her.

"We'd be glad to have you to supper, if you'd care to stay."

Both Mitch and Billy assented eagerly. After exchanging pleasantries with them and waving Bradshaw off to change, Stuart turned to say something quietly to his wife. Celia had been conversing with Jessie's guests for some few minutes, her manner one of brittle flirtatiousness that was designed, Jessie had no doubt, to infuriate Stuart. That he noticed and was annoyed Jessie could tell by the tightening of his face. The stage was clearly set for a terrible quarrel, and the knowledge made her dread the coming meal more with every moment that passed.

Whatever Stuart said to Celia was inaudible to everyone else, but it made her face redden furiously. Jessie held her breath; the explosion she had feared was clearly at hand. But Stuart headed off the threatened scene with a single warning look at his wife. Moving quickly, though without giving the least impression of speed, he then caught Celia by the arm in a hold that Jessie supposed might look loving to an observer who had no idea how things stood between them, and drew her with him toward the door.

"Jessie, you can tell Rosa we'll be ready to eat in twenty minutes," he said over his shoulder, his manner still perfectly pleasant. Jessie thought that only someone who knew him as well as she did would be able to detect the anger that simmered beneath the untroubled front he presented to their guests. She supposed that to a casual acquaintance his hand on Celia's arm would look possessive rather than confining, and despite their differences he and Celia still made an attractive couple, her petite blondness the perfect foil for his dark good looks. But Jessie had no doubt that a fierce marital quarrel would ensue in the next few minutes, and she only

hoped it would be one of their quieter ones. She had
no wish to be embarrassed before their guests.

A marital quarrel. Even such unpleasantness as
that had an intimacy about it that bothered Jessie. It
brought home to her the fact that, however much
Stuart might despise Celia, and vice versa, they were
married. Joined until death parted them. Stuart had
kissed her twice, once in gratitude and once in anger. But he was wed to Celia. Jessie knew, *knew*, that
she'd be wise to remember that.

But no matter what she knew, as she watched
them go inside together Jessie felt a funny tightening in the pit of her stomach. For a moment only,
she was surprised: as tense as she was, she hadn't
expected to feel hungry. Then she realized that what
she was feeling wasn't hunger at all.

Ridiculously, idiotically, she was feeling jealous of
Celia.

XXV

To Jessie's surprise, the evening passed pleasantly enough. If Stuart and Celia had quarreled—and although Jessie hadn't actually seen them, she was sure they had—there was no outward sign of it. Celia managed to curb her tongue for the duration of the meal and was no more flirtatious with Mitch or Billy than was appropriate. In fact, she addressed most of her remarks to her cousin Gray, and left the entertaining of Jessie's guests to Jessie herself, and to Stuart.

Jessie was almost amused to discover that the younger men addressed Stuart with veneration, as if he were a generation rather than less than a decade older than they. He, in turn, adopted an avuncular manner toward them that was equally inappropriate. Or maybe not. Chronologically, the age difference might not be that great, but there was a tremendous gulf between them in bearing and experience.

After the meal, the company, with the exception of Celia, who pleaded a headache, retired to the porch. Stuart and Gray blew a cloud, while the younger men vied for Jessie's attention. Conscious of Stuart's watchful presence even as he talked lazily to Gray, Jessie went out of her way to respond to her visitors' compliments and quips.

When it grew dark enough so that Sissie began lighting the lamps inside, Stuart stood up and tossed his cheroot over the side of the porch.

"Well, Gray and I have work to do. Jessie, you won't be out here long, will you?"

"We're just leaving, Mr. Edwards. Thank you for supper."

Mitch and Billy stood hastily at Stuart's none-too-subtle hint, but it was Billy who spoke. Mitch echoed his thanks for the meal. Stuart nodded at them both and invited them to come back anytime. Then, with Gray at his heels, he headed inside for, presumably, the library, where he did most of the plantation's paperwork.

"Thomas, you go get Mr. Todd's and Mr. Cummings' horses," Jessie called down to the shadow she saw sidling around the corner of the house. Thomas was on his way to Rosa's kitchen, she knew. After supper was his favorite time for begging tidbits.

"Yes'm, Miss Jessie," Thomas yelled back, although Jessie thought she detected a shade of reluctance in his reply. She grinned. Rosa had served fresh ham and yams for supper, followed by molasses pie. Molasses pie was Thomas's favorite food in the world, and it was clear that he feared missing out. But Rosa would undoubtedly save him a slice, so Jessie didn't feel particularly guilty about depriving him of his treat.

"*Will* you be going to the Culpeppers'?" Mitch asked in a low voice as Billy turned to retrieve his hat from the seat of a rocker.

"You'll just have to wait and see," Jessie responded with a glimmering smile. Really, she did like Mitch. He was the handsomest boy for miles around (although he paled in comparison with Stuart's hard male splendor, a thought that Jessie resolutely dismissed almost as soon as it occurred). And he was kind, and good-natured, and . . .

"Do you think it'd be all right if I stayed for a little

longer? There's something I really want to say to
you," Mitch whispered hastily just as Billy came
back, hat in hand.

"What are you whispering to Miss Jessie about?
If I didn't know you so well, I'd swear you were
trying to steal a march on me." Billy regarded his
friend with a scowl, then thrust Mitch's hat at him
while retaining his own. "Here, I got your hat for
you."

Mitch accepted the hat, but made no move to place
it on his head as Billy had his.

"It's none of your business what I say to Miss
Jessie. And you can just go on home without me.
We go back in different directions, anyhow."

"I'm not leaving you here alone with her!"

"Are you trying to be insulting? If you are, then
you better be prepared to back your mouth up with
your fists!"

To Jessie's alarm, the two young men were suddenly nose to nose, glaring at each other as though
they were mortal enemies instead of friends. Quickly
she put a hand on each one's arm.

"Mr. Todd! Mr. Cummings! Please!"

They looked down at her, suddenly shamefaced,
and turned away from each other.

"Sorry, Miss Jessie," Billy muttered sheepishly,
while sneaking in a scowl at Mitch.

"That's all right, Mr. Cummings. Just because Mr.
Todd was so nasty to you, I'll save you a dance at
the Culpeppers'."

"You *are* going!" Both young men were immediately all attention.

"I suppose."

"That's wonderful. Just wonderful! And you'll
save me a dance." Billy grinned at her, then looked
triumphantly at Mitch. "You notice she didn't say
she'd save you a dance."

"Get out of here, braggart, before I remember
we're supposed to be friends." Mitch gave Billy a

cuff on the arm, but this time it was clear that he was only funning.

Billy grinned, picked up Jessie's hand, and before she knew quite what he meant to do, carried it to his mouth.

"I suppose I'll let this bouncer drive me away, but at least I'll leave you thinking about me."

With that Billy pressed a quick kiss onto the back of her hand, then released it with a flourish to run down the stairs to where Thomas waited with his horse. Mitch scowled after him. Jessie laughed. She quite liked Billy Cummings, too. Maybe, just maybe, if she gave herself a chance, she could find someone who had the same effect on her that Stuart had. Someone available. Someone like Billy, or Mitch.

"Now what did you want to say to me?" she asked Mitch pertly after they watched Billy ride away.

Mitch looked around uneasily. "Uh—could you walk with me a little way? We won't go far, but I, uh, I would rather not be interrupted."

"This sounds interesting." Jessie placed her hand on the arm Mitch offered her, and allowed him to escort her down the stairs. It was almost dark now, and the moon was already riding high in the sky, although it couldn't have been much past seven o'clock. The wind had picked up with the setting of the sun. Jessie found herself wishing for a shawl.

Thomas still waited at the top of the drive with Mitch's horse. He looked at the pair of them expectantly as they approached.

"Mr. Todd won't be leaving quite yet, Thomas. You can take his horse back to the stable."

"Yes'm, Miss Jessie." The boy's response was proper, but there was a hint of disapproval in the eyes that watched Jessie stroll along the drive on Mitch's arm. Aware of that disapproval, Jessie tilted her chin a trifle higher in silent disregard of it. After all, how was she ever to find a man who attracted her as much as Stuart if she was never alone with one?

"So what did you want to say to me?" Jessie asked after Thomas, horse in tow, finally disappeared in the direction of the stable.

"Well . . ." To her surprise, Mitch seemed almost ill at ease. He looked around swiftly, then caught Jessie's hand and pulled her toward the orchard. Surprised, she nevertheless went with him. When the house was all but hidden from them by the thickness of the trees, he stopped.

"Good gracious, it must be something quite momentous!" Her voice was light, although she had to admit to feeling a bit nervous. Here, where the trees blocked out most of the remaining light, it was so dark that she could barely distinguish Mitch's feature. "I really mustn't stay out here long. Most everyone we know would say it's not proper."

"It will be proper, if you say yes," Mitch said on a deep breath. Turning so that he faced her squarely, he caught both of her hands and stood looking down at her for a moment while she began to get some inkling of what he must be going to say. "Miss Jessie, will you marry me?"

She was so taken aback that she nearly laughed aloud. She managed to clamp down on the impulse, but she stood looking up at Mitch with the liveliest astonishment. Half a year ago she doubted that he'd had more than a vague notion of who she was, though he'd known her all her life. At Stuart's and Celia's engagement party, he'd been mortified at having to dance with her. And now, on the strength of her altered looks and a few dances, he was proposing marriage? The notion struck Jessie as exquisitely funny.

Or maybe it was nerves that was prompting her insane desire to giggle.

"Are you serious?"

She was so flustered that some of her newly acquired poise deserted her. As soon as she said it, she knew that that couldn't be the proper response to a gentleman's proposal of marriage. But no one had ever proposed to her before, and she was not quite up on the etiquette of it.

"Miss Jessie. Jessie." Mitch took a deep breath and looked intently down at her. He was some few inches taller than she, with even, regular features whose youthfulness was only emphasized by the scraggly mustache that decorated his upper lip. His shoulders were manly, his build solid, his hands as they gripped hers strong. Jessie gazed up into his face and wondered if she might, indeed, consider marrying him. Only a few months ago her wildest dream had been to be noticed by him. Now that he was—good heavens!—actually asking her to marry him, she should be over the moon with happiness.

At the very least, she should consider the possibility.

While she had been ruminating, he had been nattering on about how her beauty near unmanned him. She came back to herself when he got to the part about her eyes reminding him of the finest chocolates, and barely managed to subvert a renewed urge to laugh. Somehow having chocolates as eyes sounded distinctly unromantic.

"You are not attending! Are you?" He broke off his rapturous description of her charms with the accusation, looking affronted. Jessie pressed her wayward lips tightly together to keep the telltale smile from them, and nodded.

"Of course I am attending. It's just that—that I've never had anyone ask me to marry him before."

"Well, I should hope not," he said, mollified. "You're very young, Jessie, yet you're ready to be a wife, I think. And I—I would cherish you."

This last he said very low, and the muttered sincerity of it touched Jessie's heart at last.

"Mr. Todd . . ." she began.

"Mitch," he corrected, his eyes fastened on hers as though mesmerized by them. Jessie was begin-

ning to find his obvious admiration very pleasant,
and in fact wondered if perhaps . . . perhaps . . .

"Mitch," she repeated, her eyelids fluttering
down and then up again as a natural instinct for
coquetry asserted itself. "I—I don't know what to
say."

"Say yes, Jessie," he breathed, and his hands
lifted hers to his lips, where he pressed a kiss on
each of her knuckles in turn.

"Oh, Mitch . . ." The touch of his lips on her
hands was warm, and not at all unpleasant. It occurred to her to wonder what would happen if he
kissed her, properly, on the lips. Perhaps his kiss
was all that was needed to break the spell of Stuart's.
Perhaps, once Mitch kissed her, all the melting heat
that Stuart awoke in her would spring to life for
Mitch, and she could wed him and live happily ever
after.

"Kiss me, Mitch," she whispered daringly. Her
eyes closed and her lips pursed and lifted even as
she issued the invitation. She felt Mitch's hands
tighten on hers, felt him hesitate, and finally his
mouth was on hers, softly kissing her lips.

Then a grim voice from the direction of the drive
abruptly ended Jessie's experiment.

"That's quite enough, Mr. Todd," Stuart said.

XXVI

"Mr. Edwards!"

Mitch jumped away from her as if he'd been shot, spinning to face Stuart with such a guilty look on his face that Jessie felt like kicking him. She, on the other hand, felt not the least bit of guilt, and she hoped the haughty tilt of her chin showed it.

"I think it's time you left." Stuart was still talking to Mitch. Except for a single condemning glance when Mitch first let her go, Stuart had not so much as looked at Jessie. He stood less than six feet away, his fists planted on his hips, his booted feet spaced slightly apart. Against the background of the low, spreading fruit trees he looked tall, solid, and formidable.

"Sir, I—I know this looks bad, but I can explain. I—I was asking Jessie to marry me."

Stuart's eyes narrowed. "Were you, now?"

Jessie decided that the time had come to put in her two cents. "Yes, he was."

Still he spared her no more than a glance. His attention was all for Mitch, who was so nervous he was perspiring despite the evening's chill.

"And what did Jessie reply?"

"She—she didn't. Yet. You—she—she hasn't said."

In the face of Stuart's icy disapproval, Mitch's

pretensions to manhood collapsed with amazing
speed. He looked like a schoolboy caught by the
headmaster with his hand in the jam pot.

"Really? Jessie?"

Stuart did look at her, finally. Those narrowed
eyes were unreadable in the shadowy gloom of the
orchard. It was too dark even to see the expression
on his face. Not that it would have been much use
if she could have seen it, Jessie mused. When it
pleased him to do so, he could keep his face as expressionless as stone.

"I have no intention of giving Mitch an answer in
front of you," she said coldly. Mitch, clearly uncomfortable, glanced from her to Stuart and back. Paying him no heed for the moment, Stuart looked her
up and down, thoroughly. Jessie knew full well that
his gaze was meant to disconcert her. If he had succeeded, she refused to admit it even to herself.

"Are you saying that you need time to think over
Mr. Todd's very flattering proposal?"

If there was a satirical edge to Stuart's words, Jessie chose to ignore it.

"Yes," she said defiantly, "that's just what I'm
saying."

"Ah," he said, nodding as if he understood perfectly. Jessie flashed him a look that should have
killed him. If he even noticed it, it was impossible
to tell. Not even his eyelashes flickered. He met her
eyes with that icy, impenetrable look she'd come to
know and hate, and said nothing.

"You'll think about it?" Mitch asked, swinging
around to face her and thus diverting her attention
from the object of her desire. Her lips pursed. He
sounded so eager! Compared to Stuart's powerful
masculinity, he looked young in the way boys are
young, tall but ungainly, a trifle awkward, with his
limbs not yet fully under control.

"I'll think about it," Jessie agreed, more warmly
than she would have had Stuart not been listening.
She already knew that eventually she was going to

have to tell Mitch no. His kiss had awakened nothing in her but a desire to wipe her mouth on her
hand when it was over. Maybe once that wouldn't
have mattered to her, but no longer. Now, thanks
to the hard-eyed man who was standing there regarding her as if she'd just crawled out from under
a rock, she knew how a kiss should feel. Craving
that feeling as she did, she'd be a fool to marry
where it was lacking.

And it was definitely lacking with Mitch.

"Unless and until Jessie decides to accept your
offer, I suggest you refrain from taking further lib-
erties with her person," Stuart said, then paused
and fixed Mitch with steely eyes. "In other words,
if I see your hands on her again outside the bound-
aries of an official engagement, I'll break them, and
you too."

Stuart's tone was still perfectly amiable, but the
threat was not an idle one, it was clear. Mitch bit his
lip, then nodded.

"I don't blame you, Mr. Edwards. I'd feel the
same way if Jessie was under my protection. It won't
happen again, I promise. It's just that—Jessie's so
lovely, I kind of lost my head."

"You have my sympathy, Mr. Todd, if not my
approbation." Stuart's dry response put a merciful
period to Mitch's groveling. "Under the circumstances, I'm sure you won't be offended if I suggest
that it's time you headed for home. I've already ordered that your horse be brought around—for what
I understand is the second time this evening—so
there's no need for you to delay. Jessie can give you
your answer another day—in the presence of a
proper chaperone."

"Yes, sir." Mitch looked at Jessie. "Shall I come
tomorrow?"

He meant for his answer, of course. Oh, Lord, if
Stuart weren't standing there she would give it to
him now. Handsome and kind and good-natured
though Mitchell Todd was, Jessie knew she couldn't

wed him. What she had felt for him had been no
more than an adolescent crush. With Stuart's coming it had withered and finally died.

"Let me think it over for a few days, please, Mitch.
It—it's a very serious decision," Jessie said softly.
The last thing she wanted was to have to face Mitch's
entreaties again the following day. Somehow, she
wasn't sure exactly how, but somehow, this whole
unpleasant situation could be laid at Stuart's door.
If he had never come on the scene, Mitch would
never have proposed to her. While she didn't precisely regret the transformation in her life that had
resulted in his proposal, she did regret that she no
longer felt inclined to accept it. In the lonely days
before Stuart's coming, if Mitch had asked to marry
her she probably would have fainted, then jumped
into his arms in her haste to agree. But Stuart had
forced his way into her life and changed everything.
Even her heart.

As that thought occurred to her, Jessie scowled
direly at him. If he noticed her displeasure, he gave
no sign of it. He stood there, broad of shoulder, lean
of hip, and immovable as a mountain, waiting for
Mitch to go.

"Well. All right, if that's what you want." Mitch
was braver than Jessie had credited him with being,
after all. In spite of Stuart's frown, he turned and
took both her hands in his. "Make your answer yes,
Jessie. Please."

The words were very soft, designed for her ears
alone. But from the sudden sardonic twist to Stuart's
lips Jessie did not doubt that he heard them, too.
Without waiting for her reply, Mitch released her
hands and took himself off through the orchard.
Minutes later they could hear his horse's hooves
clattering down the drive.

Stuart's eyes were still fastened on Jessie. She returned his impenetrable stare with as much hauteur
as she could muster. Now that they were truly alone,
his stance relaxed slightly. He leaned one shoulder

against the gnarled trunk of an ancient pear tree, and crossed his arms over his chest.

"If you'll excuse me, I think I'll go inside," Jessie said coldly. Why she had not gone earlier, with Mitch, she could not have said. It was almost as if Stuart's eyes had held her transfixed for that brief period, like a snake's might a rabbit. But for whatever reason she had stayed, his movement had broken the spell.

"Oh, no, you don't. Not—quite—yet." Stuart reached out to trap her wrist as she would have swept by him. Thwarted, Jessie turned on him.

"Let go of me! How dare you come out here spying on me!"

His eyebrows lifted and he straightened away from the tree. His hand was clamped shackle-like around her wrist, and he was so close that he loomed over her intimidatingly. Jessie, however, refused to be intimidated. She was suddenly, fiercely, angry at him. Why, she refused to let herself speculate.

"Spying, is it?" he asked softly. Jessie realized with a start that he was every bit as angry as she. Those blue eyes snapped and blazed. "You little strumpet, if you value your hide you won't take that tone with me!"

"Strumpet!"

"What else would you call a young woman who leads her beau off under the trees, then begs him to kiss her?"

"You *were* spying! How despicable!"

"Kiss me, Mitch," he mimicked ruthlessly in a mincing falsetto. "Oh, please, kiss me!"

"I did not," Jessie said through gritted teeth, "say, 'Oh, please'!"

"But you did beg him to kiss you. Don't deny it, because I heard you, my girl!"

"I didn't beg him, I asked him! Just because—because—" Jessie broke off to stand glaring speechlessly at him as it occurred to her that she couldn't possibly explain.

"Because why? There's no reason you can give me that might serve to excuse such loose behavior. Good God, being a light-skirt must run in the family!''

"A light-skirt!"

"Like your stepmother," Stuart said with relish.

"You mean *your* wife?" Jessie was so angry that she hurled the below-the-belt riposte with pleasure.

"Yes. Just like my wife. My thrice-damned wife, who'll lie down for anything in breeches. Have you lived with her for so long that her round-heeled ways have rubbed off on you?"

"If you say another nasty word to me, I'll slap your face, so help me I will!"

Stuart smiled then, a nasty, mocking smile that was as insulting as anything he'd said. "If you slap my face, you'll get exactly what you got the last time. But maybe that's what you're hoping for."

Jessie stared up at him, up into the harsh, handsome face, and abruptly felt much of her anger leave her. As valiantly as she had fought against admitting it, even to herself, she very much feared that he had hit the nail squarely on the head. Oh, not that she wanted a repeat of that bruising, angry kiss he had punished her with at their last encounter. But the kind of kiss she suspected he was capable of bestowing—the thought made her knees weaken. She looked at his mouth and imagined it on her own—and finally faced the truth. The reason that she wasn't interested in Mitch Todd any longer was simple. In fact, it stood squarely in front of her at that very moment, its hand clamped around her wrist, its chest only inches from her own as it scowled down at her. The reason was Stuart. Jessie realized with a sinking sensation in the pit of her stomach that she had fallen in love with him.

She also suspected that he cared in some fashion for her. Certainly he was furious with her for kissing Mitch, too furious considering the minor nature of her offense. After all, being chastely kissed by an

eligible gentleman whom she had known all her life
and who had just offered her marriage was not exactly the first step on a greased slide to whoredom.
Even the most protective father in the world would
not have taken such violent exception to what had
occurred. And Stuart was not her father.

For all his protestations that he had done so out
of gratitude, Stuart himself had kissed her much as
Mitch had done. Then, later, he'd kissed her far
more shamefully as well.

He didn't strike her as the kind of man who normally went around kissing his wife's relations. Especially not the way he had kissed her.

His wife. Her stepmother. For all Celia's bitchery,
Stuart was a married man. She should walk away
from him, now, and at the next opportunity accept
Mitch's proposal. To stay at Mimosa now that she
had faced the truth about her feelings for Stuart
would be nothing less than a disaster. There was no
future in it, and the best she could hope for would
be to wind up with a broken heart.

But never to have him kiss her as her body cried
out to be kissed—she didn't think she could go away
without that.

Swallowing in an effort to ease her suddenly dry
throat, Jessie lifted her gaze from his mouth to his
eyes. He was watching her intently, his eyes glittering. His face was dark with temper, his brows pulled
together over those heart-stopping eyes. His mouth
curled angrily at her. Even in the face of his wrath,
just looking at him made her pulse quicken. He was
without a doubt the handsomest man she had ever
seen in her life.

"Maybe," Jessie said at last. "Maybe it is."

"What?" He blinked, as if he couldn't for the moment imagine what she was talking about. It took
him a second or two to recall his taunt that she had
left unanswered. The instant he remembered she
could see it in his face. Those incredible blue eyes

flickered, and then he scowled down at her even more fiercely than before.

"You heard what I said."

"You want me to kiss you?" Disbelief made it a question.

"Yes, Stuart," she said, taking a step closer, so that her breasts lacked just a foot or so of brushing his chest, and lifting her face. "Please."

His expression was indescribable. "God in heaven, have you lost your senses? Are you sickening for something, like brain fever? You can't just go around asking men to kiss you! I ought to beat you!"

He sounded so horrified that Jessie had to smile. She took another step toward him, and to her amusement he took a half step back.

"I don't want *men* to kiss me. I want *you* to kiss me." She'd knocked him completely off balance, she could tell, and the knowledge gave her a delicious courage. She had a feeling that he didn't get thrown off balance very often, or very easily.

"A quarter of an hour ago you wanted that Todd boy to kiss you."

"That," Jessie said, "was just an experiment."

"An experiment?"

Jessie nodded. "I wanted to see if he kissed like you."

"Good God!"

"He didn't."

"Jessie . . ."

"Not at all." She took another step toward him. With the pear tree behind him, he was left with nowhere to go. Catching her free wrist, he slid both hands up to her elbows and held her away from him.

"Now listen here, Jessie . . ."

Cocking her head to one side, she continued thoughtfully: "But then, you were the first gentleman to ever kiss me. Maybe I've built it up all out of proportion in my mind. Maybe, if you kiss me again, I won't feel any more than I did with Mitch. Then I can marry him after all.'' Her tone was wistful. The faintest suggestion of a frown puckered her brow. If she'd suddenly grown a second nose, he couldn't have regarded her with any greater consternation.

"If you truly don't want to, of course, I'll understand.'' All at once she sounded very humble.

"It's not that I don't want to.'' Shaking his head, he looked down at her. "Christ, this is the devil of a conversation! Jessie, I kissed you the first time because—because—hell, I don't know, because you looked so sweet. The second time was a mistake. It shouldn't have happened. To do it again would be a worse mistake. Take my word for it.''

"So I should just go on with my life and pretend I don't feel . . . what I feel when you kiss me?''

"Yes,'' he said through gritted teeth. "You should.''

"I can't.'' Her words were very soft. Her eyes fastened on his. Stuart looked down into her face, opened his mouth as if he would say something, hesitated, and was lost. His hands on her elbows no longer held her away, but slid around to encircle her upper arms and pull her gently against his chest.

XXVII

"I know better than this," Stuart muttered.

Jessie was already rising on tiptoe, her breasts swelling and throbbing as they pressed against his chest, her face lifting for his kiss. His eyes flamed a brilliant shade of blue as they moved from her eyes to her mouth, and his fingers wrapped around her arms tightened almost painfully. Jessie didn't care. All she cared about was the beautiful male mouth she was stretching to reach.

"Christ," he said then, the near whisper more curse than prayer. But Jessie was not, at the moment, concerned about what might have prompted such a sentiment. His head was descending, his mouth just touching hers with the same exquisite gentleness he had shown the first time he had kissed her. Softly, tenderly, his lips brushed hers. The hot, wet melting she had experienced before flooded her, and she gasped against his mouth.

Stuart lifted his head.

"Christ," he said again, looking down into her face with an expression that was almost, she decided dazedly, bewilderment. She thought he was going to pull away from her and her hands closed pleadingly on the sleeves of his coat.

But he did not pull away.

Instead, he lowered his head again.

If Jessie had died in that moment, she would have died happy. The touch of his mouth on hers jolted through her like a lightning bolt. Her insides quivered along with her knees. Her lips trembled against his mouth.

Still he was just barely kissing her, his mouth brushing back and forth, back and forth over her shaking lips. The world whirled around her. Jessie held onto the smooth wool of his coat, eyes closed, straining on tiptoe to deepen the contact, her heart beating so fast she thought she might die.

"Ah, Jessie." He whispered it against her mouth. His breath was warm on her lips. For a moment, just a moment, she again feared he might pull away. His hands slid along her bare skin from her elbows to her wrists, raising goose bumps in their wake, then closed over hers where she clung to his coat. Gently he pried them free, then lifted them until they were linked around his neck. Her eyes opened then, to find him looking down at her with an expression that was only slightly less dazed than she felt.

As if he had no more control over his actions than she did over hers.

Without a word he bent his head to hers again, and this time his kiss was marginally less gentle than before. Jessie's eyes fluttered shut, and her arms around his neck held him tight. His hands slid down over her back, stroking the nape of her neck beneath the thick fall of her hair, tracing her spine through the thin material of her dress.

When his tongue came out to gently trace the outline of her lips, she shuddered.

"Sweet, sweet Jessie." He murmured the words as he kissed the corner of her mouth. Her fingers dug into the silky curls at the nape of his neck, and she quivered in his hold. Pressed full against him, she felt the hard, muscular strength of him with every fiber of her being. Her breasts throbbed against the solid warmth of his chest; her thighs quivered against the powerful length of his.

"I love you, Stuart." It was a mere breath, escaping of its own volition. Hearing her own voice whisper the secret she'd only just discovered herself, Jessie's eyes fluttered open in alarm

His mouth lifted just a fraction above her own. His eyes as they met hers were heavy-lidded and intense. A muscle quivered at the side of his mouth. Then his arms slid around her waist, pulling her tight against him, and his head descended again.

This time he was not gentle at all. His mouth slanted over hers, parted her lips. His tongue slid inside. As he had done once before, he invaded her mouth, his tongue exploring the contours of palate and cheeks, running over her teeth and stroking her tongue. He tasted of brandy and cigars. His tongue was burning hot, and very strong.

But this incursion was nothing like the punishment he had inflicted upon her before. This kiss rocked her world on its axis.

Jessie's arms tightened around his neck, and her head fell back to rest against his shoulder. When his tongue touched hers again, instinctively she responded, stroking his tongue with her own.

The harsh indrawing of his breath presaged the lifting of his head.

"Stuart . . ." She was sore afraid he meant to leave her.

"Shhh, darling." He pressed kisses along her cheek to her ear, where he explored the delicate whorls with his tongue. Then his mouth slid down the cord of her neck until it was stopped by the lace frill of her collar.

"You smell just like vanilla."

Whispering to her, he pressed her closer to his body. With mingled excitement and shock, Jessie realized that his hands now cupped her bottom. They were large hands, and strong. Jessie could feel the heat and strength of them through her dress as they curled around that part of her that she'd thought was only good for sitting, pulling her full against him.

There was something large and hard lying across his abdomen. As he pressed her against it, Jessie realized that it had its origin between his thighs.

It was only when he rocked her against it so that her woman-place rubbed squarely against the bulge that she realized what it was.

The knowledge burst inside her like a rocket. Her insides quaked, and that hot, sweet melting feeling intensified until Jessie had to cling to his neck because she could not stand.

He had been kissing her neck, but as she shivered and sagged in his arms, his mouth moved even lower, to find and rest against the tip of her breast. His breath burned through the layers of her dress and chemise to her skin. He bit at her nipple, and Jessie cried out.

Then he was lowering her to the ground, and coming down on top of her.

As his weight crushed her, Jessie whimpered, but not with pain. She wanted what he was doing to her, burned for it, ached for it. Her hands clung to his shoulders, then locked convulsively around his neck. His mouth descended, stopping her soft cry, kissing her fiercely while he cupped and squeezed her breasts, and pressed himself urgently against the juncture of her thighs.

He pinched her nipples, and Jessie felt a shaft of fire shoot clear down to her toes. When one hand left her breast to jerk her skirt upward, she trembled in anticipation.

Then, with no warning at all, he stopped what he was doing and lay still. One hand was clenched in her skirt, which was raised above her knees. The other cupped her breast.

"Stuart?" Her tremulous voice seemed to provide the impetus he lacked. Moving stiffly, he propelled himself to his feet despite her clinging hands. "What's wrong?"

"I'm a swine, but not that big a swine," he said through his teeth, then turned on his heel.

Scrambling into a sitting position, Jessie could do nothing but watch as he strode away.

XXVIII

By the time Clive pulled the saddle from Saber's back and turned the big horse loose in his stall, it was nearer to dawn than midnight. He could have awakened Progress, who slept in the loft so as to be near his beloved horses, to do the job, but he wasn't the man to deprive a dependent of his night's sleep when the task was one he could as easily do himself. Besides, being in the huge, echoing barn with only the animals for company was oddly peaceful. And some kind of peace was what he had ridden hell-for-leather in search of.

Clive carried the saddle to the tack room and hung it neatly on a peg, then rubbed a hand over his face. God, he was tired! Tired enough, maybe, to sleep.

Though he doubted it. Physically he might be weary, but his mind continually ran in circles, trying to find some solution to the conundrum he was facing. So far, he hadn't had a tinker's damn of luck.

Hadn't someone once said that a man had better be careful what he wished for, because he just might get it? Clive now knew just what he meant.

Saber stuck his head over the top of the stall and nudged Clive as he dropped a handful of the molasses-impregnated grain that was the animal's favorite into his trough.

"Good night, fella," Clive told him, rubbing his

velvety nose and scratching the itchy spot behind
his left ear. Saber's head bobbed up and down appreciatively at this treatment. Clive had to smile, although the smile was wry.

It was stupid, he knew, but he loved the horse.
Saber was a fine animal, with the proud head of an
Arabian and the speed of a Thoroughbred. A mount
like Saber had been part and parcel of what he had
used to wish for so intensely. And, like the rest of
his wish, it had been granted, in spades.

After years of living by his wits, he'd finally gotten everything he'd ever dreamed of. More than he
had ever dreamed of, in fact. He was a wealthy man
now, owner of a magnificent plantation of the sort
he had used to look at enviously in passing from the
deck of whatever riverboat he'd happened to be
working. His wish had been to buy some land, have
a place he could call his own, stay put, and put down
some roots. But he'd known, even as he'd been
wishing, that he'd never have a place like the vast
plantations he saw from the river. Money enough to
buy a place like that was not likely to be won on a
hand or two of cards.

But by a labyrinthian twist of fate he'd ended up
as master of a plantation that covered more territory
and housed more souls than some towns. He had
acquired more possessions than any man had a right
to own. Even Saber, whom he had purchased from
a horse breeder near Jackson, was the embodiment
of his dream. The animal had cost more than he
would ever have considered spending on a horse in
his old life. But as master of Mimosa, there was little
he couldn't afford.

More than that, he was respected, looked up to
even, when deference was something he had never
thought to imagine for himself. Clive McClintock,
river rat, professional gambler, who even his friends
acknowledged was no more honest than he had to
be, was now one of the gentry, a gentleman planter.
When he'd been wishing, that wish had been so

far out of line with what he'd considered possible
that it had never even occurred to him.

But it had come true nevertheless.

Carelessly he had wished for land, enough money
to work it, an end to the life of constantly hustling
for a living.

His wish had been granted and somewhere the
gods must be laughing.

In reaching for wealth, property, and respectability, he'd grabbed a tiger by the tail.

He had a wife whom he hated, whom it was a
struggle to keep from strangling, although he had
never in his life harmed a woman; who was a bitch
and a whore and who hated him at least as much as
he hated her.

He had a name that he was beginning to hate, too.
When he'd assumed it all those months ago, he had
not realized how much it was going to irk him to
have to spend the rest of his life being known as
Stuart Edwards.

Clive McClintock might not be the name of a gentleman, but it was his name.

There were people he'd grown fond of, such as
Miss Flora and Miss Laurel. They thought he was
their nephew. He'd told himself, when he'd begun
the deception, that'd he'd make a far better nephew
for them than the great Stuart Edwards had ever
done. And he had. He visited them, didn't he? And
he was courteous, protective of their well-being,
available for them whenever they cared to send for
him. His arrival had given them a new lease on life.
He had no doubt that both of them would live to be
a hundred.

But the fonder he grew of them, the more he felt
like a fraud.

When he'd first formulated the plan, he'd meant
to help Celia's chubby little stepdaughter come out
of her shell and find a husband, thus serving the
dual purpose of improving the girl's life and getting
her out of his hair at the same time.

Who could have guessed that under all that hair and excess weight had lurked a beauty whose merest smile would have the power to steal his breath?

Who could have guessed that her belligerence hid a soul of rare sweetness?

Who could have guessed that in trying to improve the chit's lot in life he would lose his head and his heart and wind up wanting her more than he had ever wanted anything?

And there, of course, was the jest that had set the gods to laughing. They had granted him everything he had ever wished for, more than he had ever wished for.

But he had never thought to wish for a woman to love. Love, he would have said, was something that could be pumped out of a man's system after twenty minutes or so between the sheets with his adored.

But he would have been wrong. He knew that now. Love had nothing (well, very little) to do with taking a woman to bed. It was about laughing together, and talking together, and experiencing all the myriad other details of daily living together.

It was about caring more for the loved one's well-being than for one's own.

Which was how he felt about Jessie. He loved the girl, and that was the simple, overwhelming truth. Loved her enough not to finish what he had started in the orchard. Loved her enough not to take her maidenhead and in doing so ruin her life.

The gods had offered him vast wealth, land, respect. To take it, and keep it, all he had to do was marry and stay married to Celia.

And if he was married to Celia, he could not follow his heart and wed Jessie. If he could not wed her, he could not take her maidenhead, or her love.

As he had told her, he was a swine, but not that big a swine. Although he would have been, had he not loved her.

So somewhere the gods were laughing. They had

given him everything he had ever dreamed of, and more.

Only he, fool that he was, didn't want their munificent gift any longer.

All he wanted was Jessie, and she was the one thing he couldn't have.

XXIX

Mitch came for his answer the following Tuesday. The previous day he'd sent a message over inquiring if it would be convenient for him to call then, so Jessie was expecting him when he arrived. She sat nervously in the front parlor, which Celia had recently refurbished in the newly popular Empire style. A muralist had traveled all the way from Natchez to paint intricate harbor scenes on all four walls. The pale blue of the sky and water was the predominant color in the paintings, while the furniture itself was of ebony wood upholstered in white. When Jessie had dressed, she had forgotten to keep in mind the color of the room where she would receive Mitch. Consequently she was clad in jade-green broadcloth, long-sleeved in deference to the weather, which had finally grown cool. The fitted bodice rose demurely to her neck, where she had pinned a small cameo that had once been her mother's. Three flounces ran diagonally across her shoulders to her waist in front, and three more trimmed the full skirt at the hem. With her hair upswept in back and her face framed by the short curls that Sissie had recently trimmed for her, Jessie looked lovely. She was more than satisfied with her appearance—until she took a seat in the front parlor. Then she wondered if her dress clashed with the room, and that uncertainty made her even more nervous.

"Lamb, I thought this day would never come," Tudi said under her breath as Mitch was shown into the parlor. Mindful of Stuart's edict about propriety, and fearing that being alone with him would make it more likely that Mitch would argue when presented with her refusal, Jessie had asked Tudi to stay in the room with her. Stolid and unmoving, Tudi stood behind the chair where Jessie sat. In honor of the occasion, her apron and turban were fresh and snowy. Jessie had asked Tudi to stay with her while she answered Mitch; she hadn't told Tudi that the answer was going to be no.

"Hello, Jessie. Afternoon, Tudi."

Mitch looked as nervous as Jessie felt. Too much on edge to stay seated any longer, Jessie stood up to greet him. He took her hand in his and raised it to his mouth. "You're looking beautiful today."

"Thank you."

Still unused to thinking of herself as beautiful—it seemed impossible when Jessie considered it—she flushed a little at the compliment. Mitch still held her hand in his; the imprint of his lips was faintly moist on the back of her hand.

Looking up at him, Jessie was struck anew by how attractive he was. If she had never seen Stuart, she would have considered Mitch, with his tousle of nut-brown curls, twinkling hazel eyes, and sturdy build, the ideal of manhood. If she hadn't seen Stuart . . .

Holding her hand, Mitch shot a quick glance at Tudi, then drew Jessie away, toward the window. Tudi watched them with a faint, satisfied smile. Jessie knew that Tudi, who loved her and had nothing but thoughts of her happiness at heart, would be well pleased to see her wed to Mitch.

Mitch would make a kind, attentive husband to some lucky girl. Jessie truly regretted that it wouldn't be she.

"Well, Jessie, I've come for your answer," Mitch

said softly when it became apparent that Jessie had been struck dumb.

Ever since he had first asked her, Jessie had known this moment was coming. Not wanting to hurt him, she had her answer carefully prepared. Still, it was hard to say no to this boy who'd been the object of her girlhood daydreams for years.

"Mitch . . ." Jessie began, then paused helplessly as her tongue became glued to the roof of her mouth. Taking a deep breath, she slid her eyes from his face to glance almost blindly out the window.

But what she saw outside instantly sharpened her gaze.

Stuart was out there, just beyond the curve of the drive, astride Saber. Holding onto his stirrup and looking up at him with her back to the window was Celia. It was obvious from the expression on Stuart's face and the tense stance of Celia's body that they were engaging in yet another acrimonious quarrel.

A marital quarrel.

"Is it so hard to say, Jessie?" Mitch asked tenderly. Jessie dragged her eyes back to his face. A queer, unsettled feeling churned in her stomach, making her feel almost nauseous. Anger sprang to life inside her, corrosive, eating her insides.

"No, Mitch, it's not hard to say at all," Jessie replied, her voice surprising her with its composure. "I'll be honored to marry you."

"Hooray!" Mitch shouted, startling Jessie, and gave a little jump into the air. Then, before she had recovered from her surprise, he caught her around the waist and twirled her around, then planted a kiss on her lips.

Jessie's head was whirling, from either being spun or the kiss, but almost as soon as she had said it she couldn't believe the words had come out of her mouth. Surely she hadn't just promised to become Mitch's wife!

"Oh, lamb!" Tudi hurried to hug her. Jessie returned Tudi's embrace because she couldn't do anything else. She was in a daze. Good Lord, what did she do now? "You take good care of her, you hear, Mr. Todd?"

"Don't you worry, Tudi, I will!" Mitch was beaming, radiating happiness, while Jessie felt sick to her stomach. Before she could open her mouth to deny what she had just said—could she deny it, now that she'd agreed?—Mitch was catching up her hand and pulling her toward the door.

"There's Mr. and Mrs. Edwards now, outside," he said. "We'll tell your stepparents, honey, and make it official. Yippee, we're engaged!"

He sounded so joyous that Jessie could do nothing but let him drag her after him out to the veranda. Once there, he stopped by the rail and hallooed at Stuart and Celia, who were still arguing down the drive.

"Mrs. Edwards! Mr. Edwards! Look here!"

With that he swept Jessie up in an embrace that almost crushed the air from her lungs. As she clung to his shoulders, from necessity, he proceeded to kiss her with more thoroughness than he had shown the night in the orchard.

When he lifted his head, he was grinning so widely that his face looked as if it might split in two. He glanced around, and Jessie followed his gaze. Stuart and Celia were both staring at them, looking, as well as she could tell from such a distance, equally stunned.

"It's all right this time, Mr. Edwards! We're engaged!" Mitch bellowed. Turning to face them, he grinned widely and slid his arm around Jessie's waist.

XXX

How Jessie got through the rest of that day and
evening she never knew. Once the fateful words had
left her mouth, she felt as if everything that followed
was out of her control. For once in Jessie's life she
had managed to truly please Celia, who became immediately full of plans for a lavish engagement party
and, later, probably the following summer, an even
more lavish wedding. The prospect of hostessing
such august social events while at the same time rid-
ding herself of her annoyance of a stepdaughter was
the reason for Celia's good humor, Jessie knew, but
still it was a welcome change to have Celia smiling
rather than sulking. The servants, who heard the
news from Tudi even before Jessie got back inside
the house, were excited for her. Tudi was even talking about going with her "lamb" to her new home,
and possibly bringing Sissie, too, if Miss Celia could
be persuaded to permit it.

Stuart, on the other hand, was terse as he con-
gratulated Mitch and pressed a cool kiss on Jessie's
cheek. As was usually the case when he was laboring under the grip of some strong emotion, his face
became completely unreadable. His eyes as they met
Jessie's were as opaque as stone, but Jessie didn't
need to see evidence of it in his face to know what
he was feeling. He disliked the notion of her en-

gagement intensely, but was powerless to do anything to thwart it. After all, Mitch Todd was the scion of one of the wealthiest planting families in the area. As the only son of three children, he would undoubtedly one day inherit Riverview, which equaled Mimosa for prosperity. With the best will in the world, it was impossible for Stuart to pronounce the match anything but suitable.

Of course Mitch stayed for supper, and since they were engaged, Jessie was permitted to walk with him alone about the grounds afterwards. Several times Jessie opened her mouth to tell him that she hadn't meant it, that it had all been a mistake. But in the face of Mitch's transparent happiness, she couldn't do it. So she suffered silently, secretly appalled at what she had set in motion, as he talked of plans for the future, of how they would grow old together, of how many children they would have. Later, when he was getting ready to leave, he kissed her. Jessie dutifully permitted it, not even pulling away when his tongue slipped daringly into her mouth. But for all her slight hope that perhaps, just perhaps, she might be able to wed Mitch after all, his kiss evoked merely a mild feeling of distaste.

The fireworks, she was beginning to fear, came only with Stuart.

Could she wed a man whose kiss made her want to scrub her teeth afterwards? No, she could not. But how was she to tell Mitch—and everyone else? Like a snowball rolling downhill, her engagement was getting bigger and bigger, and more impossible to deny, with each minute that passed.

Even after Mitch had gone and Jessie went upstairs to bed, her mind was so troubled that she could not sleep. Finally she gave up the attempt altogether, pulled her wrapper on over her nightdress and went along the corridor. She would sit on the veranda until the night air induced sleepiness—if it ever did.

The house was dark except for the fairy lights that

were left burning at the top and bottom of the stairs
and at the end of each corridor. The servants had
long since retired to the quarters, and Stuart and
Celia were clearly abed. Jessie estimated the time at
just gone midnight. On other nights the sound of
quarreling from the rear of the house had persisted
long after this. But tonight the house was quiet. Jessie might as well have been the only one in the wide
world who was awake.

Tugging open the heavy oak door, Jessie stepped
onto the veranda. Immediately her attention was
caught by the midnight-blue velvet of the sky. It was
ablaze with stars that twinkled like diamonds, so
many that Jessie was briefly dazzled. Pulling the
door shut behind her, she stepped to the rail. Her
hands closed around the smooth carved wood, and
her chin tilted back. The moon was huge and as
round as a wheel of cheese, surrounded by millions
of blinking stars. A slight breeze blew from the east,
sending small dark clouds like wisps of veiling scud-
ding across the glittering sky. Foliage rustled, lo-
custs sang, and night birds and their prey shrieked
and called. The sheer breathtaking beauty of the
night bestowed its own serenity upon Jessie. For
the first time since she'd promised to wed Mitch,
she felt a degree of peace.

Then, mixed with the delicate scent of lilacs and
mimosa, Jessie caught a whiff of pungent cigar
smoke.

Her head snapped around. At the far end of the
veranda she could plainly see the tip of a cigar,
glowing red. It was only slightly more difficult to
make out the massive dark shape of the man, but as
her eyes adjusted from the brightness of the sky to
the gloom at the corner of the veranda, she could
see him well enough. He was tipped back in a rocking chair, his booted feet crossed at the ankles and
resting on the rail in the posture she had favored
before he had masterminded her metamorphosis
from harum-scarum girl into lady. Despite the chill,

he was in his shirtsleeves, the elegant brocade waist-coat he had worn at dinner hanging carelessly open and his neckcloth absent. As Jessie watched, he took another drag at the cigar so that its tip glowed, then let hand and cigar drop to dangle at his side.

"Hello, Stuart."

He smiled at her. She could clearly see the baring of his teeth.

"Too excited over your forthcoming nuptials to sleep?" A sneer underlay the question.

"Yes," Jessie said defiantly, all thought of the night's beauty having fled. One hand still rested on the rail. The other clenched beside her.

"So you decided you could stomach his kisses after all."

"Yes."

"Looking forward to them, are you?"

"Certainly."

Stuart chuckled, the sound low and fairly un-pleasant. "Liar."

"At least he's free to marry me!"

"That," said Stuart, "is undeniably true."

The cheroot glowed briefly again. Then, with his other hand, Stuart lifted something else—a bottle—to his lips, tilting his head back to meet it. Jessie watched in dismay as he took a long swallow from the bottle, then set it on the floor again and wiped the back of his hand across his mouth. Never before had she seen Stuart drink, or for that matter behave in such an ill-mannered way. But at least the spirits explained his unaccustomed disarray and the biting undertone to his words.

"You're drunk!"

"Just a trifle well to live. And why not, pray? A man don't get news of his stepdaughter's engage-ment every day."

"I'm going to bed."

"To dream of darling Mitch?" The sneer was pro-nounced. Stuart lifted the bottle to his lips again, tilted it, and drank.

"That's certainly better than dreaming of you!"

"Undoubtedly."

Stuart set the bottle on the floor and got to his feet, then flicked the remains of his cheroot over the rail. Jessie stood her ground as he came toward her, his movements carefully precise but not unsteady, which she would have expected if he'd been truly drunk. Although a tiny voice deep inside her urged her to flee, she did not. Back straight, head proudly erect, she stood her ground. Only she knew how tightly her hand was clenched on the rail.

He stopped directly in front of her. It was only at times like this, when he stood so close and she had to look up at him, that Jessie realized just how tall Stuart truly was. He was taller than she by several inches more than a head, and so broad of shoulder and wide of chest that his shadow on the ground completely dwarfed her much slighter one.

His hand came up to rest against the side of her neck. The warm strength of his fingers curled around her nape under her hair, which was freshly brushed and allowed to hang loose for sleep. Even at that slight touch, her foolish heart began to pound.

"Nevertheless," Stuart said softly, "I prefer that you dream of me."

And he lowered his head to her mouth.

He kissed her softly, tenderly, his lips promising her the world. Jessie's eyes closed, and her hand clenched even tighter over the rail as she fought the urge to succumb to that tender assault. Their bodies didn't so much as touch, and the only hold he had on her was his hand curved around her neck. But her blood turned to lava in her veins.

It was only when he parted her lips to deepen the kiss that she tasted the whiskey on his tongue and lips and remembered that he was, if not drunk, the next thing to it. Would he be kissing her so if he were sober? Or would he be wishing her well in her marriage to Mitch?

Her guess as to the answer gave her the strength to push him away.

"You're nothing but a dog in the manger," she said bitterly, and to emphasize her disillusion she drew her hand across her mouth as though to wipe away the taste of his kiss.

"What does that mean, pray?"

He was looking down at her, his face in shadow but his eyes glittering as brightly as the stars.

"You don't want me yourself, but you don't want anyone else to have me, either."

"Whatever gave you the notion that I don't want you?"

Even as her heart speeded up at that, his lips curled into a nasty, mocking smile. Then, shocking her into immobility, his hand lifted to cup and squeeze her left breast. The soft globe nestled into the palm of his right hand as if it belonged there. Jessie could feel the heat of his skin burning hers through the double layers of her wrapper and nightdress. For a moment she couldn't so much as breathe.

"I do want you. And it's clear"—his thumb ran suggestively over the nipple, which sprang to desperate attention at his touch—"that you also want me."

"How dare you!" Immobile no longer, Jessie made an inarticulate sound of rage and knocked his hand away. It was plain from the obnoxious smile with which he met her outraged eyes that he'd meant merely to demonstrate her helpless response to his touch. And of course he'd succeeded, in spades.

"I'd be willing to bet that your nipple doesn't do that for darling Mitch."

"You," Jessie said through gritted teeth, "can go to hell!"

It was one of the few times in her life that she'd ever sworn aloud, and it felt good. Triumphant, she turned away, to seek shelter in the safety of her bed-room. But Stuart, the devil, was laughing.

"Ah, how fickle is woman! Was it only the other night that you said you loved me?"

Jessie couldn't have been stopped faster by a punch to the stomach. She drew in a sharp breath, then felt a rushing tide of red surge up to cloud her vision. How dared he mock the most profound confession she'd ever made in her life! Her hands clenched into fists, her teeth ground together, and she turned on him with a sound of pure rage—to find him laughing still.

"You cad!" she hissed, and flew at him, feet flail-ing, fists swinging. He grabbed her upper arms and held her off—and continued to laugh.

"Now, now," he cautioned her, the glint in his eyes belying his smirking mouth. "You love me, re-member?"

If she'd had a gun, she would have shot him. Fortunately she was weaponless—except for a long-ago piece of advice that Tudi had given her on how to defend herself against a man.

'Let—me—go!" she spat, and when he did she gave a little smirk of her own, drew back her arm, and drove her doubled fist as hard as she could into his groin.

XXXI

Then she ran. She left him doubled over, cursing like a stevedore, and ran as if her life depended upon it, which it probably did. She had no doubt at all that if Stuart could get his hands on her at that moment, his first impulse would be to put them around her neck and squeeze the life from her.

The stable was her goal. She would saddle up Firefly and ride for her life, ride until she was exhausted, until her head was clear enough or her body tired enough to sleep, ride until Stuart had had time to recover from the black temper that her blow was certain to have put him in. It didn't matter that she wore only her nightdress and wrapper, or that her feet were bare. It didn't matter that it was gone midnight. Her impulse was to get away, far away, from Mimosa—and Stuart. She would ride until she felt like coming home again, however long that might be.

The grass was cool and damp against her feet, with an occasional rock to bruise the tenderness of her sole. Jessie stepped on a spiny holly leaf as she neared the stable door, and had to stop to pull it from her foot before she could proceed. She was bending down, her wounded foot on the opposite knee while she yanked the leaf free, when she became aware of Stuart running as lightly as an Indian in pursuit of her.

Hurt foot or no, Jessie sprinted for the stable like a wild thing. It was dark as a cave inside, the horses all quiet in their stalls, Progress asleep high above in the loft. Jasper sprang up from his bed of hay with a ''Woof!'' only to quiet down when he discovered the intruder was his mistress.

With Stuart so close behind, Jessie knew that her chances of escaping his vengeance were slim. But she hoped that, with the advantage of darkness and her superior knowledge of the stable, she might be able to get a saddle on Firefly and then ride the mare out right under Stuart's nose. Once she was mounted, he wouldn't be able to stop her. If she had to, she would run him down.

The tack room was at the far end of the barn. With Jasper galloping at her heels, clearly under the impression that this was a new game, Jessie pulled the door open and rushed inside. The door shut on its own behind them, barely missing Jasper's tail. Sacks of grain littered the floor, some full, some half full. Saddles were slung over sawhorses in the middle of the room. More saddles hung from pegs, as did bridles and brushes and the countless other pieces of paraphernalia necessary to properly care for horses. A tiny window opposite the door let in moonlight. The silvery beam helped Jessie to avoid tripping over any of the various obstacles in her way as she snatched Firefly's bridle from the peg where it hung.

The bridle dangled from one hand while she scanned the pegs for her saddle. Jessie found it, and was stretching up to unhook the stirrup from the peg that held it when the door to the tack room opened on its silent leather hinges. Jasper woofed, then bounded toward the newcomer. Jessie whirled, swallowing hard. Stuart was silhouetted in the aperture, a darker, more solid shape against an infinity of darkness.

''Get him, boy!'' Jessie hissed, only to be confounded as the traitorous hound jumped up on the man, tail wagging furiously.

Stuart didn't even stagger. He gave Jasper a quick pat on the head, said, "Down!" in the voice of a master, and was immediately obeyed. Then Stuart gave the dog a shove through the door, said, "Go to bed, sir!" and closed the door with Jasper on the other side of it.

To Jessie's dismay, the dog didn't even whimper for readmittance. Her loyal protector was clearly as much butter in Stuart's hands as were everyone and everything else at Mimosa.

"Now, then, Jessie," Stuart said. From the silky tone of his voice Jessie knew that he was every bit as angry as she'd feared he's be.

"If you lay so much as a finger on me, I'll scream the rafters down!"

Despite her threat, her words were a harsh whisper. She could not be the cause of a confrontation between Stuart and Progress, and she knew it. Indeed, even if she screamed the dead, and Progress, who in his later years slept like the dead, heard her, whether he would then be on her side was doubtful. He too had succumbed to Stuart's charm long since. Was there no one who was immune to the crafty devil?

"Scream all you like, because I intend to lay much more than a finger on you."

Although there was not enough light to permit her to see his face clearly, Jessie was sure from the sound of his words that his teeth were clenched. As he approached her, looming large in the darkness, her hand fell away from the saddle and she moved back, away from him. He continued to stalk her until her back was against the wall and there was nowhere else for her to go.

"Trapped, Jessie?" The words were very soft, but no less menacing for all that. Jessie knew Stuart wouldn't harm her, but still a frisson of fear shivered up her spine. He looked so very tall and menacing in the darkness. His eyes, the only part of him that was clearly visible, glittered through the gloom like the stars in the sky outside. Her back was pressed so hard against the rough plank wall that she could feel the texture of it clear through her garments to her skin. Her bare toes curled against the grittiness of scattered bits of grain and straw. Her eyes were wide and fixed on his face—and her fingers were wrapped around the cool leather straps of the bridle.

The bridle. She was not quite defenseless, after all.

"Get back!"

Jessie lashed out at him, only to have the bridle caught and jerked from her hold.

"Oh!"

Stuart tossed the bridle aside. It landed on the floor with a jangle of metal.

"Now what? Are you going to kick me? Slap me? Scratch me? Hit me where no young lady has any business hitting a man? Or is it finally my turn?" There was something curious in his tone, something that was not anger at all.

"Stuart . . ." Jessie's heart was pounding, whether from fear or something else she didn't know. Her eyes were huge as she looked at him through the darkness. Her hands were suddenly very cold. Moonlight glinted off his eyes as he reached for her, catching her wrist and pulling her toward him. All the fight had left Jessie. Unresisting, she let him draw her forward until a mere handbreadth of space separated them. His hand circling her wrist was the only part of him that touched her, but every millimeter of her skin was tingling.

"I don't want you marrying that Todd boy." His voice was rough.

"Stuart . . ." Oddly enough, the only word that seemed able to force its way out of her dry throat was his name. He was looming over her, using his sheer size to try to dominate her, to bend her to his

will. The hard, muscular strength of him took on a
life of its own in the darkness, and she thrilled to it.

"You said you loved me."

This time the reminder didn't drive her into a
frenzy. This time he wasn't mocking her. His voice
was low, his hand on her wrist warm and strong
and yet not hurting.

"You can't wed him if you love me."

"Stuart . . ." There was an ache in her voice. Her
heart was swelling inside her even as her bones were
melting. He was barely touching her, but already he
was making her his. She was on fire, burning up
with love and something more, and he was the only
thing on earth that could put out the flames.

"I won't permit you to marry him, do you hear?"
He gave her wrist a little shake.

"Stuart." Jessie took a deep breath, then was finally able to talk. She should explain, she knew,
about accepting Mitch, but explanations could wait.
Everything could wait, except the need that was
consuming her alive. "I do love you, Stuart."

"Oh, God!" It was a groan. He might have pulled
her to him, or she might have stepped into his arms,
she didn't know. But in a fraction of a breath Jessie
found herself plastered against him, her arms wind-
ing tight around his neck, his arms locking her to
him as he bent his head to find her mouth.

There was nothing at all gentle about this kiss. He
kissed her as if he were starving for the taste of her
mouth, as if he could never get enough. Jessie met
the sweet plunder of his tongue with a wild excitement of her own, straining on tiptoe against him,
her nails digging into the vulnerable nape of his
neck. He tasted of whiskey, and since it was Stuart
who tasted so, she suddenly loved the taste. His jaw
was prickly with bristles, but since it was Stuart who
scraped her soft skin, she loved the feel of it. His
hold on her was tight enough to crack her ribs and
deny her breath, but she loved that, too. She loved
everything that he was doing to her so much that

she was dizzy with it. So much that when she kissed him back she made soft little mewling sounds into his mouth without even being aware that she was doing so. So much that when she felt the rising bulge of him, she pressed herself against it, rubbing, instinctively seeking to ease the ache between her legs.

"Christ, Jessie!" It was a groan as his mouth slid from her lips to her neck, then lower, to find and claim the tip of her breast.

As the moist heat of his mouth burned through the cloth, Jessie cried out. Pure fire shot along her nerve endings, and her knees buckled. He caught her up in his arms. For just a moment his head lifted, and he looked around. Then, even as she whimpered a protest, he moved with her, stepping over the grain sacks and saddles to lower her to the floor. Even as he came down beside her, Jessie realized that he had found a haphazard pile of empty grain sacks to use as a bed.

"I've wanted you—how I've wanted you," he whispered hoarsely as he claimed her mouth again. Jessie locked her arms around his neck and was lost. She had no thought of right or wrong, no thought of danger to her person or her heart. All she knew was that this was her man: the man she had longed for and waited for all of her life.

When he yanked the skirts of her nightdress and wrapper up around her waist, she clung to his neck and kissed him with feverish abandon. When he reached down between them to do something to his breeches, she pressed tiny kisses along his cheekbone. When his knees, still encased in cloth, slipped between hers to push them apart, she quivered and arched and cried out against his throat.

His hand was between them again, touching her in that place where no one had ever touched her, the place that was so secret she did not like to touch it herself even when she bathed. But when his hand covered her there, resting atop the soft nest of curls, the aching inside her intensified until she was shud-

dering with it, her thighs trembling, her body afire
for something—something. . . .

Then he rose a little above her, holding his weight
from her with his elbow, while he probed at the
quivering, burning softness of her with that huge
hot man-thing she had felt but never seen. It seemed
as though there was an opening in her flesh, because he was wedging himself inside. . . .

Jessie gasped, part in fear and part in ecstasy, and
his mouth claimed hers again with sudden fierce ar-
dor. His back arched, and the man-thing shoved up
against a barrier inside her. Was this what men did
to women, put their man-things inside them until
they touched the barrier? It hardly seemed worth all
the fuss. But no, he didn't seem content with that.
He was pushing . . . pushing. . . .

Some of the ecstasy that had been carrying her
away abruptly took wing. He was hurting her. . . .

"Stuart, don't!"

But her protest was swallowed up by his mouth.
Even as she tried to turn her head away, tried again
to tell him that this was going beyond the bounds
of what was pleasing, he gave a mighty thrust that
rent her in two.

XXXII

A single tear trickled down Jessie's face, which she immediately wiped away with an unsteady finger. She was lying on her back with Stuart sprawled atop her, his man-thing still wedged inside her, although minutes before he had finished the dreadful business of fornicating with a mighty groan. After that he had collapsed, pinning her down, his face buried in her neck as he drew in great, gasping breaths.

Jessie wished she could take some of those breaths herself, but his weight on her rib cage precluded any such luxury. The man weighed a ton. He was sweaty and stank of whiskey—had she really thought she liked the smell only a quarter of an hour before?— and from the feel of things between her aching thighs, he had gotten man juice all over her.

The very idea was disgusting. The thing he had just done to her was disgusting. *He* was disgusting.

And she hurt.

"Get off me!" Jessie finally found the strength to shove at his shoulder.

That, at least, had the effect of making him raise his head.

"Get off you?" There was a curious note to his voice, almost as if he didn't quite believe what he was hearing.

"Yes," she hissed, "get off me!"

Stuart obligingly rolled onto his side. Propping himself up on one elbow, he watched as she jack-knifed upright. To Jessie's horror, the moonlight spilling through the small window provided suffi-cient illumination to reveal that she was naked from the waist down. Her belly and legs gleamed palely in the darkness, punctuated by the dark triangle be-tween her thighs.

Flushing, she yanked at her nightdress and wrap-per, which had twisted around her waist, and finally succeeded in making herself decent. Then, despite her unsteady knees and her thighs that felt as if they'd been turned to jelly, she tried to get to her feet.

"Whoa, there!"

Stuart stopped her by catching her around the waist with his arm. He hauled her back down, then sat up himself to peer into her face. Angrily Jessie averted her face from him. Long fingers slid beneath her chin and tugged it toward him again.

"Don't touch me!"

With a petulant slap she knocked his hand away. Instants later one long finger was back, probing at her cheek, tracing the damp trail left by that telltale tear.

"I said don't touch me!"

"I hurt you." It was said in such a quiet voice that Jessie barely heard it. He sounded penitent, but she was in no mood to care if he was remorseful now or not. She had given herself to him without reserva-tion, and he had caused her physical pain! The place between her legs still throbbed!

"Yes, you hurt me! Of course you hurt me! You—you put that—that *thing* in me!"

Through the darkness she caught the faintest glimmer of a smile. Then it vanished. Stuart caught her hand and raised it to his lips. Although Jessie tried to pull away, he wouldn't release it.

"Jess. Jessie." He pressed her palm to his lips,

then gently kissed each knuckle. Jessie was too mentally and physically exhausted to engage in the combat she guessed it would take to get her hand returned to her. So she sat glowering at him as he played with her fingers.

"Will it help at all if I say I'm sorry?"

"No!"

"I didn't think so."

Stuart sighed. Releasing her hand, he fastened his breeches, then scooted backward until he was sitting with his back against the wall. Then, before Jessie realized what he was about, he caught her around the waist and pulled her onto his lap.

"Let me go!"

"Presently. Sit still, Jessie. I'm not going to hurt you."

"A trifle late to be promising that, isn't it?" The fine art of sneering was coming more and more easily to her.

"Will you let me explain?"

"What is there to explain? You—we—fornicated, and now it's over, and I want to go inside."

"We made love," he corrected her quietly.

Jessie snorted. Stuart shrugged. She could feel the movement of his shoulders with her back muscles, snuggled up against his chest as she was. Her now decently covered bottom was nestled against that part of him that had hurt her, and her legs were draped over his. It would have been a cozy posture—if he had not had to hold her in place with his hands clamped around her wrists so that her arms formed an X across her chest.

"Maybe *you* fornicated," he said in her ear. "*I* made love."

"Love!" The single word was scoffing.

"Love. I love you, Jessie."

"Hah!"

There was a moment of silence. Then, astonishingly, Stuart chuckled. The sound was wry, but still it was, unmistakably, a chuckle.

"Do you know how many women—full-grown, sophisticated, very beautiful women—would have given their eyeteeth to hear me say that? But I bare my soul for the first time in my life to a wet-behind-the-ears miss, and what does the object of my passion say? 'Hah!' "

"I don't believe you!"

"Why would I lie?"

"To get me to—to—you know—again."

This time he laughed out loud. Despite her imprisoned wrists, Jessie managed to reward that infuriating chortle with an elbow to his ribs.

"Ow!"

"Stop laughing!"

"Oh, Jessie, I'm not laughing. At least, not at you. Would you please, for just a moment, use that very admirable brain you possess and answer me this: if all I wanted was to—fornicate, to use your word for it—do you really think I'd have trouble finding willing partners? You're more than lovely, darling, but ordinarily my taste does not run to just-hatched chicks."

"I am not a just-hatched chick!"

"Were you lying when you told me you loved me? Maybe you just wanted to use me for—you know."

He was teasing her now. How could he laugh after what he had done? "That isn't funny!"

"This whole damned mess isn't funny. Jessie, you told me you love me. Did you mean it?"

Every traumatized nerve ending in her body screamed at her to say no, but Jessie found that, cuddled on his lap as she was with his voice warm and disturbing in her ear, she could not quite bring herself to lie about something as important as that.

"Yes!" The word emerged through gritted teeth.

"If you love me, why don't you believe me when I say I love you?" He sounded genuinely curious. Jessie shifted impatiently in his lap, only to find herself held tight. For a minute she had almost forgotten that he held her prisoner, so comfortable was she.

"Because you're so—so . . ." Jessie's voice trailed off. It was impossible to put into words all the things Stuart was.

"So what?" He was not going to leave it alone.

All right. She would tell him. She would spell the whole thing out for him, and let him maintain then that he loved her. For all he called her a just-hatched chick, she was not naive enough to believe that a man like Stuart could actually fall in love with the Yazoo Valley wild child. No doubt his disgusting male urges had driven him to fornicate with her, and he was seeking to ease her distress by dressing up in pretty words what had happened between them.

It was unnecessary. However unpleasant it might be, she would rather hear the truth than soothing lies.

"So handsome, and so smart, and so—so charming, and . . ."

"Stop, Jessie, you'll unman me." Despite the jesting note in his voice, she had the feeling that he meant it. Then he continued. "Even if all that is true, why could I not love you?"

Jessie chewed her lower lip. Her shortcomings were many, and always before in her life they had been used as ammunition to wound her. But this was Stuart. He had hurt her physically, but still she loved him more than anyone in the world. He must not pretend to love her if he didn't. It was important that there be truth between them, however bitter she might find it.

"Because I'm—I'm well enough, I suppose, but certainly no match for you when it comes to looks, and I've never been anywhere farther than Jackson, and I—I like dogs and horses better than people, and I don't know how to dress, or do my hair, or dance, or anything."

"Darling, did it never occur to you that you are

seeing yourself through a mirror fashioned by your stepmother's spite?"

The notion startled Jessie. She started to say something, but Stuart silenced her with a gesture. When he continued, his voice was very soft. "Shall I tell you what I see when I look at you? I see a young lady with hair the color of polished mahogany, masses of hair so thick that she could ride through the streets like Lady Godiva with her modesty intact. I see porcelain skin, big, innocent cocoa-brown eyes, and a face that's as delicate of feature as a cameo. I see gorgeous shoulders, breasts that are luscious enough to make any man worthy of the name lick his lips, and a waist—"

"Stuart!" Jessie protested, scandalized at the intimate turn his description was taking.

"Don't interrupt," he responded severely, and went on. "Where was I? Oh, yes, a waist that's small enough not to need the stays she rarely wears anyway—oh, don't think I haven't noticed!—and a sassy little derriere that makes me want to grab it every time it flounces past."

"Stuart!"

"Hush, I'm not finished. To sum up all those distracting physical attributes, when I look at you I see an extraordinarily beautiful young woman. But, Jessie . . ."

"Yes?"

"That's not why I love you."

"It's not?"

"No." He paused for a theatrical moment. When he resumed, he was almost whispering in her ear. "I love you because you're gallant. You've taken every handicap life has thrown your way and emerged triumphant. You've known more adversity in eighteen years than most young ladies will know in a lifetime, yet you've survived with your courage and your sweetness intact. What you are, my Jessie, is a rara avis, and that is why I love you."

As he ended, his lips caressed the delicate shell of

her ear. Jessie sat motionless for a moment, hardly feeling his touch, while she mentally reeled beneath the impact of his words.

Perhaps, just perhaps, he did love her.

It was the most beautiful thought she had ever had.

"Do you mean it, Stuart?" she asked humbly.

"I mean it, Jessie." His lips slid from her ear to nudge aside her hair and nibble at the silky column of her neck. A shiver coursed through Jessie's body. She rested her head against his shoulder to give him easier access to her neck.

"You're not just saying that to get me to—to make love with you again?"

"Praise the Lord, at least we've gotten past 'fornicating.' No, Jess, I am not just saying that." Something that sounded suspiciously like amusement laced his words. Eyes narrowing, Jessie slanted a look back at him. He took advantage of the slight turning of her head to recapture her mouth.

His kiss was soft and very sweet, and completely took her mind off the ache between her thighs. Jessie shifted in his lap so that she could put her arms around his neck, and closed her eyes. As he deepened the kiss she sighed into his mouth. When she dreamed of Stuart, and of his kisses, this was how she dreamed that he would kiss her. The hard passion with which he had kissed her previously had gentled. His lips were soft as they moved over hers, warm and undemanding. Jessie discovered that the faint taste of whiskey that lingered on his lips and tongue was not so repulsive after all. In fact, she was quite coming to like the taste again.

He took his time with her mouth, tracing the outline of her lips with his tongue, probing gently between them and then retreating until her mouth parted of its own accord for him. Still he played with her mouth, until her breathing grew uneven and she quivered with impatience for him to deepen the kiss even more. When he retreated yet again, she bit down on that tantalizing tongue to punish it for its teasing.

"Ouch!" he protested, and lifted his head. Jessie pulled him down to her with a tug on the curls at the nape of his neck.

"Kiss me properly," she commanded, and he obliged. As his mouth claimed hers once more, Jessie sighed with satisfaction. He was kissing her as he'd taught her to want to be kissed, kissing her so that the now familiar hot longing rose up inside her to initiate the melting of her bones. Despite the fact that she knew where all this kissing must lead, despite that pain that she knew awaited her at the culmination of the sweet clamoring that sprang to life in her veins, she could no more stop herself from responding to his touch than she could stop herself from breathing. She loved him. How she loved him! If it was a woman's lot to be hurt by the man she loved, then so be it.

He kissed her thoroughly as her head fell back against his shoulder in a gesture of absolute surrender. One arm encircled her back, supporting her as she leaned against its strength. The other hand stroked the soft skin of her neck, caressed her shoulders, cupped her breasts. His thumb rubbed over her nipples, abrasive through the thin cloth that covered them, and the growing heat inside her quickened urgently. Instinctively her breasts thrust into his sheltering palm. Her nipples ached for his touch. But his hand was already sliding down, down through the valley between her breasts, down over the sensitized skin of her belly, down, while she quivered and quaked and burned. It was only when that hand stopped to press hard against the secret place at the apex of her thighs that the memory of pain came flooding back.

Despite her brave resolution, Jessie stiffened. Stuart had hurt her there. Her lashes flickered, then lifted.

"No, please," she whispered, and when he would have kissed her, she avoided his mouth.

Her soft protest and the rejection of his kiss smote him like a blow. He lifted his head just enough so that he could look down at her. Jessie's face was tilted toward him, her mouth soft and rosy with his kisses, her head resting against his shoulder, the thick fall of her hair spilling like dark, waving silk around them to puddle on the grain sacks and the floor. Those cocoa-brown eyes were wide with uncertainty, remembered pain and present fear lending dark shadows to their depths. Faint blue smudges beneath her eyes attested to both the lateness of the hour and the trauma he had put her through. The moonlight shimmering over her features lent her a haunting beauty that he knew would linger in his mind long after this night had passed. Her arms were looped around his neck, trusting in their very passivity in the face of the pain he had already inflicted and, for all she knew, meant to inflict on her again. The white frill at the neck of her nightdress exposed the tender hollow of her throat. The thin cotton gown clung to the round firmness of her tip-tilted young breasts. Pert nipples thrust at the cloth, drawing his eyes. Her wrapper had come untied at some point, leaving her nightdress to act alone as a flimsy veil for her form. The soft white cotton was more opaque than not, but still he could make out the gentle curve of her belly, the lissome line of her legs, and the dark triangle between them.

He had hurt her, though he'd never meant to. Guilt coursed through him as he recognized that. He'd done much this night that he'd never meant to do: he had never meant to bed her, to take her maidenhead, to make her his. But the combination of whiskey and her promise to wed another man had proved explosive, ripping the lid off his unaccustomed nobility and setting free the fierce hunger for her that had festered inside him for so long.

He had gotten himself drunk, and then she had made him angry. Along with his temper he had lost his good intentions and in a fit of passionate madness had taken what he wanted. Now he was sober, but despite the despicable nature of what he had done in taking her virginity, he could not truly regret it. Not at the moment, anyway. Maybe when dawn came and he was no longer dazzled by moonlight and kisses, he would curse himself for the selfish bastard he had once again proved himself to be.

But not now. Not when the girl he loved lay across his lap, her arms looped around his neck, her body all but naked, her eyes dark with doubt and fear and yet, transcending all, aglow with love for him.

If anyone else in his life had ever truly loved him, he couldn't at the moment remember it.

His eyes were full of Jessie, and his heart was full of Jessie. She was everything he had ever wanted, and he had made her his.

Somewhere the gods might be laughing, but he would take what he could get for now and worry about the morrow on the morrow.

Just one thing he promised himself, and her: because he had hurt her with his first claiming, he meant to take good care that neither he nor anyone else hurt her again.

For better or worse, the deed was done and she now belonged to him. And if he knew nothing else, Clive McClintock knew how to take right good care of himself and all that was his.

XXXIII

"Jess. Let me teach you about loving."

"I—I—you already did."

Jessie's eyes flickered away from his. Her passion was fast ebbing as the memory of pain reasserted itself. With the best will in the world, she didn't think she could submit herself to that again. Then she looked back up at him. He was facing the window, and she could read his expression quite clearly. For once his face was open to her, his eyes tender as they met hers, his mouth not quite smiling. The moonlight painted a silver wash over the night-black waves of his hair and glinted off his azure eyes. The exquisitely carved symmetry of his features was bathed in a soft glow, giving him the unearthly handsomeness of a young god come to earth to woo a mortal maiden. His neck was strong beneath her hands, his shoulders and chest broad and solid as she rested against them. Beneath her bottom she could feel the strength in the powerful muscles of his thighs—and the growing hardness of the man-thing between them.

"I—I just can't," she added miserably, and hung her head.

To her surprise he hugged her, wrapping both arms around her and rocking her back and forth like

a hurt child. Then he loosened his hold, and tilted
her chin up to drop a quick kiss on her mouth.

"It won't hurt again, you know. Only the first
time hurts for females, I suppose to discourage them
in case they should be tempted to fall into a life of
depravity. But after that . . . after that, Jessie, it can
be so good."

"If you don't mind, I'll just take your word for
it."

He grinned then, and the effect was like the sun
bursting through the clouds on a rainy day. The
sheer beauty of the man temporarily dazzled Jessie.
She began to think that maybe she could, to please
him, after all.

But maybe she couldn't, if it was going to hurt.

"We can just skip the part that you don't like, for
now," he said obligingly. "Maybe we can start by
getting you out of that very fetching nightdress. I
have a fancy to see you naked in the moonlight."

Shocked, Jessie clutched the neck of her nightdress and vehemently shook her head.

Stuart looked her up and down with a smile.
"That's out for now, too, hmm? All right, my shy
little violet, how about if we reverse things and I let
you see me naked in the moonlight?"

The leer he gave her was absurdly exaggerated.
Suddenly it occurred to Jessie that he was teasing
her. Her brows snapped together, and she scowled
at him.

"You're doing it deliberately," she accused.

"What?" He looked the very soul of innocence.

"Embarrassing me!"

"Not I."

But Jessie knew better. He had purposefully set
out to ruffle her feathers, and in so doing restore
some vestige of her fighting spirit. Aggravating
though his method was, it had achieved its goal.
She no longer felt so—tremulous. Her scowl eased,
and her eyes ran down as much of his body as she
could see, which wasn't all that much since she was

sitting on his lap. The idea of seeing him naked in the moonlight was intriguing, to say the least. Never had she even dared to wonder what he looked like naked, although . . .

"I've—occasionally—wondered—what you look like without your shirt," she confessed, running the last words together in a rush. Her eyes fell away from his as maidenly modesty threatened to get the upper hand over her sudden boldness.

"Have you, now? I'm entirely at your disposal, Madam Curiosity. Why don't you find out?"

Jessie looked up at him again, sorely tempted but more than a little uncertain how to—or if she should—proceed. Seeing her dilemma, Stuart covered her hands with his and lifted them to where the first shirt button was fastened, some little way below his open collar.

"Well, go on," he encouraged her when her fingers rested against the rumpled linen covering his chest but made no move to do anything else.

"You want me to . . . do it?" It was very close to a squeak.

"You do know how to undo a button?"

That urbane question caused Jessie to shoot him a look. He almost sounded mocking, but the expression in his eyes was far from mockery. They were bright and glittering, possessive, hungry—hungry for her. He wanted her fiercely. It was there in his eyes.

The idea that she could so affect him gave Jessie the courage she needed. Taking a deep breath, she shifted her gaze to his chest, and her fingers began to clumsily work that first small button free.

By the time she had undone three, Jessie was so distracted by the widening expanse of chest her handiwork had exposed that she quite forgot what she was about. Her fingers abandoned the diminished row of buttons to reach out, tentatively, to touch the whorls of black hair she'd revealed. The solid wall of muscle radiated heat. Jessie probed fur-

ther, touching the silk-over-steel skin of his chest,
running a questing finger over the wide V she had
opened in his shirt. His mouth tightened, but he
made no other move. Jessie got the impression that
he was deliberately holding himself on a tight rein
so as not to frighten her.

The idea that he would not seek to reciprocate her
exploration of his body in kind made her bolder.
Stroking the hair-roughened skin, Jessie grew more
intoxicated by the moment. She loved the way he
felt, loved the masculinity of ridged muscles covered
by hair, loved the very scent of him. It was all she
could do not to bury her nose in his chest and just
breathe.

"See? Nothing to be afraid of at all," Stuart murmured as her hands moved over him. His eyes were
slightly narrowed, their opalescent blue opaque. His
expression was again impossible to read, but his
heart—Jessie could feel its hurried beat beneath her
hand. Ta-dum, ta-dum, ta-dum, with a strong, fast
rhythm, as if he were involved in some taxing physical contest. A tiny smile curved Jessie's mouth. Finally she had found a way to gauge what he was
feeling.

"What's funny?" There was a gruffness to his
voice. Jessie's eyes slid from that fascinating chest
to his face.

"Your heart's pounding."

"Is it?"

"Umm-hmm."

"And that's funny?"

"Umm-hmm."

"Do you mind telling me why?"

"It's a secret."

"Is it, now?" He was looking at her as if he did
not quite like the sound of that.

Jessie's fingers spread out, burrowing through the
thick mat of hair. Her eyes flickered down again to
the object of her attention.

"You have the most magnificent chest."

"Thank you. Though I don't think you've seen enough of it to make a truly informed judgment."

"Oh."

The hint worked. Jessie finally remembered what she had been about when the attraction of his chest had diverted her, and slid the remaining shirt buttons from their holes. When she finished, his shirt hung open, laying bare a wide expanse from his neck to the waistband of his breeches. Taking a deep breath, Jessie ogled the exposed swath of hard-muscled, hair-roughened chest. Before she had quite recovered from the sight enough to touch the flesh she had revealed, he shrugged out of both shirt and waistcoat and tossed them aside.

Which left Jessie sitting on his lap, faced with the first bare-chested man she had ever seen. At extremely close quarters, yet. Her lips parted, and she stared.

He was beautiful. Were all men that beautiful? Jessie was sure they couldn't be. Like his face, Stuart's shoulders and arms and chest and belly must be extraordinary. Of course, she had known that his shoulders were wide. That was obvious even when he was clothed. But what she had not known was that they would be sleek, and bronzed, and solid as a stone wall. She'd seen his strength demonstrated a thousand times, doing everything from yanking Mr. Brantley from his horse to slinging sacks of grain onto a wagon. But she had never guessed that his arms would bulge with muscle. She'd been held against that chest and never suspected that it was covered with a wedge-shaped pelt of hair as black and thick as the hair on his head. Neither had she imagined that his belly would be as hard as a board and ridged with muscle—or that he would have two hard male nipples, their aureola more brown than pink.

When Jessie just sat there, unmoving, her eyes fastened on his chest, Stuart caught her hands and lifted them so that they were pressed against the

flesh she had revealed. She felt the heat of his skin
against her palms, the fine texture of his chest hair
as it curled around her fingertips, and her breath
caught. The thrill that surged through her as she
touched him was totally unexpected. Her breasts
swelled, and the remembered sweet clamoring between her thighs began anew.

Impossibly, her body seemed to have forgotten the
pain that followed such stirrings. Her bedazzled
mind soon forgot it, too.

Sliding her hands along the breadth of his shoulders to stroke over his muscled arms, Jessie marveled at the hardness of his muscles. Then her hands
returned to slide down his chest, sensuously exploring the hard, flat planes that were rendered even
more seductively masculine by their liberal covering
of hair. Her fingers trailed over his belly and traced
along the waistband of his breeches, thrilling to the
board-solidness of the muscles there. Stuart sat motionless as one questing finger dived inside his belly
button, part of which was just visible above the
breeches he had not quite managed to return to their
proper position. His eyes flickered as that finger
made a slow rotation before being withdrawn, but
his hands continued to rest without pressure on Jessie's waist, letting her learn about his body as she
would. But when her fingers at last found their way
to his nipples and rubbed lightly across them, his
control finally slipped, though just a little. His hands
tightened perceptibly on her waist, and he sucked
in his breath.

The small sound drew Jessie's attention. She
glanced quickly up at him, only to find herself mesmerized by the hot glitter in his eyes. Incredible as
it seemed, though he made no move to do anything
about it, he was clearly wild with wanting her. Jessie
realized then just how tight was the rein he'd been
holding himself on as she touched and caressed him.
But still he'd done nothing to hurt or frighten her,
leaving it to her to learn only what she would of

lovemaking. She knew suddenly that what she wanted to learn was what excited him. Then an idea so daring that it shocked her occurred to her.

When he had kissed her in the orchard, he had put his mouth on her nipple. The resulting conflagration had turned her bones to water.

Would her mouth on his nipple affect him the same way?

Jessie bent her head and tried it.

"Christ, Jess!"

To her disappointment, Stuart's hands rose to cup her face and push it away from him. Frowning, she looked from the distended nipple she had just licked to his face. Had she hurt him? Or did females not perform such intimacies on gentlemen?

"Don't men like that?"

He laughed. At least Jessie thought it was a laugh, although the unsteady sound could just as easily have been a groan.

"Too much, darling. I think you'd better forget that for the present. Unless you want to end up flat on your back right quickly."

"Oh."

"Yes, 'oh.' "

The warning was enough to dissuade her from repeating that particular experiment. Instead Jessie confined herself to running her hands along the width of his shoulders, over his hair-roughened chest and muscled back, along the strong column of his neck until the glitter in his eyes had exploded into pure flame and his heart was pounding beneath her palm as if he'd run for miles.

It was good to have that to judge just how her touch was affecting him. Except for the conflagration in his eyes, his face gave her no clue. Only the thudding of his heart revealed just how hungry for her he was. A slight, satisfied smile curled Jessie's lips as she pressed her hand against the telltale part of his chest. He would never again be able to completely hide from her what he was feeling.

"I do have more buttons, you know."

Stuart's voice was hoarse. With Jessie's attention thoroughly taken up with the state of his heart, it was a moment or two before that comment filtered through.

"More . . . ?" Jessie's voice trailed off as she looked up, puzzled. Then her frown cleared. Of course she knew what he meant.

Did he really expect her to unbutton his breeches? Did she want to? Jessie thought about it for an instant. Oh, yes, she did!

Reaching down to where his belly button peeped coyly over his waistband, she sought and found the first button. It was much larger than the bone buttons that had closed his shirt, and thus should have been easier to manipulate. But her fingers fumbled and slipped, and what should have been a simple task became endlessly complicated by the feel of his ridged abdomen as her fingers worked beneath the cloth. Finally Stuart brushed her hands aside and did the job himself.

The sides of his breeches parted to reveal more hard male flesh. The wedge of hair on his chest narrowed to a dark arrow that led past his belly button, over his abdomen, to disappear where the breeches again cut off her vision. Tantalized, her eyes followed the trail, only to widen as she caught a glimpse of something that swelled turgidly against the black cloth just beyond the opening.

His man-thing, of course. Shuddering, Jessie shut her eyes.

"Coward," Stuart chided in her ear. Jessie's eyes stayed tightly shut. He made a sound of half-exasperated amusement, his hands tightening around her waist as he lifted her off his lap.

Jessie's eyes opened as she was abruptly deposited on the littered floor.

"If we are to continue this interesting experiment, I need to take off my boots," he answered her in-

quiring look. Then, while Jessie watched speechless,
he proceeded to do just that.

When his feet were bare, he stood up, and his
hands went to the waistband of his breeches. Jessie's eyes clamped shut. But the rustle of cloth told
her that he was shucking his breeches as well.

"Open your eyes, Jessie." There was an undertone of laughter to the words.

Jessie shook her head.

"Just looking won't hurt you, will it?"

Probably not. But she just couldn't bring herself
to.

"Come on, Jess." Despite the gentleness of his
tone, it was clear he did not mean to take no for an
answer. He caught her upper arms and hauled her
up to stand before him. In the process, as he had no
doubt intended, Jessie's eyes flew open.

She kept them fixed firmly on his face.

He was smiling at her, closer to the window now,
so that the moonlight pouring in over that handsome face highlighted every feature. His eyes
glowed with their own light, burning bright as they
moved over her. His mouth was crooked, twisted
into something that was not quite a smile.

Of its own accord her hand came to rest on his
chest, just over his heart. It was pounding like a
kettledrum.

She should have dropped her hand, of course,
once she had determined that. But instead her fingers lingered, seduced by the feel of his flesh. His
skin was so hot, the muscles beneath it so hard. . . .

His hand rose to catch her wrist, draw her hand
down the center of his chest, over his belly. Jessie's
fingers tingled at the feel of him. A shiver raced
along her spine.

"Touch me, Jessie," he whispered. Even as her
eyes closed in protest, his hand led hers to the man-thing that had caused her pain.

Her fingers found it, recoiled. He would not release her wrist.

"Please, Jess."

Jessie's fingers shook, but she responded to that husky whisper in the only way she could. She allowed his hand to guide hers again—and this time, at his unspoken direction, her hand closed over him.

He sucked in his breath. She opened her eyes.

His face was set, his lips slightly parted as he breathed through his teeth, his eyes narrow slivers more silver than blue as they blazed down at her. Jessie looked up into those eyes for a long, shuddering moment, and then her gaze moved down the length of his body slowly, so slowly, to the enormous pulsing thing she held in her hand.

Against the whiteness of her skin it looked very dark. Her eyes ran along the length of it, more fascinated now than afraid. It had felt huge when he had plunged it inside her, but she saw that it was not as horribly enormous as she had thought. It reared up from a thick nest of wiry black hair to which the arrow that trailed past his belly button had led. It was so hot it burned her palm, but its skin was smooth and velvety and just slightly damp. When she squeezed it, just to see what would happen, Stuart flinched and grimaced. Jessie's eyes flew to his face. Sweat had broken out along his brow, although the tack room was cool. Despite his extreme physical reaction, he watched her steadily, his eyes glittering like diamonds in the moonlight.

"See? There's nothing so fearsome." The words came unsteadily through his teeth. As Jessie's eyes moved back down over the broad-shouldered, narrow-hipped body to the thing she held, she saw that his fists were clenched at his sides. It occurred to her then that perhaps it was hard for him to have her touch him and nothing more. Maybe gentlemen had need to do that hurtful thing to females, or hurt themselves. Maybe that was why the man-thing was so large and swollen. Maybe, if it did not disgorge its juice, it ached.

Curiously, the longer she held the man-thing in her hand, the more her fear of it receded.

"No," Jessie agreed, and tightened her hand again. This time she saw the muscles of his thighs tighten as if to brace themselves against her. When she sneaked a quick glance at him, she saw that his eyes were half closed, his mouth compressed.

"Does it hurt you when I do that?" she asked, curious.

He shook his head. "It pleases me." His voice was thick. His eyes closed. Then they opened again, and his hand moved to catch hers. To Jessie's surprise, he pulled her hand away from him.

"If it pleases you, why may I not do it?"

"It pleases me too much."

That guttural explanation made no sense to Jessie. She was about to demand elucidation when his hands moved up her arms to her shoulders, where they slid beneath the edges of her wrapper.

"Will you let me take this off?" There was still that oddly hoarse note to his voice.

Jessie looked up at him, uncertain. But this was Stuart, her Stuart, whom she loved with all her heart and soul. What he wanted her to do, she would do.

"Yes," she whispered. His eyes crinkled at her encouragingly, and then he was easing the wrapper from her shoulders. It fell unheeded to the floor.

Jessie stood before him in the thin cotton of her high-necked, long-sleeved nightdress and knew what was coming next.

"You're not afraid of me, Jess?"

"No." They were both whispering. Jessie was mesmerized by the hot, tender glow of his eyes.

"Let me take off your nightdress."

His fingers were already at her neck, undoing the tiny buttons there.

"Stuart . . ."

"I won't do anything you don't want me to. I just want to look at you. All right?"

Jessie could no more have denied that husky coax-

ing than she could have stopped breathing. The very
hoarseness of his voice was awakening shivers inside her. Despite her knowledge of where this dangerous game must end, her body was coming to life
again, her nerve endings atremble with anticipation,
her breasts swelling, her nipples tightening. The
ache between her thighs had changed in character,
becoming more pleasurable than painful.

Was it woman's lot to want the very thing that
hurt her?

"All right, Stuart," she whispered, and bowed her
head.

A laugh shook him. "Don't look so scared, Jess. I
won't hurt you," he breathed, and then he was
pulling her nightgown up and over her head. It
joined her wrapper on the floor.

Jessie stood there, bathed in moonlight, feeling
more hideously vulnerable than she had ever felt in
her life. No one save her maid had ever seen her
completely without clothes, and having Stuart's eyes
on her was very different from being tended to by
Tudi or Sissie. Instinctively her hands moved to
shield her body in the age-old gesture of woman.
Stuart caught her hands, held them wide. His eyes
ran over her body. Too embarrassed by her own nakedness to look down at herself, she watched his
face instead.

That expressionless face remained expressionless,
save for the narrowing of his eyes and the tiny muscle that tightened at the corner of his mouth.

"Christ, Jessie, you stop my breath."

His eyes were fastened on her breasts.

XXXIV

Naked, she was the most beautiful creature Clive had ever seen. Awash in luminescence, her skin was an unearthly glowing white, so pale and pure that he felt that to touch it would almost be a sacrilege. Her shoulders with their delicate bones were stiffly held, both proud and shy at the same time. Her breasts were even more glorious than he'd imagined, firm round globes that thrust wantonly away from her chest, the shape and color of her nipples reminding him of fresh, ripe strawberries. Her rib cage was narrow, her waist small and supple, her hips softly rounded. There was the slightest feminine curve to her stomach, where her navel nestled, a small, perfect circle. The sweet center of her womanhood was veiled by a modest triangle of reddish curls. Her thighs were pressed tightly together, as if she sought to keep herself from him. Her legs were long and lissome, with dimpled knees and small feet.

He might love her for her mind and soul, but her body was certainly a wonderful bonus.

It was all he could do to keep from reaching out and fondling a ripe breast, then tossing her on her backside and easing the burning tumescence between his legs in the quickest, most basic manner possible.

But because this was Jessie, sweet, sweet Jessie,

he most nobly refrained. Indeed, he had already exercised more restraint with her than he had ever had occasion to show to a woman and he was like to burst from it.

But because she was his, and shy of him, he would take the time to gentle her. Her first time had been fueled by whiskey, anger, and long-denied lust. Her second would be the stuff of rapturous female dreams. He meant to bend all his considerable experience to making sure of it.

But at the moment she was blushing furiously, her eyes averted from his in what looked very much like an agony of embarrassment. If he had not been holding her hands, he knew she would be using them to cover herself.

"Don't be shy, Jess," he murmured coaxingly. When she still wouldn't meet his eyes, he dropped one hand to catch her chin. That worked. Her eyes as they rose to his were wide, their walnut depths glowing with a combination of newly awakened passion and, he feared, fear. With a mental kick to the seat of his own pants, he castigated himself for hurting her before. But, of course, she'd been a virgin, and pain the first time was a virgin's unavoidable lot. With the best will in the world, he couldn't have saved her that.

"I can't help it," she whispered, sounding every bit as nervous as she looked. Clive smiled down at her tenderly. What a child she was still! It would be his pleasure to teach her to be fully a woman.

"You're beautiful, Jessie."

"Thank you."

She sounded like a well-mannered schoolgirl, and looked like one, too, except for her mouth-watering nakedness and the scarlet blush suffusing her cheeks.

"Your breasts are the most gorgeous things I've ever seen in my life."

"Stuart!"

That "Stuart" was beginning to grate on his

nerves. With every fiber of his being he wanted to
hear her call him Clive. But of course he never
would, and he mentally swatted the notion aside
like a bothersome gnat.

"I want to kiss them."

"Stuart!"

She sounded truly horrified. Her eyes were wide
and shocked. A smile tugged at the corners of Clive's
mouth even as his hand slid down from her chin to
caress the satiny skin of her neck. His palm itched
to cup her breast, but he knew better than to rush
his fences. What Jessie needed was wooing.

"I want to kiss every inch of your skin. Starting
with your mouth, and working my way down. Do
you mind?"

"Yes! No! I don't know! Oh, Stuart, please—"

Whatever request she was going to make of him,
he was never to know, because he dipped his head
at that moment to taste her open mouth. Just taste
it, no more.

"Please what?" He kept the presence of mind to
inquire when just a moment later he lifted his head.
Her eyes appeared dazed as she blinked up at him. A
good foot of space separated her flesh from his. Only
his hand on her neck linked them. But that kiss had
left her looking dazed. That boded well for the even-
tual outcome of his wooing.

"I don't know. Oh, Stuart, I do love you, but . . ."

"If I didn't know better, Jess, I'd think you were
trying to tell me that you're a tad reluctant." He
bent his head and kissed her again, more lingeringly
this time but still hardly more than a taste. "Are
you?"

"What?" In the aftermath of that second kiss, she
seemed to have trouble following the gist of his conversation. Her lips trembled, and her eyes had an
unfocused look to them that pleased him very well.

"Never mind." He kissed her a third time, his
tongue just grazing the surface of her lower lip. To
his satisfaction, she sighed into his mouth and

stepped closer without any urging on his part. Her breasts nuzzled his chest, and her arms slid around his neck.

"I love you, Jessie." He murmured it caressingly against her mouth even as he deepened his kiss. Every male instinct he possessed was now thoroughly awake and aroused, demanding that he take what was his without further ado. But still he held back. No matter what else was wrong in his life, he meant to make this right for Jessie.

"Oh, Stuart." It was a sigh as she nestled more fully against him. Despite his good intentions, he was unable to keep his arms from encircling her and pulling her closer yet. With every millimeter of his skin he felt her against him, the soft fire of her breasts with their hard tips snuggling against the muscles on his chest, the gossamer down of her pubic hair brushing his thighs. He ached, and swelled, and lusted, but still, still, he did not take more than a kiss.

It was Jessie herself who told him when she was ready for more. He held her close, his tongue exploring her mouth, when she gasped and rose up on tiptoe, her arms tightening around his neck.

Clive could feel her trembling in his arms. Inwardly he permitted himself a smile, although he was too far gone with passion to manage one physically, even if his mouth had not been thoroughly occupied with kissing Jessie. Then one hand slid down her back to stroke a softly rounded buttock.

Her skin was silky smooth, the curve of her cheek just right for the span of his hand. Clive surrendered to temptation and squeezed. She cried out against his mouth.

Good intentions or no, this was almost more than he could withstand. To his amazement, his arms began to shake. He hadn't trembled so over a woman since he was a green boy.

"Stuart?" She felt the tremors and was questioning them. Clive took advantage of the slight backward arch of her body to do what he had been wanting to do for what seemed like forever: he bent his head and took one pert nipple in his mouth.

Jessie cried out, trembled. Her hands burrowed in his hair, tugging as she gripped his scalp, but she didn't try to pull him away from her. Instead she held him close and arched her back still more, offering her breasts to him with an instinctive voluptuousness that thrilled him more than the most practiced courtesan with all her tricks had ever been able to do. With his tongue he rolled her nipple around, sucked on it, savored the sweetness of it, and all of a sudden found himself past the point of no return.

As he lifted his head to claim her mouth again, he discovered that he was shaking like a schoolboy, burning with need for her, aching and throbbing until he feared that the part most vitally concerned might explode.

If he didn't ease himself with her soon, he would spew his seed ignominiously into the cool night air.

That was an indignity that had not happened to him since he was a boy of thirteen, and he did not mean to suffer it again tonight. Scooping Jessie up in his arms, Clive lowered her to the pallet of grain sacks, kissing her all the while. She clung to his neck and kissed him back, with all the sweet passion that he'd been delighted to discover came to her so easily, and never protested once.

Not when he lay her on her back and knelt beside her, not when he fondled her breasts, not when he stroked her belly and the soft skin of her thighs. Not when he slid his hand up her inner thigh to the place he longed to enter, and touched her there.

Not only did she not protest, but she cried out in pleased surprise and arched her mound against his hand.

Clive shut his eyes, gritted his teeth, and abruptly gave up the fight. He could hold off no longer. He had to have her now, or die.

Still he tried to make it easy for her. Even as he loomed over her, his knees wedging between hers,

his hand stayed on that place he had learned was
the secret to pleasuring women, rubbing and stroking and making her ready for his entry.

From the way she trembled and gasped, and from
the wild little plunges with which she answered the
thrusts of his tongue in her mouth, he judged she
was as ready as she was ever going to be.

His heart was pounding so furiously that blood
drummed in his ears. He held his weight from her
with arms that trembled, kissed her mouth, and
spread her legs wide.

Then he entered her, as gently as he could. But as
the fiery wetness of her closed around him, he lost
all control and plunged fiercely inside.

She clutched him and bucked beneath him, moaning that despised name that she thought was his. But
Clive was so lost in the throes of his own savage pleasure that he could not have said if she was with him
or not as he strove mightily toward the sweet finish.

In the end, when he cried out in satisfaction at the
hot explosion of seed, she cried out too, shuddering
in his hold. Was she crying out from pleasure or
from pain? God, he hoped it was from pleasure, but
for the moment he was too spent to find out, too
spent, in fact, to do more than collapse atop her and
pant for air.

It was some while later that he recovered himself
sufficiently to roll to one side. Propping himself on
one elbow, he looked down into her face.

Her eyes were closed, her lashes dark, feathery
crescents against her cheeks, her beautiful hair
spread out in a wild tangle around her head. Strands
of it were caught up in the hairs on his chest, and
waved over his arm. He stroked a wayward curl back
from her forehead, and looked down at her lovely
naked body with an overwhelming sense of pride of
ownership. She was his, marked with his sweat and
juice and hair. His, and he meant to keep her.

"Jessie."

No reply. Her eyelashes didn't even flutter.

"Jess."

She didn't respond, didn't move so much as a muscle. Only the gentle rise and fall of those distractingly pretty breasts told him that she still lived. His brow knit in consternation. Then, and only then, did it occur to Clive that the love of his life had fallen fast asleep.

"Good God," he said blankly. Then his mouth twisted into a wry smile. Whatever reaction he had been expecting from her in the aftermath of his lovemaking, it was not the gentle snore that at that very moment issued from between her parted lips.

He leaned over and kissed her, very gently so as not to waken her, and got to his feet. Within minutes he was dressed. Then he picked up her nightgown and wrapper, shook them to rid them of any wayward bits of straw or grain, and knelt beside Jessie. Lifting her into a sitting position, he maneuvered her nightgown over her head.

That woke her. "What . . . ?"

"Shhh," Stuart said, smiling a little at her owlish blinks. Then he tugged her nightgown down, threw her wrapper over his arm, and stood up with her in his arms.

"Stuart?"

"Hush, darling. I'm taking you to bed."

"Oh."

He shouldered his way out of the tack room, quelled Jasper with a word, and let himself out of the stable. The side yard seemed flooded with moonlight after the darkness of the barn. He strode quickly toward the house, ever conscious of the soft, trusting bundle in his arms. Her head lolled against his shoulder, her arms looped loosely around his neck, and she seemed to alternate between almost sleeping and wakefulness. A fierce sense of protectiveness was born in him as he carried her to the bed she would occupy alone. If anyone should discover that Jessie had lain with him, Jessie would be the one to suffer. Therefore, for her sake, no one must discover it until he had figured a way out of this god-awful mess.

"Stuart?" Her head was lifting from his shoulder, and she was blinking at him again.

"Hmm?" He smiled at her indulgently.

"You were right."

"About what, darling?"

"The second time didn't hurt a bit."

"Didn't it, now? Just wait till you sample the third time."

"I don't think I can. Wait."

Discretion or no, that breath-stealing reply called for a kiss. Stuart stopped, answered the call thoroughly, then resumed his journey. He carried her inside the sleeping house, all the way up to her room, where he brushed aside the mosquito netting and laid her on her bed.

When he kissed her again and would have left her there, Jessie caught his shirtfront.

"Stuart." She was smiling sleepily, already curling up in the dainty, white-linened bed, one hand resting on her pillow beneath her cheek. Looking down at her, holding aside the curtain of netting, Clive thought that never in his life had he seen a female appear more desirable than she did in that moment.

"What is it, darling?"

"I guess I won't marry Mitch after all."

"No," he said positively, scowling despite the glint that gave her teasing away. "I guess you won't."

"Dog in the manger," she said softly.

He bent to kiss her. Every cell in his body longed to climb into that bed with her, but he knew that, for her sake, he absolutely could not.

"Now there you're wrong," he told her when he lifted his head. "I do want you. Go to sleep, Jess."

And he left her there, smiling into her pillow, while he made his way to his own lonely bed.

XXXV

A meadowlark was singing when Jessie awoke
the next morning. It must have been perched in the
large loblolly tree that provided perennial shade on
the west side of the house, because she could hear
its song clearly even through her closed window.
Jessie stretched, smiling, and thought, How appropriate. She felt like singing, too.

Getting out of bed, she crossed to the window to
look out. There was a slight soreness between her
thighs as she moved to tell her that the night before
had been no dream, but she didn't really hurt anywhere. Despite the scant amount of sleep she had
had, she felt good, Jessie decided, happy and care-
free and tingling with energy. Outside the window,
the grass seemed greener than ever before and the
sky bluer. Smiling foolishly at the world in general,
Jessie leaned against the window frame. The reason
that she felt so marvelous was that she felt loved.
Stuart loved her! Was that not a miracle worthy of
the name?

It was early yet. The sun had not yet cleared the
tall oaks, and the grass was still wet with dew. There
was a great deal of bustle in the vicinity of the gin
building. Jessie remembered that the last of the cotton was scheduled to be picked that day. Mule wagons loaded down with large woven baskets filled to

overflowing with cotton stood in line before the two-story wooden structure, just beyond the quarters, that housed a gin machine on its upper level. After the cotton fiber was separated from the seed, it would be sent on to the lint room and then the cotton press. Finally it would be baled, and rolled to the landing just this side of Elmway, where the riverboats docked. As always at the end of the cotton-growing season, the river was clogged with traffic as the cotton was transported from the plantations to a large cotton port such as New Orleans. From there the cotton would be shipped to England. The noise and activity that surrounded the successful conclusion of the cotton season had always been something that Jessie looked forward to, and this year was no exception. But now she saw the wagons and heard the braying of the mules and smelled the fresh-picked cotton with senses far keener than they ever had been before. Being in love clearly increased one's awareness of the everyday pleasures of life.

Stuart would no doubt be out there in the vicinity of the gin building. Jessie blushed a little at the thought of confronting him in broad daylight after all that had passed between them during the night, but her hunger to see him outweighed her instinctive shyness. Turning her back on the scene outside the window, she hurried to dress.

Sissie had left a can of hot water outside Jessie's door as she always did. Jessie retrieved it, poured the water into the basin, and washed her face. Her body felt vaguely sticky. She would have liked a bath, but ordering one in the morning when her usual practice was to bathe at night might cause Tudi or even Sissie to wonder why. Happy as she was, Jessie was fully aware that what had happened between her and Stuart last night would be condemned by the rest of the world as wickedly scandalous. It was shameful enough that she had lain with a man to whom she was not wed, but when that man was married already, and to her dead fa-

ther's widow . . . It was downright sinful, and Jessie
knew it. Should anyone discover the truth, she
would be branded a scarlet woman and tittered
about and shunned. But she refused to let grim reality dim her enjoyment of the day. There would be
time enough later to ponder the more distressing
aspects of loving Stuart.

Shucking her nightgown, Jessie sponged her body
as well as she could. Brownish stains on the whiteness of her inner thighs puzzled her briefly, until
she determined that they were blood. Her virgin's
blood, meant to be her gift to her husband on their
wedding night. For the first time it truly hit Jessie
that she was no longer a virgin. As far as the marriage mart was concerned, she was now soiled
goods. Marriage was out of the question for her after
last night. A niggle of fear rose inside Jessie as she
considered that. She loved Stuart madly, and trusted
him to resolve the siuation in some unforeseen way
that would result in the two of them being together
forever, but the grim truth of the matter was that he
was already wed and could not marry her. Was she
to spend the rest of her life at Mimosa as his paramour while her stepmother claimed the honorable
title of his wife? Was their true love to be confined
to stolen trysts at midnight? Or would Stuart try to
get a divorce, the very idea of which made Jessie
shudder? The reality of the situation into which she
had tumbled began to rear its ugly head, but Jessie
determinedly beat such unpleasant thoughts back.

For today, just today, she would enjoy being
happy. She loved, and was loved in return. For just
a little while she would pretend that none of the
barriers between her and Stuart existed, and that
they were free to love as they would.

Jessie dressed quickly in the peacock-blue riding
habit that was so wonderfully becoming, then sat
before her dressing table brushing out her hair. Ker-
nels of grain and bits of straw were caught up in the
thick mass, and she thanked heaven that she was in

the habit of tending to herself in the mornings. If Tudi or Sissie had seen such debris in her hair, there would have been some highly awkward questions asked.

When she had finished styling her hair, Jessie gathered up every little bit of straw and grain that she had brushed from it and threw them in the back of the fireplace where they were unlikely to be noticed. Then she shook out her nightgown and wrapper to check them for bloodstains, and was relieved to find none. Finally the bloodstained cloth with which she had bathed her thighs was rinsed until no stains remained, and the murky water emptied into the slop jar.

Doing all this, she felt as guilty as a murderess. But when it was done, and she paused before her cheval glass for a final check of her appearance, her spirits rose again. Soon, soon she would be with Stuart. Nothing else mattered.

The morning was cool, though not as cool as the night. The long-sleeved, nip-waisted riding dress was welcome in such weather, and she had tied her hair with a blue ribbon at the crown and left the rest of the curly auburn tresses to hang down her back to her hips. The style made her look very young, she decided as she turned this way and that to admire her reflection in the mirror, and also, she hoped, very pretty.

Stuart had said she was beautiful. Could he really think that?

Smiling beatifically at the memory, Jessie left her bedroom and headed for the stable by way of the back stairs. She passed Tudi, who was carrying an armful of linen up, and startled her by giving her a quick hug in passing. From Rosa in the cookhouse she snitched a corn pone, bestowing on her a radiant smile in the process. Despite her utter unawareness that she was behaving in any way out of the ordinary, her unaccustomed ebullience left both women staring after her as she went merrily along.

"Don't my lamb *never* grin like that," Tudi muttered starkly to the stairway at large, and turned completely around on the landing to watch Jessie skip the rest of the way down the stairs. In the kitchen, Rosa just shook her head and continued with the preparations for luncheon.

Jessie, unaware of the speculation she was leaving in her wake, went on to the stable, where she bade Progress a cheery good-morning, bestowed the last of the corn pone along with a pat on Jasper, and swung nimbly into the saddle. Firefly greeted her with a dancing sidestep that exactly suited Jessie's mood. She patted the mare, too, and rode out of the barn near giddy with anticipation. In just a few minutes she would see Stuart again.

Celia was picking her way across the ground that separated the house from the privy, her skirts lifted high with exaggerated care that they not come into contact with the fresh-scythed grass. Even at such a distance she looked exceedingly cross, and even thinner than Jessie remembered.

Celia glanced up then and saw her stepdaughter. Jessie felt some of her precarious happiness fade. She would have ridden away from her stepmother with no more than a token wave, except Celia beckoned. Reluctantly, Jessie reined Firefly toward the wife of the man she loved.

"You look to be in exceptionally high spirits this morning," Celia observed coldly, regarding Jessie with distaste as the younger woman drew rein in front of her. Her face was very pale, and her hair was slightly untidy, which was so unlike Celia that Jessie wondered if she might be ill. And there was something in her tone, some edge that had never been there before. Of course, Celia was habitually unpleasant toward her, her animosity increasing daily as Jessie's looks began to eclipse Celia's own, but still . . .

Could her stepmother possibly know what had passed between her and Stuart during the night?

No, of course not. No one knew, save herself and Stuart. Still, Jessie could not help the tide of guilty color that rose in her cheeks.

"Did you want me for something in particular, Celia?" she asked, hoping to get away before Celia could notice the telltale blush.

"If you run across my husband, as you usually seem to do, I wish you would send him to me. Honestly, the man is never to be found—by me, that is. I understand you manage to find him a good deal." The petty disagreeableness in Celia's voice was no more pronounced than usual, Jessie told herself. For months Celia had been making insinuations about the time and attention Stuart accorded Jessie. Celia's comments were no more than another salvo on the same old front—were they?

"If I run into him, I'll send him to you." Already Jessie was edging Firefly away.

"Oh, I'm sure you'll run into him. You make it a point to, don't you?"

"I'll tell him you want to see him," Jessie said evenly, and turned Firefly toward the road.

"On second thought, don't bother," Celia called after her, malice plain in her voice. "What could be more appropriate than having *you* be the bearer of my good tidings? Just give Stuart a message for me. Tell the randy bastard that he finally got what he wanted: I'm fairly certain I'm with child."

XXXVI

Jessie boarded the *River Queen* early that afternoon. Once she had made up her mind that leaving Mimosa was the only thing she could do under the circumstances, the details had become surprisingly simple. For a while after Celia had blown her world to smithereens Jessie had ridden blindly, sick at heart and stomach, her mind in turmoil. Then, when she forced herself to truly face the realities of the situation, an icy calm descended upon her, and she knew what she had to do. She returned to the house, packed a small valise, and wrote a note, which she left between her coverlet and pillow so that it would not be found until Sissie came by that evening to turn down her bed. Getting out of the house with her valise did not even present the difficulty Jessie had feared it might. The house staff was busy with the usual tasks, and Celia was either in her room or absent from the house altogether, which she usually was during most of the daylight hours. Jessie encountered no one as she left by the front (rather than the back, where she might have run into Tudi or Sissie) stairs.

Money had been the greatest obstacle when she had formulated the determination to leave, but it turned out not to be a problem. At this time of the year everyone, including Graydon Bradshaw, who ordinarily spent most of his working hours in the plantation office, was busy in the fields. The office, a small, separate brick building some way from the main house, was deserted. It was also locked, but Jessie knew where the key was kept. Running her hand along the top of the doorjamb, she found it just where she expected it to be. That key unlocked the door. Once inside, Jessie went straight to where the strongbox, containing enough cash to cover any contingencies that might arise, was concealed beneath a loose plank in the floor. Lifting the board and removing the strongbox was the work of a moment, but like the door, the strongbox was locked. Fortunately the key was in the top drawer of Bradshaw's desk.

The theft was ridiculously easy.

Jessie was careful to return the strongbox to its hiding place and lock up behind her so that no one would be alerted to what had happened until her note was found. Then she mounted Firefly and rode to the landing where the riverboats docked. Getting Firefly safely back home again was another problem, though she could have just turned the little mare loose. Firefly would have returned to her stable before the day was out, but again Jessie did not want to alert anyone at Mimosa to her plan until it was too late to stop her. Fortunately some supplies for the Chandlers were being unloaded. Jessie knew the two Elmway hands who were piling the goods on the wagon. The obvious solution was to ask them to tie Firefly to the back of their wagon and convey her to Elmway for the day.

"You goin' on a trip, Miss Jessie?" one of the men, George, asked her in some surprise as he accepted Firefly's reins.

"Yes, indeed. I'm going to Natchez for a spell. Doesn't that sound lovely?" Jessie hoped that the gaiety in her voice didn't sound as forced to George's ears as it did to her own.

"It does, Miss Jessie. You got your girl Sissie with you?"

Half the bucks in the valley were sniffing around Sissie's skirts. Jessie made a mental note to talk to Stuart about finding the girl a husband amongst the people at Mimosa before she could lose her heart to someone from another plantation, which could cause endless complications. Only as the thought was filed away did Jessie remember that she was leaving, and thus would not have the opportunity to talk to Stuart about anything, much less Sissie's love life, for a very long time.

Anguish smote her even as she lied brightly for George's benefit.

"She's already gone aboard. I'll tell her you asked after her, shall I?"

"You do that, Miss Jessie."

With a pat for Firefly and a wave for George, Jessie headed up the gangplank. She had a bad moment then, since it occurred to her that she had not the least idea how to go about securing passage. Fortunately the captain was more concerned with his cargo than his passengers, and seemed to require no more than payment to let her aboard. After the money changed hands, and she was walking along the deck with a key to her cabin in her hand, Jessie allowed herself a moment of relief. Funny, wasn't it, how terribly easy it was to tear one's life up by the roots?

Except for her trip to Jackson with Miss Flora and Miss Laurel, Jessie had never traveled. If she hadn't been so sick at heart over Stuart, she would almost have enjoyed the journey downriver. The Yazoo River had never seemed to her particularly small, but when the *River Queen* churned out of the tributary into the vast muddy waters of the Mississippi, Jessie was awed by the sheer grandness of it. Boats of every size and description chugged up and down the huge waterway. Along the silty banks activity flourished.

When the *River Queen* docked briefly at Vicksburg,
Jessie moved off the deck and returned to her cabin.
Ladies rarely traveled alone, and to do so left her
open to insult. One or two gentlemen on board had
already eyed her in a fashion she could not like. It
would be best to keep to her cabin as much as possible until the *River Queen* reached her final destination of New Orleans. She could use the time to
plan what she would do when she finally had to
disembark. The eight hundred dollars she had ap-
propriated from the strongbox would not last forever.

It was conceivable that she might at some point
have to find paid employment, but as what? And
how did one go about securing a position, anyway?
Panic threatened to swamp Jessie as it became clearer
by the moment just how very sheltered her life had
been, but she refused to give in to it. If she was ill
equipped to make her own way in the world, well,
she would just have to learn how best to go about
things. Somehow, some way, she would manage,
because she had to. She was young, healthy, intelligent, and unafraid of hard work. So why should
the world beyond the safe confines of Mimosa seem
so overwhelming?

Of course she could always send to Mimosa for
funds. Jessie had a strong feeling that Celia would
pay handsomely to keep her despised stepdaughter
from returning home. But it was a step that she
hoped she would not have to take. Sending for
funds meant that she would have to reveal her
whereabouts to the folks at home. As sure as God
made little green apples, someone from Mimosa
would come after her—and that someone would
probably be Stuart.

Jessie didn't think she could face Stuart again. Not
without falling into his arms and begging him to take
her home. As the *River Queen* steamed farther from
Mimosa, Jessie felt her resolve falter more than once.
Night fell, and homesickness reared its ugly head,

made far worse by the knowledge that she couldn't, ever, go home.

As sleep refused to come and Jessie tossed and turned in her bunk, the only thing that kept her from turning around and heading for home as soon as dawn broke the sky was the knowledge that in leaving Mimosa, and Stuart, she had done the right thing. The only thing.

Celia was Stuart's wife, whether any of the three parties most closely concerned was pleased with the fact or not. There was no magic solution that would make all come right. Now that the line had been breached and Stuart had become her lover, all the ingredients for disaster were in place. Add to that the child Celia expected—whether or not it was Stuart's, and the possibility that it was not was something that had occurred to Jessie early on—and one thing became perfectly clear: there was no room for Jessie at Mimosa.

Whether or not she loved Stuart, or he loved her, didn't matter. Celia was his wife, and Celia was expecting a child that would be raised as his. The only thing that Jessie could possibly do under the circumstances was take herself out of the picture.

If she had not already lain with Stuart, she would have wed Mitch without delay and thus put herself permanently beyond Stuart's reach. But she *had* lain with Stuart, given him her maidenhead as well as her love, so that option was closed to her. She would not go to Mitch as soiled goods. The only remaining solution was to build a life for herself away from Mimosa, however much her heart bled to leave it.

Though what that life would be she had not, at the moment, the least idea.

Her heart ached as she tried to force it to accept the truth that, in renouncing Stuart, she renounced everyone and everything she loved: Tudi, Sissie, Rosa, Progress, Firefly and Jasper, Mimosa. . . .

Tears stung Jessie's eyes as, one by one, the beloved faces appeared in her mind's eye. Stuart she

tried not to picture at all, but in the end she lost the
fight. She saw him in scores of different poses: the
handsome stranger whom she had hated on sight,
when he'd come to Mimosa as Celia's fiancé; her
first sight of him in a black temper, after she had
told him that Celia was a whore; Stuart being kind
to her that long-ago evening in the garden at Tulip
Hill, when she'd wanted to die from sheer humiliation; how unbelievably handsome he had looked in
his formal clothes at his wedding; the arrested look
on his face when he had seen her in the yellow
dress, his gift to her; the first time he had kissed
her. The image of him as she had seen him last arose
and stubbornly refused to be banished: Stuart, smiling tenderly at her when he had tucked her into bed
just the night before, those sky-blue eyes that she
knew she would remember until the end of her days
aglow with love for her. . . .

Finally the tears that had been pooling in her eyes
burst forth to roll down her cheeks. For once she
didn't even try to stop the flow. With a sob she
turned on her stomach, buried her face in the pillow, and cried until there were no tears left. When
the deluge was over, she was utterly exhausted. Her
eyes burned, her nose was stopped up so that she
could scarcely breathe, and still her heart ached.
Tears helped nothing, as she had learned long ago
and should have remembered. Curling into a ball of
misery, Jessie at long last fell into an exhausted
sleep.

Jessie stayed in her cabin until the *River Queen*
docked at Natchez early the following afternoon.
Despite her soggy wretchedness of the night before,
she had risen early and dressed in a gown of
emerald-green broadcloth with befrilled, elbow-
length white sleeves, a fitted bodice, and a full skirt
trimmed with bows and ruffles about the hem. The
gown bared her shoulders in the fashionable mode,
yet it was still modest and well suited for travel.

She'd brushed her hair, pinned it atop her head—
and sat down in the cabin's one chair. There she had
remained, watching the passing river through the
small square porthole that afforded her an excellent
view, until the *River Queen* steamed into port and
maneuvered into position between two other steam-
boats that made the *River Queen* look small in comparison. Finally, as ropes were thrown to men
standing ready on a vast wooden wharf, and hordes
of people swarmed over the wharf toward the boat,
Jessie put on her hat with its huge upstanding brim
and left her cabin. Surely, amidst all the excitement,
no one would harass or even notice one young lady
traveling on her own.

As she threaded her way through the crowd
thronging the upper deck, Jessie realized that she
was hungry. Perhaps she might disembark briefly
and purchase something to eat from one of the
quayside carts of the type she had seen in Vicksburg. The *River Queen* had a dining room, but Jessie
had not yet summoned up the courage to visit it.
The intricacies of ordering a meal in a public dining
room, coupled with the fact that she would have to
eat alone, were something that she felt inadequate
to deal with, at least for the present. Although she
would have to, of course, sooner or later. She would
have to learn to do many things for and by herself.

"Hey, missy, need somebody to show ya the
sights?" The speaker was a man, fortyish, wearing
the gaudiest waistcoat Jessie had ever seen. It was
of silk, with bold red-and-white stripes, and nearly
succeeded in distracting her attention from the in-
gratiating grin on his florid countenance as he approached her. Averting her face as soon as she could
tear her eyes away from the ridiculous waistcoat,
Jessie hurried along the deck without replying.
When she reached the gangplank she looked over
her shoulder and was relieved to see that she was
not being followed.

The gangplank was used for both boarding and

disembarking, while another gangplank at the stern
of the boat was used for cargo. There was a crush of
people moving in both directions on the passenger
gangplank, so progress toward the dock was nec-
essarily slow. Jessie found herself squashed between
a stout, well-dressed elderly lady carrying a parasol,
who was hard of hearing, judging from the volume
of the remarks shouted at her by her less-well-
dressed female companion; and a flashy couple who
had eyes for no one but each other as they inched
their way toward the quay arm in arm.

"It ain't safe for a young lady such as yerself to
sashay around Natchez by her lonesome. Harley
Bowen, at your service."

Jessie was horrified as the man in the gaudy waistcoat squeezed around the flashy couple to pop up
beside her with a triumphant smile. Hoping that if
she ignored him he would take the hint and leave
her alone, she quickly turned away.

"You're a real looker, aren't you, sweetheart? But
you don't need to put on that cold face with Harley
Bowen. Ain't never been a female yet that wasn't
safe with me."

Jessie cast him a desperate glance out of the corner
of her eye. She had no reason to be frightened of
the man, not out here surrounded by people, but
dealing with a fellow of his stamp was something
she'd never had occasion to do. Still hoping that if
she ignored him he would give up and go away, she
lifted her chin and fixed her eyes firmly on the ebb
and flow of the crowd along the wharf.

"There's some places under the hill that I'd sure
like to show you."

Jessie's feet moved slowly forward along with everyone else's as she tried to affect both deafness and
blindness to the dreadful creature who pestered her.
The *River Queen* was only one of the many steam-
boats tied up along the dock, she saw. A great deal
of the hustle and bustle at quayside was caused by
boisterous dockhands loading cotton. The iron

wheels of the cotton wagons rolling over the uneven boards of the wharf resulted in a constant clatter. The dockhands' frequently profane shouts to one another added to the din. Vendors hawking their wares from portable carts, and friends and relatives of arriving passengers pushing through the crowds to call to their loved ones, combined with the rest to create general bedlam. From a large paddle wheeler just docking farther down came a sudden burst of gay calliope music. Jessie had to fight the urge to put her hands over her ears.

"So what do you say, pretty thing?" Harley Bowen persisted, and had the audacity to actually put a hand on her elbow.

That brought Jessie's head jerking around. "Take your hand off me," she hissed, tired of pondering the correct way to deal with the situation. Ladylike reticence had never been one of her virtues, and she saw no reason to practice it on the lout beside her!

Harley Bowen's nearly lashless gray eyes widened as she turned on him. Instead of dropping, his hand tightened on her arm. "Oh-ho! Hoity-toity, ain't we? Be careful of your tone, missy. I ain't a man to tolerate no snot-nosed females."

"Take your hand off my arm!"

"Are you having problems, dear?" The primly dressed companion of the hard-of-hearing lady looked around to inquire. Gray-haired beneath a hat that resembled a flattened pancake, and much thinner than the lady she accompanied, this woman was clearly not the sort to stand much nonsense. Glancing at her, Jessie was reminded of the Latow children's stern governess. Jessie half expected her to smack Mr. Bowen's encroaching hand.

"Well . . ." Jessie was reluctant to involve a stranger in her difficulties, but she was growing less confident by the second of her ability to deal with the situation on her own. The hand on her elbow tightened.

"Mind your own business, old woman," Harley Bowen snarled.

"Indeed! An innocent young lady being molested is the business of any God-fearing citizen, sirrah!"

The stout woman turned to look as her companion bristled and exchanged glares with Mr. Bowen.

"What is the matter, Cornelia? You know how I dislike loud voices." The words were trumpeted.

"This . . . gentleman—and I use the term advisedly!—is pestering this young lady, Martha." Cornelia voiced the disclosure in tones loud enough to make Jessie want to sink through the floor—or, in this case, gangplank.

"Is he?" Martha looked interested as her gaze swept from Mr. Bowen to Jessie, who was trying without success to pull her elbow from his hold. They had almost reached the end of the gangplank, Jessie saw with relief. Once she was free of this crush of people, perhaps she could rid herself of Mr. Bowen without causing the dreadful scene she feared was imminent.

But what if she couldn't?

"Who asked you to stick your spoon in, you old lard bucket?"

Martha's hearing was apparently good enough to catch that. Her mouth popped open and her eyes bulged with outrage. Before Jessie or Mr. Bowen or anyone else had any inkling of what she meant to do, Martha brought her parasol down with a crack on Mr. Bowen's head.

"Oh! Help! Bitch!" Mr. Bowen howled, throwing his arms up to ward off the blows that proceeded to rain down upon his head. Staggering backward, he knocked against the flashy couple. The lady stumbled and fell against the rope railing.

"Henry! Help!"

"Why, you . . . !" The lady's gentleman friend caught her with one hand and turned on Mr. Bowen menacingly at almost the same moment.

"I'll teach you to call people names!" With her

befrilled parasol, Martha was the very image of an
avenging fury.

"Get him, Martha!" Cornelia was practically
jumping up and down as she egged Martha on.

Just as the altercation seemed about to explode
into a free-for-all, Jessie reached the end of the gangplank and the combatants spewed out upon the
wharf, propelled by the people behind them. Caught
up in the ebb and flow of emerging humanity, Jessie
felt her arm grabbed again.

But Mr. Bowen, face purple with rage as he advanced on Martha, who was regarding him like a
prize fighter ready to take on all comers, was in front
of her. Surely she was not being accosted by another—?

Jessie looked around. As she identified her assail-
ant, her face paled even as her heartbeat quickened.

"What the bloody hell is going on here?" Stuart
demanded.

XXXVII

Loath as she was to admit it even to herself, Jessie's first reaction when she saw Stuart was pure, unadulterated joy. Her heart pounded, her lips curved into a smile, and it was all she could do not to throw herself into his arms. He looked very much the gentleman planter in a tall black top hat, a black frock coat, and a buff-colored pair of the new, fashionable trousers that were beginning to replace breeches for everyday wear. The bright afternoon sunlight picked up blue glints in the black hair that curled beneath his hat. Long hours in the fields had darkened the color of his skin to a deep bronze, making his eyes seem more vividly blue than ever in contrast. Tall, broad-shouldered, and narrow-hipped, he was so handsome that even Martha stopped ranting to goggle at him. Jessie barely managed to restrain herself from throwing her arms around his neck, but in a very few minutes all the reasons why she must not be glad to see him flooded back.

With Stuart's arrival on the scene, the squabble almost resolved itself. Taking one look at the size and style of the gentleman who clearly had prior claim to the object of his fancy, Mr. Bowen took himself off. The flashy couple followed suit. Deprived of her prey, Martha was prepared to accept

Stuart's thanks for her intervention on Jessie's be-
half when the disjointed tale was explained to him.
Cornelia, with a monitory sniff, looked Stuart up and
down. Unlike Martha, she was not to be bamboozled by a handsome face and good manners, and
said so.

"Will you be all right with this one, dear?" Cornelia asked Jessie, ignoring the fact that Stuart was
standing right beside her, his hand still curled
around Jessie's arm.

"Oh, yes, ma'am. Thank you."

"Very well, then. Shall we be on our way, Martha? You must be dying for a cool drink after all that
exertion."

"Well, you know I am. But did you see the way
that rudesby scurried off? I imagine he'll think twice
before he insults another lady!"

"Indeed, so do I! You gave a most impressive account of yourself."

The two ladies were still vivaciously discussing the
particulars of Martha's schooling of Mr. Bowen
when they moved out of earshot. Stuart's hand on
her arm pulled Jessie in the opposite direction. Only
when they reached a tiny park just beyond the hub-
bub of the wharf did he stop. An iron bench was
located under one of the three trees in the park. Stuart pushed her down upon it and stood over her.
Jessie had to crane her neck to look up at him.

"Now, then," he said, crossing his arms over his
chest. Jessie saw that the urbane smile with which
he had soothed Martha and Cornelia had quite faded
away. His sky-blue eyes were angry, his mouth
grim. "Suppose you tell me just what you hoped to
gain from this damn-fool escapade. I had to leave
Gray and Pharaoh to do the work of four men to
come after you, and for all I broke my neck getting
here, it appears that I barely made it in time. There
are places in Natchez where a young lady could step
over the threshold and never be heard from again,
and from the looks of things when I arrived, you

were about to discover one of them firsthand. Good God, Jess, do you have any idea what could have happened to you? No, of course you don't. God save me from women who haven't cut their eyeteeth yet!''

This last he uttered in such a savage undertone that Jessie realized he'd been frightened for her. The knowledge was all that saved him from a blast of her temper by way of reply.

"Are you quite finished?" Jessie was proud of the evenness of her rejoinder.

"No, I sure as hell am not!" He fished in his pocket and produced a crumpled wad of paper, which he waved at her. "This, I'm assuming, is garbage?''

Jessie recognized the note that she'd left to explain her departure. Since it said that she couldn't bear to hurt Mitch by refusing his offer outright, but she couldn't marry him either, and thus was taking an extended trip in the hope that he would forget about her by the time she returned, the note might rightly have been described as ''garbage.''

"What did you want me to write? The truth?''

"Exactly what is the truth? Pray enlighten me." Stuart was speaking through his teeth. The hand that held her note clenched into a fist, crumpling the paper again.

"Celia is with child.''

"If she is, it isn't mine.''

"Whether it's yours or not is not the point. The point is that I—that you—that Celia is your wife, not I.''

"Very elucidating." It was a sneer. He was very good at sneering, and it maddened Jessie when he did it.

"You know what I mean!''

"No, I don't. The last time I saw you—and very lovely you looked, too—it seems to me that we pledged our love and sealed the bond most thoroughly. Or is my memory faulty?''

"You know why I left as well as I do, so stop pretending you don't!" The outburst was so loud that several people passing on the cobbled street turned their heads toward them. Jessie lowered her voice to a hiss. "Did you really think we could go on as before, after that? Oh, I see, you thought you'd have a wife in the parlor and a mistress in the barn! How very cozy!"

His eyes narrowed. "Sarcasm doesn't become you, Jess."

"Sneering doesn't become you, either, but you do it often enough!"

Angry, she jumped up from the bench, brushed past him, and stalked out of the park and down the street toward town, the wide feather that curled up over the brim of her hat bobbing indignantly as she walked.

"Jessie." Stuart was behind her. Jessie's nose lifted higher in the air as she deliberately ignored him.

"Jess!" He caught her arm. She whirled on him so fast that her skirts swirled and a few inches of lace-trimmed white petticoat were revealed, attracting more glances from passersby.

"Just go away! Go back to the wife you married for her money and the child that you might or might not have fathered, and leave me alone!"

"If Celia is with child, which is open to doubt, it can't possibly be mine. I haven't lain with her since two weeks after our wedding."

"Hush!" As the sound of a shocked gasp behind her penetrated her rage, Jessie all at once became aware that they were the cynosure of half a dozen pairs of eyes. Cheeks pinkening, she frowned fiercely at Stuart, then glanced meaningfully around, hoping to silence him.

"My taste doesn't run to whores, whether I'm married to them or not."

"Stuart!"

Two ladies exchanged shocked glances, lifted their

noses, and hurried past. A couple slowed down to
listen, their eyes avid. Excruciatingly aware of the
growing audience, Jessie, her face becoming more
pink, tried without success to get Stuart to look
around.

"You love me, Jess. And I love you."

"Would you please look around you?"

Her anguished moan must have penetrated, because, finally, he did look around. As he saw the
small crowd of onlookers who had slowed down or
stopped altogether to gawk, he stiffened. Under the
glare of his icy blue eyes the passersby immediately
began to move on.

Stuart's hand tightened on her arm, and he turned
her around. Jessie found herself being marched back
toward the wharf.

"Where do you think you're taking me?"

"Where we can have a little privacy. You have a
cabin on the *River Queen*, right? We'll finish this discussion there."

With the memory of the crowd their quarrel had
attracted still fresh, Jessie bit her tongue and let him
drag her aboard the *River Queen*. She tried to look
marginally pleasant as Stuart hurried her along the
deck in the direction she reluctantly indicated. They
didn't attract any undue attention, for which she was
thankful.

Stuart stopped outside her cabin door and held
out his hand. "Key." Jessie extracted it from her
reticule and held it out to him without a word. He
opened the door, ushered her inside, pocketed the
key as if he owned it, and closed the door again,
leaning against it as he eyed her.

Jessie crossed to the opposite side of the small
cabin, where she had spent the morning sitting in
the sole chair, and turned to face him with the width
of the room between them.

"I'm not going back to Mimosa." Her voice was
very quiet.

"That's the most ridiculous statement I've ever

heard in my life. You damned well are going back to Mimosa. It's your home. You love the cursed place."

"Nevertheless, I can't go back there. How can I, feeling about you the way I do?"

He swore. The succinct profanity brought color to Jessie's cheeks, but she did not look away from him.

"There's no need to swear."

"I'll swear if I feel like it. And I damned well feel like it."

He broke off, scowling, then took a deep breath and pulled the cheroot case out of his pocket. Extracting a cigar from the case and lighting it was the work of just a few moments, but it gave him enough time to think.

"Did it ever occur to you that we could go away together? The two of us?" The question was carefully casual, but the almost nervous way he puffed on the cigar belied his tone.

It took a minute for that to filter through. Jessie's eyes widened. "You would leave Mimosa?" A wealth of disbelief colored her voice.

"What a pretty opinion you have of me! Yes, I would leave Mimosa. With you."

"You married Celia to get it."

"It was a mistake. I should have known that nothing on earth was that easy."

"Are you actually suggesting that we should—run away—together?" Jessie practically held her breath.

"Why not?" He smiled then, a roguish smile that gave him a devilish charm.

"And never go back? What about Tudi, and Sissie, and Progress, oh, and your aunts . . . ?"

"We'd write them every week." He was flippant, but Jessie was starting to believe that he meant it.

"How would we live?"

"Don't you trust me to support you?"

"You'd still be married to Celia."

"Maybe we could change that, somewhere along the line."

"You mean you'd try to get a divorce?"

"Something of that nature. What do you say, Jess? Shall we run away together?"

"Think of the scandal."

"Why? We wouldn't be there to see it."

"Oh, Stuart." She was tempted, so horribly tempted. She'd been prepared to give up everything for him, but it was almost more than she could bear that he should give up everything for her.

He took a last drag on his cheroot, dropped it to the floor, and ground it out with the toe of his boot. Then he crossed to stand in front of her, throwing his hat on the bunk on the way.

"Well, Jessie? Will you give up your home, and your friends, and all the rest of it for love?"

"That's what I was doing. Only I never thought you'd want to come along, too." Her reply was almost inaudible. Her eyes were wide as saucers as she looked up into his face.

"Is that a yes?" He took her hands. Jessie felt the warmth and strength of his fingers as they curled around her suddenly cold ones.

"Stuart, are you sure?"

"Am *I* sure? Jess, anything I'm giving up was never really mine. It's you who will be sacrificing home, and friends, and security."

"None of that means anything, without you."

He smiled then, warmly, tenderly, and pulled her closer. "That's precisely how I feel," he bent his head to whisper, and then he was kissing her mouth.

XXXVIII

Jessie wrapped her arms around his neck and clung with such fervor that after a moment he lifted his head and laughingly protested that she was strangling him.

Then, looking down into her face, he saw something that chased the laughter away and made his eyes narrow.

"Tears, Jess?" he whispered, and reached up to wipe the telltale moisture from her cheeks with his thumb.

"I thought I—would never see you again," Jessie confessed, leaning her forehead against his shoulder so that he could not see the tears that persisted in squeezing past her closed lids.

"I'm harder to lose than a bad penny. Besides, you should have known that I would come after you. Did you think I would just let you go?"

"I thought you'd stay—at Mimosa."

"You thought I'd choose Mimosa over you." There was censure in his tone.

"You married for it."

"I wasn't in love then. I am now." His hand beneath her chin coaxed her head up until he could see her face. "Crazy in love, Jessie."

"You must be, if you're willing to give up Mimosa." That inspired her to assay a shaken laugh, which was immediately followed by more tears. Stuart groaned, gathered her up in his arms, and sat in the hard-backed chair with her on his lap. Jessie let him settle her against him and attempted to hide her face in his neck, only to be thwarted by the wide brim of her hat.

"Don't tell me you're going to turn into a watering pot. I can't abide females who cry." But his hands were gentle as he removed the pin from her hat and tossed it on the bed to join his, then pushed her head down to lie against his shoulder.

"I'm sorry." She swallowed a sob, and immediately hiccuped.

"That's all right." He turned his head to kiss her mouth again even as his hands explored the intricate swirls of her hair in search of pins. "I'm prepared to make an exception—for you."

"Have you had many women, Stuart?" His remark about "females who cry" had awakened her curiosity about any other who might have wept on him.

"What a question!" He removed the last of the pins from her hair. It fell around them like a sable cloak. Stuart smoothed the tumbled mass with a stroking hand.

"Have you?"

He sighed. "A few, Jessie. I'm almost thirty years old, and I stopped being a virgin about the time, I reckon, that you were learning to walk. But I've never taken a woman who wasn't willing, and I've never loved any of them. Until now."

"Is that the truth?" She sat up to regard him suspiciously.

"On my honor." He held up his hand as though to take an oath, a grin twisting his mouth. "Good God, I've got a feeling you're the jealous type."

"I think I must be." Jessie said it quite seriously as she settled back against his shoulder. "I hate the idea of you with anyone else. You're mine."

Stuart turned suddenly serious, too. "I won't

cheat on you, Jessie, and I won't lie to you. I'll take good care of you, I promise. You won't have what you had at Mimosa, but you won't be in want. I've got a little money put away. And I can make more."

Jessie sat up again as a dreadful thought occurred to her. "Oh, do you think that Miss Flora and Miss Laurel will be so shocked by what we've done that they'll write you out of their wills?"

"It's very likely." Stuart's voice was extremely dry.

"You're giving up so much. . . ."

"But I'm gaining you, and you're what I want. Now hush your blather, woman, and kiss me. All the squirming around you're doing has made me randy as a goat."

"Stuart! How crude!"

"You'll have to get used to it, and all my other bad habits, too."

"Gladly." The word was muffled by his mouth. Jessie twined her arms around his neck and kissed him back. When his mouth left hers to move along the line of her shoulder, bared by her dress, she made a sound much like the purr of a contented kitten.

"I don't like you showing so much skin in public." It was a growl as his mouth traced the neckline of her bodice.

"This gown is perfectly modest," Jessie protested.

"If you say so. In future I'll take you shopping for your clothes. My aunts apparently have a pretty broad view of what's proper for a lady." As he spoke his fingers found the hooks at the back of her bodice and began to undo them, one by one.

"If this gown was any more proper, I'd be covered from my chin to my ankles!"

"That," said Stuart with a wicked grin, "is precisely what I had in mind. In public."

And with that he tugged her bodice down. Beneath it was a filmy chemise and lace corset cover.

Stuart looked at them—and the flesh they revealed as much as concealed—with interest. Jessie flushed rosily, but made no move to hide herself from his gaze.

"But in private," he continued after a moment, during which his eyes feasted on the creamy tops of her breasts, which swelled out of her chemise, "in private I may never let you wear any clothes at all. I may just keep you naked."

With that he stood up with her, and set her on her feet. Her dress, already unfastened, dropped to the floor with a rustle. Jessie stepped out of it and kicked it aside.

"Very pretty," Stuart said approvingly as he surveyed her in her underwear. He reached out to hook his hands beneath both straps of her chemise and slide them down her arms until her breasts were completely revealed.

"But that's even prettier," he finished in a husky whisper, and lifted his hands to fondle her breasts. Jessie's knees went weak. She swayed toward him, her eyes closing. He squeezed her breasts, dropped a quick, hard kiss on her mouth—and with his hands on her shoulders turned her away from him.

"Stuart . . ."

"We're going to do it the way it should be done this time: slow and easy and in a bed. Hold still a minute. These laces are in a knot."

He was fumbling with the tapes to her stays. Jessie caught her breath at the image his words conjured up, and had to grab hold of the back of the chair to steady herself. Her eyes closed, then opened again as he freed her stays and tossed them aside.

After that, it was the work of a minute to rid her of her petticoats. Then he turned her around to face him again and lifted her chemise over her head.

Jessie was left standing naked in front of him except for her garter-tied stockings, which ended at her thighs, and her pointed-toed shoes. His hand came out to sweep aside the thick fall of hair that partially covered her. Then, for a long moment, he simply stood there and stared.

"You are the loveliest thing I've ever seen in my life," he murmured, and knelt at her feet.

For just a moment Jessie stared blankly down at his wavy dark head. Then his hand circled her silk-clad ankle, lifted her foot from the floor, and slid from it her elegant new shoe. She balanced on her stockinged foot as he repeated the treatment with the other one. Then his eyes—and hands—lifted, to slide slowly over her calves, her knees, her thighs.

Jessie quivered as his fingers, untying her garters, brushed against the smooth bare skin between her legs. With his head bent so that she could feel his warm breath against her thighs, his expression was hidden from her. But Jessie could feel the quickening of his breathing, the slight unsteadiness of his fingers as he rolled her stockings down her legs, first one and then the other, and tossed them aside.

She expected him to get to his feet. But still he stayed on his knees before her. Her heart began to pound as he lifted his head and she saw that his eyes had heated to pure blue flames.

Naked, she stood before him, unresisting as his hands slid back up her legs to curve around the back of her thighs. He pulled her toward him, and for all that she loved him, for all the passion that was rising in her as swiftly as sap in a young tree, she started in shocked surprise when he pressed his face to the curly triangle of hair at the apex of her thighs.

"Stuart, no!"

Her fingers twined in his hair and tugged as she looked down, wide-eyed with horror, at his face snuggled so intimately against her. But instead of heeding her, he pulled her legs slightly apart. Jessie was about to protest more vehemently when she felt something warm and wet touch her in that secret place between her legs.

His tongue! He was touching her there with his

tongue! Jessie tried once to pull away, but he held her fast. Then she no longer wanted to escape, no longer had the will to do anything but clutch his hair and moan as he took his pleasure of her with his tongue and mouth.

At some point, just when Jessie was sure her knees would not support her any longer, he backed her up to the bunk and pushed her gently down upon it. Without knowing quite how it happened, she found herself flat on her back with her legs extending over the sides of the mattress. As his mouth left her briefly, modesty threatened to surface and she tried to close her legs. He stroked them apart, knowing just where to touch her to send shooting stars of pleasure sizzling through her veins, dazzling her so that she scarcely realized when he lifted her thighs to rest on his shoulders while her feet hung down his back. Then his face was nuzzling its way between her legs again and he was kissing her there.

Jessie thought she would die with the sheer, shameful pleasure of it.

Then he took her past the point of shame, took her to where the only thing that mattered was the exquisite tremors that racked her body, took her to where she sobbed and moaned his name without even realizing that she did so.

Finally his hands reached up to fondle her breasts, rubbing her nipples between the thumb and forefinger of each hand while he worked his special brand of magic between her legs, and he took her farther yet.

Sensation exploded inside her like a too tightly packed charge of gunpowder. Jessie cried out, writhing, her nails digging deep into the nubby coverlet that was twisted half on and half off the bed.

While she was still floating back to earth, he stood up, lifted her in his arms, stripped the tangled coverlet and top sheet back, and placed her properly in the bed. Jessie felt the smooth coolness of a pillow beneath her crimsoning cheek, but she kept her eyes tightly closed. She was too embarrassed to open them.

The memory of what he'd done, and the disgraceful way she had responded, were searing themselves permanently into her brain. It was quite possible that she would never again be able to look him in the face. A lady would never moan, or squirm, or—or permit him to do such a thing in the first place.

Clearly she was no lady, but a shameless, abandoned hussy. She wished she were dead.

"Jessie."

Still her eyes refused to open.

"I thought you'd like that."

She shuddered.

"If you don't open your eyes and look at me, I'm going to do it again."

That threat, uttered in a purposeful tone, served the purpose. Jessie's eyes shot open. Stuart was standing by the bed, still fully dressed even to his coat. The slight disorder of his hair was the only visible sign that he had been as much a party to what had happened as she. He was smiling faintly, his eyes possessive as they moved from her face to run over her body. Jessie realized then that she lay atop the sheet, naked as a babe, with nothing at all to shield her from his eyes. Jackknifing into a sitting position, she grabbed the top sheet from where he'd tossed it to the foot of the bunk and jerked it up around her chin.

"Shy, Jess?" He was chuckling at her even as he shrugged out of his coat. Jessie realized that it was the middle of the afternoon, broad daylight was streaming in through the small window that overlooked the river, and any secrets her body might once have held for him were secret no longer. He must have seen everything, places even she herself had never glimpsed, private places that no one should see. The thought made her crimson anew.

She could feel the heat of the blush spreading over her from the top of her head to the tips of her toes.

"Don't worry, we'll get you over it."

If that was meant to be comforting, it was not. Before Jessie could assure him that she didn't *want* to get over it, that she never had any intention of doing anything again that would require she be over it, it occurred to her that he had removed his cravat and was in the process of unbuttoning his shirt.

"What are you doing?" There was squeaky disbelief in her voice. Surely he didn't intend to . . .

"Taking off my clothes." He sat on the edge of the bed to pull off his boots. Jessie stared with reluctant fascination at his broad bare back. As he tugged at his boots, the muscles flexed and bulged beneath his skin. Her hand stretched out to touch that back, but she recollected herself in time and snatched her hand away.

"You surely don't mean to—"

"I told you we were going to do it slow and easy and in a bed. The other was just to take the edge off. I don't want you scratching up my back." He was grinning at her as he stood up to slide his trousers down his legs. Then he was naked, and climbing into bed.

XXXIX

Jessie did scratch up his back, after all. She never would have believed that he could arouse her to that degree of passion so soon after the other, but he did. And as to taking it slow and easy—it started out that way, but the finish was quite otherwise. It was hard, and fast, and glorious—and exhausting.

For some time afterward neither of them moved. Stuart lay sprawled out on his back with Jessie cuddled against his side. They dozed, and half woke to mutter love words, then dozed again. By the time Jessie opened her eyes with some real degree of wakefulness, long shadows filled the cabin. Beyond the porthole what she could see of the sky was a magnificent panoply of orange and gold.

From the feel of things, the *River Queen* was under way.

"Stuart!"

Jessie sat up, shaking the hair from her face and clutching the sheet to her breast. Turning to look at Stuart, she discovered that her instinct toward modesty had left him fully exposed. Stretched out on his back with his arms lifted above his head, he was a stirring sight. Jessie regretted that she had so little time to admire it.

"Stuart! Wake up! We're moving!"

"Moving!"

That opened his eyes. He sat up, shook his head to clear it, and looked around as his eyes widened. Clearly he was digesting the unmistakable evidence of movement, just as she had.

"Looks like I'll be traveling kind of light, this trip," he said, and fell back against the mattress, grinning.

"But—but you don't even have a change of clothes! Or anything!"

"Don't worry. It's not the first time I've found myself in this situation. Although usually such a paucity of possessions has been the result of my having to get out of a particular place in a hurry. Oh, well, the inn where I have a room bespoke will likely hold my clothes until I return, and if they don't—" He shrugged. "Clothes aren't hard to come by. In the meantime, I'll be rinsing my linen out at night and putting it on damp in the morning. I've done it before."

"What about Saber? You did ride Saber, didn't you?"

"I started out on Saber, but he threw a shoe just south of Vicksburg. I left him at a stable there, and hired a job horse that is presently eating its head off in the stable behind the inn where I meant to stay the night. I rode all last night, so I am somewhat lacking in sleep, which accounts for the fact that I dozed off. You led me quite a dance, my darling."

"Are you sorry?" The question was quiet.

"No. Hell, no. What's one of the richest cotton plantations in Mississippi compared to a redheaded chit whose blood is as hot as her hair? I'll take a hot woman over riches any day."

He was teasing her. That had the idiotic effect of reassuring Jessie completely. She lifted her nose in the air. "I do not," she said with dignity, "have red hair."

"Oh, yes, you do." The grin he gave her was wicked. "And not only on your head. Down—"

"That's enough!" Jessie stopped him, scandalized, but she had to grin back at him in the face of his amusement. "Your civilized veneer is slipping, Mr. Edwards."

His eyes flickered at that. "Now, truer words were never spoken," he muttered obscurely.

When Jessie would have questioned the meaning of that, he reached for her and dragged her down to lie beside him.

"You always smell so good," he whispered in her ear, and then he was kissing her mouth.

If Jessie's stomach had not interrupted with a loud, rumbling growl, he would have done more than kiss her. But at the incongruous sound he lifted his head to look at her in surprise.

"I'm starving," she said plaintively, and evaded his arms to sit up. This time she didn't bother with the sheet, and his eyes feasted on her rosy-tipped breasts.

"Me, too," he answered, and would have pulled her back down again if she hadn't slid off the bed. This time she did take the sheet with her.

"No, I mean it," she insisted, wrapping the sheet around her as she padded to where her valise awaited with a change of clothes. "I haven't had anything to eat since—my goodness, since breakfast yesterday."

"Why didn't you go down to the dining room? They have one, you know."

"I didn't like to eat all by myself. I kept thinking that someone would think it was odd, that I was traveling alone. Besides, I don't quite know how—the only time I ever ate in a public dining room was when Miss Laurel and Miss Flora took me to Jackson, and they handled everything."

"Good God." Stuart sat up again and swung his long legs over the side of the bunk. He stood up, not a whit bothered by his nakedness in her presence, and walked over to the pitcher and bowl in the corner, where he proceeded to sluice his face with water. Jessie watched his buttocks with a great

deal of interest. She already knew that they were
sleek and hard to the touch, but this was the first
good view she had had of them. Nice, she decided,
very nice.

He turned, caught her looking at him, and grinned
at her as she blushed and turned away. "Let's get
some food into you. I'd hate to have you waste away
into nothingness. I like my women to be shaped like
women."

Jessie struggled to dress while keeping the sheet
modestly around her, but it was difficult. Stuart finished long before she did and stood watching her
with a grin playing at the corners of his mouth. Finally, exasperated, she dropped the chemise she'd
been struggling to pull over her head and snapped
at him.

"Would you please go for a walk around the deck
or—or something? You're making me nervous."

"You'll have to get used to me."

But he picked up his hat and took himself off. Jessie was able to dress, and take care of other personal
needs, without his disquieting presence.

When at last she emerged, she was wearing a low-
cut gown of deep rose silk that she considered the
most suitable for dinner of those she had brought
with her. Her hair was pinned high atop her head,
and her beaded reticule was clutched in her hand.

Stuart was lounging against the rail just outside
the cabin door, smoking one of his ever-present cheroots. When he saw her, his eyes widened and he
straightened away from the rail, flicking the cheroot
overboard.

"I thought you said you were getting dressed."

"This dress is perfectly proper!"

"Don't you have a shawl or something you could
wear with it?" His eyes slid down to the valley between her breasts, which was visible to him only
because of his height, Jessie thought with annoyance. Still, she could not help tugging at her bodice.
Stuart grinned.

"If you're going to be ridiculous, I'll eat by my-self!" She flounced away from him.

"Grumpy little thing when you're hungry, aren't you? I'll have to be sure to keep you well fed." He caught up with her, captured her hand, lifted it to his lips, and tucked it into the crook of his arm. "You look lovely, Jessie. I like the gown—what there is of it."

"Oh!" She tried to pull her hand free, but he held it in place, chuckling. When she would have hit him with her reticule, he cringed and held up his hand to ward her off.

"I'm only teasing you. Come on, let's eat. I seem to have worked up an appetite myself."

In the interests of satisfying her hunger as expeditiously as possible, Jessie allowed herself to be mollified. When they reached the dining room, she was positively glad of Stuart's presence. She shrank a little closer to his side as they waited to be shown to a table. The room was aglitter with chandeliers and crystal and white tablecloths—and people.

The meal was excellent. Stuart insisted that she try a fancy, French-named dish that turned out to be snails swimming in butter, and laughed uproariously when it arrived and she refused to eat it. To pacify her he ate it himself, and gave her his plain old Mississippi catfish, which she tucked into with relish. Only as she sat back, replete, after the last bite did it occur to Jessie that the aggravating creature had probably meant to switch meals all along. He was much more the snail-eating type than she was.

Stuart drank most of a bottle of wine, though he refused to pour her more than a single glass. It was on the tip of Jessie's tongue to remind him that he was her illicit lover now, not the guardian of her morals, but in the interests of harmony she held her tongue. Later, when a gooey gateau was brought to the table, she was about to refuse when he insisted that she be served a slice.

It was delicious, and left her quite in charity with him again.

The dining room was on the lower deck. As they left, Stuart had a low-voiced conversation with the steward. He was smiling when he returned to where she awaited him by the door.

"How much money do you have with you?" he asked, steering her outside.

"About seven hundred dollars. Why?"

"And I have a little over a thousand. That should be enough."

"For what?" Jessie was thoroughly mystified.

"For increasing our stake. Come on, Jess, and let me broaden your experience a little."

He refused to tell her more, but led her to a small parlor at the bow end of the upper deck. There he knocked on a closed door and was admitted to a smoke-filled room that appeared, at first glance, to be overflowing with gentlemen in various stages of inebriation playing cards.

"Be quiet, stay beside me, and if you should see any cards, try not to give my hand away," he whispered to her as he led her across the room to a table where some kind of card game was apparently just getting started.

"Mind if I join you?" Stuart addressed one of the men at the table.

"You got a thousand?"

"Yes."

"Have a seat, then. Name's Harris, this here's Ben Jones. Don't know the other gent, and don't suppose it matters. He's got a thousand, too."

Stuart pulled out a chair for Jessie behind the one he took, saw her seated, and then appeared to forget all about her. Jessie watched the steady progress of the game for a while, then got bored and allowed her attention to wander. She knew as much about cards as she had known that French dish Stuart had ordered at dinner. But he seemed totally absorbed in the game, which he had obviously played before.

Jessie realized that there was a great deal about Stuart's life before he came to Mimosa that she didn't know.

There were women in the room, Jessie saw, perhaps half a dozen or so, and such women! Dressed in sumptuous gowns of silk and satin that made hers look positively Quakerish, they laughed and tossed back drinks just like the men at the close of a hand, and stood quietly behind the tables during play. Jessie watched them with some interest, wondering if they were females of ill repute. Surely not, but they were certainly very bold in the way they behaved.

Stuart seemed to have some difficulty with his scarred hand when it was his turn to shuffle the cards and deal. Jessie realized that the wound had affected the dexterity of the muscles controlling his fingers to some small but telling degree. He compensated for the injury by holding his cards in his injured hand and making most of the moves necessary for the game with the other. But the cramped position required for him to hold the cards must have strained the muscles, because about half an hour into the game he unobtrusively transferred the cards he was holding to his other hand, and dropped his injured hand below the level of the table. For a moment he flexed his fingers, stretching them wide; then he shook his hand vigorously. Jessie's first instinct was to catch that hand and massage away the spasm in the muscles as she had done once before, but even as the thought occurred to her, she realized that he wouldn't appreciate her mollycoddling in front of a roomful of strangers. So she sat back, and seconds later he resumed play, with no one save herself as witness to the small byplay with his hand.

"You have an ace up your sleeve." The comment, made by Stuart, was very quiet, but there was an edge to it that immediately brought Jessie's wandering attention back to him. He was addressing the man directly across the table, who at that point seemed to have most of the money in the game piled in front of him. As he spoke, Stuart's face was the hard, expressionless mask that she had seen maybe once or twice before. He looked like a different man from the laughing lover of just a few hours before, and Jessie felt her stomach tighten. When Stuart looked like that, there was trouble coming.

"The hell I do!"

"Shake out your sleeve."

The two other men at the table were dividing suspicious glances between Stuart and his opponent.

"I didn't see no cheatin'," the man Stuart had first addressed—Harris, Jessie thought his name was—said testily.

"I did." Stuart's voice was icy, his eyes cold as they fixed on the man he accused. "You can always prove me wrong. Shake out your sleeve."

"Won't hurt to do that," Harris said, as if reasoning it out. The third man nodded, but the man Stuart accused of cheating jumped suddenly to his feet.

"Don't nobody accuse me of cheatin'!" he bellowed, fumbling at his belt. Jessie bit back a scream as Stuart leaped up, diving across the table to catch the man's hand and twist it. A knife clattered to the floor. Then, still holdig the man's hand in a grip that caused an expression of agony to twist his mouth, Stuart unfastened the man's cuff and gave his arm a shake.

A card fluttered out to land facedown beside the knife on the floor.

"By gum, he *was* cheatin'! We owe you one, sir!"

Stuart bent, scooped up the knife and the card, which was the ace of hearts, then released his victim's hand. Red-faced, the man backed away from the table, turned, and swiftly left the room.

"How'd you know? I didn't see a thing!"

With an assessing glance at Jessie, which apparently told him that she was holding up as well as could be expected, Stuart resumed his seat.

"I've played a few hands of cards in my time," he said by way of an answer. He and the two re-

maining players retrieved their money from the pot,
and split the cheater's leavings between them as
matter-of-factly as if that was the way it was supposed to be done—and for all Jessie knew, it might
have been. A man who'd been standing beside the
door apparently watching for an opening walked up
to the table.

"Looks like you could use a fourth."

"Got a thousand?" It was apparently Harris's favorite line.

"Sure do."

"Have a seat."

Cards were reshuffled and redealt, and the play
was just getting under way again when a woman
came rustling toward the table. Stuart's nose was
buried in his hand, but Jessie, with nothing else to
do, watched her come. She was smiling broadly, a
voluptuous woman with most of her considerable
charms on display.

"Clive!" she exclaimed when she was close
enough, and came around the table toward Stuart,
who finally looked up. "Clive McClintock, as I live
and breathe! Where've you been hiding yourself,
sugar?"

"Good God," Stuart said, staring at her. "Luce!"

XL

Clive's first crazy instinct was to be glad to see her. Luce was an old friend from the days when he'd been riding high as one of the best riverboat gamblers around; one, moreover, for whom he had a certain soft spot. But as he started to get to his feet to envelop her in a big hug, he remembered Jessie, sitting so primly quiet behind him. His jaw clenched with trepidation, and he regarded Luce with as much horror as he would have a scorpion crawling out from between his cards.

He could have pretended not to know her, of course, but he'd said her name in his first surprise, and anyway, Jessie for all her youth was no fool. It was pretty obvious from the way Luce swooped to plant a smacking kiss on his mouth that they were well acquainted. Clive endured the kiss because he didn't know what else to do, while the skin between his shoulder blades tingled as he imagined Jessie's eyes boring into him.

Then it hit him. Luce had called him Clive. He hadn't even caught it at first, had been mainly worried about Jessie's reaction to encountering one of his previous mistresses. He'd been feeling like Clive, like himself, since he'd made the decision just that afternoon to beat those laughing gods at their own game by throwing their munificent gift of riches back in their teeth. He was sick and tired of playing at being Stuart Edwards, who'd been a back-stabbing thief and a general no-good, from everything he'd been able to discover. Money, as he was certainly not the first man to learn to his cost, was not everything, or even the most important thing. The green-as-grass chit sitting behind him was that.

He'd meant to tell her, he really had, but he'd thought he'd introduce her gradually to the idea that he was not *quite* what she thought him. First he'd warm her up to the intricacies of loving so that she'd be as hot for him as he was for her, and at the same time introduce her a little to the life he'd led before, so that when he revealed the truth—that he just happened to be Clive McClintock, river rat and former gambler, instead of Stuart Edwards, scion of the South Carolina Edwardses and heir to Tulip Hill— it would not come as such a shock.

Still, he had not anticipated the denouement with much pleasure. And now here it was thrust upon him with no time to prepare at all.

"I see your hand healed pretty well." Luce was beaming at him. Clive put his cards down on the table and got slowly to his feet. He was scared to look behind him, scared of what he'd see on Jessie's face, so he looked at Luce instead.

"It healed," he agreed in a hollow voice, then nodded at the men with whom he'd been playing. "Sorry, gentlemen, I'm out."

Picking up his money, he tucked it carefully into the pocket of his waistcoat. Then, and only then, did he turn to look at Jessie.

She was wide-eyed and pale, sitting there as if Luce's advent had frozen her to the chair. Except for the fiery glints in the masses of hair she wore piled on top of her head, and the dark slashes of her brows above those big-as-boulders eyes, she could have been carved from white marble. Not a vestige of color remained in her cheeks.

"Jess." His voice was not his own. It sounded

more like it should have belonged to a croaking frog—or the quaking coward that Clive McClintock had never, until this moment, been.

"Oh, Lord, Clive, am I causing you problems?" Luce sounded half amused, half rueful as she looked from his face to Jessie and back.

Neither of them bothered to answer. Her eyes fastening on his, Jessie rose slowly, with almost sinister grace, to her feet.

"Clive?" she said then. *"Clive?"*

"What's wrong with her?" Luce asked, puzzled. "She sounds like she don't know your name."

"Clive?" Jessie's voice was rising. Clive moved swiftly then, not oblivious to the attention they were starting to attract, but not concerned with it, either. He reached Jessie's side, tried to take her arm. She shook him off, took a step back, and looked at him as if she'd never seen him before in her life.

"Clive?" His name, now carrying an undercurrent of rage, seemed to be all she was able to say.

"I can explain, Jess." The words were feeble even to his own ears, and he was not surprised when she disregarded him to focus those huge eyes on Luce.

"His name is Clive? Clive—McClintock?"

Luce turned swiftly to Clive. Luce was a good friend, she wouldn't want to cause trouble for him if she could help it, but she was clearly in a quandary. Clive shrugged helplessly. There was no way now to make the truth easier for Jessie to hear.

Taking that shrug as permission to agree, Luce nodded. Her face was a study in fascination as she looked from Clive to Jessie again.

"Have you known him long?"

Clive didn't try to stop Jessie's questions. As Shakespeare—or somebody—had once said, the truth will out. And it was coming out now with a vengeance, far beyond his ability to contain it or even lessen the damage.

Again Luce looked at Clive for guidance. When

none was forthcoming, she answered uneasily, "About ten years."

"You've known *Clive McClintock* for about ten years." It was a statement, not a question. If possible, Jessie went even paler than before. "But you haven't seen him for a few months, have you? Since right after he hurt his hand?"

"That's right." Luce sounded almost as puzzled as she was intrigued.

"So who," Jessie said, getting to the meat of the problem, her eyes swinging from Luce to Clive at last, "is Stuart Edwards? Or did you just make him up?"

The last was a sibilant hiss.

"No, I . . ." For once in his life Clive was fumbling for words. But Luce, getting into the spirit of things, answered for him. Clive winced.

"Stuart Edwards? Wasn't that the name of that thief you killed? Oh, did you ever get your money back?"

"You cheating—lying—fornicating—bastard." Jessie wasn't even shouting. Her fists were clenched at her sides, her eyes blazed fury at him, but her voice was scarcely louder than a whisper for all it flailed him with the stinging lash of a whip. The room had gone completely silent as one pair of eyes after another had become aware of the diversion going on in their midst. Neither Jessie nor Clive noticed that they had a large, and fascinated, audience. Luce did, but being the center of attention had never bothered her.

"You lied to us all from the beginning! Everyone—Celia—Miss Flora and Miss Laurel—and me!"

"Jessie. I know it sounds bad, but—"

"*Sounds* bad!" She laughed then, a high, hysterical titter that alarmed Clive. She looked on the verge of hysterics, with her eyes grown black as coals and glittering in that paper-white face, and her neck stretched high above tense shoulders so that the cords in it stood out visibly. Memories of other hys-

terical women he had seen, hooting in grating peals
of laughter before dissolving into mindless shrieks,
caused the hairs on the back of Clive's neck to rise.
He had to get Jessie out of here, get her someplace
where he could talk to her, force her if need be to
listen to reason. What he'd done sounded bad, he
agreed, but once he'd explained it all, surely she'd
see that it wasn't nearly as terrible as it sounded.

He hoped.

"I can explain," he said again, feebly. And again
she laughed.

There was nothing for it but to take her back to
their cabin, sit her down on the bed, and spell things
out for her. He was pretty sure that what was making her so mad was the fear that, if he had lied about
everything else, he had lied about loving her, too.

Even if nothing much else he'd told her was, that
particular statement was the truth.

"Come on, Jessie. We need to talk," he said, hoping to head off her impending explosion with his
own calm reasonableness, and took her arm again.

Jessie looked down at his large bronzed hand on
her bare white skin as if it were a copperhead ready
to bite her.

"Don't you ever," she said distinctly as she jerked
her arm free of his touch, "lay a hand on me again."

Then she turned on her heel and started toward
the door. A wild chorus of cheers and clapping broke
out amongst the onlookers to mark her progress. If
Jessie heard them, she ignored them magnificently,
sweeping toward the door with as much stateliness
as a queen. For the first time noticing his audience
more than vaguely, Clive felt the urge to preserve
as much of his masculine dignity as he could. Taking
care that Jessie didn't see, he shrugged as if to say,
"Women!" and followed her toward the door.

She had almost reached it, and he had almost
caught up with her, when she suddenly turned on
him. Her eyes blazed with fury, and her body quiv-

ered with it. She was so angry that even her hair seemed to throw off sparks.

"You lowlife scum," she hissed through clenched teeth. Then, before Clive had the least inkling as to what she was about, she drew back one clenched fist and launched a roundhouse punch that caught him squarely on his unsuspecting nose.

It was a punch worthy of a champion. Clive howled and staggered a pace backward, his hand flying to his injured nose, which felt as if it might be broken. When he took his hand away, he saw to his disbelief that his fingers were covered in blood.

Jessie had already turned her back on him and sailed out the door. The onlookers were shouting with laughter, hooting at him and bombarding him with snippets of mostly obscene advice that he didn't even register. Luce laughed, too, although she tried not to show it as she hurried to his aid. With a shake of his head and a swipe at his bleeding nose, Clive shrugged aside her offer of assistance. He had more important things to worry about at the moment than a bloody nose, such as shaking some much-needed sense into Jessie.

In hitting him, Clive realized, Jessie had really done him a favor. He was no longer quite the cringing penitent he'd been just moments before. His own temper was starting to heat.

He'd be damned if he would put up with much more in the way of abuse from a wet-behind-the-ears snip of a girl!

As he stalked out the door in Jessie's wake, he caught one final contribution to the general hilarity.

"Round one to the lady!" some wag cackled.

Clive gritted his teeth. Somewhere, he knew, the gods were laughing again. He could almost hear their raucous chuckles at his expense.

XLI

Jessie slammed the door to her cabin, turned the key in the lock, and leaned against it, still in shock. Rage bubbled like boiling liquid in her veins, but overriding that and every other emotion was sheer, quivering disbelief. The man she had loved had never even existed. Stuart Edwards was no more than a role Clive McClintock had assumed to gain control of Mimosa. And Clive McClintock was a slimy, low-down confidence man whose business it was to take advantage of everyone with whom he came into contact, including herself.

In short, she'd been had, in more ways than one.

A brisk rap made her jump away from the door and turn to survey it as if it had suddenly come alive and tried to bite her.

"Jessie. Let me in."

How dared he even foul her name with his mouth! Jessie glared at that closed panel as if her eyes could bore right through it and stab him.

"Jessie. Open the door. Please."

Hah! It was all she could do not to say it aloud, but she refused to give him the satisfaction of exchanging so much as another word with her. She was going home, home to Mimosa and people who were what they seemed whether they all loved her or not, as soon as the blasted boat touched dry land again. As for him—Jessie would take great pleasure in trumpeting his infamy to the skies! If he ever dared to show his face in the Yazoo Valley again, he'd be lucky not to be run out of there on a rail!

"Jessie. I mean it. Unlock this door!"

So he thought he could still give her orders and have her obey, eh? Was he in for a shock! The man she obeyed was the man she had looked up to with sickening adoration, and that man was not Clive McClintock, curse the name!

"Jessica!" The knob rattled. A sneer curled Jessie's lip.

"Damn it, Jess!" The knob rattled again. "If you don't open this damned door right now, I'll break it down!"

His voice was getting progressively angrier. So Clive McClintock was upset that his little game had been disclosed before he was quite done playing, was he? Jessie wondered what his next step would have been. After seducing and ruining her, would he have abandoned her somewhere and gone back to Mimosa to play at being Stuart Edwards until it no longer suited him? Or had he looted the plantation of its operating cash and the profit from the cotton before leaving, intending all along not to go back, but rather to live high on the hog on Mimosa's money until he could locate another victim?

There was a thud, and the door shook as if he'd thrown his shoulder against it. Eyes widening, Jessie took another step backward as she realized that he truly meant to break down the door. On the third try the lock broke and the door crashed back on its hinges, leaving Clive McClintock looming large and threatening in the frame. For just a moment he was a darker shape against the gathering night beyond, and then he was strolling almost casually into the cabin. Annoyingly, he didn't even seem out of breath.

"Get out of here!" Jessie hissed at him. He didn't so much as look at her as he gently closed the damaged door behind him. With its lock broken, it immediately swung open again. Crossing the room with a purposeful stride that made Jessie jump out of his way, he picked up the chair that was his objective and set it beneath the knob, this time effectively closing the door.

"Get out of here or I'll scream!"

"I wouldn't do that if I were you." There was the slightest edge to his voice.

"I will! I'll scream! I'll scream so loud that they'll hear me clear up to the bridge!"

"If you even try it, I'll gag you and tie you up and sit you down and *make* you listen to me. If you don't believe me, just let out a yell."

Oddly, the very levelness of his voice was convincing. Jessie was left with no doubt that the swine would really do as he'd threatened if she screamed. So, prudently, she did not.

"Sit down." It was an order, not an invitation. When Jessie continued to stand where she was, silently defying him, he took a step toward her. The cabin was dark, and she could see no more of him than a large, menacing shadow. It occurred to Jessie suddenly that she did not know this man at all. This was not Stuart Edwards, whom she loved. This was Clive McClintock.

"I said sit down!" The words cracked like a whip. Jessie was standing near the end of the bunk, upon which she abruptly sat.

"Very wise."

He crossed the cabin to where the lamp hung from a center beam. There was the click of flint on steel, and then the lamp was lit. Its warm glow flickered and gradually grew, illuminating the cabin. Jessie sat as he had ordered, warily watching his broad back as he crossed to pull the curtains over the porthole and thus shut out the night.

"If you run out that door, I'll catch you within three steps."

Either he had eyes in the back of his head or he

knew precisely how her mind worked. Guessing that it was the latter, Jessie regarded the back of his head with renewed rage. She had indeed been on the verge of bolting for it. But, as he threatened, he'd have her back within seconds. Even if she did manage to get away from him for a while, he would track her down. On a steamboat the size of the *River Queen*, there was nowhere to go.

Then he turned to face her. Jessie gasped as she saw the mess she'd made of his beautiful face.

Blood was smeared around his mouth and over his cheeks, and his nose was already slightly swollen from the blow she'd landed. More blood oozed from his nostrils. As Jessie stared, just a little appalled at her own handiwork despite the fact that he'd mightily deserved what he'd gotten, he moved over to the washstand, dipped a cloth into the water that remained in the basin, and held it to his nose. Looking at him, Jessie felt a quiver of trepidation. What would he do to her in revenge? Never had she thought to physically fear him—but again she reminded herself that he was not the man she thought she knew.

But then her gaze lifted. Above that damaged nose were the clear blue eyes and black hair of the man she'd loved. Lying, cheating scum or not, Jessie suddenly wasn't afraid of him anymore.

"I hope it hurts." She meant it, too.

"It does, thank you very much."

"You deserved it, and more."

"If I didn't agree with you, I'd have paddled your backside by now."

"If you lay one hand on me . . ."

He sighed, and shifted the cloth beneath his nose. "Don't threaten me, Jess. If you'll just let me explain, you'll see that this whole unfortunate situation is nothing more than a—misunderstanding."

"Some misunderstanding!" She snorted. "I suppose you're going to try to tell me that you introduced yourself as Clive McClintock, and we, poor backward fools that we were, somehow misunderstood you to say Stuart Edwards?''

He eyed her in a way that told her that her sarcasm was not appreciated.

"I love you, you know. Whatever you may think, I wasn't lying about that."

"Oh, I believe you." Clearly, from her tone, she did not.

He removed the cloth from beneath his nose, which had apparently stopped bleeding, and turned to the mirror over the washstand to wipe the bloodstains from his face. There wasn't much he could do about the stains on his shirt. He swiped at them with the cloth, with no perceptible result. Grimacing, he decided to let them be.

Turning back to her, he crossed to the bunk and stood in front of her. Fists resting lightly on his hips, he looked down at her with a considering expression. Jessie had to tilt her head way back to see his face, and immediately felt at a disadvantage. Still, if she got to her feet she would be practically in his arms, the very idea of which she could no longer abide. So she stayed where she was.

"I'm still the same man I was an hour ago. I haven't changed, except for my name. Wasn't it Shakespeare who said that a rose by any other name would smell as sweet?'' There was a coaxing note to that last. If he was trying to be funny, the effort fell dismally flat.

"Or stink as bad,'' Jessie replied tartly, and crossed her arms over her chest as if to erect a symbolic barrier against him.

"I was going to tell you."

"Oh, yes?'' Jessie inquired politely. "When? It seems to me that you passed up several excellent opportunities—such as before you seduced me."

"I did not seduce you,'' he said, sounding nettled. "Damn it, Jessie, I fell in love with you. And you fell in love with me. Me, not Stuart Edwards. Me."

"I don't even know you. Clive McClintock and I have never met."

"You're determined to be difficult about this, aren't you?"

"I suppose I must be. It's contrary of me, I know, but I find it hard to overlook the fact that everything you've ever told me is a lie."

"Not everything."

"You'll have to pardon me if I don't believe you."

"You want the truth? I'll give you the truth. I'm a gambler, and I used to work the riverboats up and down the Mississippi. One night I won big, enough to set me up for life if I was careful with the money. But it was late at night, and I had to keep my winnings with me until morning. Two men broke into my cabin that night, stole the money I had won, and put a knife through my hand. I chased them and killed one—the real Stuart Edwards—but the other got away with my money. Then I found out that my hand—I'd never be able to make a living as a professional gambler again. Too much damage."

"So you decided you'd pretend to be someone respectable—I assume that Stuart Edwards really was Miss Flora and Miss Laurel's nephew? You didn't lie about that, too? No?—and see if you couldn't rob people just like you were robbed, only in a slightly more genteel way."

"I thought I was telling this, not you."

Jessie made a gesture with her hand that told him to proceed.

"With my hand like it is—hell, you know what I'm talking about—I had no way to make a living."

"Honest labor never occurred to you?" Sarcasm was beginning to come naturally to her, she discovered.

"Will you let me finish?"

"I'm sorry. Please, continue. I'm fascinated, really."

"I went looking for my money. I'd meant to buy a piece of property with it, to set myself up as a sort

of gentleman farmer. Oh, nothing on the scale of
Mimosa, of course, but a place that I could build into
something one day. I was sick of gambling, sick of
the river anyway. But I never found the bastard who
got away with my money. I did find out that Stuart
Edwards had two old aunts who wanted to leave
him everything they owned. Stuart Edwards was
dead. But I wasn't. I thought I'd just go see the old
ladies, let them think I was their nephew. If they
were on the verge of death, I thought that a visit
from their nephew might even comfort them."

"How very noble you are!" Jessie marveled.

He held up a hand as if to acknowledge a hit. "All
right, I thought I might inherit their property in the
real Stuart Edwards' place. After all, he stole what
was mine. And he was dead. Somebody had to inherit from the old ladies."

"There's no need to sound so defensive. I'm sure
anyone would have thought exactly the same
thing."

The look he shot her was enough to silence her.
"Then I got to Tulip Hill. It was clear that the Misses
Edwards weren't going to expire for quite a few
years yet. I was going to take myself off again—until
I met Celia."

"At least your thought processes are consistent.
Consistently opportunistic."

"Hush your mouth, Jessie, and let me talk. I met
Celia. Aunt Flora's an inveterate matchmaker, and
it was she who told me that the widow Lindsay was
as rich as a damned Midas. I had a look at Mimosa
and liked what I saw. Hell, you knew months ago
that the only reason I married Celia was for Mimosa.
Marrying for money's not a crime."

"No."

"It's not as if I forced her to marry me. She was
hot after me from the moment she first laid eyes on
me—it was all I could do to keep her out of my bed
until the wedding."

"That must have been a chore. Being a fortune hunter does have its problems."

"Jessie, if you don't keep quiet I'm going to strangle you! Celia and I both were getting exactly what we wanted from the marriage, so what was wrong with that?"

"*You* were getting exactly what you wanted. Celia wanted to marry Stuart Edwards, gentleman. Not Clive McClintock, rat."

"All right. I grant you, she probably wouldn't have married me if she hadn't thought that my bloodline made me her social equal. But did I do badly by her, or Mimosa? Did I do badly by you, Jess?"

He had her there. She was a different person now from the backward girl he'd befriended. If he'd only left their relationship at friendship, she would be stoutly defending him now, instead of wanting to rip out his heart.

"I meant to make life better for all of you. Even Celia. But she—you know what she is. By the time our honeymoon was over, it was all I could do not to murder her. But I didn't. I took over Mimosa for her—that damned overseer you had was robbing you blind when he wasn't in bed with Celia—and I tried to help you have a happier life than you'd had up till then. Hell, I felt sorry for you. I knew Celia must have led you a hell of a life."

"You felt . . . sorry for me?" If he'd thought to appease her with that, he was sadly mistaken.

"Just at first." He saw his error and quickly tried to retrieve it. "Well, actually, at first I believed everything Celia had told me about you, and concluded that you were an ungrateful little brat. Then, when I saw how—uh, how you didn't quite fit in socially, I felt sorry for you. I thought you should have a chance to be like other girls your age, to dance and flirt at parties, to find a nice young man to marry. I discovered that you were really a sweet little thing under all that hair and bluster, and that you

were pretty in your own way. All you needed was
the right clothes, and a little experience in handling
social situations, and you'd do just fine. I saw that
you had both, didn't I? But then you changed from
an awkward young girl to a beautiful woman. In a
month or two, right before my eyes. That was something I never expected."

Jessie was silent. He paused and stood looking
down at her for a minute. Then, before she realized
his intention, he hunkered down so that his face
was level with hers. His hands were braced on either side of her as she sat on the bed, effectively
imprisoning her.

"You were the joker in the deck. I was richer than
I'd ever dreamed of being, I had everything I ever
wanted and more—and then I had to go and fall in
love with you. I never meant to, Jessie."

If he was waiting for some response from her,
none was forthcoming. She looked at him, merely
looked at him, forcing herself to harden her heart
against his words. He was a practiced deceiver, but
she was not to be bamboozled twice. He'd not get
around her with pretty talk again.

"So you decided to add me to the list of things
that the bogus Stuart Edwards had acquired."

He moved then, impatiently, his hands catching
her upper arms just above her elbows. Leaning
closer, he balanced on the balls of his feet.

"It wasn't like that, and you know it. Hell, Jessie,
just this afternoon I gave up everything for you! I
have just over a thousand dollars in my pocket, a
little more in my own name in a bank in New Orleans, and the clothes on my back. If I didn't love
you to the point of insanity, why would I give up
Mimosa? It's worth a fortune, and as long as I stay
Stuart Edwards it's mine. Only a fool or a man crazy
in love would whistle a prize like that down the
wind!"

Jessie studied him. Notwithstanding his injured
nose, he was, she concluded reluctantly, still the

handsomest man she had ever laid eyes on. And also the biggest liar!

"I don't believe a word you've said," she announced coldly. Then, as he opened his mouth to continue the argument, she thrust out her hands and shoved him, hard. With a surprised exclamation he fell over. Before he could recover, she sprang to her feet, dragged the chair out of the way, and bolted out the door.

His curses singed the air.

"Damn it, Jessie, you come back here!" he bellowed. But Jessie lifted her skirts and ran. She knew he'd be coming after her, knew it as well as she knew that the sun would rise in the morning, and she meant to get safely away.

XLII

Of course he caught her. It took him a few more than three steps, but he caught up with her before she could reach the top of the stairs leading to the bridge. She'd fully intended to run to the captain and beg him for help. After all, she had paid for the cabin, and Stuart—no, curse him, Clive—had no right to stay there at all. But she never made it.

"Damn it, Jessie, you're more trouble than you're worth." He grunted furiously as he grabbed a handful of material at the back of her gown and yanked. She was about four steps up, leaping nimbly for the bridge, and the yank threw her off balance. With a wild cry of fear she tumbled backward, to be caught in his arms.

Threats or no, Jessie screamed. He silenced her instantly by covering her mouth with his. Jessie kicked, beating at his head with her fists, but he subdued her with ridiculous ease. His arms around her stilled her struggles and held her fast. His tongue took full advantage of her cut-off scream to thrust inside her mouth.

"Any trouble down there?" An officer of the ship must have heard her scream. He'd left the bridge to stand at the rail at the top of the stairs, and was frowning down at them.

Clive's reaction time was much faster than Jessie's. He lifted his head, grinned broadly at the man, said, "Just a lover's tiff," and was thrusting his tongue back down her throat again before Jessie could recover her wits enough to make any kind of protest.

The officer withdrew. Jessie seethed, and bit down on that encroaching tongue so hard that it was a wonder she didn't bite it in two. He yelped and jerked his head back. As soon as her mouth was free she screamed again. Clive silenced her this time with his hand over her mouth.

"You little hellcat, I'm giving you fair warning: the next injury you do me, I'm going to repay in kind."

He was walking along the deck with her held high against his chest. Her skirts spilled over his arm and her head was nestled forcibly against his shoulder in what must, to any chance observer, have appeared a loving pose. Stars twinkled brightly overhead, visible for miles in either direction above the clear swath cut by the river. Gleaming moonlight reflected off the night-dark surface of the water, making the deck brighter than it otherwise would have been. The rising wind would have chilled Jessie if she had been in any state to feel it. But she was so angry that she burned with the heat of it, and the drop in temperature that had come with the night passed unnoticed.

They had almost reached her cabin when another couple came into view, strolling arm in arm toward them. Jessie squirmed and tried to kick, squealing against his hand in an effort to alert them to her situation. But Clive's arms clamped around her so hard that they hurt, and his hand over her mouth tightened until she could scarcely catch her breath. Her face was turned to his shoulder, and the couple passed without, apparently, noticing anything out of the way.

Then they reached her cabin, and Clive carried her inside.

He dropped her without ceremony on the bed. Jessie cried out as she landed with a bounce, but was already preparing to scramble to her feet when he swooped over her, pinning her down with his hands.

"I've had a bellyful of your tantrums tonight," he said through his teeth. "Give me any more cause and I'll paddle your backside until you can't sit for weeks. You have my word on it."

His eyes were stormy with temper. One look at them, and Jessie knew he meant it. She sat up as he released her and went to prop the chair beneath the door, but made no further move to escape.

"Get undressed." He had turned back to look at her. His boots were planted apart, and his fists rested on his hips. The very set of his chin bespoke belligerence.

"I won't!"

"Oh, yes, you will!" There was an almost predatory glint in his eyes as he watched her.

"I won't!"

"To hell with that," he snarled, and was upon her in a single stride. Jessie swatted at him wildly, but before she could do any damage he had her flipped onto her belly with her face pushed into the mattress so she could not scream. Then he sat on her back.

The weight of him alone was enough to quell her struggles.

Jessie was forced to lie helplessly, burning with fury, as he stripped her clear down to her chemise. When the last petticoat was tossed aside, she expected to find herself naked in the next instant. Instead he lifted himself off her and rolled her onto her back.

Enraged, Jessie shot into a sitting position and tried to punch his nose again. This time he was ready for her. He plucked her fist out of the air, grabbed its fellow, and held them for just long enough to wrap her silk stocking around her wrists, tying her hands together.

"What the devil do you think you're doing?" she hissed, glaring down at her bound hands.

"Getting ready for bed," he said through his teeth, and with his hand in the center of her chest he shoved her onto her back. "I'll sleep better knowing that you're safe at my side and out of mischief."

"How dare you tie me up! I'll—"

"Scream and I'll gag you," he warned, and at the look in his eyes she believed him. Fuming, Jessie made no outcry while he used her other stocking to secure her bound hands to the top of the bunk.

Then he stood up and took off his clothes. Jessie refused to watch. Instead she stared furiously at the opposite wall until she felt him jerk the tangled bedclothes out from beneath her. The unexpectedness of it made her look around. He was naked, and looming over her.

She kicked at him. It was a mistake. The hem of her chemise flew up to somewhere in the neighborhood of her belly button. Powerless to cover herself with her hands tied, Jessie could only look down at her long bare legs and the curly triangle of hair between them with mortified fury. How dared he do this to her! He was every bit the villain she'd known him to be! If he touched her, if he dared . . .

Clive placed one knee on the bed and reached for her.

"If you touch me, I'll kill you. So help me God, I will!" It was a fierce hiss.

Clive merely lifted an eyebrow at her mockingly. Then his hand found its target, and he twitched the hem of her chemise into place so that she was minimally decent once more.

"I hate to disappoint you, Jessie, but I'm too tired to do anything but sleep. Though I'll be glad to accommodate you in the morning, if you like."

With that he blew out the lamp and rolled into bed beside her. In a disgustingly brief period of time he was fast asleep, while Jessie, lying rigid on her

sliver of the mattress, was left staring into darkness
as she fought not to let her body slip toward the dip
his weight created in the bed. Fury and hurt warred
inside her, but as she closed her eyes at last, fury
had the upper hand.

Sometime during the night he rolled over, pulling
the covers clear off her body. Half asleep, Jessie
gradually registered that she was cold. Of its own
accord her body sought the nearest source of heat.
Clive, of course. He had his back turned to her, and
she snuggled close against it, her front against his
back. Then she fell back asleep.

Jessie dreamed that she was at Mimosa again, safe
at home in her own snug bed. She was watching
Stuart smile at her, one hand over his head as he
lifted the mosquito bar out of his way. Then he was
crawling into bed beside her, reaching for her, his
hands stroking her body, which was mysteriously
naked, caressing her breasts and belly and thighs
until she was moaning with need.

He was looming over her, his knee sliding between hers to part her legs, probing at her as he
sought entry. In her dreaming state Jessie felt the
burning heat of him, the moistness of his mouth on
her breasts.

Then all of a sudden he found the opening and
thrust inside. At the shattering impact Jessie's eyes
flew open to discover that this was no dream!

She was flat on her back and he was over her,
possessing her, kissing her breasts even as he moved
inside her with slow, careful ease. Part of her wanted
to beat at his head, to cry rape, but the quivering
hunger of her body told her that this was no rape.
Though he'd done it somehow in her sleep, he'd
roused her to the fever point where her fury at him
no longer mattered next to the urgent demands of
her flesh. Her hands weren't even bound any longer,
she discovered when he withdrew nearly all the way
and she clutched at his shoulders to stop him.
Sometime while she'd slept, he'd untied her wrists.

This time he was slow, and careful, and relentless, pushing her nearly to the brink time and again, only to draw back until she was mindless, pleading for him to finish, pleading for him never to finish.

Her arms wrapped around his neck and her legs wrapped around his waist. With each slow, sure thrust she cried out, arching her back. Finally he lifted his mouth from hers to whisper in her ear.

"Tell me you love me," he commanded hoarsely.

Dizzy with need, she did as he said.

He moved inside her again, then almost withdrew.

"Say it again."

"I love you! I love you! Oh, Stuart, I love you!"

He thrust deep inside her, once, twice, taking her quivering to the brink.

"Clive," he rasped in her ear. "Say 'I love you, Clive.' "

"I love you, Clive," she gasped obediently into his mouth, then repeated it again and again, mindlessly, as he took her over the edge with him.

XLIII

When he awoke the next morning she was gone. Clive lay for a moment in luxuriant peace, his eyes still closed, before it registered that Jessie was not curled beside him any longer. He opened his eyes to make sure. Except for the silk stocking that still hung down from where he had secured her bound hands to the headboard, there was no trace of her in the bed at all. He had only tied her hands because he was furiously angry and too damned tired to think up some other way to keep her with him, and safe, until he could calm her down. When he'd awakened during the night and seen how uncomfortable she'd looked, he'd had a pang of conscience and freed her hands. Then one thing had led to another, and he'd thought that the situation between them had been resolved. Obviously he'd been wrong.

Clive sat up, looked around, and cursed. The cabin was empty, not only of Jessie but also of all her belongings. Clive's eyes widened in disbelief as he shot out of the bunk to make sure.

The little witch had run out on him! While he'd blissfully caught up on the sleep that she'd cost him in the first place, she'd dressed, packed her things, and vamoosed!

It was only then that Clive realized, with a sinking

sensation in the pit of his stomach, that the *River Queen* no longer throbbed with power, but rocked gently up and down in time to the river's swells.

While he'd been sleeping, they'd docked again! As the realization came to him, Clive leaped for the door, kicked aside the chair, which she'd apparently positioned as well as she could from the outside, and as the door swung open, stood naked in the aperture staring out at the busy port that he knew all too well.

Damn, he'd have a hell of a time tracking her down in a town the size of Baton Rouge!

Embarrassed titters from a trio of passing females brought him to full awareness of his position. They were giggling behind their hands, two of them averting their eyes as they passed while the third ogled him boldly. No lady, that!

Clive felt unaccustomed color rise to his cheeks as he stepped back and slammed the door, which of course immediately swung open again. Cursing, he kicked it shut and shoved the chair against it to hold it so.

This time when he caught up with her, she'd be lucky if he didn't resort to beating some sense into her! He loved her, damn it, and she loved him, Stuart or Clive, he knew she did, whether she would admit it or not. She was just having a totally unnecessary temper tantrum to punish him for his slight deception, and if he didn't teach her a lesson she wouldn't forget, it wouldn't be for lack of the inclination to do so!

He'd get dressed and . . . Where the bloody hell were his clothes?

The little baggage had taken his clothes! Everything from shirt to trousers even down to his boots, was gone!

His purse, too, with every cent they'd had between them in it!

He was naked, penniless, and mad enough to chew nails. Just wait until he caught up with her!

When he got his hands on her, he would wring her neck—so help him God, he would!

Clive stomped about the cabin, cursed, and finally kicked the end of the bunk to relieve his feelings. What he did, instead, was hurt his big toe.

When he quit hopping about on one foot, he snatched the coverlet off the bunk, wrapped it around himself toga-fashion, and hobbled onto the deck to procure assistance.

He only hoped Luce was still on board.

Jessie was both tired and unhappy as she stood at the rail of the *Delta Princess* late the following afternoon. She'd done the right thing, she knew, in leaving Clive McClintock—the dirty swine!—and heading for home, but the knowledge didn't make her feel any better. For the life of her, she couldn't stop confusing that treacherous piece of scum with the Stuart she had loved, and her heart ached badly.

The only thing that made her feel even slightly better was imagining how angry he must have been when he'd awakened and found her, his clothes, and all the money gone. She wondered how he'd ever managed to get off the *River Queen*, or even if he had. Perhaps he'd simply accepted the inevitable and allowed the boat to take him on to New Orleans.

Where he still would have had to disembark naked.

The picture that that thought conjured up caused a reluctant smile to tug at Jessie's lips.

The *Delta Princess* was steaming up the Yazoo River toward the dock just to the west of Elmway, and already Jessie was beginning to see the familiar plantations along the river. Makepeace, the Bensons' place, fronted on the water, as did the Culpeppers' Beaumont and the Todds' Riverview. Mimosa sat some way back from the river, facing the road, so that the house itself was not visible from the *Delta Princess*'s deck. But Jessie knew when they steamed past Mimosa land. She was almost home again! Her heart swelled at the thought. How had she ever thought to leave it?

The Mimosa she returned to would not, of course, be the Mimosa she had left. Stuart would be gone, and Celia would be in sole charge once more. As for herself—what would her role there be now? She was far from the child she had been before Stuart—no, Clive, curse him!—had helped her to grow up.

Heavyhearted, Jessie tried to imagine what Mimosa would be like in the future. Celia's former patronizing contempt for her stepdaughter had jelled over the past months into near hatred. She would do her utmost to make Jessie's life a misery, especially when Jessie told her the truth about Stuart— no, Clive! (Would she ever accustom herself to thinking of him by that dreadful name?) Or perhaps, since Celia's marriage had clearly been unhappy for some time, Celia would thank her for being the catalyst that ended it. But where would that leave Celia's coming child? Whether Stuart/Clive was the father or not—and Jessie tended to believe him about that, as Celia's proclivities were well known to her— the baby would be the object of infamy from the moment of its birth if the truth came out. To further complicate the situation, if Stuart was not Stuart at all, but Clive, the legality of Celia's marriage might be called into question. Would the child, even as the supposed offspring of Stuart/Clive, be considered legitimate if the marriage was not? Jessie wondered, bitterly, if Clive McClintock, wherever he was, was finding any enjoyment in contemplating the disaster he had left behind him.

The scandal, when it broke, would be appalling. When word got out that Stuart Edwards had been nothing but an impostor, had been found out and had subsequently vanished, the talk would swell loud and long. Celia wouldn't thank her for making them all notorious, and Jessie didn't much like the idea herself.

Yet, if she said nothing, Clive McClintock would be free to return and resume his role as Stuart Edwards for as long as it suited him. Jessie didn't think she could bear that. To see him every day, have to treat him publicly with at least a modicum of respect, and watch him living a lie as her stepmother's husband and the Misses Edwards' nephew and her own—what? Nothing. Stuart, or Clive, it didn't matter. He was no longer anything to her.

Except a fraud, a cheat, and a liar.

If she told, his goose would be effectively cooked in the Yazoo Valley. If she didn't, he might come back. But then again, Jessie thought hopefully, he might not. Perhaps she should just hold her tongue and await events. She could say that she had never even seen him while she was away, but had decided to return to Mimosa on her own. Stuart Edwards could simply be allowed to vanish, and over time be forgotten.

Perhaps that would be best. As long as he didn't come back.

Jessie clung to that thought until the *Delta Princess* approached the dock. She was standing at the bow rail, the wind snatching her hair from its pins, her wide-brimmed straw hat hanging from its ribbon around her neck so that she could enjoy the sun on her face. A line of mule wagons carrying cotton waited on the bank to be unloaded; a dirt farmer and his family stood to one side, watching the paddle wheeler come in. A little way back sat a man on a big black horse.

Jessie's eyes widened. Leaning forward, she stared as if unable to believe what her eyes were telling her. The black horse was Saber—and the man was Clive McClintock!

The *Delta Princess* was tied up, the gangplank lowered, and what few passengers there were on board disembarked. Still Jessie stayed where she was, frozen in place by sheer disbelief. Her eyes were fixed on Clive, who had swung down from Saber and was leisurely making his way to where she stood transfixed.

"Need some help with your bag, miss?" The speaker was one of the ship's officers. Jessie tore her eyes off Clive to glance at him distractedly.

"No, I . . ." she began.

"The lady has help, thanks," said the smooth voice that she had thought, hoped, never to hear again. As Jessie looked around, Clive came up behind her, dismissed the man with a smile and a nod, and bent to pick up her valise, which sat on the deck at her feet. Then he put his hand on her arm just above her elbow.

"I hope you brought my boots. I have a fondness for that particular pair."

"How did you . . . ?"

"Presently, Jessie. Presently."

Without causing a scene, Jessie could do nothing but let him escort her from the boat. His grip on her elbow was perfectly polite, his smile urbane. But he didn't speak again. Nor did she. When they were on dry land, he led her toward Saber in total silence.

After they had reached the big horse's side, he dropped her valise in the grass and turned to face her, tipping back his hat. Jessie's eyes ran over him, disbelieving. How had he managed to get here before her, and fully clothed at that?

"How did you *get* here?" she asked, because that was the question that burned in her mind to the exclusion of all else.

"Did you think I wouldn't? You cost me another night's sleep, but I'll survive."

"Your clothes . . ." He was dressed in a dove-gray trouser suit with a cream-colored waistcoat that was every bit as elegant and well fitting as the clothes he customarily wore. He needed a shave, but the black stubble on his cheeks and jaw just added to his rakish appeal. Even the gray top hat on his head was bandbox fresh!

"Taking my clothes wasn't nice, Jessie. I had to

borrow some from Luce's current gentleman friend.
Quite a good fellow, actually, but rather short.''

''But . . .'' Jessie's eyes ran over him again. She
was practically speechless with shock. She had left
him, little more than a day ago, naked and penniless
a good two hundred miles downriver. Now here he
stood before her, not only fully clothed but also immaculately dressed, having reached her destination
before she did! And if those clothes belonged to
someone's too-short gentleman friend, she would
eat them!

''Fortunately I was able to pick up my own things
when I rode through Natchez. I've been riding almost continually since you left me, Jessie, on three
different horses. So if you find me in not the most
pleasant of tempers, I'm sure you'll understand.''

The shock was beginning to wear off. Here he
was, no apparition but Clive McClintock the rat in
the flesh, smiling smoothly at her while his sky-blue
eyes glinted a warning that he was far from the civilized gentleman he appeared.

''I knew you were no gentleman the first moment
I laid eyes on you!''

''How very perceptive of you.''

''You shouldn't have come back. When everyone
finds out what you've done, the consequences won't
be pleasant.''

Despite what he had done, one tiny, ridiculously
soft spot in her heart did not quite like the idea of
seeing him driven from the valley, or arrested, or
whatever would be his ultimate fate. Her mind knew
what he was, but a niggling piece of her heart kept
getting him confused with the Stuart she had loved.

''You mean when everyone finds out that Stuart
Edwards has been dead for some time and that I'm
really Clive McClintock?'' He was still speaking to
her with that awful affability, while his glittering
eyes conveyed quite another message.

''Yes. That's precisely what I mean.''

''And just how will everyone find out? You don't

mean that you would expose me?'' Clive raised his brows in mock surprise. ''Surely not! Think of the consequences—for yourself.''

Jessie was briefly taken aback. ''What consequences could there possibly be for me?''

''Well, my darling, much as it would pain me to do so, if you were to tell tales out of school, I would be forced to retaliate in kind.''

''I don't understand you.''

''Don't you? Let me spell it out for you, then. Should you feel it necessary to inform the world— or even one other person—that I am not Stuart Edwards at all, why, then I would have to disclose certain—intimate—acts that have occurred between us. Who do you think would be more reviled—the impostor, or the once virginal young thing who had sunk to being his mistress?''

As the import of his words sank in, Jessie felt a rush of blood surge directly to her head. ''You— cad!'' she cried.

''I would only do such an ungentlemanly thing if you forced me to it, of course.'' The apologetic tone he affected was pure mockery. ''What do you say, Jessie? Shall we keep one another's secrets?''

''I hate and despise you,'' she said bitterly.

''You'll get over it,'' he answered, apparently taking her words for the agreement they were. Bending, he picked up her valise and hooked its handle over the horn of his saddle. ''Can I give you a ride home?''

''No!''

''Come, Jess, don't be childish. It's a long walk.''

''I'd sooner walk all the way to Jackson than ride with you!''

''Suit yourself.'' Shrugging nonchalantly, he swung into the saddle, saluted her, and rode off.

Jessie was left glaring after him, unable to think of any words bad enough to describe him, even to herself. She'd thought to hitch a ride on one of the mule wagons but discovered, to her dismay, that they were not yet being unloaded.

If she wanted to get to Mimosa anytime soon, she would have to walk.

It really wasn't all that far, she told herself as she trudged along the dirt road that, with its mud puddles and fresh ruts, gave silent evidence of a rain the night before. But the weather was humid, and though the tall pines on either side of the road blocked the sun, they were little protection against the sultriness of the air.

Mimosa wasn't much more than five miles distant, Jessie calculated, but she was wearing her new shoes with the cunning little French heels, and after a while they began to pinch her feet. Her gown, bought in Jackson at the same time as the shoes, was styled in the latest fashion. It was a lovely shade of deep blue, baring her shoulders in the current mode, but the skirt was longer in back than in front, and she had to constantly pick it up to keep it from trailing in the mud. The ribbon of her hat began to irritate her throat, and when she put the hat on her head, it only made her hotter. She was miserable, and her feet hurt, and like everything else that was wrong with her life, it was all Clive McClintock's fault!

Then Jessie heard the faint rumble of thunder. Even as she looked up in trepidation, the heavens opened and rain began to fall in great silvery sheets.

By the time she had rounded the bend in the road where Clive waited on Saber beneath the sheltering overhang of some juniper trees, Jessie was soaked to the skin. Her hat had wilted long since, the brim tipping soggily at the sides to allow water to pour down on both shoulders. Her gown, as wet as her hat, felt as if it weighed a ton. Water sloshed inside her shoes. The wet leather was, she was sure, rubbing blisters on her feet.

Still, she was not quite ready to give up the ghost. When she saw Clive waiting for her, she lifted her nose and stomped right past him. The knowledge of how utterly ridiculous she must appear, soaked to the skin and hobbling through the still pouring rain, goaded her. When he nudged Saber into keeping pace with her, she flashed him a look of loathing.

Her one consolation was that he was every bit as wet as she was. Although, of course, his hat had not wilted. No hat of his would dare!

"Changed your mind yet?" The question was maddeningly genial. Jessie threw him a look that could have sliced granite, and continued to stalk through the rain with her nose in the air.

"Stone in your shoe?" The falsely solicitous inquiry made her want to pick up a rock and brain him with it. Ignoring him, she slogged on.

Then Saber, through what she suspected was no mere mischance, shied. The big horse did a little sideways dance step before Clive could bring him under control. At the conclusion of the performance, the animal's rear end swung around to collide solidly with Jessie's back. Caught by surprise, she stumbled forward and lost her footing, falling face-down in a puddle.

In the minute before she could recover her breath enough to pick herself up, Clive was off Saber and hunkering beside her.

"Jessie! Are you hurt?"

"You did that on purpose!" she accused, turning over and sitting up to glare at him.

"Obviously not," he answered his own question, then took one look at her, with the straw brim of the already ruined hat crushed now to dangle over her nose and reddish mud coating her person from her eyebrows clear down to the hem of her skirt, and started to grin.

"If you laugh, so help me, I'll kill you," she warned through gritted teeth as he gave every evidence of doing just that.

"I guess I'll simply have to risk it," he managed, before succumbing to a fit of the chuckles that made her look longingly at his still just slightly discolored nose.

Jessie glared at him. Before she could make any other move to carry out her threat, he picked her up out of the puddle and stood up, still chuckling, to deposit her on Saber's back.

If she hadn't been so wet, and so muddy, and so tired—and if he hadn't cannily kept his hand on the rein—she would have kicked Saber into a gallop before he could swing himself up behind her, and left him standing there.

But she didn't. Clive got up behind her, turned her so that she was sitting sideways between his body and the saddle horn, and slid his arms around her to reach the reins.

Her only satisfaction was that, in doing so, he got himself nearly as muddy as she.

"I hate you," she said to the trees at the side of the road, refusing to look at him and keeping her body rigid so that she didn't have to touch him any more than was absolutely necessary.

"No, you don't. You're just mad," he told her comfortably. Jessie had to clench her hands in her lap to keep from hitting him.

And so they rode the rest of the way to Mimosa, with Jessie, muddy and sullen, not quite sitting on Clive's lap, and Clive, grinning widely, enjoying himself for the first time in two days.

But when they reached the turn-in to Mimosa, he stiffened.

"Something's happened," he said.

Jessie slewed around in the saddle to look at the house. Half a dozen carriages were parked in the drive, and twenty or so of Mimosa's people were gathered in the front yard despite the slackening rain.

"That carriage belongs to Dr. Crowell," Jessie said suddenly, recognizing the battered buggy that was a familiar sight at houses where there were birthings, sickness, or death.

"Good God." Clive nudged Saber into a canter. Jessie hung on to the saddle horn for dear life as the animal slipped and slid on the muddy drive until Clive reined in at the foot of the steps. Then she slid down, ducking under Clive's arm before he could help her.

"Miss Jessie, oh, Miss Jessie!" Amabel, Pharaoh's wife, was one of the small group in front of the house. " 'Twas Pharaoh what found her!"

"Found who, Amabel?" Jessie asked, fighting to stay calm. Clive was beside her, tying Saber's reins to a newel-post in the absence of Thomas or Fred, who in the face of the current crisis had apparently deserted their posts.

"What's happened?" Clive demanded sharply.

Just then Dr. Crowell, accompanied by Tudi and Rosa, appeared on the veranda above them.

"Oh, lamb, where you been?" Regardless of the rain, Tudi hurried down the steps toward her.

"What's happened?" Clive demanded again, more sharply this time, as Tudi folded Jessie, mud and all, into her arms.

"I'm sorry to be the bearer of ill tidings, Mr. Edwards," Dr. Crowell said heavily as Stuart climbed the steps toward him. "But I'm very much afraid your wife is dead."

XLIV

Celia lay in the front parlor, on the settee where Jessie had sat as she had waited for Mitch to call to receive her answer to his proposal. A quilt covered Celia's body, but the tip of one small muddy shoe was just visible. Jessie felt her stomach tighten. It was impossible to comprehend that Celia was dead.

With Dr. Crowell murmuring something at his side, Clive moved toward where Celia lay. He reached for the quilt to twitch it back from her face. Jessie turned quickly away.

"God in heaven!"

Apparently, from the sickened tone of Clive's voice, whatever had happened to Celia wasn't pretty. Jessie's stomach heaved, and she clapped her hand to her mouth as she fought against casting up her accounts. Clive looked sharply at her.

"There's no need for you to see this," he said to her, then spoke over her shoulder to Tudi, who hovered just behind her. "Take her upstairs and help her get changed."

"Yessir, Mr. Stuart."

"Oh, God!" At the reminder that Stuart was not Stuart, Jessie felt a fresh wave of nausea overtake her. She was thankful for Tudi's arm to help her up the stairs.

Tudi undressed her while Sissie, summoned from

the back hall, where the house servants had gathered, prepared her bath.

"Was it the baby?" Jessie whispered as she slid into the steaming water.

"The baby?" Tudi asked, seemingly uncomprehending. Jessie, still so nauseated from shock that she could barely lift her head without gagging, lay back against the lip of the tub as Tudi washed her like a small child.

"Celia. What happened? Was it a problem with the baby?"

Tudi and Sissie looked at each other over Jessie's head. "No, lamb," Tudi said, gently running the wet cloth over Jessie's neck. "It wasn't the baby."

"She was kilt!" Sissie, who was laying out fresh underclothes for Jessie, added in a rush.

"Killed!" Jessie sat up straight, looking wide-eyed from one woman to the other.

"The doctor, he said somebody done beat her to death," Tudi said. Then, before any of them could say anything more, there was a tap at the door. Sissie went to answer it, and had a low-voiced conversation with the person on the other side. When she closed the door and turned back into the room, her eyes were wide.

"Dr. Crowell, he said you should come on down into the library when you're ready, Miss Jessie. Judge Thompson is here."

"Judge Thompson!"

"Miss Celia was murdered, lamb. He's probably come to see if he can discover who did it."

"Get me dressed!"

Something niggled at the back of Jessie's mind. She couldn't quite bring it forward so that she could consciously examine it, but it was there, nonetheless. Whatever it was urged her to go downstairs quickly, before events could be put in motion that she would be helpless to stop. Although just what those events might be she couldn't quite express, even to herself.

She stood up abruptly and stepped out of the tub. Tudi said something in a low voice to Sissie. As Tudi enveloped Jessie in a drying cloth, Sissie slipped from the room. By the time she had returned, some ten minutes later, with a black dress hanging over her arm, Jessie was clad in her underwear and Tudi was pinning up her hair.

Jessie's eyes widened when she saw the black gown. But of course she had to wear black. Her stepmother was dead, and she was officially in mourning.

"It was Miss Elizabeth's." Tudi answered her un-spoken question as she deftly threw the dress over Jessie's head. "From when your grandmama died."

The dress was a trifle too short and a trifle too snug in the bosom, but Jessie didn't care about that. As she looked at herself in the cheval glass swathed from neck to ankles in black like a crow, the reality of the situation hit her like a blow: Celia was dead.

"I can tell 'em you're not feeling well, lamb," Tudi offered as Jessie hesitated before leaving the room.

Jessie took a deep breath. "No. I'm all right." Then, with Tudi behind her, she went down the stairs.

As promised, Judge Thompson was in the library. So, Jessie saw after she opened the door, were Dr. Crowell; Seth Chandler, who held the largely honorary post of county coroner; and Clive. Seth Chandler looked tense; Clive wore his icy mask. The tension in the room was palpable.

All four gentlemen turned to look at her as she entered. Tudi closed the door quietly behind her but remained outside, in the hall.

"Gentlemen." Jessie's voice was steady despite the churning in her stomach that would not go away.

"Ah, Miss Lindsay," Judge Thompson greeted Jessie. "Please join us. You have my deepest sym-pathy on the loss of your stepmother."

Seth Chandler and Dr. Crowell murmured similar sentiments. Jessie sat in the leather chair farthest from the desk where Clive perched on a corner, inclining her head in acknowledgment of their words.

With an odd feeling of detachment, she saw that, unlike herself, Clive had not had a chance to change. He was still wet, with smears of mud marring his gray suit. For once his hair was disordered, curling wildly about his head as it dried. His face was composed, but very pale.

"I'm sorry to have to distress you with these details," Judge Thompson continued when Jessie was seated. He pulled up a chair beside her and lowered his voice as if in respect for the somber subject he must broach. "Mrs. Edwards was discovered shortly after noon today, lying out behind your privy. Your man Pharaoh found the—uh, her. I understand he's been with your family for a long time?"

"All his life. He was born on Mimosa."

"Ah. And do you have any reason to suspect that he might have wished to do Mrs. Edwards harm?"

Jessie's eyes widened. "Pharaoh? No. He would never hurt anyone."

Judge Thompson exchanged a look with Dr. Crowell. "Miss Lindsay, again I hate to distress you, but I understand that you left the house some four days ago in a state of some, ah, emotional disturbance?"

Clive made a sudden movement as though he might be going to protest, but Dr. Crowell moved to stand beside him, silencing him with a hand on his arm.

Jessie's attention shifted back to Judge Thompson. "Yes."

"And Mr. Edwards came after you?"

Jessie looked fleetingly at Clive. His thoughts were hidden by that expressionless mask that she realized now was the mark of a professional gambler. But what, this time, had he to hide?

"Yes."

"When and where did Mr. Edwards locate you?"

"In Natchez, the day before yesterday."

"I see. And has he been with you ever since?"

Suddenly Jessie saw where Judge Thompson's questions were leading. He was trying to find out if Celia's husband had an alibi for the time of her murder. Fortunately for Clive, he'd been with Jessie. Then her blood froze as the truth dawned: he had not been with her at the time Celia was killed. She had run away from him yesterday morning and had not seen him again until he'd met her at the dock some two hours ago. Of course, he'd ridden clear from Baton Rouge in that period, but had he somehow found time to stop by Mimosa and beat Celia to death before he met Jessie at the dock?

Preposterous! Wasn't it?

"Yes, he's been with me ever since," Jessie answered clearly, her eyes moving to Clive again. Was it her imagination, or did he look just the tiniest bit relieved by her answer? She waited, but he didn't contradict her.

"I see. Thank you very much, Miss Lindsay. Of course, Mr. Edwards told us the same thing, but we have to corroborate everything, don't we?"

As Judge Thompson got to his feet, seeming relieved, Jessie looked at Clive again. He met her eyes, his expression as unreadable as it had been when she'd entered the room. Those sky-blue eyes were as unfathomable as the sea.

There'd been much she could have told Judge Thompson, above and beyond the fact that Celia's husband had no alibi for the time of her murder. But she had held her tongue, and even lied. The question was, why?

Jessie was all too afraid she knew the answer. And so, she feared, did Clive.

It lay in the vagaries of her foolish heart.

XLV

Celia was buried the next day, in the small cemetery where Jessie's parents and grandparents had been laid to rest. It was raining, not the pouring sheets of the day before, but a steady drizzle. Like everyone else present, Jessie was both cold and thoroughly damp. Beside her, Clive, soberly clad in black as befitted a newly bereaved widower, held his hat in front of him and bowed his head at the Reverend Cooper's solemn words. He seemed completely oblivious to the rain. Droplets of water beaded on his black hair and rolled like tears down his face.

He looked so much the perfect picture of the grieving husband that Jessie's lip curled. Fraud! she wanted to scream at him, even as he was throwing the first clod of dirt on the coffin. He had not loved Celia, had hated her, in fact. He'd made no bones about having married her strictly for Mimosa. Now, since he was Celia's nearest survivor, Mimosa was his.

The question was, had he killed Celia to get it?

Miss Flora and Miss Laurel stood behind him, their faces puckered with concern for the man who, if they did but know it, was not their nephew at all. Neighbors crowded the small family plot. Beyond the iron fence stood Tudi, Sissie, Rosa, Progress, Pharaoh, and all the rest of Mimosa's people in a large, silent mass. Jessie thought that she would by far rather have stood with them than where she was. They were her family now, the people who truly loved her and whom she loved.

Except they weren't her people now, but Stuart's. No, curse him, Clive's.

The fortune hunter had played his hand perfectly, and had got up from the table with the prize.

"Come, Jess, it's over."

Jessie's thoughts had taken her far away from the soggy graveside. Clive's hand on her arm and his whispered words brought her back to reality with a start. The service was over, his hat was firmly in place on his head, and the neighbors were parting to let the grief-stricken family pass. Jessie kept her eyes lowered as Clive pulled her hand through his arm, turned her about, and escorted her through the sympathetically murmuring crowd down the hillside to the buggy that waited on the road below. It was only a short distance to the house, an easy walk in fine weather and one that Jessie frequently made, but in times of tragedy the family invariably chose to ride. Today, the rain had made it doubly necessary.

Now, according to custom, the mourners would retire to Mimosa to offer sympathy to the bereaved and partake of refreshments. In this instance, there would be the added attraction of speculating about who the killer might be. The most obvious candidate, the new husband who inherited all, was taken out of the running by the stepdaughter's alibi. That left the field open for the most farfetched of theories. Jessie did not doubt that the crowd in Mimosa's formal rooms today would enjoy itself very much by exploring them all.

"Are you all right?" Clive asked Jessie in a low voice as he handed her up into the front seat, where she would sit beside him.

Miss Laurel and Miss Flora, as the widower's sup-

posed aunts, rode in the buggy with them. Their
presence kept Jessie's reply brief.

"I'm fine," she said. Ignoring his frowning look,
she lapsed into silence as he helped the old ladies to
their seats.

The remainder of the day was a nightmare. Forced
by common courtesy to circulate amongst the neighbors who crowded into her house, Jessie developed
a blinding headache. It was hard enough to pretend
a grief she didn't feel. Except for the shock of it, and
her niggling suspicion that maybe, just maybe,
Clive's infamy might stretch to the extent of clob-
bering his wife over the head, she could not really
be sorry that Celia was gone. But to see Clive pretending to be Stuart, accepting compliments on how
well he was holding up and looking suitably grave,
made her want to shriek the truth to the skies. More
than at any other time, during the course of that
endless afternoon Jessie had a chance to observe
firsthand what a consummate actor the man really
was. Of course, always before when he had played
at being Stuart Edwards, gentleman, Jessie had not
known about Clive.

It was later, near suppertime, and the crowd had
begun to thin out, when Jessie saw Clive pull aside
Mr. Samuels, Celia's lawyer, for a low-voiced discussion. Jessie's lip curled. Clive no doubt wanted
to discuss the will.

"Lamb, why don't you go upstairs now? You've
done what was needful, and won't no one say a
word against you if you go to lie down."

"Oh, Tudi." Jessie put the untouched cup of cof-
fee she was clutching on a table at her elbow and
turned to lay her head on Tudi's comfortable shoulder. She was tired, bone tired, not only in body but
also in spirit. At the moment all she wanted in the
world was to be a small child again and let Tudi
chase the bad things away.

"There, child, there." Tudi patted her back, and

for just a second Jessie was comforted. Then Miss Flora came up behind her.

"Jessie, Stuart asked me to ask you to please join him and Mr. Samuels in the library."

Jessie straightened and turned to look at Miss Flora. Tudi bowed her head and faded away. "Did he?" She was sorely tempted not to go. Clive McClintock might be master of Mimosa now, but he didn't give her orders, and never would.

But in the end she went. Miss Flora ushered her there so kindly that Jessie had not the heart to demur. Besides, what difference could it make? She would go, and play her part a little longer. Then the next day, or even the next, this stunned feeling might leave her and she would be able to decide what she should do.

Miss Flora knocked, then opened the door. "Here's Jessie," she said, and gave Jessie an encouraging little nudge when she was slow to go inside.

So Jessie found herself in the library again, with Clive seated behind his big desk for once and Mr. Samuels ensconced in a chair he'd pulled up to its other side. Miss Flora gently closed the door behind Jessie, leaving her alone with the two men, who rose politely to their feet as she entered.

"Pray accept my condolences on the death of Mrs. Edwards, Miss Lindsay," said Mr. Samuels. Jessie had heard the same sentiments so many times since yesterday that they scarcely registered, but still she managed a polite "Thank you."

"Did you want me?" she asked then, looking at Clive. His expression was still suitably grave, but there was a glint in his eyes that told Jessie he would recover from his wife's death with indecent speed. In fact, though no one who didn't know him as well as she did would ever detect it, Jessie thought he looked almost relieved.

"Sit down, Jessie."

The gentlemen could not sit until she did. Although that wouldn't stop Clive, no gentleman he, if they were alone. Jessie took the same chair as before, when she lied to Judge Thompson. Clive frowned a little as she sat so far away, but said nothing as he and Mr. Samuels settled into their seats.

"Of course, you know that I am—was—Mrs. Edwards' lawyer." Mr. Samuels turned slightly in his chair to address Jessie. She inclined her head. "At his request, I've been going over her will with Mr. Edwards. It contains no surprises. Upon Mrs. Edwards' remarriage, of course, ownership of Mimosa and all its chattels passed to Mr. Edwards, and her death doesn't change that. Nor does it change the provision in your father's will that left you with the right to live at Mimosa for the rest of your life. Since that might be problematical now that Mr. Edwards, who is no real kin of yours, will be living in the same house without a wife, I've suggested to him that he buy out your interest. Did he follow that suggestion, you would be able to live anywhere you liked, in comfort, for the rest of your life."

"Buy—me—out!" Jessie was almost speechless. Was she to lose Mimosa on top of everything else? She turned huge, shadowy eyes on Clive. Surely he wouldn't do that to her.

"Hear him out, Jess," Clive advised quietly. With a quick look at him, Mr. Samuels continued.

"But Mr. Edwards, for reasons of his own—which I am sure are sound ones, although they are strictly contrary to his own interests and, in fact, my advice—has refused to follow that course. The course he has chosen instead is not, in my opinion, in his best interests—but, of course, I am here only to give advice."

Mr. Samuels and his flowing sentences were losing her. Jessie grasped that Clive had declined to buy her out, and thought that was good. Or did he mean to kick her out without any compensation at all? Surely he wouldn't do that! But this was not the man she had thought she knew. This man was a stranger, and might be capable of anything at all.

"What Mr. Samuels is trying so nobly to say is that I've signed it all over to you, Jessie. Lock, stock, and barrel, no strings attached." Clive watched her with the air of a cat at a mouse hole. Jessie frowned. She heard the words, but they made no sense. When she said nothing, he went on with a slight touch of impatience. "Mimosa's yours, as it should have been in the first place."

Jessie looked at Mr. Samuels. "Do you understand what you just heard, Miss Lindsay?" he asked gently, no doubt believing that her incomprehension could be laid at the door of her new and numbing grief. "Mr. Edwards has renounced all rights to Mimosa. The property is yours."

Jessie's eyes widened. Slowly they moved back to fasten on Clive. He didn't grin at her—but he might as well have. There was amused satisfaction in those sky-blue eyes.

"It's quite a magnificent gesture, I must say," Mr. Samuels continued, shaking his head. "And he had no need to do such a thing, of course. Everything came to him. Perfectly legal. But he thought, in light of the fact that he has only come lately to Mimosa, the property should be yours."

Admiration and respect for the man who would renounce such a rich prize as Mimosa were clear in Mr. Samuels' tone. Jessie had no doubt that this evidence of Stuart Edwards' true nobility of character would be all over the Yazoo Valley by nightfall the following day. "What a gentleman he is!" everyone would say.

"It's all yours, Jessie." Clive spoke very gently, as if he thought that shock at his magnanimous gesture was the reason for her silence.

Still Jessie said nothing. Her eyes were wide and almost unfocused as they stared at him. In his well-tailored black suit, he looked every inch the elegant gentleman and as devastatingly handsome as always. His expression was sober, but there was a gleam in his eyes that told Jessie he was feeling pleased with himself.

It hit her then that the riverboat gambler was taking the biggest chance of his life: he was risking everything on a single turn of the cards. And it was clear from the look in his eyes that he expected to win.

Jessie started to laugh.

XLVI

Hysterics, everyone said as Clive, followed by an anxious Tudi, carried the still giggling Jessie up to bed. Held high against Clive's chest, gasping as she fought to breathe in between the gusts of laughter that claimed her, Jessie wondered if they might not be correct. But she didn't think so.

It was all just so funny. So hysterically funny.

So Clive had thought that he would sign her home over to her as proof positive that he was no longer the fortune-hunting gambler who had lied his way into ownership of Mimosa, eh? What masterful strategy on his part! She would really have to congratulate him when she could find the breath! But, of course, a leopard didn't change its spots, and a gambler didn't lose his eye for the main chance. He must know that his deception, if revealed—and Jessie could certainly reveal it at any time—would make his inheritance of Mimosa something less than a sure thing. In fact, he probably wouldn't inherit at all. Which tended to clear him as far as Celia's murder went. But then, if he'd committed the deed, she had no doubt that he had done so in a fit of temper, with no premeditation, so perhaps he hadn't had time to consider that he was killing his meal ticket.

In any case, with Celia dead, and Jessie already knowing him for the opportunistic cad that he was, he stood a very real chance of losing all that he had gone to so much trouble to acquire. How, then, to keep it? Why, give it to sweet, naive little Jessie, of course, who would be so touched by the gesture with all its ramifications that she would melt with love for him and hasten to accept the proposal of marriage that he would no doubt immediately tender! Then Clive McClintock, river rat, would have it all again: Mimosa and respectability. And this time, Jessie was sure that he would take whatever steps were necessary to make certain that, whatever happened, his marriage was perfectly legal.

Once a fortune hunter, always a fortune hunter. Only this time he'd outsmarted himself. Jessie couldn't wait to tell him so.

"Get Dr. Crowell up here," Clive said over his shoulder to somebody as he bore Jessie through the door of her room. His face was taut and anxious as he laid her carefully on the bed and remained for a moment, bending over her.

"Everything's going to be just fine, Jess," he murmured, his hand stroking briefly over her cheek. Then, before she could even think about knocking that hand aside or throwing his base intentions in his teeth or doing anything at all but laugh and wheeze, Dr. Crowell entered the room. Tudi, scandalized at the idea of having any man but a doctor in her lamb's bedchamber, shooed Clive out.

From the darkness of the room and the utter stillness of the house, it was very late at night when Jessie awoke from the sleeping potion that Dr. Crowell had administered. It took her a few minutes to orient herself, but at last she remembered what had happened, and realized, too, that she slept in her own bed. Gentle snores ensuing from the truckle bed across the room told her that she was not alone. Getting to her feet, Jessie tiptoed over to discover Tudi fast asleep.

Dear Tudi, guarding her lamb.

Jessie turned back to her bed, where her wrapper was laid out neatly across the foot. Shrugging into it, she tied the sash, then made her way out of the room on noiseless feet. Tudi was a great believer in the efficacy of fresh air at night for one's health, and had left her windows cracked despite the chilly November night. Through the slightly open windows had come the smell of a rainwashed world—mixed with the pungent aroma of cigar smoke.

Clive, apparently unable to sleep, was smoking on the upper gallery. Jessie meant to join him there.

The fairy lamps were lit in the hall, and the interior of the house was scented with the flowers for the funeral that had not yet been removed. An eerie stillness lay over everything, as if the house somehow sensed that its mistress had died just the day before. The queen was dead. Long live the king!

The door to the upper gallery was ajar. Jessie stepped through it quietly and turned to look for Clive.

He was seated, as he had been before, in the rocking chair at the farthermost end. Barefoot, she moved toward him over the rain-slick boards. As yet unaware of her presence, he rocked slowly back and forth, staring out into the drizzle and puffing on his cigar.

When at last he looked around at her, his hand holding the cigar froze midway to his mouth, and his eyes widened. Jessie realized that, in her white wrapper, with the dark shadows of the gallery obscuring her identity until she drew close, she must look disconcertingly like a ghost. The notion pleased her, and she smiled. But his alarm, if alarm it was, did not last long. In less than a minute his eyes narrowed in recognition, and his cigar resumed its journey to his mouth.

"Did you think I was Celia?" It was almost, but not quite, a taunt.

He ignored her question. "What are you doing up?"

"I smelled your cigar."

He looked at her again, a faint smile curling his mouth. "So you came out to join me. Does that mean you've decided to forgive and forget, Jess?"

"It means I think we should talk."

"Talk away." He took another puff from his cigar. "Suppose you start by telling me whether or not you killed Celia."

His mouth quirked. "So it's going to be that kind of conversation, is it? Let me ask you something, Jess: What do you think?"

"That's no kind of answer."

"That's the best I'm prepared to give. I'm in no mood to be cross-examined at the moment."

"You wanted me to lie to Judge Thompson."

"Did I?"

"Yes. You'd already told him the same thing yourself."

"Maybe I just wanted to see if you loved me enough despite our disagreement to lie to protect me."

"I don't believe that."

"What do you believe, then? That I rode nearly two hundred miles in two days to beat you back here, and on the way decided to take a little detour and murder my wife?"

"You could have stopped to change clothes and found her—with—someone." Jessie vividly remembered how furious he had been when he'd come across Celia with Seth Chandler. He'd threatened her with murder then—and had looked perfectly capable of carrying out his threat.

"I could have."

"Why won't you give me a straight answer?" Jessie clenched her fists in frustration.

"Because I'm tired of your questions." He stood up suddenly, tossed his cigar over the railing, and caught her by the upper arms before she could so much as take a step back. "In fact, I'm tired of talking altogether. Come to bed with me, Jess."

"You can't be serious!"

"Oh, I am, believe me. Very serious."

"We just buried Celia today!"

"I didn't love her, and you didn't, either. Don't be a hypocrite, Jessie."

"A hypocrite!"

"A very lovely little hypocrite." Before Jessie had any inkling of what he meant to do, he scooped her up in his arms and started walking back along the gallery with her.

"Put me down!" He was carrying her into the house.

"Shhh! You'll wake Tudi. Think how shocked she would be, to know I'm carrying you off to bed with me."

"I don't want to go to bed with you!"

He turned down the corridor that led to his bed-chamber. "One thing I have learned about you, my darling, is that you don't know what the hell you want."

Then he bent his head to catch her mouth. Jessie didn't even try to turn her face away. Suddenly she realized the truth: this, *this* was why she had crept out on the gallery to join him. Her bruised heart ached for his kisses, she discovered as his mouth sought and found hers. Her body burned for his touch.

In the morning would be soon enough to do what she had to do, and call his bluff. Tonight she would give in to the devil's temptation one last time.

As he shouldered through his bedroom door with her, Jessie slid her arms around his neck and kissed him back.

"You know you love me, Jess," he murmured maddeningly near her ear as he kissed the soft hollow beneath it. Then he found her mouth again, and she was given no chance to reply. His boot shoved the door closed behind them. The latch caught with no more than a soft click.

What passed between them was wild, and glori-

ous, and wanton, both shaming and exhilarating.
Clive left not so much as a centimeter of her body
unexplored, and insisted that she return his ministrations in kind. When at last he allowed her to doze,
the sky was turning gray in preparation for the
dawn.

Jessie didn't sleep long, not more than an hour,
but when she opened her eyes the sky outside his
uncurtained bedroom windows was bright salmon
pink. He was already awake, sitting up in bed, naked except for the sheet he had dragged over his
lap, and smoking one of his cigars. His eyes were
possessive on her as she stretched like a contented
cat against his side.

"Good Lord! I have to get back to my room. Tudi's probably already awake." Suddenly realizing
how bright the dawn was, Jessie sat up as she spoke.
She was naked, her bare breasts rosy from where
his jaw had scraped them the night before, her
mouth slightly swollen from his kisses, her hair a
mass of tangled curls.

"If she's scandalized, you can always tell her
you're going to marry me."

That stopped Jessie in her tracks. Her head turned,
and she looked at him without answering. Broad-
shouldered and lean, his skin dark against the
sun-bleached whiteness of the sheets, he was so
handsome he took her breath away. The black hair,
the blue eyes, even the red-tipped cigar, were the
stuff of every girlish dream she'd ever had.

Was she going to allow Clive McClintock to dazzle
her into giving him on a silver platter everything
he'd schemed and tricked and cheated to take?

Jessie climbed off the bed, found her nightgown
where he had tossed it on the floor, and pulled it
over her head. Then she recovered her wrapper, too,
and shrugged it on.

"Is that a proposal?"

"It is. Are you going to accept?"

The sound that came from Jessie's mouth then was

a creditable imitation of a laugh. "I'm a fool, I admit, but not quite fool enough to agree to marry an admitted fortune hunter when I've just acquired a fortune. You signed Mimosa over to me—how very generous of you, considering the fact that your marriage to my stepmother was probably illegal!—and now you want to marry me to get it back! Was last night supposed to seduce me into agreeing? It didn't succeed. In fact, since you've been so very obliging as to give my property back to me, I want you off it before tonight."

He went very still. Even his hand holding the cigar froze. Watching his eyes, Jessie saw them flash. Then all outward signs of what he was feeling disappeared beneath a curtain of silver-blue ice.

"If you want to cut off your nose to spite your face, then go ahead. Now get the hell out of my room, fast. Because if you don't, I'm liable to lose my temper and kick the new mistress of Mimosa right in her very pretty ass."

XLVII

Clive couldn't remember ever being angrier in his life. He was so furious that it was all he could do not to rant and rave and curse, not to storm down the hallway and kick in Jessie's door and apply his hand to her backside until her soft white skin was red and blistered. He loved the little bitch, damn it, loved her as he'd never loved a woman in his life. Loved her as he'd never thought to love anyone. After the night they'd just passed, to have her call him a fortune hunter and, sneering, throw his love and the only heartfelt marriage proposal he'd ever made back in his face infuriated him. If the reason he was so furious was because she'd hurt him, badly, well, that was something he refused to even think about.

His newly vulnerable heart was not lacerated; he was just damned mad!

So he dressed, slammed a few of his belongings into a bag, clapped his hat on his head, and stomped out of the house. Without waiting for Progress, whom he could hear moving around in the loft but who had not yet made it down the ladder, he saddled Saber himself (he'd given Jessie everything else; the horse she couldn't have, even if she had him clapped up for horse stealing!), tied his bag behind the saddle, and was up and away.

She wanted him off Mimosa, so, by God, he'd give her what she wanted, and be damned to her!

Jessie, still in her wrapper and nightgown, was standing at a window in her bedroom as Clive rode down the drive and turned west, toward Vicksburg, less than an hour after she'd fled from his room. She'd told him to go, and he was going. She should feel deliriously happy. What she had done was absolutely the sensible thing. So why did she feel so desolate?

Tudi, behind her, evidently saw Clive leaving, too.

"That's Mr. Stuart," Tudi said, surprised. "Where can he be goin' at this time of a mornin', and in such a hurry too?"

"I sent him away," Jessie said in a voice that, for all her fine protestations, sounded suspiciously hollow.

"Lamb, you never did that!" Tudi's hand on her arm turned Jessie around to face her. "Why, it's been as plain as the nose on your face that you're crazy in love with that man! I was scared, while Miss Celia was with us, of what was gonna happen, but I never said anything. But now—why on earth would you go and send him away?"

Jessie hesitated, but the temptation to confide in someone was too great. Besides, Tudi was the one person who might be able to help her make sense of her feelings. And Jessie knew that her secrets would go with Tudi to her grave.

"Oh, Tudi, he's not what you think," Jessie said. Sinking down upon the bed, she proceeded to tell Tudi, in detail, about Clive McClintock and his schemes.

"That boy's been *bad!*" Tudi exclaimed when Jessie had finished, her eyes wide with shock.

"But I love him," Jessie ended miserably. "Or at least, I loved him when I thought he was Stuart. But I keep telling myself that I don't even know who Clive McClintock is."

"Lamb, you've done gone and bedded with him, too, haven't you? Last night, that was where you went, and not out on the gallery at all like you said."

Jessie hung her head. Tudi hugged her. "Just never you mind. Lots of ladies have done worse. Let's just hope and pray there are no consequences to worry about. If your baby was to be born in this house without a marriage, your granddad would rise from his grave at night and haunt me, he'd be that mad."

"Oh, Tudi!" At the idea of the shade of her grandfather, the kindest man in the world, frightening Tudi, who had been known to rout copperheads with a broom, Jessie had to smile. Then, as she considered what else Tudi had said, her smile faded. "I never thought about getting with child."

"Well, we'll cross that bridge if and when we come to it. No point in worrying your head about it, because it's in God's hands now."

Jessie looked up at Tudi then, her eyes wide and shadowed. "I never thought being in love could hurt so much."

Tudi shook her head and pulled Jessie's head against her shoulder. "Lamb, love hurts us all. Ain't nothing we can do about that."

A week passed, then another, and a third. Life at Mimosa resumed its usual pattern. Sad as it was to say, Celia was not much missed, although an investigation into the circumstances of her death was continuing. With each day that went by, Jessie became more and more convinced, in her own mind, that Clive could not have murdered her stepmother. He was an unprincipled liar, a rake, and a cad, but she did not think he was a killer. If he had returned to Mimosa and found Celia with a lover, he would likely have wiped the ground with the man but left Celia relatively unharmed. And if he *had* caught Celia with a man, where was that man?

If Clive had not killed Celia, who had?

The idea of a murderer at large in the vicinity of Mimosa caused Tudi to start sleeping in Jessie's room each night. As an extra precaution, Progress gave up his beloved spot in the loft and slept in the still room off the back hall. Such evidence of their devotion touched Jessie deeply.

Gray Bradshaw and Pharaoh between them did the best they could to take care of the day-to-day work of running the plantation. Jessie thanked the Lord daily that Clive had not left during the cotton season. It was amazing, considering that he'd been at Mimosa such a short time, how much he'd learned and how much of the actual running of the plantation he'd assumed. With no one but Jessie to make final decisions on everything from the amount of new harness to purchase to the best time to shoe the mules, she was spurred to a renewed appreciation of exactly what Clive had taken on when he'd married Celia for Mimosa.

If nothing else, the man for all his elegant good looks was a workhorse, she had to give him that. But he was also a scheming, conniving opportunist, out to acquire riches any way he could. Despite the fact that the plantation missed him, the servants missed him, the Misses Edwards missed him, and she missed him (though she was loath to admit it, even to herself), she had done the right thing, absolutely the right thing, by sending him away. So why did her heart ache so, growing more painful instead of less so with every hour of every day?

It was generally agreed that Jessie's downcast demeanor was the mark of genuine grief for her step-mother, and the community rallied around her in consequence. Mitch was the most frequent of the many callers who came by regularly to cheer her up. Dear, loyal, faithful Mitch, who, having decided that Jessie was the wife for him, seemed unable to shake the notion. When she'd run away, Clive had had a message sent over to Riverview tersely breaking Jessie's engagement, but Mitch held no grudge against her for that. If anything, it seemed to make him view her as a more valuable matrimonial prize.

To the neighbors, Jessie said only that Stuart had gone away to tend to some business matters of his own. It was common knowledge that he had deeded Mimosa over to Jessie, which one and all agreed was an uncommonly handsome thing to have done. So his image in the community gleamed brighter than ever. In fact, Jessie reflected bitterly as she listened to the dozenth caller that week heap praise upon that absent black head, if Clive were ever to return, he'd probably be greeted as a conquering hero, rather than the cad she alone knew him to be!

Clive, in the meantime, was growing progressively drunker, dirtier, and more dispirited. He'd made it to New Orleans the first week and was back in his old haunts with his old cronies. The problem was, he no longer felt like his old self. For better or worse, Clive McClintock was not the devil-may-care gambling man he'd been less than a year before. Jessie and Mimosa had marked him, and when he was drunk enough to admit the truth to himself, Clive was conscious of a longing to go home.

Home! Home to vast cotton fields with the sound of spirituals rising over them, and a big white house with shady verandas, and the smell of Rosa's delicious home cooking. Home to wrestle with the never-ending planter's problems of boll weevils and tobacco worms and blight. Home to good, honest physical labor and a sound night's sleep.

And most of all, home to Jessie.

In his drunkest moments, he considered that he knew exactly how Adam and Eve must have felt when God cast them out of the Garden of Eden. He felt just as bereft, and just as alone.

He was living in a hole in the wall in the Vieux Carré, in a single room over a saloon because he didn't care to find better, and because it made staying drunk easier. It might have been days and it might have been weeks since he'd bathed, and it didn't bother him either way. When he was halfway sober he played pickup card games in the saloon for eating money, but he found that he didn't even care much for cards anymore.

Dear God, he wanted to go home! But Jessie had called him a fortune hunter, a cad, a liar, and a thief. The bad thing about it was, he decided dismally as he reflected over the self he'd been, he could see where she'd been at least half right.

Much as he hated to admit it, he was ashamed of what he'd done. And there was no way he was going back to Jessie with his tail between his legs and beg her to take him back.

Clive McClintock was going back riding high, or not at all.

But still he wanted to go home.

Miss Flora and Miss Laurel were the first ones to bring Jessie the news. They'd ridden over, as they did practically every other day, to see if Jessie had had word of their supposed nephew. Although Jessie had grown to love the old ladies dearly, she was always uncomfortable in their presence. What could she say to them when they inquired about when dear Stuart would be coming home? "Never, and his name is Clive"?

But on this particular afternoon, nearly a month after Celia's funeral, Miss Flora and Miss Laurel were far more interested in imparting the news they'd just heard than in talking about Stuart.

Jessie would never believe it, they assured her, but they'd learned through Clover, who'd heard it from her sister Pansy, who was married to the Chandlers' man Deacon, that a search had just that morning been conducted at Elmway. A poker with traces of blood on it had been found hidden in a greenhouse, and Seth Chandler had been arrested for Celia's murder!

Did Jessie think he could possibly be guilty?

* * *

At first Clive wasn't even interested in playing. The game was twenty-one, not one of his favorites because it required a great deal more luck than skill, and he'd been drinking all day and felt lower than a snake's belly in consequence. But the man who suggested the game was insistent, and since he had nothing better to do, Clive sat down. Then they started to play, just the two of them. Soon it became clear to Clive that his opponent had wanted the drunken ne'er-do-well that he, Clive, was doing a remarkable job of imitating to play because he'd thought he'd found a pigeon to be plucked.

Clive's interest in the game immediately picked up. He'd been drawing money from his nest egg in the bank only as he'd needed it, but he had a little on him and he resolved to use it to punish this cocky fellow for his presumption in thinking he could fleece Clive McClintock.

At first he deliberately lost, small sums, until he had the fool well pleased with himself. Then Clive allowed himself to be persuaded to increase the stakes.

When his opponent lost, he seemed to believe that it was just a run of bad luck that would soon improve. Doggedly he stayed in the game, and lost some more.

Clive was feeling better by the minute. If ever a man deserved to be taught a lesson, it was this clumsy fool who thought to take advantage of a poor drunk.

Finally Clive won all his opponent's money, some three thousand dollars, and was ready to call a halt. But like many amateurs, the fellow didn't know when to stop.

He had, he said, one more valuable: the deed to a piece of property just north of New Orleans. It was worth a lot, how much he didn't know because he'd just won it off another fellow two days before, but he was willing to wager it sight unseen against the three thousand he had lost, and three thousand more of Clive's money besides.

Clive had been a gambler long enough to know that even when Lady Luck smiled on a man, she could be a mighty fickle mistress. It was also entirely possible that the paper his opponent waved was the deed to a dirt farm worth approximately five cents. On the other hand, the cards had been running his way, and he was feeling lucky.

So he shoved his money to the middle of the table, and his opponent threw the deed on top. And when the cards had been dealt, and drawn, Clive was the richer by three thousand dollars and one deed.

It was some two days later before he bestirred himself enough to go visit his newly acquired property. Fetching Saber from the stable where he'd been kept in the luxury that Clive had denied himself, Clive rode north until he reached Lake Pontchartrain. A few miles to the east, along a road that followed the contours of the bank, he came upon the property that, according to coordinates on the land map he'd acquired before setting out from New Orleans, was now his.

He had to check the coordinates twice. There was no mistake. This was the place.

By Mimosa's standards, of course, it wasn't large. A thousand or so acres, with fields gone to seed and outbuildings that needed repair. The house was a sprawling two-story frame farmhouse, sound enough, though it could use a coat of paint and probably some fixing up inside. The place was deserted. Clearly there'd been no planting done on it for some time. But with hard work, and hands to do it, and Clive himself to supervise and plan, he'd have a property that any man would be proud to call his own.

Somewhere the gods might be laughing, but this time, praise be, they were not laughing at him. He'd just been handed the means to go home riding high!

XLVIII

When Jessie received the note asking her to call at Tulip Hill that afternoon to discuss a most urgent matter with the Misses Edwards, she made a face. Undoubtedly the old ladies meant to grill her about Clive's whereabouts. At Mimosa, she'd always been able to wriggle out of conversations with them that got too difficult by pleading the press of work. At Tulip Hill, she would be at their mercy.

But there was no help for it. If they specifically asked her to call on them, she would have to go.

Accordingly, she dressed in one of the long-sleeved full-skirted, high-necked black gowns that were her daily attire, and would be for the year she was in mourning for Celia. Sissie brushed her hair out, pinned it in a smooth coil at the back, and trimmed the curls surrounding her face. She'd lost weight since Celia's death, Jessie decided without much interest as she checked her appearance in the mirror while tying on her bonnet. She was almost too thin now, with shadows under her eyes that made them look huge and very dark. Her skin looked very white, almost translucent, against the somber black silk of the dress.

Tudi, who had taken to watching over her like a hen with one chick since Clive had left, rode over to Tulip Hill with her. They took the buggy, and Prog-

ress drove. At the house, Miss Laurel was in the hall
to greet Jessie, while Tudi was sent around to the
kitchen to chat with Clover for the duration of the
visit.

"Hello, dear. How are you holding up?" Miss
Laurel greeted her with a kiss on each cheek.

"I'm doing just fine, thanks. It was nice of you to
invite me over."

"Well, we know how it is when one is in mourning. One doesn't get much opportunity to go out."

Miss Laurel sounded almost nervous, and Jessie
had never before in her life been kept standing in a
hall. She frowned.

"Is everything all right with you and Miss Flora?"

"Oh, yes, yes—oh, good, here is Flora now. Flora,
here's Jessica."

"Well, bring her into the parlor, silly."

"I didn't want to do it alone. . . ."

"You didn't want to do what alone?" Jessie inquired, mystified. No one replied. Miss Flora beckoned her and Miss Laurel imperiously toward the
front parlor.

"Oh, dear, I hope you won't be too angry. I didn't
want to do it like this," Miss Laurel muttered, to
Jessie's complete bewilderment, as Miss Flora slid
open the pocket doors and shooed them ahead of
her into the front parlor. "I thought we should come
over first and get you used to the idea."

Jessie had been in this room many times since the
disastrous evening when the furniture had been removed and she had danced with Mitch and Clive. It
was a pretty room, decorated in the style of perhaps
twenty years before, but kept so clean and fresh with
vases of just-picked flowers that it never seemed out
of date. Today the curtains were open (they were
usually kept pulled so that the furniture would not
be faded by the sun) and there was a lovely view
over the sloping front yard. A small fire burned in
the hearth.

Miss Flora had closed the pocket doors behind her

and stood with her back to them. Miss Laurel stood beside her, her hands clasped in front of her. Both ladies looked absurdly nervous. Suspicious, Jessie opened her mouth to demand an explanation. But the words never left her mouth.

"Hello, Jess," said a husky voice. Jessie's heart leaped. She whirled so quickly that her skirts belled out behind her to see the heart-shakingly familiar form of a tall, black-haired man rising to his feet from one of the wing chairs before the fire.

"Clive!" she gasped, then immediately clapped her hands over her mouth as she realized she had given him away before his supposed aunts.

Incredibly, he smiled, a crooked smile that lit up his face with devastating charm. "It's all right. They know."

"They know!" Jessie looked sideways at Miss Flora and Miss Laurel. Miss Laurel nodded vigorously.

"He told us everything, Jessie, dear," Miss Flora said. "He shouldn't have pretended to be our nephew, of course. But you know, the real Stuart had never visited us once in his life, and he probably never would have. This Stuart is everything we'd ever hoped our nephew would be. He's been good to us, Jessica, and we've grown to love him. Our feelings haven't changed, just because his name has."

"No, indeed," Miss Laurel chimed in.

"And we've talked about it, and decided that he's as much our nephew as ever. In our hearts, which is where it counts."

"Oh, yes," Miss Laurel said.

"He wants to tell you something, Jessica. We think you should listen to him."

"We'll be just outside if you should need us," Miss Laurel added as her sister opened the pocket doors again.

"Now, why should she need us?" Miss Flora

scolded her in an undertone as the two ladies whisked themselves out of the room.

"I don't know. Don't take me up so, sister. 'Twas . . ." The rest of their argument was cut off by the doors sliding shut again.

Jessie's heart began to pound erratically. She was alone in the room with Clive. Clive, whom she'd both longed for and dreaded to see. . . .

Slowly her eyes swung back to him. He was as handsome as ever, devastatingly so, his black hair waving faultlessly back from that perfectly carved face with the incredible blue eyes. He looked very tall and masculine in the dainty, feminine room. Jessie had to fight the urge to run straight into his arms.

"Don't look so scared, Jess. I'm not going to eat you." He moved away from the chair to stand in the center of the room a few feet from where Jessie herself stood. He was clean-shaven and as immaculately dressed as always, but as Jessie looked at him more closely she realized that, like herself, he was a good deal thinner than when she'd seen him last. She realized something else, too: despite the crooked smile that curved his mouth, and the teasing glint in those sky-blue eyes, he was at least as nervous as she.

"I'm not scared," she said, although it was less than the truth. She was afraid, not of him but of herself and the way he made her feel.

"I'm glad one of us isn't," he muttered, and Jessie wasn't sure if she was supposed to hear that or not.

For an awkward moment they merely looked at each other. A hundred words crowded Jessie's mouth, but she rejected all of them for one reason or the other. The curse of being tongue-tied, which she'd thought she'd long outgrown, afflicted her just as it had in this same room so many months ago— until it occurred to her that Clive was having difficulty finding words, too. For silver-tongued Clive McClintock, that was eloquence in and of itself.

"Miss Flora said you had something to tell me," Jessie prompted. The thought of Clive being ill at ease in her presence lessened her own discomfort a little. Never in her life would she have imagined him at a loss, and certainly not because of her

"I do." But he said nothing more.

"Well, what is it?" Such hesitancy on his part was so uncharacteristic that Jessie began to worry. Perhaps it wasn't awkwardness in her presence that was the cause of his unaccustomed reticence. Please God he was not going to make some dreadful confession that she'd rather not hear.

"I won a property, playing cards. It's nothing like Mimosa, of course, but with time, and money, it can be made profitable."

"How nice." Was that what he wanted to tell her? Surely not.

"I also have some money in a bank in New Orleans. My money. Not one cent of it came from Mimosa."

"Oh, yes?" She must have sounded as bewildered as she felt, because his eyes twinkled suddenly.

"I'm not doing this very well, am I? The point I'm trying to make is that I don't need your damned money, or Mimosa. I can manage quite nicely on my own."

"I'm glad to hear it." If he'd come all this way to tell her he didn't need her . . . !

"Don't get huffy, Jess. I'm not finished. I also want to make it clear to you that I did not, repeat *not*, murder Celia."

"You don't have to tell me that. I had already decided you didn't. Besides, they've arrested Seth Chandler."

"Chandler?" Clive was momentarily diverted. "I wouldn't have thought him the man to—well, never mind. The point is that I didn't kill her."

"I never really believed you did."

"So I don't need your money, and I didn't murder your stepmother. Do you have any other major objections to me?''

Jessie blinked at him. ''What?''

His lips tightened, quirked. ''Oh, sit down, Jessie. If I'm going to do this, I may as well do it properly.''

''What are you talking about?'' she asked, completely at sea. She was so mystified by his circumlocutions that she let him take her hands and lead her to the settee, where he pushed her into a sitting position. When he dropped to one knee before her, while retaining his hold on her hands, she still did not catch on.

''I love you, Jessie, and I'm asking you to marry me,'' he said quietly. ''Me, Clive McClintock. Not Stuart Edwards.''

''Oh, my!''

''That's not much of an answer.'' His eyes never left her face as he lifted her hands, one at a time, to his mouth. He kissed the backs of her hands, and Jessie felt a shiver run down her spine at even that soft touch of his mouth. Only Clive had ever affected her like that. It was likely that only Clive ever would.

''Whatever will we tell the neighbors?'' she whispered.

It took a minute for that to register. When it did, those sky-blue eyes blazed into hers.

''Is that a yes?''

Jessie nodded. He grinned, stood up, and pulled her with him into his arms.

''Do you mean it?''

''Yes, of course.''

''Oh, God.'' He hugged her tightly. Jessie's arms went around his neck, and she closed her eyes. Against her breasts she could feel the fierce beating of his heart. At that telltale sound, a smile curved her lips. He was not the only one with gambling in his blood, it seemed. Foolish or not, she was going to take a chance on following her heart.

''I've missed you,'' she whispered, and caressed

the back of his head. He kissed her temple, her cheek, the lobe of her ear. "I'm sorry I told you to leave. It was stupid of me. But then, I didn't really think you'd go."

"I've missed you, too," he said, his voice very low. "More than you'll ever know."

Then, when she thought he would kiss her, he held her a little way away from him with both hands on her upper arms. For just a minute he looked down at her without speaking, his expression sober. "You can trust me to take good care of you, Jessie. I've decided that when it comes to scheming, the game's not worth the candle."

"I trust you," she assured him, her eyes tender. Her hands slid along his broad shoulders, absently smoothing the dark blue superfine of his coat. Then they slid back, oh so softly, to catch the lobe of his ear. "I have just one question for you, sirrah: Have you spent the last month with that friend of yours, Luce? Because if you have . . ."

She tugged his ear sharply. He yelped, caught her hand, and grinned. "I've been as celibate as a monk, I give you my word. In fact, I'm ready, willing, and able to prove it anytime."

Jessie eyed him. "Lucky for you," she said, satisfied, and slid her arms around his neck to kiss him. Then, finally, he pulled her close against him and bent his head to find her mouth.

When at long last he lifted his head, Jessie was breathless and tingling. "I love you," she whispered, shaken, into the warm skin of his neck below his chin. His arms tightened around her.

"Say it again," he murmured into her ear. "But properly this time."

Properly? Then Jessie knew, and smiled. "I love you," she repeated obediently. Then she added what she knew he wanted to hear: "Clive."

He kissed her again. Just as Jessie's bones were melting and her knees were threatening to give way, she heard a faint sound behind them. Clive, appar-

ently, heard it, too. He lifted his head, and Jessie
looked around.

The noise they had heard had been the opening
of the pocket doors. Miss Flora, Miss Laurel, and
Tudi stood in the aperture, their faces identical stud-
ies in suspense.

"She said yes," Clive reported over Jessie's head,
and Miss Flora and Miss Laurel immediately broke
into huge smiles. Tudi, however, stalked forward.
Watching her old nursemaid come, Jessie felt a niggle of alarm. In defense of her lamb, there was no
telling what Tudi might say or do.

"Now, Tudi . . ." she began, hoping to ward her
off.

"Miss Jessie, this is between him and me," Tudi
said, and walked right up to look Clive, who stood
a good foot taller but was not nearly as broad, in the
eye.

"It's all right," Clive said to Jessie, but she
thought he winced a little as he met Tudi's stern old
eyes.

"What you done just ain't right, not in my book
nor anyone else's." There was a wealth of repri-
mand in Tudi's voice. "But I'm telling you the truth:
if you hadn't showed up hereabouts pretty shortly,
I'd have come myself and fetched you. My lamb
here's been missin' you real bad."

Clive smiled then, a slow and charming smile that
made Jessie's heart turn over.

"Thank you, Tudi. I appreciate your saying that,"
he said quietly. Then, putting Jessie aside, he held
out his hand to Tudi. She looked at it for a moment
before pushing it aside.

"You're family, Mr. Clive," she said, and, wrapping her arms around him, rocked him almost off
his feet. He hugged her back, grinning, and Jessie
felt moisture rise to sting her eyes as she watched
the two people she loved best in the world together.
Tudi stepped back, frowned, and said as an after-

thought, ''That is, so long as you're good to my lamb.''

Clive laughed out loud. ''I'll be good to her, Tudi, I promise you that.''

Then Jessie went into his arms again, and Tudi walked away, satisfied.

EPILOGUE

It was some nine months after Celia's death, and Jessie had been Mrs. Clive McClintock for eight of them. Under the circumstances, the wedding had taken place in the courthouse in Jackson, with only Miss Flora, Miss Laurel, and Tudi, who'd refused to let her lamb get married without her, present. But the honeymoon—that had taken place on the magnificent steamboat *Belle of Louisiana*, and it had been something to remember in more ways than one.

As Jessie had prophesied, explaining the change in her husband's name to the neighbors had proved a little tricky. But with Aunt Flora and Aunt Laurel to stand by them, to say nothing of the staunch partisanship of all Mimosa's and Tulip Hill's people, they had brushed through the awkwardness tolerably well. The community's acceptance of the Stuart Edwards-who-wasn't was helped considerably by everyone's ongoing fascination with the events of Seth Chandler's trial for Celia's murder. Just when his conviction had seemed a foregone conclusion, Lissa Chandler had confessed tearfully that she, not her husband, had done the foul deed.

Jessie and Clive had not been the only witnesses to Seth Chandler's rendezvous with Celia on the night of his birthday party, it seemed. Lissa, unnoticed by them all, had seen that kiss, too. Later, she had confronted her husband, who not only confessed to having an affair but also said he was considering divorcing her to marry Celia. Lissa, terrified at the prospect, had seized the first opportunity to ride to Mimosa and try to reason with Celia. But before she had reached the house, Lissa had seen Celia headed for the privy. So she had waited until Celia came out, passing those few minutes by idly studying a refuse heap behind the privy. Amongst the objects discarded there was an old poker with a broken handle. When Celia had emerged from the privy, Lissa had confronted her with what she knew, and begged her to leave her husband alone. Celia had laughed and taunted her, then started to turn away, still laughing. Lissa, beside herself, had picked up the poker and brought it down on Celia's head. The first blow had probably been fatal, but Lissa, hysterical, had hit her seventeen times.

The daughter of the circuit judge down in Vicksburg, Lissa had quickly been declared insane. It was doubtful that she would ever face trial.

When the matter was finally settled, the citizens of the Yazoo Valley breathed a collective sigh of relief. Between Celia's murder and the Chandler trial, they'd never had so much excitement in their small community. In the context of those events, the change in Stuart Edwards' name was worth no more than a lift of eyebrows or a shrug. A man could call himself anything he pleased. But what would happen to those poor Chandler girls?

On this particular day in mid-August, Jessie sat fanning herself on the upper gallery, disgruntled at having to stay home while Clive was out in the fields. But she was eight months gone with child—a living memento of their honeymoon—and he insisted upon treating her like spun glass. In fact, he'd forbidden her to ride Firefly for the duration, which she thought was unbelievably high-handed of him. Backed up by Tudi, who was his ally in nearly every pronouncement concerning Jessie's welfare that he made, Clive was adamant. Jessie rode in the buggy, or not at all.

But she didn't have to like it.

The bell announcing the end of the workday had rung just minutes before. Clive would be home at any second. Already the workers, on foot and in mule wagons, thronged the road toward Mimosa. Thomas waited for Saber in the yard. From the house came the tantalizing smell of country ham and yams, Clive's particular favorites.

When he did ride up, he greeted Jessie with a wave, then swung down from the saddle and exchanged a few words with Thomas before the boy led Saber away. Then he climbed the stairs. Jessie waddled over to greet him.

"How's my little watermelon?" he inquired with a grin, placing a hand on her rounded stomach as he bent to give her cheek a peck.

Jessie smiled sourly. "In no mood for jokes about my belly," she replied.

"Crabby, are we?" he answered blithely. "Cheer up, darling, it'll all be over soon. Tudi says you're coming along marvelously."

"Oh, does she?" Jessie muttered as she followed him into the house. He would bathe and change before dinner, and she would lie on the bed and watch him. He wouldn't even let her scrub his back. And Tudi was almost worse than Clive. When she was around, Jessie wasn't permitted to do so much as tie her own shoes.

Both Jessie and Clive shared Jessie's room now. As always, a steaming bath waited for him. He started stripping off his shirt as soon as he entered the room. Jessie closed the door behind him and leaned against it, watching him undress.

He was dirty, sweaty, bulging with muscles, and utterly magnificent. Just looking at him as he pulled off his boots with the help of the bootjack, then dropped his trousers, made her feel warm all over. The one thing he had not forbidden her to do during her pregnancy was make love with him. Jessie rather suspected he felt he should abstain, but when faced with temptation he simply could not. In any case, the fact that they still managed to have intimate relations was the one tidbit of information about her pregnancy that he did not share with Tudi.

Tudi had been very frank with him about the need to spare his wife his attentions in her later months. Jessie had heard the lecture he'd been given, and every time she thought back to it she grinned. It had been the one time since she'd known him that she'd seen Clive blush.

Every now and then, when he approached her and she was feeling devilish, she threatened to tell Tudi on him.

"Jess, shouldn't you be lying down?" he called from the tub.

There was nothing to be gained by arguing. If she did not lie down, he would simply get up, pick her up, and place her on the bed. Which could get interesting at times, but at the moment she was perfectly content to watch him bathe.

Jessie obediently stretched out on the coverlet, her hand on her stomach as she watched him vigorously lather his arms.

"I've been thinking," she began as he sluiced his face.

"I didn't hear you."

"I said, I've been thinking," she said again, louder.

"I wish you wouldn't do that."

"Oh, you!" Jessie snatched the pillow from beneath her head and threw it at him. "Seriously, Clive."

"Seriously, Jess," he repeated, mocking her with a smile as he stood up, wrapped a cloth around his waist, and came to sit on the bed beside her. He put his hand on her swollen belly, and she guided it to where he could feel the child turning somersaults. "What have you been thinking this time?"

"If it's a boy, I know what we'll name him."

"What?" His eyes widened as the baby kicked his hand. Watching him, Jessie felt her heart swell with love.

"Stuart," she answered, and grinned wickedly.

Clive looked at her, groaned, laughed, and bent to kiss her. "You've got to be joking."

But she wasn't, it was, and they did: Stuart Clive.